I0822168

THE ORIONIDS

WYATT WERNE

The Orionids

Book cover design by ebooklaunch.com

ISBN 979-8-9887257-0-1 (ePub/Digital Online)

ISBN 979-8-9887257-1-8 (paperback)

ISBN 979-8-9887257-2-5 (hardcover)

First Edition: August 2023

For Alison and Katie,
with love.

1

Vandenberg Space Force Base, California
April 2041

Helena Darcy and her husband Nolan had a balcony view overlooking the control room's four titan screens.

A deadpan voice said, "T minus three minutes."

Nolan squeezed her hand and shifted forward on the sofa. Project Phoenix, her baby, three minutes from a ring of fire. She winced, feeling a spasm. Under her t-shirt, another baby, hopefully would wait longer.

Ceiling-tall displays framed the silver rocket against an obsidian sky. The first stage's new nuclear thermal thrusters swayed and danced onscreen as mission control completed final gimbal tests. The second stage's polished aluminum skin grinned for the camera as the launch pad's lights reflected off its curves. She'd never seen a rocket launch on the far side of the moon. The displays were eerily still and grayscale. No stars. No white puffs of fuel vapor. The agency spent billions on a high-bandwidth, deep-color satellite link. Yet, the only hint was the red-white-and-blue flag atop the third stage. A tranquil, metallic ballet. No hues of the imminent violence.

Nolan's blue eyes and thick, long, brown hair framed a unibrow, now furrowed, and pursed lips. Five hours ago, he said there was no logical reason to be in the control room. The launch was happening on the moon's far side, four hundred thousand kilometers away, and was broadcast worldwide. She told him *she* was going to see it with her work family. *He* could stay home. Lying to Nolan wasn't her intent, but now she couldn't breathe, and her body ached to squat. Too late for meds, her own ring of fire would burn soon. Despite Nolan's heroic effort dragging the sofa from the agency lobby, sitting on it did not relieve the intense pressure in her abdomen. But she held it. If she told him, he would call the medics, who would cart her out. She could hold on for two minutes and thirty-eight seconds.

She squeezed his hand to reassure him they were leaving immediately after the launch. He shook his head, sighed, and looked away.

The deadpan voice again, "Fueling complete, strongback retract."

When the new Director, Blakely, hired Helena, Project Phoenix was a rescue. Before him, Congress defunded it three times and resurrected it four times. The staff called it Project Phoenix, not by its congressionally approved acronym, because of its repeated rebirth in fiery congressional hearings and because it was going to another sun.

Between the project's lives, the agency was the Wild West. Employees behaved like street mutts. Managers fought for crumbs, and corruption ran rampant. People did what they could to survive. Predictably, rot drove out competent engineers. Director Blakely's first initiative was to fire the engineering team and bring in fresh recruits. Her first lesson was that incompetence had no consequences. The old team sabotaged the project, deleting plans and pilfering hardware. She resented that no one went to jail for that. Director Blakely called it *providence* and told her to focus on the future. The new mandate: Showcase the agency's new nuclear thermal propulsion system and the use of drones for space colonization.

Movement onscreen. The launch pad's aluminum scaffolding twitched, shifted, and then a silver arm uncorked the payload faring. She prevented herself from squeezing to uncork her own pressure. She pulled her hand back for fear she'd crush Nolan's knuckles. He looked at his hand, then up at her. She didn't let go. Instead, she smiled, thinking it more like a grimace, then glanced back to the launch feed.

She tended to Phoenix like her own child. Demanding perfection. Director Blakely made her the unofficial trainer-in-chief, ensuring new hires knew how to do their job. The new engineers revamped the engines and adopted drone technology, allowing the agency to lift supplies to orbit and build a launch facility on the moon's far side.

She ran her hand over the bump under her blue-green t-shirt. If something went wrong today, Phoenix would be aborted. Her baby would turn to ashes on the launch pad.

Waiting to see it grow up would be the hardest part. For the next twenty-eight years, the Interstellar Image Relay Array System, IIRAS, would traverse space to Earth's nearest companion system, Alpha Centauri. First, the rocket would lift thousands of microsatellites from the solar system. Next, a massive laser would accelerate them across the void at mind- and time-stretching speeds, nearly two hundred million kilometers per hour or almost one-fifth the speed of light. Along the way, some would position themselves to establish a relay system to transmit images across space. At Proxima Centauri, one-third of the remaining satellites would decelerate into orbit around a habitable Earth-class exoplanet. The final cluster would continue to habitable exoplanets orbiting the Alpha Centauri AB twin stars. Ones that telescopes and sensors claimed had liquid water, carbon dioxide, and oxygen. All the correct conditions for life. Four and a quarter years later, IIRAS station would receive pictures. And five-point-two seconds after that, she would process them as IIRAS's image technician.

The relay satellites, each with its own power to re-broadcast messages over billions of kilometers, would form the longest transmission line in human history, sending clear images of an extrasolar planetary system and Earth's Sun, as viewed from Alpha Centauri. Her other child, Dilan, would be thirty-two when those images returned. Rubbing her bump, she wondered if his great grandkids would live there.

"IIRAS Primary in startup. T minus one minute thirty seconds."

Nolan mumbled something about Director Blakely between her pangs. She winced and smiled.

Despite Director Blakely's commitment to keeping the agency tidy, he would not have been her choice. IIRAS-the-agency had become a goliath bureaucracy. Within earshot, Director Blakely lectured her the way a pastor gives a sermon, emphasizing *science* as if he expected a *hallelujah* in the hallway. He said IIRAS would make countless scientific discoveries. It would be investigating dark matter and energy. He asked staff to imagine images of quasars, or black holes, or holograms of a red dwarf flaring in real time. She corrected him: Not real time. With a four-point-two-four-six year lag because of the speed of light.

He looked at her, silent, the way her pastor used to quiet the pews, then continued his lecture. So-and-so in astrophysics told him they could use the spectroscopy of our own sun, as seen from four light years away, to understand interstellar space. IIRAS was *not* a half-a-trillion-dollar wild goose chase searching for aliens. It was *not* space tourism. It was *not* a billionaire's pet project. *The mission of this agency is taxpayer-funded science, Helena.* Amen. When the new IT assistant, Bill Catwell or Cadell or something, showed up to wire her new computer, he wore a black and blue graphic shirt with the logo, *They said there would be aliens.* She told him to leave that one at home.

Those were Blakely's private sermons. In public, Blakely climbed Congressional Hill to spin bedtime stories. *Whatever makes our sponsors sleep at night, Helena.* And keeps the money flowing. When Senator X asked an ignorant question about aliens, instead of a lesson on science, Blakely delivered a hologram of a blue-green planet orbiting a red dwarf star like Proxima Centauri, then entertained the committee with sketches of the type of purple alien plants that might evolve on that planet. He came down the mountain converted. He added a dozen programs to search for extraterrestrial life. Staff showed up to the Halloween party as lavender aliens. Now, below her on the first floor, every control room desk had the agency's stuffed blue alien mascot propped in a corner.

Fairytales. There would not be aliens. Proxima Centauri was a red dwarf. Its periodic flares would incinerate life. Axyl Dover, a capable engineer she respected, warned her that the instruments showing an oxygen-rich atmosphere and carbon dioxide were likely false positives. His euphemism, *wishful thinking*. Her opinion, more like agency-learned incompetence. Director Blakely listened, said it was better to handle it privately, then handed her a batch of new hires to train.

She tried not to squeeze Nolan's hand. This contraction was lasting too long and something wet dribbled between her legs. Fifty-eight seconds would not make a difference now.

Then the live picture in the control room scrambled and cut out. Her body stopped obeying. An earthquake of pain radiated across her stomach and back and she started pushing. Painful yet relieving at the same time. Her body wanted it out.

"Space weather disturbance, standby."

She wanted to scream.

"LUNSAT 6 Buffer overload switching."

"Clearing. Visual link established."

She exhaled slowly, breathing through the contraction.

The rocket was back up on the monitors.

"IIRAS primary is go for launch."

The control room collectively exhaled, except hers was more like a grunt.

The clock ticked down. She couldn't restrain the push. The pressure moved lower. She tried to breathe slowly, evenly, and ignore Nolan's stare. How could he not know what was happening? Forty seconds. Her stomach, angry, squeezed.

"Director confirms go." Cheers in the control room.

Thirty-eight seconds. This contraction was too soon after the last and far worse than before. What would waiting thirty-two years be like?

"T minus thirty seconds."

Deep breath, inhale.

"T minus fifteen seconds. Main engine startup."

Yes, it was happening now. So much pressure on her pelvis. The control room counted down from ten seconds, then erupted in cheers and applause as IIRAS lifted off.

Helena ignored her swollen ankles and the bowling ball in her hard belly. She pushed herself off the seat to join the standing ovation. She clenched Nolan's wrist, then doubled over and dug her nails into Nolan's arm. He shook his head, eyes on the pink and yellow running down her legs. Nolan said, *breathe and don't push, Helena.*

Too late. She was on the floor, legs up, feeling her own ring of fire. People scrambling. Nolan again, *Jesus Helena, you are crowning.* She laughed. When the EMTs arrived, they told her something, but instinct had taken over. This is where she wanted to deliver Dilan. She pushed and squeezed. Nolan's hands were bloody. Dilan was much more painful than Phoenix.

2

United States Lunar Colony
Procellarum Improvement District, Texas
October 2073

Kate Devana strode through the metal doors into the critical care wing of the colony hospital. Miraculously, the wedding melee and stampede had resulted in only one patient, Helena Darcy, female, sixty-four years old. The intake monitor at the nurses' station confirmed Helena was in stall fourteen, at the far back corner of an otherwise empty ICU.

Nothing had changed in the eight months since Kate herself had been a patient here. The smell of blood and disinfectant. Hospital-standard oatmeal paint. One human nurse and two nursebots staffed the nurses' station, wearing identical hospital-issued green scrubs and disinterested fake smiles. A nursebot engaged her with an approving *proceed*, which Kate took to mean it had scanned her face and validated her credentials.

She was here because twenty minutes ago, she finished evacuating a wedding party from the transparent dome enclosing The Crown Oasis, the lunar colony's most luxurious hotel-casino.

An hour before that, the newlyweds, he in a cinnamon tux and she in a burgundy dress, had no forewarning of the impending chaos.

The October wedding kicked off the holiday season. The colony's designers did a spectacular job making people forget they lived on the moon. Bouquets of orange mums and purple African daisies decorated butterscotch tables. The barrel planters along the walkways brimmed with white gourds, pumpkins, and squash imported from Earth. The transparent fifteen-story dome covering The Crown Oasis and its outer gardens was a window to the lunar night outside that reflected the wedding. Under it, guests chatted as effervescently as the champagne in their hands. They debated the romantic constellations they might see if the lights dimmed or asked one of the human or drone servers for more of the delectable mushroom caps stuffed with crab and crisp bacon, while swigging billion-year-old water, mined from premium comets, twice distilled, with perfect mineral balance.

A superb wedding. One she could picture for herself in the unlikely event two things happened. One, she and Rae had the tens of millions of dollars needed to blow on a lunar wedding. Two, both of them went insane enough to spend that kind of money.

Although, she'd change a few things.

Like the protest and murder halting the nuptials.

It started with one protester disguised as a server, shouting "Earth First," then ripping off his hotel uniform to unveil a blue and green graphic shirt with an image of Earth. One hundred and thirty-three guests rolled their eyes.

A staff server messaged security, *someone is smashing glasses.* Meanwhile, human and drone servers continued serving hors d'oeuvres. Then, more protestors unveiled themselves wearing identical blue-green shirts and screaming the same slogans. The four protestors toppled the server drones and overturned the barrel planters, sending gourds rolling under tables. Then they started chanting, singing, slapping food and wine out of the guests' hands, and scolding them for eating lunacultured vat-grown meat. Some guests responded with choice profanity, others with shoves and punches. Protestors returned fire with flowers and food.

Kate and her new deputy Jin arrived, moving through the ruckus toward the protestors. Her initial impression, seeing millionaires in a food fight, was to grab some bacon-wrapped scallops before they were wasted. Vat-grown or not, they were delicious, and the Icy Comet brand water served here was outstanding. Cool, refreshing, always good to be hydrated before a brawl.

That didn't make it to her report, because thirty-eight seconds later, the lights cut out and paused the melee. The guests looked up with mouths agape, thinking a planetarium event was planned. Guests and hotel staff were treated to thousands of stars while the protestors used the darkness to escape. Kate kept her eyes on the protestors until four loud thuds reverberated in the dome.

Then the lights flickered on. Four objects resembling human bodies had spattered against the outside of the transparent aluminum dome, like the world's grisliest bloody mosquitos on the solar system's largest windshield. Blood and gore foamed and rolled down the dome's outer surface, streaking and freeze-drying, leaving blood and human organs smearing the dome's south quadrant.

Kate recognized the props. They were realistic fluid-filled silicone torsos that the military used for weapons testing. Unfortunately, none of the guests had Kate's insight. At once, one hundred fifty people gasped, panicked, screamed, and stampeded for the doors. Except one. The burgundy bride elected to ignore everyone's safety and her own, standing with a camera on the bridal party table, live-streaming the event to the lunar server.

Burgundy's new husband pleaded with her to run. Kate tapped him on the shoulder and told him to get to the exit. Kate had to wrestle burgundy bridezilla down from her perch, twist the phone from her hand, then drag her to safety. Bridezilla kicked and screamed. Not even grateful to be safely reunited with her sobbing groom and guests. She demanded her device with her wedding holovideos back. Kate shook her head. It was now evidence.

All the guests made it safely into the hotel, save Helena Darcy. Kate found her under one of the tables, her wife Kenna and first husband Nolan kneeling beside her and shouting for help. Upon seeing Helena, Kate knew she had two problems, but Helena had one much bigger one.

Kate's first problem was that the protesters had vanished in the stampede. Her second problem, she did not have time to chase them because Helena Darcy's butterscotch dress was blotched red.

Helena had not been trampled. In fact, no one had. Even the guests that meleed with the protestors were no worse than bruised. On inspection, Helena's problem turned out to be four deep stab wounds to her back and chest. Rolling Helena over, her butterscotch dress was soaked, and she was lying in a pool of blood. Kate rendered first aid as best she could, but Helena was already unresponsive with a weak pulse. Jin found a stretcher and assigned two drones to speed Helena to the hospital with Kenna and Nolan in tow.

Kate triaged the wedding riot, tasked Jin with taking statements and collecting evidence, then bolted to the hospital twenty minutes behind the EMT drones. She found an electric cart on I-10, the staff-level colony superhighway connecting wings. Drones, maidbots, and human staff cleared a path as she sped along the corridor.

A hospital notice pinged her phone on the way up the hospital stairs. Helena Darcy was in stall fourteen. A second message followed from Brigadier General Kelli McMichaels.

Sorry I couldn't warn you.

Kate balled up her fist. The last time her ex Kelli made her punch a wall, she landed in the hospital with a boxer's fracture. Kate exhaled and marched through the curtain to stall fourteen, where Kenna was in tears, unable to speak. Kenna sat beside the bed, sobbing, mascara smeared, blood and makeup plastered on a formerly butterscotch chiffon dress, holding Helena's ashen hand.

The medical machines marked Helena Darcy's death with silence.

Kenna rose, and Kate let her sob and shudder on her shoulder. Kenna's face was hot with grief and her hair smelled like blood. Kate might have whispered, I'm sorry for your loss, or some other irrelevant thing people say when someone dies. She'd said it dozens of times. Every time it felt pointless. Of course she's sorry. Everyone is sorry, except the person who stabbed Helena.

Kate said, "Is there anything I can do?"

Kenna pulled away. "Find who did this and make them pay. That's what you do, right?"

Kate inhaled and looked away. Helena was on the gurney, uncovered. An oxygen tube hung from her bloodless, gray lips. Her eyes were glassy and staring through Kate, resigned, saying, *there is nothing you can do.* She looked cold and Kate wanted to cover her up.

Kenna made justice sound simple. The colony was eight hours and four hundred thousand kilometers from Earth. Like a cruise ship in the middle of the Indian Ocean, far from everything—except farther. The witnesses would be gone in a few days, scattered across the globe. She couldn't hold them. Helena Darcy wasn't a billionaire or a celebrity, so no mediabots would demand that police put a mobile lab on a rocket to collect evidence and then run fancy algorithms to analyze it. The

Feds that did come here were more interested in investigating political enemies, not ordinary crimes like murder.

Staring into Helena's eyes, her temples throbbed. In her experience, once a human learned it could kill with impunity, there would be more killing. Maybe in her jurisdiction. Maybe even Kenna, because who knew what this bastard was up to.

She looked back at Kenna and offered another hug. "Of course, I will." She felt like it was a lie. Another irrelevant thing people say when someone is murdered.

Her biggest problem, maybe herself. Not seeing things clearly had become a bad habit of hers recently. Hubris and hominess had crept into her life.

But she needed to do something. She needed to get the guy who did this. Even if she had to deliver frontier justice by crawling into this guy's bedroom at night to knife him the way he did Helena. Or reach through satellites to deliver a billion volts. If only to send a message, nobody came to her jurisdiction to murder people. It didn't matter if it was Helena Darcy or one of the pros in fishnets plying their services in the red light district. Not here, not on her watch. That's why she advocated for this job. Can't let this place become the Wild West.

3

United States Lunar Colony
Procellarum Improvement District, Texas
August 2073

Eight weeks earlier, three voices echoed as the elevator doors opened to a sea-salt-colored hallway on a Piscis penthouse floor. The loudest was that of Kate's new partner, Jinho Knight, shouting *sit down*. Then, as she passed the first brass-trimmed door, a crackle emanated from a half-open threshold four suites away. Then silence. Kate smiled.

Five minutes ago, the message from Jin read, *outside Gil's place. put me in coach.*

While the lower levels of Piscis were leased to affluent, long-term residents, the penthouse floors eleven through fifteen were the most distressing. Spacious suites, rented monthly, usually to celebrities with heavy baggage.

She could have said no. But she needed to take his training wheels away some time.

He had answered a call to the eleventh floor of Piscis for a domestic disturbance. The two disturbers were Jaxton and Leni Gil, and neither were domestic. They were rarely sober, multimillion-dollar celebrities known for bad holomovies, bad press, and bad behavior. If this weren't her third visit, she wouldn't know their names.

Six weeks ago, she greeted Jin at the spaceport on his first day. He disembarked the lunar cruise ship *Independence* on July 6th in a red, white, and blue outfit, still decorated for the holiday two days prior. So far, the colony had been quiet. Today he would experience the penumbra of the August 2073 lunar eclipse, a total eclipse and a blood moon, which meant absolute bloody mayhem on the colony. Tourist hordes had rented every square centimeter to party, spectate, and have sex as the moon blocked out Earth's sun.

In May, nine weeks before Jin disembarked *Independence*, Kate picked his name out of a hat. Not literally, although Dr. Apul Mulawarman's supersize quantum computer felt like rolling dice. He was the CEO of Lunar Foundries, which made computer chips in their factories on the moon for seventy-five percent of the devices in the solar system. He was also on the Lunar Tourism Board and was one of her bosses. His computer scoured applicants' curricula vitae and resumes, scraped servers, and ingested social media around the globe, plugged it all into his black box algorithm, then gave her a shortlist of five names.

Her first question reviewing the applicant pool was whether there was some as-yet-undiscovered narcotic in the billion-year-old ice at the poles. Something that made two hundred A-list high achievers want to blow their career moving from elite cybercrime or tactical units to breaking up one-sixth-g-bar fights in the red light district of the colony. Or answering domestic disturbances for celebrities. She had no illusions about her job. She was the head of a one-person, soon to be two, cruise ship security detail. Except this cruise ship traveled fifty times the speed of the fastest ocean liner, on the moon, with multi-multi-millionaires as guests.

Her younger brother Greg, who jumped on a job referral to be a bouncer at a strip club in the red light district, said, *It's the moon, Katy. Thirteen billion people want a job here.* No, she told him, thirteen billion minus one. Doctor Rachel Torres' smiling hazel eyes and ample curves attracted her to the colony, not the job. In the mirror, she saw a rent-a-ninja with shoulder length, curly black hair and brown eyes keeping drunk tourists from getting violent. Which was fine because she also saw something else in the mirror, something she'd never seen, a future.

The algorithm distilled the sour mash to five suckers, all dumb enough to want to give up promising careers to work for her. She sighed and swiped right to interview all of them. She questioned their sanity, and her own. She was as clear as she could be with all five candidates. The colony was glamorous. The job wasn't.

Of the five she interviewed, only Jin was sober about the job. Jin had three things in his favor and one that wasn't. First, he had a stellar resume, including a degree from a big-name school in cybercrime. Second, he had Homeland Security experience, and before that was in the military, so he understood *hurry up and wait*, *planning to plan*, and filing pointless reports that the brass would squirrel away in a dank room and ignore.

She explained during the interview that crime was voluntarily reported, bad for the colony's image, so few hotels volunteered to report it. In fact, none volunteered. Guests didn't stick around long enough for police or Feds to arrive and follow up. Her department—she couldn't suppress the grin when she said that because her department was just her—mostly focused on priority one calls: immediate threats to life, sexual assaults, human trafficking, and the like. Hotel-casino security focused on the rest.

Jin nodded, saying he was eager to help. The third attribute in his favor, he exuded athletic confidence. He did not have the expected flabby physique of a cyber desk jockey. Instead, he had the look and disposition of a brindle boxer. Kate was tall, at one hundred eighty centimeters or five foot eleven. He was twenty centimeters taller, as tall as her brother Greg. He had smooth brown skin and broad, muscular shoulders and biceps. He was shy during the interview. Once the ice broke, he showed he could flash a fierce, intimidating frown or sad puppy dog eyes. He was as sweet as cotton candy and eager to please. She did not count his innocence and willingness to please in his favor. She said those were virtues, just not for this job. She warned him he couldn't be a lapdog and allow the uber-rich celebrities and residents to bully or manipulate him. He needed to be guarded and stand his ground.

He nodded, saying, *stand my ground, I can do that, boss.* She offered him the job on the spot, and he accepted.

Today was going to be his first test.

Stepping into the Gil's apartment, a war zone, her first question: How long would Jin last? Based on the red, white, and green shards of glass decorating the floor like glitter, not long. Her previous partner, Cris Davis, quit after a week. But there were bullets involved in that. Here there were only thrown dishes and scuffed and dented walls. And exploded bags of mustard and ketchup mixed into fiery orange puddles on the kitchen floor. Also, brown coffee-scented liquor and red wine peppered the floor. She grew optimistic, thinking no bullets, until she saw the gun bagged up on the kitchen counter.

As glass and debris crunched under her feet, Kate counted days. Today was Tuesday. The eclipse was Thursday. If Jin had any sanity in that genius brain, he would quit by Friday. Intelligent people didn't cosplay janitor to entitled celebrities.

Kate crunched a path between the red and chocolate puddles to find Jaxton and Leni Gil sitting sullen, exhausted, and handcuffed together on the sofa, beyond an overturned table and chairs. Their clothes smeared with food, wine, and broken glass. Jin stood over them, wearing a big grin and wagging his head. Jaxton had a bloody hand, a gash on his face, and a red welt forming above his eye that would be black soon. Leni seemed relatively unscathed, except for two char marks between the red stains on her white blouse. Both had bloodshot, half-open eyes that rolled in disapproval at Kate's arrival.

Kate looked from Leni, to Jaxton, to Jin, then back to Leni. Kate knew the script by heart. So did the Gils, as this wasn't her first visit. Still, she needed to do the read-through. Today, she was adding a twist at the end.

"Leni, do you want to explain first?"

Leni huffed and rolled her eyes to the side.

"How about you Jaxton. Want to talk about the bloody hand and gash?"

Jaxton looked at Leni, then glared at a point a thousand meters behind Kate.

"Do either of you want to press charges? Go to the hospital?"

Jaxton and Leni both shook their heads. Kate turned to Jin. "What happened before I got here?"

"I could have handled it better. This one started to throw bottles at me. I tazed her. This one tried to punch me. He ran into my fist."

"Are you hurt?"

"Nah. She has horrible aim. His face is soft."

She smiled. "One-sixth g. People overthrow. Weapons?"

Jin pointed to a clear bag on the kitchen counter. "One gun from the safe in the bedroom."

"Used?"

"Not on me. Or each other."

"Video?"

"What I got off their phones is 2D and choppy." Jin read notes off his pad. "I can't tell what the argument is about through all the screaming. She started throwing dishes and food. She winged him in the hand and head. He threw a bottle back then hid in the bathroom. After she stopped pounding on the door, he came out of the bathroom and tackled her. That's when the video cuts off. When I got here, they were wrestling on the floor. When I separated them, they both attacked me."

"Make sure we get a copy of all the video."

Leni finally opened her mouth. Kate shushed her. "Exercise your right to shut up. You are doing so well. Jin, message Piscis security. Get them an escort to the spaceport. I want them on a shuttle yesterday."

Jaxton spoke. "Don't talk to Leni that way. And I can't leave. I'm filming."

Kate ignored him, surveying the room.

"You can't send me home. The producer will have your job. You won't work—"

"Jin, make sure you get good holograms of all the damage. Also, their injuries. Note that they waived medical attention."

"Done and done."

"Did you hear me, cunt? If you send me back to Earth and shut down this film, I will have you fired."

Leni's eyes narrowed as the nerve impulse traveled to her arms. Kate wasn't going to block it. Leni balled her fists. The swing. Yeah, Leni didn't like that word. She missed, sailing high.

Jaxton doubled down, insulting Leni. Kate pictured finishing him with a kick. Neck broken, head lolled to the side, a death smirk on his face. Then she had a different image, that of Jaxton in boot camp, going into the mess hall the first day then coming out with the entitlement beat out of him. It worked wonders for her teenage bad attitude. After, he'd be plopped into a war zone where the real zingers were bullets, not words. She had nine skulls tattooed on her arm, friends who didn't come home, none killed by petty insults.

In a few hours, he wouldn't be her problem. She said, "Shh. Both of you. Sit still or Jin will taze you both."

"I can't leave. You're ruining my career."

Leni rolled her eyes. "Your acting is so bad they will be glad to get rid of you. You only got that part because you screwed the casting assistant." Leni yanked her handcuffs. "Do I need to sit next to him on the shuttle?"

Jaxton had a retort forming on his lips, but he looked beyond Kate and held it. Glass crunched behind her. Kate turned to see a woman in a baby blue pantsuit, white blouse, and black flats, with blond hair in a ponytail. The woman was sticking out her right hand while standing one-legged, her right leg bent behind her, using her left hand to shake and smack debris off her shoe.

Masterful coordination in lunar gravity. The woman was either an Olympic gymnast or had a lot of practice cleaning the Gil's debris off her business clothes.

"Annelle Gray, two N's two L's. I am the Gil's publicist and family attorney."

Kate did not shake her hand. "I like the double irony."

"What irony?"

"That this is a family, and the drama is getting publicized." Kate pointed at the couch. "These two are on the next shuttle. They both waived medical."

Gray pinched her lips and then waved her hand like a magic wand to shut her clients up. "Send the bill to—"

"The production company. Check."

"Can we clear the hotel while we take them to the shuttle? They can't be seen like this."

"Piscis security will take them out the staff level. They won't be seen."

"Can we clear—"

"We are not clearing the hotel." Kate shook her head.

"Handcuffs?"

"I'm flattered Annelle with two N's, but I am seeing someone."

Gray looked to Jin for backup. He smirked and looked at his pad.

Gray said, "Funny. I meant them. Can we take them off?"

Kate looked the couple over. Leni rolled her eyes. Kate said, "Can they behave?"

Gray said, "I don't like your attitude towards my clients."

"It's all I have. Your brats threw a seven figure tantrum and nearly killed themselves and my deputy."

"I told you, the production company will pay."

"Next time, they book separate rooms. Ideally in the Chinese colony."

The Chinese lunar colony was a two hour rocket ride across the moon.

Gray said, "Or what? You can't—"

"Or next time Jin will drag them through the casino and talk to every camera on the way. Real family publicity. Right Jin?"

Jin smiled a great big tail-wagging smile.

"You can't do that. Do you know who they are?"

"I know who they are. Look me up. I don't bluff."

"I can have you fired."

Kate shook her head and smiled. "I am not that lucky today. Jin, let's go. Annelle with two N's and two L's needs to have a family meeting and these two probably want to change into something more comfortable for the trip home."

"What about the gun, boss?"

Kate looked at Gray, then her sulking clients. "It's Tuesday. Leave it here."

Jin squinted and furrowed his face.

"Rae doesn't like me bringing her dead bodies on Sundays. But today is Tuesday, so if they shoot themselves today—"

Kate smirked. Annelle opened her mouth but didn't take the bait.

Leni raised the arm cuffed to Jaxton. "Handcuffs, bitch?"

"When your security escort gets here, they can decide whether you are behaving."

Kate expected another protest from Annelle, but it didn't come. Gray knew the script as well as Kate, and if she were any good, anticipated the twist. She and Jin crunched out of the room.

In the hallway, Kate thought Jin finally grasped the colony's eclipse mayhem.

"The whole eclipse going to be like this?"

"Worse. All I ask is that you give me a week's notice before you quit."

In a week, the eclipse would be over. The circus would ebb with depleted tourists on their way home. At the beginning of September, Kate planned a belated six-month anniversary getaway with Rae. After Jin quit, she could focus on hiring another deputy.

"Are you kidding? That was fun."

Kate paused at the elevator, studying the closed door, thinking, he was as loco as she was. "Did you get yourself zapping Leni on video?"

"No. I forgot—"

"Good. Last thing we need is something out of context on the server. Remember I told you, there is no such thing as privacy on the colony." She paused to quiz his face. "Why did you taze her?"

"She was throwing bottles at me. What would you have done?"

His face. Innocent and sweet. He didn't enjoy it as much as she would have. Good for him.

"Shot her," she said, deadpan. "I wouldn't have gotten that close."

Jin paused, then laughed. "My way is more efficient. Less paperwork."

"Less satisfying, too." The crackle echoed in her head. She grinned and slapped his back. "You handled it great."

"How do you want me to write this up?"

"Well, that depends."

"On what?"

"Do you want to testify at their divorce and slander trial, or not?"

"Definitely not."

"Me neither. So spread the blame around. Make the report a land mine so no one will want to step on us."

"So, the truth."

"Mostly. Stick to what can be documented on video. Leave out the fun part."

"What about if—"

"If it's not on video, did it really happen? And will you remember it four years from now well enough to swear to it at their divorce and slander trial?"

Jin was silent, facing the doors. Kate called the elevator and told it I-10.

"Meat memory is unreliable. The worst. Stick to what's on video."

Jin opened his mouth, seemingly to debate the point, then said, "10-4 boss."

4

Earth-moon Lagrange point L5
Spaceship *Tesseract*
September 2073

Two weeks after the eclipse, miraculously, Jin was still Kate's deputy, and she and Rae were accelerating to their getaway. Rae wanted to paint, so she had Kate perform a poor impression of an art model on *Tesseract's* bed.

Behind Kate, the stars drifted outside *Tesseract's* panoramic windows as they cruised towards High Frontier Grill, where a five-star steak, a ninety-nine point Cabernet, and a stellar view at the Earth-Moon Lagrange point L5 awaited. The cabin lights were low. Stars shimmered through the blue and purple bottles stacked on *Tesseract's* mirrored bar. Her cool violet reflection glittered as if lit by a celestial disco ball.

"Lie still, sweetie."

Kate tried. She did not earn the call sign 'Kinetic' by lying still and posing. She had forward, reverse, and afterburner. Neutral only redlined her heartbeat and made her suck air. After the fourth *lie still*, Kate got up, donned her bathrobe, then shuffled to *Tesseract's* wine cabinet behind the bar.

Time for a wine break.

Rae's head swiveled, tracking Kate to the bar, then put down her brush. Kate rooted through the wine fridge and hoisted two glasses and a bag of Bien Courage Estates Merlot. Rae got up, tying her bathrobe, then coasted to the bar. Kate poured as Rae sat, framed by the starlight of the Milky Way, with an unfinished portrait of Kate in the background.

Kate raised her glass, clinked, then chugged her wine and poured another.

Rae sipped her wine, mumbling *mmmhm*, the sound she made when her son Axio was into something nefarious. Today, Rae's hazel eyes were cool green, not like the Atlantic Ocean, but more like the handle of a Damascus steel knife Kate bought in Tokyo. Detached and scalpel sharp. Rae brandished those eyes during autopsies or when excising Axio's problems. Kate's stomach clenched. Those eyes had never been deployed at her.

"What did Aria say about the apartment?"

Kate sipped her wine and looked away. "No problem. It reverts to the Tourism Board at the end of the month. She will hold it open."

Rae raised her eyebrows. "For you? Did you ask—"

Kate waved her empty palm. "No. No. She has plans. Serves some plot point in her four dimensional real estate strategy." Kate took another sip.

"Don't be nervous about meeting my parents."

"I've already met your parents. And your sister, Meloni."

"Virtually. Not in person."

Kate smiled, more like a wince. "Looking forward to it. You sure about my place? They could stay—"

"Meloni will use the pull-out couch. I will move the table to storage and rent a spare bed."

Kate had operated from a sub in the middle of the Indian Ocean. Drunk sailors. Cramped quarters. There were always fights. She swigged her wine.

"But if your parents stayed at my place—"

"—then we have to pay for it, Kate. My parents don't have that kind of money. It's not practical. And unnecessary."

"But I—" Kate swirled her wine and shut her mouth. Rae made more than Kate, but Kate's expenses were lower—practically zero for years—so Kate had stockpiled her money. A cache any supply clerk would envy. Meant to be used though, not just hoarded. Extra space, so everyone was comfortable, seemed worth it. But if Kate offered to pay, she would get the lecture on independence and frugality. Salted with practicality and necessity.

Rae smiled. "It'll be cozy. The six of us. We've done it before."

Six of them. Rae's sister Meloni, Rae's son Axio from a previous marriage, and Rae's parents all crammed into Rae's tiny flat. Kate had lived that cramped on boats and space stations, but not by choice.

"We'll make it work." Kate slurped, then refilled the glasses.

Rae sipped her wine, then said, "Do you want to tell me about Kelli?"

Kate stared at the counter, teeth clenched. "No." She scarfed her wine. "But I will anyway."

"When I start an autopsy Kate, I usually find it best to start with the basics."

"Name, rank and serial number?"

Rae smiled and tapped her finger on the bar. Rae's autopsy patients didn't feel the green eyes flaying them. Kate looked around the bar for anesthesia. From a shelf, she grabbed a bottle of vodka and shot glasses. Rae put her hand over her shot glass.

"You said your relationship was volatile."

Kate blew out a breath, then poured herself a shot. "You could say that." How to explain the scars on her elbow and wrist? Those were Kate's fault, punching walls.

Rae frowned and then tapped her finger on the bar again. "You did say that."

"She saw us as a military superpower. A Washington D.C. power couple. We fought over the dumbest things. She forced me to Presidential galas. Showed me off. General so-and-so meet Kate the well-bred show dog. Look how many medals she has." Kate shook her head and downed her vodka. "So we fought. I punched a door on my way out. Got stitches. Then I put on a nice dress and went anyway."

Kate studied the grain on the bar counter. Real wood was too heavy for space, but this countertop was a good imitation.

She drew a circle with her finger and sighed. "And around it went. Then my fifteen-year service anniversary came up, and I'd had enough. The next time, I didn't punch a wall. I just left. I thought, *Nope, game over.* Left all my stuff—" Kate shrugged. "The important stuff was on base anyway, so I wasn't leaving much behind."

"So what happened Wednesday?"

"How exactly do you know about Wednesday? It's supposed to be—" Kate interrupted herself. "Doesn't matter. I am not cheating, if that's what you think."

Rae smirked over her wine glass. "Kate, if I thought for a nanosecond you were cheating we wouldn't be here. Give me credit." Rae sipped her wine. "And if you do, take it somewhere without a satellite and internet connection. Cause I will know."

Kate exhaled. "How did you hear?"

"I heard Wednesday from Doctor Rheese."

Kate counted the tawny specks in Rae's hazel eyes. Some days they were warm brown. Today they glowed red under the reflected light.

"Doctor Rheese?"

"Aria's doctor. He treated her for extreme anxiety and talked to me like I already knew what happened. Then he wanted to know what I knew. Imagine how embarrassing that was for me since I knew *nothing* because my *partner* does not talk to me."

Kate stared at the shot glass. The first night they spent together, Rae said, *everyone knows everyone's business here at the speed of light.* A lesson Kate kept re-learning.

"It's supposed to be classified."

"That's not an excuse, Kate. Your ex dragged you to god knows where, and Aria—" Rae shook her head and slurped her wine.

Kate thought another shot of vodka would smooth the next part. She chugged it. Then said, "There is no good way to say this, so I just will. I am going to quit this job. I can't do this project. Maybe we shouldn't make it official until I get my shit together. Not fair to you."

Rae laughed. Her full face and belly into it. "Quit."

Rae's eyes had the same smirk as the wine glass, her tone mocking as if quitting was in the same category as seeing extraterrestrial aliens and a nine hundred foot Jesus. *Oh, you saw bigfoot. You're quitting.* The same tone.

Out loud it sounded dumb to Kate too.

"I don't see a choice. I'm not worried. Private security for these billionaires—"

Rae wound her left hand. The right one sloshed the wine. "Rewind. Tell me how Aria had a panic attack. What project?"

"Hangar C. That's where Kelli had us meet. We all got the same message. Jin, me, and Aria. We were picked up in a personnel carrier and transported to the military base." Kate stared at her empty shot glass, then said, "I was assigned to the Presidential Security detail. Project Orion."

"So—the rumors are true. Assigned?"

"They needed someone to direct colony security. Since I am the Chief of Colony Security..." Kate shrugged and refilled her anesthesia. It wasn't working.

"When does President Latham get here?"

"She arrives late October or early November. The exact date will be announced at the last minute for security reasons."

"Why all the secrecy?"

"Security. While she's en route she will be extremely vulnerable."

"She will be on a rocket—"

"In space, hundreds of thousands of kilometers from defenses, with vulnerability in four dimensions."

"Four?"

"Time is your enemy on an eight hour rocket ride."

"This will be the first off-world visit of a U.S. President. Olicia Barron must be thrilled."

"Aria says she hates it. Olicia supports her opposition. But she can't say no to a Presidential visit."

Rae mumbled *mmmhm*.

"Aria is on the security committee since the President will be staying at The Crown Oasis."

Mmmhm, again. Then Rae said, "Who else is on the committee—besides you three?"

Kate fingered the vodka bottle's label, hoping her spacesickness would pass. The vodka was expensive, came in real glass. Odd, she felt acceleration and weight. They were going six thousand kilometers per hour to L5. But the stars outside floated and she couldn't tell which way they were going. Had she lost her space legs?

"Security is tight. It's being run out of the Pentagon."

"You're saying the Space Force is running security."

Kate's calves tightened and her stomach squeezed. Run, hide, or fight. Or option four, pour a shot. When did she drink the last one? How many was that?

"Fucks sake Kate. You're telling me Kelli is on the committee."

Rae's eyes dissected Kate. She understood how Axio must have felt. Kate raised her shot glass and swallowed. It refluxed in her throat.

"Worse. Wednesday I found out she *is* the committee. The President handpicked her and promoted her to Brigadier General. She is overseeing all lunar Presidential security. We were whisked across the lunar surface to a secure facility on the military base."

Kate paused to let the news and vodka settle.

"I was serious about quitting. Fuck her. I am not going to be her little parade Pomeranian again. She can find another face to sit on while she climbs the ladder."

"Why couldn't she come here?"

"She treated it as though she were planning World War Three. Had to be secure. Lectured us about leaks. Then halfway over Aria got claustrophobic and hyperventilated."

"Half the colonists would have vomited. What was she thinking? You were in a windowless space casket only a millimeter thick without suits."

"We calmed her down. The experience is going to leave a scar."

"She's good at that. Leaving scars."

"My scars were my own dumb fault. I should have just—well what I should have done is broke it off earlier." She inhaled. Then said, "Which is why this time, I think—"

Rae shook her head. "So, what'd she say?"

Kate refilled Rae's wine glass, then fondled the vodka bottle.

"This vodka is good. It's made in Alaska from sugar cane. Charcoal filtered. Real glass bottle."

"Not interested in the bottle, Kate. What did she say?"

Kate stared at the bar countertop and puffed her cheeks. It wasn't what Kelli said. Kelli had been trying to wheedle her way back into Kate's life for six months. Kate had used every tool she knew—dodged, postponed, and canceled—but couldn't ignore her messages because she needed to cooperate with the military on colony security issues.

On Wednesday, Kelli set a trap, carpet bombing Kate's senses in person. Kelli ditched the battle dress camo, instead holding Wednesday's briefing in civvies—white high heels, pants, and a handsome wide-lapel gray jacket exposing a low-cut white blouse. She dyed her hair blond and styled it in a short bob.

Kelli spent the hour spewing nonsense buzzwords while standing too close, leaning into Kate, and wafting a musky scent. Kelli punctured Kate with her kryptonite-blue eyes, then flirted. The moisture rushed to Kate's libido, which habitually fell for the deception and that low-cut blouse after every fight.

Kate held the air in her cheeks a few heartbeats to let the nausea pass, then let the air out.

"Just nonsense. She said she's looking forward to working closely together again."

"You mean looking forward to stealing credit for another of your successful assignments on her way up the ladder."

"Tomato, to-*mah*-to."

"She said that, *closely together*?"

Rae stared at her empty shot glass. Kate poured two.

"You went to her turf. I am surprised Aria went along with this plan."

Why did Kate go? She searched for something that didn't sound like an excuse.

"You are right. Kelli hounded us about security. It was not a good plan."

A *terrible* plan. Her gut knew it. What was she supposed to do?

"How was she dressed?"

Kate waved her arms. "Look. It doesn't matter. I am going to quit. Problem solved."

Rae glared and shook her head. "The run and hide Kate is not the one I fell in love with. You are hiding from my parents and now Kelli."

Kate scrunched up her forehead. "I am not hiding. If I stay on this job, I have to stay on this detail reporting to her. I thought you would be happy—"

"So you are going to run and hide every time an ex comes out of the woodwork? You have a lot of them."

"No, but—"

"But what?"

It was true, Kate did have a lot, but Rae didn't have to point it out. Kate didn't respond.

"You are not fighting. I don't know what that means. What happened to the Kate that rides the lightning bareback?"

Kate watched the stars on the vodka bottle spin around. Which direction was she going?

"But if I keep this job—"

"So you just let her take your job."

"I don't need it. Private security pays—"

"You told me this is the best job you ever had."

"It is but—"

"But what?"

Waving her arms, Kate said, "She's a Brigadier General for chrissake. I can't just tell her to fuck off, Rae."

"Kate Devana can." Rae flicked her pointer finger. "*You* just don't want to. I understand. I knew you were like this. You military brats are all the same." Rae puffed her cheeks and pushed off from the bar.

"Like what?"

Walking away, Rae said, "Veni Vidi Vici Vaginae."

Kate opened her mouth, then closed it. She had a retort. A good one. She canceled it. Better to shut up when a superior officer gave a well-deserved ass-chewing unless you wanted a dishonorable discharge.

"Where are you going?"

"To the bathroom. I need a break. The wine went right through me."

Kate exhaled and stared out the window. She was dizzy. The stars barely moved. Space was deceptive. Thousands of white dots outside. But each trillions of kilometers from the other. In between, empty. Thousands of lifetimes apart. She would survive alone in an EVA suit for a few hours at most. Humans needed a fragile cocoon of life support to survive space travel.

And if the debris detectors went bad, and a tiny unseen piece of garbage hit the hull, *boom*, life over. Fuck, why didn't she see this coming?

Rae yelled from behind the bathroom curtain. "Maybe you're right about your place. It's going to be crowded with all six of us."

"I don't mind paying for another month."

"I think that's a good idea. Maybe two."

Kate's face flushed, burning. Her fists clenched. This was her own stupid fault. She kicked the bar, rattling the bottles behind her. Her ankle hurt. She turned to see no blood. Just a scuff on the bar. *Shew.*

She straightened the bottles. In the mirror, her reflection scowled and then held up a wine glass to toast her, "Good job Kate. Good effing job."

5

United States Lunar Colony
Procellarum Improvement District, Texas
September 2073

Helena Darcy's door binged. She checked the security video, then opened it to a woman in a pressed blue suit with closely cropped brown hair. The woman peered over Helena's shoulder, attempting to see inside. Helena and her family, her husbands Nolan and Paul and wife Kenna, had just moved to their new Cygnus flat on the lunar colony a few months ago. Nicer than her previous colony apartment. It had much more room for Nolan's booming candle business, Scents of Earth.

Helena kept the door half-closed. Floral candle scents wafted out, blocking the stench of the Fed from coming in. Not even a thousand of her husband's candles would get that smell out of the seat cushions.

"If you are here about your monthly delivery, the drones are running behind because of an outage."

This woman wasn't a customer. Helena wanted to give the agent a chance to back out politely.

The woman flashed her badge and credentials. "Special Agent Milya Bolkov."

Helena sighed. There was nothing special about this agent. All these Feds were clones with the same constipated half-frowns and the empathy of robots.

Helena started to swing the door closed. Bolkov put her hand on the door.

"I need to talk to you about your—"

"Leave my fucking son alone."

"I think he's getting himself in trouble."

"So, what else is new. He's halfway across the moon managing the far side station. He and his boyfriend Ted. Not much trouble he can get into there."

"I think a lot."

Helena sighed again and tried to close the door. Bolkov stiff-armed the door.

"I need you to leave."

Bolkov shuffled the pressure from her arm to her foot, then took out her phone. She swiped through it and then turned it around to display two videos as a split screen. The right video, Bill Caddell's bespectacled face, sweaty, round, bloodless, and in his office at eleven thirteen pm at night, based on the time stamp. He looked like a vampire, but he was really a snake. The left, Ted, Dilan's boyfriend, sleepy and in his underwear. The station was dark. Low light from the computer paled his face.

Bolkov reached around the phone with her index finger and pressed play. It was a recording of both sides of a video call to the station.

Ted said, "Bill. It's late."

"What am I hearing about you upgrading the software."

Ted's eyes widened and he jolted upright. "Sorry what?"

"Upgrading the software. Who gave you authorization to do that? And why was the signal down for nineteen hours?"

Ted looked over his shoulder, then rubbed his face.

"And where is Dilan? He should be here too."

"It's three-fifteen am Bill. He's asleep and I am not waking him up." Ted paused. "It took me a while to find the problem this time. It was on the third floor. Signal is back though."

Helena wanted to pause the video and ask questions. The agency told her the station was down due to a space weather disturbance. That a solar flare had interrupted the signal. What problem had Ted fixed?

"Wake Dilan. I want to discuss the software upgrade."

"He's asleep. Helena authorized it."

She didn't authorize anything. But the less the Fed knew, the better. She let it go.

"I don't know—"

"Check your messages, Bill."

Ted was lying. Whenever her son and Ted wanted to lie to Bill, they said check your messages. Bill never checked them. She was so tired of Bill Caddell. He didn't belong at the agency, but the agency kept him around for political reasons.

"Well, I need you to roll it back."

"My mother authorized it, Bill."

A hand appeared over Ted's right shoulder, then the video's image pixelated. The station's archaic software couldn't decide whether Dilan belonged in the video's foreground or edited from the background. Helena smiled. Three-quarters of Dilan's head was clear, the rest of him masked.

Dilan said, "You would know that if you read your damn messages."

Helena grinned. Just like she taught him.

"Whatever you two did has people thinking the images are fake. I need—"

Right, Axyl. She had heard he was spreading rumors based on outdated tests.

"Every other day Bill, Ted risks his life going out to save your piece of shit project. Right Ted?"

Ted nodded. "Eleven times in August."

Helena squinted. Eleven times just in August? For what?

She peeked over the phone at Bolkov, who was watching her every eyebrow raise. Helena inhaled and tried to deadpan her face.

Dilan leaned over the seat and into the camera. The pixelation vanished, and his head and pale chest were clear in the image. Dilan looked thin. He'd been drinking too much again and not exercising.

Dilan said, "Nobody thinks they are fake, Bill, so don't give me your bullshit."

Dilan was right. Why would Bill believe Axyl's rumors? She couldn't let the Fed see her confusion.

Not even the station's archaic AI could correct the red flush on Bill's face. Dilan liked to stir things, but it was a bad idea with Bill. He was a snake who would bite back three times as hard and squeeze the life out of his prey.

Still, she smiled at seeing Bill mad.

Dilan said, "This should have been done years ago Bill."

"I need you shits to roll it back. This is a trillion dollars worth of equipment you are toying with."

"Ever sucked a dick virtually, Bill?"

Helena gasped.

Dilan said, "You are full of it. Where did the money for the replacement parts go, anyway? How much does a Georgetown home go for these days? Or one of those ancient pollution pipes you drive around?"

Shit, no Dilan. What are you doing?

Caddell said, "What are you accusing me of you little shit?"

Dilan said, "Read your expense reports. You signed for all of this." Dilan's hand waved around. Ted looked like the blood had drained from his face. Helena's heart was in her throat, and she felt light-headed. Why was Dilan provoking Bill?

"I am going to fucking kill both of you."

"You broke it, you bought it asshole." Dilan gave Bill the middle finger, then the call ended.

Helena couldn't catch her breath. Dilan hadn't told her anything. What was Ted fixing on the station?

Bolkov asked, "What does Caddell mean, the images are fake?"

Helena shook her head. Her hands were shaking like after watching a horror movie.

She inhaled and tried to compose herself. "If I had a quarter for every time some conspiracy-loving nut said aliens were going to reach across space and come to earth to kill us because of this project. Or that the images were fake."

No one ever said the images were fake before Axyl and his damn outdated tests. If her son was fixing something on the station he must have a reason. Caddell smelled blood. She couldn't allow that snake to strangle her son.

Helena retrieved her phone. "You have two minutes to take your foot off the door, special agent whatever-your-name-was." And then to her phone, "I am being assaulted in my apartment. A woman in a blue suit. Please send security."

Bolkov said, "What do you think this was about?"

"It's none of your business. Leave my son alone." Helena looked down the hall. She wanted to scream *help me, I'm being assaulted*, but no one was around.

Bolkov looked down the hall then shook her head. "What does he mean, roll it back? Roll what back?"

"Security will be here. This is private property. When they get here, you are going home."

Bolkov moved her foot. "Caddell is headed here. Whatever your son is into, he's headed here to fix it."

Helena wanted to vomit. "What? Why is he coming here?"

"You tell me."

Helena's heart was thumping out of her chest. Shit. Why was he coming here? What was her son thinking instigating Bill like that? Her walls were closing in and she didn't have the energy to fight it anymore.

"Caddell scares you. I can tell. I can help you if you help me."

The lunaresin cracked against the door frame as she slammed the door on Bolkov.

She took a few deep breaths, then the door binged again. Not the Fed. This time, the woman that the Tourism Board hired to run security. Helena opened the door. She had seen pictures of this woman, Katera Devana. In person, she was almost towering. A half-head taller than Helena, and pretty, with soft, curly black hair and olive skin, wearing blue and silver camo fatigues. She looked like one of those recruiting holograms for the Space Force.

"Hi, I'm Kate Devana. Someone called about an assault?"

Not what she expected. Unassuming. This woman introduced herself like no one knew who she was. Everyone knew who she was. Behind those gorgeous brown eyes was the woman that burned down Lunar Foundries three years ago and cost the company trillions. The CEO was on the Tourism Board. All that, and the CEO still helped Devana get this job, as if he was still paying penance.

The smile and brown eyes made her want to tell this woman everything. But this wasn't a colony problem. There was nothing this woman could do about agency politics.

The woman looked down the hall. "I saw a Fed duck into the stairs. This have anything to do with that?"

"Everything is fine now."

"Can I call a medic? You look a little pale."

What would happen if she told this woman everything? Her son was in trouble, god knows how, and Caddell was coming here like a tornado to rip through her life.

Nothing, that's what would happen. Nothing. This was her problem.

"Coming down with the flu is all. "

The woman looked Helena over, then down the hall where the Fed used to be.

"Well, you call me direct if there is any trouble."

Helena closed the door. The door security camera showed the woman walking down the hall. Maybe she should change her mind, scream *help* down the hall again. Make the woman come back.

But Caddell was vicious. No point getting more people savaged than necessary.

She needed to take care of this herself.

6

Kailua-Kona, Hawaii
September 2073

The Hawaiian Hawk's name was Kiai, and she studied Axyl Dover from her perch on the topmost branch of the Koa tree at the corner of his ten-acre property. She arrived in March. Axyl called her Kiai because, since June, she stood guard over her brood. His property sloped down the mountain towards the coast, and Kiai was three hundred meters away and eye-to-eye in a direct line of sight. He had come out to the sunporch a half hour ago. Enough time, he thought, for Kiai to relax. With her male partner out hunting, Kiai disagreed. Her head swiveled, and her sharp eyes evaluated his shift in the chair.

Axyl lowered his eyes to his laptop and ran image data through his algorithm again, this time in debug mode. The image he received had the wrong encoding. He knew Ted had been updating the software. But incorrect encoding meant there must be a bug somewhere. He couldn't blame Ted for taking a shortcut. The hardware was forty years old, as persnickety as his one-hundred-twenty-year-old grandmother, and equally unwilling to adapt.

He sipped his coffee as he watched his algorithm run through its battery of regression tests. The progress bar read *estimated time: 5:32.*

Below the sunporch, Emma traversed the garden and had made her way to the macadamia nut tree. She knelt, with her brown sundress and long black hair flapping in the cool Hawaiian breeze, gathering nuts that had ripened and fallen into the grass. He wanted to shout to her to grab some of the mangoes. But she was too far down the garden and without her phone.

Emma must have sensed his stare because she stood up, her face framed against the Pacific sun setting behind his grove of coffee trees. Emma signed *I love you*. He signed back *I love you too. And I would love a mango.*

Emma looked left and nodded. She crossed the pineapples, wrestling two into her basket, then followed the green sand walkway to the mango trees. She inspected the mangoes, then turned and shook her head. He signed, *thanks for trying*, then a heart.

From her perch, Kiai was also tracking Emma. Kiai's existence was divisive. While he and Emma considered Kiai a conservation success, Kiai was either an abomination or new invasive species, depending on who was yelling at the council microphone. Thirty years ago, Hawaiian Hawks only nested in native ʻōhiʻa lehua trees, which were dying due to an invasive beetle from Asia. Both would die out, so biologists at the Department of Land and Natural Resources decided to speed up evolution and introduce a genetic alteration that adapted the Hawaiian Hawk to nest in the island's most common trees, most of which were now non-native.

He didn't live here when the No Hawk Virus! yard signs were more common than breadfruit trees. Today, that decision still made voices and fistfights boom. But also the hawk population. The virus worked. As a bonus, the new hawks ate invasive beetles and lizards, making Hawaiian arborists and ecologists like he and Emma merry.

On his computer monitor, the algorithm finished tests at the same rhythm as Emma's footsteps up the path. Forty years of marriage, watching her legs slink toward him still turned him on. Emma clicked through the garden gate, strode up the weathered wood stairs, then set her basket on the table next to his coffee. She leaned over, and they kissed.

"Pigs are back. They are digging at the Macadamia tree."

"I can message Mele Monday morning."

"Anything?"

"Not so far. I am rerunning the tests."

The images that IIRAS software was producing were impossible. Debugging IIRAS code was different from how he envisioned his retirement. He bought this property because it was far from dark agency scandals. So that he could sit here and watch the sunset over the Pacific. Not watch his laptop confirm something invasive slithering into the agency.

"What are you going to do?"

"Not much I can do. Agency is publishing them."

"But—"

Axyl shrugged. "I think Ted screwed up something with his latest upgrade. He will have to quietly roll it back."

"What did Helena say?"

"I didn't tell her."

"Honey, you have to. She is the Executive Director."

"Really? How do I start that conversation, Em? Hi Helena, this is your conspiracy loving friend Axyl here who you haven't spoken to in three years. Your ne'er do well son and his boyfriend screwed up the images we've waited thirty-two years to see, and the agency is publishing them anyway."

Emma shook her head as she emptied her basket onto the table. "She needs to know."

Axyl stared at his computer as the progress bar filled up. A screwed up image. Forty trillion kilometers and two hundred lifetimes away.

"The agency is hiding something, sweetie."

"The agency is always hiding something. Anyway, I have no proof. What am I supposed to say, I got an anonymous message?"

"A message with very specific details that your tests have confirmed—"

His algorithm binged. The same result as before—the images had spectral peaks between five hundred and six hundred nanometers and not enough redshift—all wrong for a rocky exoplanet orbiting a red dwarf star four-point-something light years away. All the code tests passed. Again. There were no bugs in the code that could explain the encoding. It didn't make sense.

Axyl rubbed his eyes trying to massage his headache. Maybe his blood sugar was low.

"You have to tell her something."

Emma started to slice the pineapple. The wood cutting board *thunked*, complaining that her technique was harsher than usual.

"The first rule at the agency, Em, is no good deed goes unpunished. You know that."

"You can't let Helena publish those." *Thunk*. Her knife felled a chunk of pineapple.

"That ship sailed. Helena shut me out years ago. She shut everyone out."

"She only wants what's best for the project. She put her whole life into this."

"At what cost? Her kids hate her."

"Without her, the project would've never lifted off. This was her baby. She needs help, sweetie."

He shook his head. How was he supposed to help someone who refused to be helped?

Beyond his garden, the sun had descended below the Pacific Ocean, silhouetting his neighbor's pines with a thin band of brilliant orange and pink clouds. He picked this place for its tranquility. He had ten acres of reasons not to get involved in another agency scandal. Especially one involving Helena's troubled son Dilan and the agency's cursed project, Phoenix.

Against the dusk sky, Kiai was now only a shadow in the Koa tree, although he could feel her eyes. Hawaiian Hawks nesting in Koa trees was still considered island lore, so when Axyl mentioned Kiai at the June arborist club meeting, his credibility hinged on evidence. Someone messaged someone, and yes, someone in Natural Resources was interested in pictures of Kiai's clutch. The trouble was that Kiai did not allow him near the tree. Kiai would puff her wings and screech if he got closer than forty meters. So the club voted to send a drone to investigate her four—four!—nestlings. Four was a new record for a Hawaiian Hawk brood. Very rare.

Attempting a picture was a mistake he wouldn't repeat. Kiai dived the drone and attacked it with her talons. Then she and the male took turns shattering it with their beaks. Kiai had perfect three-hundred-sixty-degree overwatch from her treetop. Since then, she'd spent most of her time looking in his direction.

"I am retired. I shouldn't even have looked into it."

Emma's slicing stiffened against the wood cutting board.

"I don't have proof. Not really."

Emma pointed her knife toward his computer. "Have your tests ever been wrong?"

"No. But it might not be a software problem. I can't find the raw data to compare."

Emma shook her head and resumed thunking pineapple. "They took away your access?"

"I've been retired for three years. It had to happen sometime."

"You put your whole life into that agency."

"Doesn't change the fact that I can't prove anything. Without proof, I am just another crackpot."

"Well, someone will run the same tests. They will come to the same conclusion and post them to a server. They can't hide from the truth. You are saving the agency the embarrassment. When those images get out, the real nuts will have a field day."

"Agency has survived worse scandals, Em. They classify anything embarrassing, it'll never get out. Anyway, there is probably a simple explanation I am overlooking."

Emma stopped slicing and plated the pineapple and macadamia nuts next to crumbly soft cheese from the farm up the road. She set his plate next to his now-cold coffee. It looked delicious, but he wasn't hungry.

"Sweetie, your blood sugars are low. You need to eat."

He fork-stabbed a slice of pineapple and let the juice drip onto his computer as he ate it. The sunset's orange and pink had changed to cool blue and gray dusk. The motion sensor light on his garden shed flickered on. In the shadow, he thought he saw an animal. Emma sat next to him and held his hand. She was watching his blood sugar tick back up.

"You could message Paul. Or Leyna."

She patted his hand, but it was because his blood sugars were returning to normal. He nodded and stabbed another slice of pineapple. Paul knew the software as well as he did.

"I can try. He might be able to get through to Helena." He paused as a shadow crossed from the shed to the macadamia nut tree. "And I will talk to Mele about the pig tomorrow."

7

Two days later, Axyl watched Kiai and her mate spread their wings and soar. It was the first time in four months both had left their outpost on the Koa tree. Her mate flew towards the coast, where the sun hovered low between orange and blue clouds and the horizon. Kiai circled, then dropped on the Macadamia nut tree. She ignored the critters on the ground, instead snooping at his computer.

Emma slinked up behind Axyl, smelling of barbeque sauce. "Still nothing, sweetie?"

For the last day, nothing appeared in his messages except half-naked women selling genetic mods. Axyl, your hair can be its natural brown again! Or news the president was rumored to be planning a colony visit.

"It's only been a day, Em."

"It's twenty-seventy-three. That might as well be infinity." Emma rubbed Axyl's shoulders. "I have some pork sliced. Do you want a sandwich?"

"Not hungry. But thanks." Axyl rubbed his forehead.

"You haven't been eating. Loss of appetite can be a symptom of—"

"It's not cancer, Em." Axyl clicked his inbox to see if there were messages. According to Em, he had cancer four times a day. He'd already had his booster shot for the main kind he might get. Equally as irritating, nothing in his inbox.

Axyl shook his head, then nodded at the Macadamia tree. "Kiai's brood fledged. That's the closest she's ever come to the house."

"She's calling a truce."

"You tend to anthropomorphize—"

"Hawks are monogamous. They mate for life and usually reuse the same nest. Add to it each year. She wants to coexist with the other top predator on this island."

Axyl met Kiai's eyes. Kiai cocked her head, then swiveled it to the descending Pacific sun.

"She's welcome to the garden pests and the lizards."

"Speaking of the nest, I think the skylight in the kitchen is leaking."

Before Axyl could answer, he heard rustling by the garden shed at the end of the green sand walkway. Kiai's head pivoted towards the rustling. She screeched and then flew off. He heard screams, squeals, and Mele's voice.

"I think she's got a pig, Em."

Axyl stood up as his phone *binged*. Mele, better get down here. He descended the sunporch stairs, clicked through the gate, and rushed down the footpath. At the bottom, Mele came out of the shadows with a zip-tied and struggling woman. Her face and voice were familiar.

"The fuck is this, Axyl?"

"She says she knows you."

Axyl brushed the woman's long brown hair aside to see Leyna Darcy's baby-blue eyes blinking and squinting. Her hair was messy, her face muddy, and leaves and grass smeared her gray shirt and beige shorts.

"Untie her and let's go up to the porch. Mele, this is Leyna Darcy."

"I'm going to stay here, Mr. Dover."

Axyl nodded as Mele stuck her knife between Leyna's arms and cut the zip-ties with an ouch bitch.

"My mom wasn't answering you. Neither was Paul."

Axyl shook his head and waved Leyna up the sand footpath.

"You could have messaged me, Leyna. You can come in the front door."

Leyna didn't respond.

"How long have you been here?"

"Mom and Nolan told Paul to block you. I got here and I was deciding."

Axyl clicked the gate and let Leyna ascend ahead of him. As the two of them rose to the top of the stairs, Emma slid open the screen door. Emma bounced forward to hug Leyna.

"Deciding what, sweetie? You know you are always welcome here."

"Who to listen to."

Axyl said, "You are twenty-one now Leyna. The great thing about being twenty-one is you don't have to listen to anyone. You get to make up your own mind."

Leyna slumped in a chair at the sunporch's wood table as if the thought hadn't occurred to her.

"You look starved sweetheart. When was the last time you ate?"

"I had some of your pineapples. And nuts."

"Oh, sweetie. Let's get you some protein and coffee. You still eat meat?"

Leyna nodded and sulked while Emma went inside. Axyl sat next to her, letting the dusk breeze fill the silence. Leyna's thin hand crept over the table, and he held it.

"I missed you guys."

"We missed you too."

"You really think my brother is in trouble again?"

"I don't know what to think, Leyna. After you eat, I will show you what I found. You can decide for yourself."

Emma returned, carrying a tray with a pot of coffee and a sandwich piled high with sliced smoked pork, fresh garden tomatoes, and lettuce. Its tongue of horseradish mayo smiled at Leyna. Emma set the sandwich in front of her and poured her a cup of coffee.

Leyna nodded thank you and scarfed the sandwich. She talked between bites through a mouthful of bun.

"I forgot how good the food is here. The meat tastes like—what is that?"

"The pigs eat the macadamia nuts."

"I love it here. Is that what Mele was doing?"

"Hopefully, before they destroy the garden again."

"Serves me right. I feel like a pig. I should have messaged."

Axyl didn't say anything. Emma sat down and held her hand.

"You know how mom is about Phoenix, and how Nolan is about mom."

Axyl nodded. Helena considered IIRAS, Phoenix, her baby. Leyna and Dilan had grown up in the shadow of a sibling that set expectations impossible to meet. Phoenix burned most of Helena's energy. Leyna had practically raised herself.

Axyl said, "Did you know Dilan got a job at IIRAS station?"

"Her, Nolan, and Paul fought about it. Nolan said it was a horrible idea. He and Paul were against it. I think Dilan manipulated the therapist and guilted mom into it."

"Kenna?"

Leyna shrugged. "Kenna is Kenna. She agrees with everything mom says."

"I see."

Leyna swallowed her last bite, then glugged her coffee. Emma reached for a dish towel on the tray and started wiping Leyna's face. Leyna shrank, then took the towel and wiped herself.

Emma said, "I am glad you came. Come in the front door next time, though."

"I was deciding."

"Listen to yourself, sweetie. You are almost graduated—"

"What I meant is, whether I wanted to know what my brother is into this time."

Axyl said, "Maybe nothing. I don't have proof. But—something is off with the images."

"The ones they just released?"

"I think they rushed them out. But, I couldn't find anything in the code." Axyl described his results.

"My brother could not code himself out of a gym locker. He could barely get the car to take him to school without my help."

Axyl shook his head. "True, but his boyfriend Ted works at the station too."

Leyna paused to finish her coffee and pour another cup. The dusk breeze had picked up, and her brown hair was waving. As she took a scrunchy off her wrist to pull her hair into a ponytail, Axyl marveled that Leyna had matured into her mother's twin.

"I could see him manipulating Ted into something stupid."

"Do you want to take a look? My skills are—"

Leyna half-smirked. "Ancient."

The color had returned to Leyna's face. Axyl returned a smile and pushed his computer toward her. Leyna pouted at Emma. Before Leyna voiced the request, Emma was on her feet.

"Did I put enough horseradish on it?"

"It was perfect. Times two please."

"I will make up the spare room for you, too. But, I don't have any clothes that will fit."

"I do. My backpack is in the mango trees."

Axyl looked down the garden path. It was dark, and it would be hard to find. He messaged Mele, Leyna lost her backpack in the mangoes. His shed's motion sensor light blinked on. Then more rustling and squeals. Then a crash. His phone pinged, got it, with a bow emoji.

"Mele'll look for it."

Leyna pulled the computer closer and connected her neuroface.

"Ok, brother, let's see what trouble you're into this time."

8

Axyl woke to grinding noises in the kitchen and the smell of fresh coffee. The undercurrent of applewood through the open window told him that Mele had started smoking last night's pig.

His phone read 6:21 am, the first time he rose at dawn in three years. Last night, Leyna and Emma badgered him into messaging Bill Caddell, an old friend and the Technology Director for IIRAS, to ask for access to the raw image and signal data. Since Caddell was on the East Coast, he needed to get up early.

Bill was old school. While the world advanced around him, Bill eschewed genetic mods, holovids, and drones. He didn't have a neuroface, an implant that allowed human brains to interface directly with computers, instead preferring his fingers. Shunning the latest technology was an odd quirk for a Technology Director. Nevertheless, the agency kept Bill around for two reasons. One, IIRAS technology was old, and finding graduates willing to learn it grew exponentially harder each day. Two, Bill knew where the agency bodies were buried—because Bill had buried them himself. Three reasons, if he counted Bill's refusal to retire.

When Axyl messaged Caddell last night, Bill's response was, *sure get some sleep. ttyl.* Axyl imagined laughter too. Bill would only believe it was urgent if Axyl flew across the country and barged into his D.C. office. Or the next best thing: interrupted his retirement, woke at dawn, and direct-dialed.

Bill would prefer a face-to-face in some downtown D.C. café that served sugary margaritas and cheap beer. Somewhere with greasy burgers and away from the prying ears of his staff. Bill's obsession with secrecy had helped him survive multiple agency scandals.

As Axyl donned a polo shirt and shorts and brushed his gray hair in the bathroom mirror, he told his reflection that a phone call would have to be enough. Leyna and Emma had badgered him into a phone call, not a ten-hour flight to D.C.

The stairs did not cooperate with his attempt to let Leyna and Emma sleep. He winced and cringed as each wood step creaked. At the bottom, he realized Leyna was already up. She was in the kitchen, with her wet hair slicked back, wearing one of Emma's pink bathrobes, and was pouring a cup of coffee.

"Sorry, did I wake you?"

Leyna poured a second cup and held it out for Axyl. "Black, right?"

Axyl nodded and blew the steam. "I need to call Bill. It's almost lunchtime on the East Coast." He paused to sip his coffee. Leyna had the same smile and figure as Helena, except forty-something years younger.

Leyna smiled. "So, we convinced you."

"You didn't. He's going to say no. But it's worth a try."

"Can I listen in?"

Axyl weighed his answer as he sipped his coffee and eyed Leyna. Bill might take him more seriously if at least one of the Darcys were beside him. Helena wasn't, but her forty-years-younger twin might be a good surrogate.

"Go get dressed."

Leyna thanked him and bounced up the stairs. Yelling to tell her to be quiet felt pointless after all the creaking. Fortunately, Emma was a heavy sleeper. He refilled his cup and took his computer out to the sunporch.

He was rarely up early enough to see the mountain behind his house cast its shadow onto the Pacific Ocean. Blue smoke from Mele's smoker rose in front of his neighbor's pines at the corner of his property. He heard something sizzling behind him and turned to see that Emma's sleep did not survive Leyna's stomping.

Emma was up and was now cooking breakfast. Leyna was coming back down the stairs, so he gulped his coffee and pressed his neuroface into service to call Bill. As Bill answered, Leyna sat across the table with a mug and pot of coffee. Bill appeared in 2D, swiveling his chair, framed by the bright light of his D.C. office window.

"Axyl. Good morning. You are up early. It must be—"

Axyl motioned for Leyna to come around the table. As she sat, he positioned the computer so they were both in the frame.

"Bill, good to see you. You remember Leyna?"

"I do but she probably doesn't remember me. Last time I saw you was your sixth birthday party. You've grown up."

"Hi."

"You are the spitting image of your mother. Has anyone told you that?"

"Literally everyone."

Axyl's phone binged with a message from Leyna. A hologram of Caddell's face on a pooping dinosaur. He tried not to laugh. Leyna got Helena's looks, but the personality must have skipped a generation because no one in the Darcy house had cracked a joke in decades.

Emma came up behind them and refilled their coffee.

"Bill. Nice to see you again."

"Nice to see you too, Emma. Ok, talk to me Axyl. I have a hard stop in fifteen. What gets you up at dawn to call me?"

"You know Ted has been upgrading the software?"

"Who authorized that? And how do you know and I don't—"

Axyl bluffed. "My guess would be Helena."

"Shit. Ted is—" Caddell paused. His eyes darted to the side as the veteran of multiple scandals calculated scenarios. "What did Dilan screw up this time?"

"Leyna and I are not sure. I need access to the raw data to track it down."

"Tell me what you found."

After Axyl explained his test results, he said, "It sounds like a hardware problem Bill, but we need the raw signal data to rule out software."

"How did you find out?"

While Axyl weighed whether to tell Bill about the anonymous tip, Leyna lied. She said, "My brother told me. He messaged me."

Caddell said, "Did you tell Helena?"

"I told my mom. She denied it. Dilan can do no wrong. I told Paul."

"What did he say?"

"Denial. Which is why I asked Axyl to talk to you."

"Well, you did the right thing."

Axyl said, "So Bill, the access—"

"I'll see what I can do. Meantime, let's keep a tight circle on this. It's probably nothing. There is a lot we don't know about interstellar space."

Leyna asked, "When will you get back to us?"

"I'll look into it after our meeting with the advance team."

Axyl asked, "Advance team?"

Caddell said, "Oh, you didn't hear. President is going to the colony first week in November. Science Secretary Hoff and I volunteered for the advance team. We are arriving—" He paused, his finger moving over something.

Axyl furrowed his brow.

Caddell continued, "Director and I are going to scout exhibits and lunar historical sites for the Presidential team. President is going to advance her science agenda. John says IIRAS will play a big role."

John Adkins was the President's Chief of Staff.

Axyl said, "I didn't know. It hasn't been announced."

"You know how these things go, Axyl. They didn't announce it. That way if they cancel it they can avoid the embarrassment."

"I do." And that's one of the million reasons he retired. "Well, say hi to Helena for me."

"I will. Will we see you at the wedding?"

What wedding?

Caddell didn't wait for a response. "Listen thanks for the heads-up Axyl. I have to run. I will be in touch. Maybe we'll see each other at the wedding in a few weeks."

Caddell closed the call. As Axyl sat back, he felt a sharp pang that was not hunger. Emma came from the kitchen and dropped two plates with strawberries, pineapple, pancakes, and sausage. He pushed it away with his eyes. Emma looked at him disapprovingly.

"You didn't ask him to pull the images."

"His first question, how did you find out?"

Emma froze. She glanced at Leyna, who was trying to cram a pancake, fruit, and sausage forkful into her mouth.

"What else did he say?"

"He and Secretary Hoff are going to the colony with the advance team."

Emma's eyes widened. She looked somewhere between shocked and panicked, which made Leyna freeze mid-chew. Axyl inhaled, watching the sunlight peek over the mountain onto the tops of his neighbor's pine trees. He saw Kiai perched at the tip of the neighbor's pine tree, scanning for breakfast.

Leyna choked down her mouthful. "I don't get it. So what if he's going to the colony?"

Emma said, "Bill's never been to the colony. He swore he would never go. He passed on two promotions to avoid it."

"Well maybe—"

Axyl said, "And he didn't question our results."

Emma said, "Bill likes to argue the minutiae."

"I don't get it."

Axyl said, "It means he knows already. He asked us how we found out and who we told. He's known for a while and is already in damage control mode."

Emma said, "Enough damage to go to space despite his anxiety. He's probably going to talk to Helena."

Axyl said, "What about this wedding, Em? Who's wedding?"

"Oh. I didn't tell you. I didn't think you'd want to go."

He didn't.

Axyl watched Kiai spot breakfast and swoop into the green brush. Bill said, I'll look into it. He wouldn't. If Axyl asked again, he would get another excuse. The slow no, the agency's ritual, no one would outright tell him to stop wasting his time asking for access. He would get excuse after excuse. Until he ran out of people to ask and got tired and quit.

He imagined Kiai and her partner taking their beaks to the station's equipment, like the drone. He wouldn't get access to the data. Or a solid explanation how humanity's greatest advancement in astrophysics was destroyed. Or why. Project Phoenix, in ashes again. He pitied Helena. Phoenix was her baby, and no one should outlive their children.

Usually, the agency's politics frustrated Axyl. But, for the first time in decades, he felt grateful Bill was keeping him in the dark. Whatever was happening was going to eat someone alive. What the agency needed was a Kiai, a predator that could keep the snakes in check. It wasn't him. He felt too old to be the agency's breakfast.

Axyl's hunger overcame his unease. He sectioned his pancake and a forkful of sausage, then ate them together.

"Breakfast is delicious." He blew Em a kiss. She blew one back.

"Why would he want to talk to my mom?"

Emma shook her head and returned to the kitchen. Axyl took another bite of breakfast and shook his head. He said, "To get your mom to get your brother to stop doing whatever he's doing."

"Like that will work. My mom will tell Dilan to speed it up."

Axyl nodded. She understood the family dynamic better than he did. Whatever *it* was.

9

New York City, New York
September 2073

Nathaniel Kirkwood spent his last day as a wattsucker on his rooftop deck overlooking Central Park West. He could rise from his seat, take one step, and be over the edge with his arms wide and wind rushing. With a bit of extra push-off, he'd sail over 72nd Street.

No one would look up. All the two-legged things that pretended to be human were busy with their headsets and phones and neurofaces. How many could he crush? Two, three? If he landed on the food truck and spattered, four? Plus himself. Five fewer cyborgs on the planet. Shit, best thing he'd have done with his life. They should put up a statue. Right where that damn food truck is, where the fucking wattsuckers congregate. With a bronze plaque that read, *September 2073, the 'Earth First' revolution started here. It was on this day humans took their planet back from cyborgs.*

The moon's waxing crescent smirked and called him a coward. Like Mylah three weeks ago. He raised his vodka bottle like a middle finger, then sucked a mouthful.

Not that it was much better on Earth. It was a clear night, and he came out hoping to see meteors streak across the sky. But it was too bright. The Manhattan sky was a dusky haze of light pollution. Joggers, walkers, scooters, all using their devices to blowtorch Central Park pathways into a blue-gray blur. Everyone below treated their electronics like appendages, like clothes, or shoes, or jewelry. They weren't appendages.

They were parasites, using their humans to suck wattage off the grid, sending some of it back to their humans' brains to make them think everything was ok. It wasn't. There was nothing normal about being codependent on machines.

Nate was a cyborg, too. A human with nanowires and a chip implant so his brain could talk to his phone, laptop, or video game console. Sometimes, it screamed, *we're out of vodka* at the refrigerator. Other times, it just screamed.

He was a monster, which made his parents Mr. and Mrs. Frankenstein. They were up there, sucking fake air and mocking him from two hundred meters below the lunar surface while dehumanizing Earthers, making neurochips like the one in his spinal cord stabbing his brain. His mother said, *you're not a cyborg, Nate.* So did his therapist. Sometimes, when he was on his medication, he believed them. Most times he didn't. His mother made the damn chips, and his therapist was an AI algorithm. What else would they say?

A red and yellow drone cab scurried down 72nd Street to offload more obnoxious people into the park. Three got out and then lined up at a food cart. Scan, order, pay. If he sailed just right, maybe he could dive bomb the taxi and flip it into the food truck line.

On the benches, at least some of the wattwraiths seemed part human. Couples jogged, then sat. Their primitive biological circuitry drove them to perform rituals like holding hands and kissing. His mother called sexual reproduction quaint, claiming it would fade like hieroglyphics and religion. She said it was for animals and troglodytes. *We've evolved, Nate.* Evolution according to Harlee Shay Kirkwood: Algorithms to choose the sperm and egg. A nutrient bath for fertilization. Then the embryo finished in a surrogate uterus rated nine-point-four out of ten by the HarvMed AI. Baked, like he was some gucci French pastry. All that genetic engineering and he still wasn't *evolved* enough for her, so she had to implant wires in his head.

He tipped his middle-finger vodka bottle into the air. "Look how I turned out, mom. Practically perfect in every way. Like you." Then he swigged his vodka.

His phone binged, *Rnng gold. Thumps up.*

The message meant, *Raining gold,* and it was accompanied by a hologif of golfball-sized gold hail smashing drones. Mylah was testing him. And he was going to fail.

He smiled and swished some vodka in his mouth, and then entered, *cm vr* followed by a heart. His neuroface corrected his message to *come over.*

The messages were a code between him and Mylah. A test which he failed. His neuroface autocorrected his messages, so she knew he was using it again. He sighed and took another swig from the vodka, then a second.

He thought, *well at least she's talking to me again*, which his neuroface translated to a message that he had to delete. Three gulps of the vodka bottle later, she responded, *u r nt offline.*

His neuroface typed, *lonely and miss you* then he deleted that too. Do cyborgs get lonely? Did alcohol interfere with the neurochip? Mylah would be mad. So what he was back to using his neuroface? He hadn't seen her in weeks. He wanted to run his hands down her side, slowing to explore her hips. Kiss that little spot right inside her hip bone.

Something he didn't understand—if his mother was so against sexual reproduction, why didn't she have the Docbot edit his libido out of the genes? Maybe the AI screwed up and gave him a double dose. His neuroface retyped, *i miss you*, and sent the message before he could stop it.

Mylah didn't respond for several seconds. *yv bn drnkng. f ur neuroface and tulk t m.*

Shit. This was bad. She was going to call him. He set his bottle on the table, this time noticing all the other empty bottles. Maybe it was better Mylah didn't come over since his place was a mess. Dirty dishes. Laundry on the floor. The recycling needed to be taken out. He couldn't remember when he changed the sheets in the bedroom. Fuck, his life story. She wanted to talk, and he wasn't ready.

If he wanted her to come over, there was only one thing he had time to clean up. So he swiped through his phone, closed his eyes, and switched off the neuroface software. He tried to message Mylah, but his brain seized, like trying to switch languages in the middle of a conversation. Then he found his fingers.

dun.

Nw tulk t m.

Nate stared at his phone, expecting her to call. Nothing happened. Then he heard a voice behind him.

"Here, dummy."

Mylah bounded through the sliding glass door, her black hair flopping in the night breeze and her breasts bouncing hello from under a tight army-green knit sweater tucked into her even tighter jeans. Her skin was a lighter shade of brown around her right ear. Weeks ago, there was a scar there where hot oil had burned her. She'd had it removed. She hugged him. He touched her light-brown patch and tried to kiss her. But she turned her big brown eyes to her phone.

"Look."

"Shit. Where did that come from?"

"Someone named Dilan Darcy. The money came with a message."

"Who's that?"

"Ben's working, looking him up. He and Rily are on their way over."

"They're here?"

"They took the train from DC."

Nate ran his hands through his hair and surveyed his apartment. There was no time to clean.

"Fuck this place is a mess. Maybe we should—"

Mylah pulled away and surveyed the bottles. She picked up the bottle Nate had been drinking, then put it back.

"How much have you been drinking?"

"Just one."

Mylah eyed the half-full bottles, then picked through the empties. Nate shrugged.

"Jesus. I should have never left. You are wallowing in your self-loathing again."

Nate felt something warm in his eyes. He was so happy to see her.

"It'll be fine, Nate. It will all be fine soon."

Mylah turned, but Nate stopped her.

"Mylah, I don't know why you're mad at me."

"Yes you do. Just stop."

She looked him over, then grabbed his phone from the table and tossed it off the deck. Starbursts blinded his vision when it smashed on the concrete thirty stories down.

"This too. It makes you relapse."

She picked up the vodka bottle he'd been slurping and emptied it over the edge. The vodka glugged from the bottle, bubbles rising inside the glass, vodka spraying into the wind. Mylah raised her arm as if she would throw the bottle. Instead, she slid it on the table between two other empties.

"I don't remember—"

Nate ran his hand over the back of his neck.

"You said I was controlling, Nate."

Maybe the starbursts helped him remember. He was drunk and high at the last protest. They fought about him using his neuroface.

"I am not controlling you. I just want what's best for you. For all of us."

He remembered now. He said she was controlling like his mother.

"Look, I'm sorry for whatever I said."

She put her fingers on his lips and then wiped his eyes with her thumb. Her big brown eyes and long eyelashes were soft and comforting.

"I've looked into it. We can have it removed."

"I know, Mylah. My parents won't pay for it, and the doc says I could stroke out."

"The action fund paid for it." Mylah ran her hand over Nate's chest and leaned up to whisper, her brown eyes and peppermint breath pleading with him. "Live free or die. Right?"

Mylah's coconut shampoo and perfume opened a flood of memories. Four weeks ago, they could barely leave the bedroom. Her skin was as soft as her sweater. If he wanted her back, he needed to do something. There was no point pretending, his pants gave it away. She was playfully smiling and tickling his stomach because she knew it too. He leaned in to taste her peppermint tongue, but she pushed away.

"When you are free."

Or dead. The door buzzed. All the hormones his body had been channeling to lust were rerouted to panic. Ben and Rily walked onto the deck, and a short man stayed behind in the shadows.

"What's going on?"

Ben said, "Intervention."

Rily said, "Don't blame us, it was her idea."

Mylah leaned up and kissed Nate on the cheek. "Do you love me?"

Of course, he did. It was a foolish question.

"Will you do this for me?"

He wasn't sure what he was being asked to do. Then, a thin elderly man stepped out of the shadows wearing green scrubs, thick glasses, and holding a giant needle. She'd said, *live free or die*. Did she want him to choose? The needle's sharp metal tip threatened him. It was as long as his finger and would puncture the base of his skull. He closed his eyes and stepped to his left. He wasn't a coward. Bottles clinked and fell as he climbed onto the table. Then he plunged over the edge. He was a meteor, hurtling thirty stories, crushing the wattsuckers below. He stretched his arms wide and tried to aim for as many as possible. Only they saw him and moved out of the way. The socketfuckers laughed at him as he hit 72nd Street. Then white starbursts.

He opened his eyes and mouthed *free*. The man stepped forward, brandishing the needle. Tears ran down Nate's face. He was so scared his heart jumped out of his chest as he blacked out. At least if he died, the last thing he would see was Mylah's soft brown eyes.

10

Nate stood in his Central Park West bedroom in the moonlight. Naked. A full moon hovering over his rooftop deck, so big he could step over the edge and walk on it. At his bedroom threshold, a doctor with green scrubs, holding a needle. Nate turned to the moon through the doors, now outside, arms outstretched. The moonlight felt cool on his skin. But he couldn't feel anything. He was disconnected. Half of him was—somewhere. He stepped over the edge. He was on a white Pegasus, Orion, flapping its huge wings. Flying to the moon. Behind him, starbursts.

Nate woke up unable to feel his phone. It wasn't on the nightstand either. He was in his own bed, the sheets smelling like laundry detergent, and the dirty laundry gone. More smells of bacon cooking and coffee brewing. A knife stabbed him at the base of his skull as he tried to sit up. He had the worst hangover of his life, although he didn't recall drinking that much.

He could only manage a meek sound as he lay back down. Mylah floated in on a smile and the smell of breakfast, holding a tray with bacon, eggs, pancakes drenched in maple syrup, and a cup of coffee next to a pitcher for cream, although he didn't take cream.

"Don't try to get up."

"No shit. Thanks for the warning."

Mylah sat on the bed. He loved her autumn look—tight black leggings stretched across her hips, and a light-gray chunky turtleneck. His head throbbed, but so did the rest of him. Her brown eyes smiled as she smothered the pancakes in butter and syrup. She cut a forkful, scooped bacon and eggs, then held it to his mouth. He was drawn like a magnet, forced to lean forward to eat.

"How do you feel?"

"Like I drank a case of vodka."

"Close."

"I dreamt about an old doctor in green scrubs and a big needle. I can't feel my phone."

"Not a dream. You are disconnected." Mylah smiled, filled another forkful of breakfast, and held it to him. "Human now. The infection is out. Doc says you will make a full recovery."

"Out?"

Mylah nodded and then showed him the contents of the pitcher, which held dozens of big white pills but no cream.

"He left these. Take two a day. And no alcohol or drugs."

Was no alcohol her rule or the docs? It didn't matter. Her warmth said they were back together. So he would follow it either way.

"I signed you up for N.A. too."

He nodded. Neuroface Anonymous, for people addicted to electronics. "Maybe I should join the other one too."

"One step at a time. How is your pain?"

"Like hot rebar through my skull. Weird, though I feel good. Like—"

Mylah lifted a syringe from the tray. The needle's point smirked at him.

"For the pain."

Then what were the white pills for? He had to close his eyes, he couldn't watch. A jab and a rush, like a narcotic. His headache receded, still a dull thud in the background, but a million miles away.

Eyes open. Another forkful of breakfast was headed his way. "I could get used to this."

"Well don't. Once this wears off—"

"I meant being served breakfast."

"Oh. Well this is fun except for the dribbles of syrup on my new sweater."

Nate put his hand on her thigh and ran it under the sweater. "You could take it off."

Her eyes smiled and she bit her lip. She put the tray aside, but as she leaned in for a kiss, Ben stomped into the room wearing jeans and a black and white I ♡ NY t-shirt. His brown hair was wet and slicked back.

"So, how does it feel to be human again?"

"Loud and ugly like your face. Try stomping louder next time."

"I didn't want to walk into the middle."

Doubtful. Nate shared a flirty smile with Mylah. Whatever was in the syringe was working, so he tried to sit up again. As he grabbed the coffee off the tray, Rily stomped in, brown hair flowing over her shoulders and dressed as Mylah's twin. Rily wanted to be Mylah hard. She was useful, understood all the technology stuff, but didn't have—something. Nate wasn't sure. Maybe Mylah's edginess.

Rily said, "Four tickets to the colony—booked."

That made Nate splash his coffee. "What?"

Mylah said, "Remember sweetie, we got a big donation?"

"Honestly, I don't."

"The other day, when I came over. I showed you. Some guy named Dilan Darcy said he saw our protest in D.C. He gave us money."

"Protest in DC? Who is Dilan Darcy?"

Ben said, "I am researching it."

"I remember being jabbed by Doctor Bigneedle and my phone being smashed, that's all."

She put her hand inside his and squeezed. "He did say it might affect your memory for a while."

Nate rubbed the back of his neck and felt the gauze. "What else did he say?"

"There may have been a little bruising. He said it's like a minor concussion. It will go away."

Ben said, "The good news is you are human again, right?"

Nate nodded, but what were the pills for? If he asked Mylah, it would make her defensive. She would say she went to a lot of trouble to find a doctor willing to risk their license, and why are you questioning me? He bit his tongue.

"So, why are we going to the colony?"

Nate spied the analog clock on the wall and realized he had been unconscious for three days. No wonder he was so hungry.

Mylah rubbed her hand up his arm. "Well, it got me to thinking. I think it's time. Your infection is out."

They had talked about it—long before Ben and Rily joined. This was why Mylah was the leader. She was fearless and willing to take big risks. The scar she'd removed, she got that protesting a server farm. She dumped fuel over the servers, lit it, and it splattered her face.

"I dreamt about it. Flying to the moon."

Nate instantly regretted saying it. Rily believed dreams predicted the future. He could see her arms shaking with joy. As far as she was concerned, they were disembarking tomorrow.

Rily said, "It's going to be great. I booked drones. We are going to drop human torsos onto the dome of that famous hotel. A disgusting display of death from above, just like the chips they make up there."

Nate shook his head. Rily was into performance art. He said, "This is risky. It needs to be worth it. We'll be in a tin can for eight hours getting there. We show up, they arrest us."

Mylah pointed at Ben. "Ben is printing masks."

Ben nodded and grinned. Another reason Mylah was the leader, she just did things. The plan was in motion. He was arguing with himself.

"We wear masks for the whole time? You sit next to someone for eight hours, they will notice your silicone skin and makeup."

"So we keep our helmets on." Mylah squeezed his hand. "This time we go big."

Nate rubbed the base of his neck. The bandage was small, like it covered a pimple. He looked at six eager eyes. If he said no—it meant the other three would go without him.

Rily clapped her hands. "We go *big*."

Mylah swiveled her head, her eyes stabbing Rily. "Can we have some privacy?"

Ben asked, "Go big how?"

Nate slurped his coffee. "She means it's time to unplug a toaster."

Rily's eyes widened. Mylah shooed Rily with her eyes. Nate said, "Can I rest? Mylah and I need to discuss this."

Rily shook her head, huffed, and spun out of the bedroom like an angry ballerina. There was a moment of awkward silence as Ben glanced from Mylah's face to Nate's. Then, he slunk out of the room like a hurt puppy, closing the door behind him.

"This is risky. Are you sure? What if we are arrested?"

"Nobody knows who we are, sweetie. We'll be two-hundred-fifty-thousand miles from any Feds. But just in case, I asked Rily to get us fake IDs to travel."

Nate sipped his coffee. "I'm not sure about Rily. Ben—" But they were a pair and without Rily there was no Ben. Nate already knew what Mylah would say.

Mylah said, "We need them. We need them to work their magic on those cyborgs. And the systems." She grinned. "And drones."

"What do you want to hit first?"

"Researching, Ben came across all the weddings they do at that gold hotel."

Nate said, "The Crown Oasis."

"Someone will be livestreaming it. So they can't censor it. We disappear like we always do then—"

"That place is crawling with wattsuckers."

Mylah leaned in. Face to face, breathy, she said, "I know. We'll have our pick of next targets. I want to build a bomb. Too bad we won't get all of them at once."

Nate was nodding, picturing a riot, then an explosion. He put his coffee on the tray, then pulled Mylah closer. "Maybe we can. First, we need a name for our group. All good secret agencies have a name."

She whispered, "The Orionids. Like the President's codename for going to the moon, except there are four of us. We can be an October meteor storm" She guided her hands between his legs. "We are going to hit *hard*. Let's be an extinction level event for the wattsuckers."

"Does all this talk of violence turn you on?" He put his hand under her turtleneck, then pushed her leggings off and smiled. A silly question.

11

United States Lunar Colony
Procellarum Improvement District, Texas
September 2073

Kate spent a considerable time in Olicia Barron's office gazing at the paintings on its stark white walls. A black moonstone desk faced the door and was positioned like a throne in front of a sweeping floor-to-ceiling window. During the two-week lunar nights, like today, the floor-to-ceiling window was a mirror, reflecting Olicia Barrons' bright office interior and her priceless art. During the lunar day, the window overlooked the Barron empire outside, a gravelly chalk-white, olivine, or brown-tinged lunar regolith that covered the people living underground.

Kate's reflection stood between a Renoir on the right and a new painting on the left she had not seen. In that spot previously, *Monet's Woman in a Parasol—Madame Monet and her son 1875.* Kate knew the Barrons had another private gallery at their residence. But this was her office, her public face, so each painting here was a statement. Or a trophy. *Woman in a Parasol*, maybe both. Whatever purpose *Woman in a Parasol* served was now finished, the painting rotated to her private collection.

Until today it had been Kate's favorite painting. In it, Kate saw Rae in Madame Monet, and Rae's son Axio resembled Monet's son. Kate could picture herself strolling on a windy day with them, blue sky and flowers, just like the painting, although Rae would be the artist, not her.

The new painting replacing it was Alan Bean's *Jack Schmitt Skis the Sculptured Hills,* textured acrylic with moon dust on plywood. Rae, who read all the art rumors on the server, said Barron bought this at auction for forty million dollars and gifted it to her daughter-in-law Aria to celebrate breaking ground on a new golf course. Aria was more than Olicia's in-law, though. Aria was the operations manager of the colony, Olicia's left *and* right hand running the place, and she used Olicia's office as her own most of the time. So naturally, *Sculptured Hills* hung here.

In *Sculptured Hills,* an Apollo 17 astronaut was having fun, turning his upper body, and pretending to ski on the moon. The way the astronaut held the pole, he could be holding a golf club and pointing to the next hole. Or out the window, pointing to the Barron empire. The lunar regolith was depicted as beige, tan, and in the foreground, almost mustard. The sky was midnight purple. From being topside, she knew digital photos did not capture the moon's color the way the human eye did. Often, the images looked grayscale or washed out. There had always been conspiracy theories about the Apollo landings—mostly but not entirely squelched when Apollo National Park opened so people could tour the ruins and see for themselves. This artist rendered the colors perfectly. The way she saw it. Proof, to her, he was there.

Kate smiled as she studied Schmitt's swing. Hips aligned. Knees flexed. *Swing*. Recruit her traps and rhomboids. Then pecs and lats to rotate. Finally, glutes. *Crack*. She could hit the ball a kilometer on the moon. Maybe more if she started doing box squats and reverse cable flys at the gym again. Of course, a bulky EVA suit would cut her range by two-thirds. There would be no satisfying crack because there was no air. And good luck finding a white ball in a sea of chalk-white gravel. But she would play, maybe Axio too, with Rae painting them afterward.

"You like that one?"

Kate had turned to face the painting. While she daydreamed, Aria snuck in. Aria was petite and athletic, wearing night-blue tights, white sneakers, and a pastel blue tank top. Her sandy blond hair was tied in a ponytail, and her cheeks were rosy. Unusual for Aria, no makeup today.

"I like them all Aria."

"You're being political. Feeling ok?"

Kate looked around the room. All the abstract art had been relocated.

"Ok, well now that we got rid of the shit that looks like graffiti, I like them all."

Aria smiled and walked to the conference table. "Mum is going to have a stroke."

Mum was always having a stroke. Or a heart attack. Typically over the real estate project du jour. Mum had several lung transplants to cure cancer caused by her decades-old bad habit and two coronary artery transplants—all grown from her stem cells. Rae said a liver transplant was on deck. But she had not yet had a stroke.

"Why? Golf course?"

"Shit no. That's going great. We changed the design and eliminated the dome. Cut two and a half years off the build."

Kate eyed the moonwalker in the painting.

"What's the yardage?"

"Each hole is a kilometer-ish. But we have a lot of doglegs."

"It's a gravel pit out there."

"Drones will rake the surface and we'll have astroturf. The color is the problem."

"Finding the ball will be a problem. How is the color a problem?"

"We are looking at blaze orange balls and embedded trackers. The astroturf color is a problem because the engineers are worried the turf will heat too fast in lunar day. They want something reflective to keep it cool."

"Too much glare."

"What I said. I want green."

Kate took another pretend swing. "Sounds fun."

"Take my spot anytime. Honestly, I fucking hate golf, Kate. I don't see the point in hitting a ball a thousand meters then chasing it. Not on Earth. Not here."

Aria put her hands on her hips and groaned into one of the chairs at the conference table. Kate scrunched her eyebrows.

"Aria, the reason I'm here is—two things really. First is Project Orion—"

Kate wanted off project Orion. Or the next best thing, a way to stay on the project but away from her ex Kelli. She hadn't decided how to frame the request.

Before she could decide, Aria said, "Mum is having a stroke over it. Do you want to sit?"

Kate looked at the chair. "I think better on my feet."

"Well good, you're going to help me think up a way out of this mess."

"Say again?"

"Mum is livid. Latham is desperate to make this her first campaign stop. Mum wants me to do everything I can think of to cut them off. And you are going to help me."

"Mind if I ask why?"

Aria raised her eyebrows and looked at the ceiling. "417C is why. Rumor is Defense Secretary Cruz will resign and run against her."

Kate followed Aria's gaze. Defense Secretary Gaby Cruz was a longtime friend of Olicia Barron. Thirty years ago, Barron's company sold drones and rockets to the Pentagon. Between then and now, the company morphed into a real estate company, using those drones and rockets to develop lunar real estate. One floor up, Cruz owned a vacation suite.

Aria reached behind her into the wall fridge and retrieved two water bottles. Aria slid one across the conference table towards Kate. Then she swished the second open and took a swig.

"So we can't come out and tell Latham to fuck off. God knows Mum would like to. So plan B is a wish and walk."

"Wish and what?"

"Make our demands so high they can't possibly say yes and force them to walk."

"We can't say no, but we can make demands?"

"You always surprise me. So tough yet so naïve. They are desperate. So yes, we make demands. Tell them all the stuff we need to make this happen."

"Politics was above my pay grade. I ran the kinetic solution."

"Perfect. So help me think up some kinetic things to demand. How about new anti-meteor missile batteries? They've turned us down for years on that. How many would you say we need?"

Kate blew out a breath and looked in the reflection, counting the green water lilies in the painting behind her. Too many. Maybe just the red and yellow ones.

"Five?"

"We have two domes and two high-rises. Which, as you know, are in high demand. People want to see the stars from their bedroom—want to *pay* to see the stars from their bedroom. Surface domes are high risk—but you know the problems. Five more missile batteries would lower the risk calculations and make engineering very happy."

Surface domes and high-rises were rare. Most of the colony was underground to protect against the unfiltered sun, radiation, and meteors that hit the surface. Above-surface structures were expensive and needed to be rated for what engineers categorized as a class 3 meteor strike, about a once-in-hundred year event. If a larger meteor hit the dome, thousands would die.

The Crown Oasis was an exception. With the fifteen gold-painted stories above ground and surrounding gardens under its dome, it was the Barrons' showpiece property, where the elite of the elite stayed. Engineering summaries claimed the gold paint reflected the lunar sun, keeping its occupants cool two weeks a month. A half-truth. At the right angle, the gold paint reflected the sun so that thirteen billion people on Earth could look up and imagine themselves here, like a big marquis. Barron never let the opportunity to advertise herself go to waste.

Kate squinted, not recalling the second dome. Maybe it was new. Then she smiled. "In the military, when I needed one pallet of ammo, I requisitioned three, hoping to get what I need. So, ask for—fifteen?"

Aria grinned and glugged her water. "I knew there was a reason we hired you. Come up with a wish list. Multiply by six."

"On it. When do you need it?"

"Last week, before we went to the base."

Kate grimaced. "No problem. I have Jinho Knight. He can send electrons back in time."

Aria smiled. "Throw in some toys for you, too."

"What if they say yes?"

"They won't. If we do our jobs. What did you want to talk about? You said Project Orion and something else."

Kate smiled. Project Orion was getting canceled, and along with that, her issue with Kelli. She was happy to help. "We are good on Orion. Now. I think—"

"This about your ex? You are welcome by the way."

Kate's mouth opened and closed.

"Is that the only face you're going to make today, Kate? I know a woman in need of being rescued and you, girl, needed rescued."

Kate put her hands in her pockets and searched the corner of Olicia's office floor for an answer. She saw nothing except dust. "Really?"

"If you were a Great Dane, she was a steak, and you were drooling all over your clothes."

"Shit." Kate puffed her cheeks. "I don't want to get back together with her. I swear."

"What the brain wants and what the bean wants—" Aria shrugged and sighed.

"I think I should stay away from her for a while."

Aria smirked. "If we do our jobs, you don't have to worry about it."

Kate chuckled and picked the water up off the table. She swished open her bottle and drank. Icy Comet brand, always cold and refreshing.

Aria grinned over her water bottle. "What was the second thing?"

"Oh, my old apartment—"

"Oh, good news. You are off the hook. We found a buyer."

"Oh." Kate took a swig of water. "Wonderful."

It was Aria's turn to look confused. "Were you going to ask for an extension?"

"It's not a problem."

"Your voice sounds like it's a problem."

Kate exhaled. "Not really. Rae's family is coming. Her parents. Meloni. Axio. We will figure something out."

"Figure something out? Where are they staying?"

"Rae's—our place."

"Christ. Homicidal much? Her place is tiny for six people."

Kate winced. Aria shook her head then pulled her pad closer. "I am going to send you something. No obligation but I want you to take a look."

"What is it?"

"It's an apartment. We could work a deal. It's—well full transparency, Kate, it's a scratch and dent. A model apartment. Been on the market for a while. Been used for short term stays too."

"Like a hotel? How scratched and how dented?"

"Not very actually. You should look. Nobody wants it."

"Why doesn't anyone want it?"

"Wrong floor plan. People want custom built. People want new." Aria put her index finger on her nose, pushed it high, and affected a high-society British accent. "Oh my *gawd* Katera Lynn, it's been used. Can you believe it?" Her voice returned to normal. "Honestly, it's almost pristine. But we have to get it occupied."

"Why the hurry?"

"It looks bad when we have a place we can't sell. Perception is reality. People think we ran out of money. Or something's wrong with it. One prospect told me she was afraid by the time she moved in, squatters would have it, and it'd take years. Suddenly, there were rumors all over the server we have squatters. Granted, that happens in cities, but it's not like you buy a ticket to space, program your prints into the system and move right the fuck in." Aria shook her head. "People are ridiculous. Anyway. Empties are bad publicity, so we gotta discount. Fire sale. Maybe your lucky day. Make a reasonable offer, I'll say yes."

"One dollar?"

Aria laughed. "Reasonable. It has four bedrooms. A balcony. Floor to ceiling holowindows." Aria swished her water and studied Kate. "But it would not be unreasonable to offer what you were paying before." She winked. "But I didn't tell you that. No obligation. Look. If you say no, no one will get upset. So have two-hundred-thirty-nine other people."

Aria touched her pad, and Kate's phone dinged in her pocket.

"Thanks. I'll look. Rae and I will look."

"Oh. Forgot. I've been so tired. Jeong Moon. Go talk to him."

"Jeong Moon?"

"Someone broke into his penthouse over the weekend."

"What did they steal?"

"Nothing."

Kate's phone binged again. "Nothing? Like they were chased off?"

"No. I just sent you the report from his private security. I have a theory, but I want you to look at it."

"On it."

"Thank you. So sorry to be rude but I am kicking you out now. I need a nap. Imagine having someone inside you sapping your energy then being dumb enough to go to the gym."

"Say again?"

Aria stared at Kate over her water. "I said that out loud didn't I?"

"Congratulations?"

"I am not announcing it. You might say it's classified. As classified as anything can be around here, anyway. But vomiting in the truck was not claustrophobia. The doc said it would take two years and we just started trying four months ago. I'm nine weeks."

"Wow. That's awesome."

"Not really. I am overwhelmed. I wasn't ready. I thought it'd take another year and by then I would be." Aria took another swig of water. "Every time I sit down I feel like napping. You'd think it'd be easier in one-sixth gravity. And Oliver is irritating the shit out of me with his nesting and moving everything around." Aria was waving her hands around, miming moving furniture. "I just want to give him my fucking uterus so I can get work done."

Aria looked misty, so Kate walked over and leaned in to hug her.

"Thank you."

"Anything I can do?"

"Break Oliver's arms so he stops moving things."

Kate laughed. "Maybe your brother's job."

"Now go. While I'm napping, I'll be dreaming of you getting me a huge fucking list so we can get this damn visit canceled. Then we are both off the hook."

On the way out, Kate slowed to eye *Sculptured Hills*. The colors were absolutely perfect. She did like that one.

12

Jeong Moon lived in a two-floor suite at Gemini, a half dozen floors up from Rae's apartment. On the way over, Kate skimmed the report Aria forwarded from Moon's private security. Someone invested a lot of time and effort hacking their way through the locks and security systems. Moon's security suspected hacktivists, but there was no graffiti or property damage. Nor had he been the target of recent protests. Nothing was reported stolen, and as far as Moon's human butler Cain stated, not even a dust bunny was out of place.

When she and Jin arrived, Cain—dressed in a white tuxedo and spartan black bowtie—directed them to sit on Moon's plush cotton corner sofa. Moon was worth countless billions, and his suite smelled like it. He was a retired technology magnate whose second career was as an outspoken critic of almost everything. It would be hard to open a media or financial server without seeing his avatar jabber jawing and skewering something or someone. According to Jin, he trended to political commentary recently, but he did not hold back on anything.

Kate wasn't religious, but when she entered Moon's apartment, Cain's haughty attitude and spotless black shoes indicated she would have an epiphany. Based on the angle of Cain's nose, Moon was too busy solving world hunger and curing cancer to meet. Kate considered it more likely he was with a hooker or masturbating.

Cain disappeared stating, *he would confer*. If Moon canceled his plans *for them*, he would appear in godlike form with magical flowing robes. Probably floating down from the second floor to deliver a twenty-seventy-three update patch for the Talmud. She hoped it wouldn't be written in programming code or Hebrew because the last time she read either was in high school.

As she awaited her epiphany, or for Moon to clean up, she surveyed his penthouse. While she knew it was not the largest on the colony, it was two floors, the largest she had been in so far. The interior was almost entirely cream, with large bright holowindows that simulated an outdoor forest. The corner where they sat had a vaulted two-story ceiling. A floating chalk-white staircase, nearly invisible against the wall, rose to a second-floor landing guarded by a minimalist aluminum railing. The landing bordered three sides of the second floor. A seating area at the top of the stairs had another sofa. She counted six rooms upstairs, all with closed doors. On the first floor, the doors were open. She eyed a spacious office, kitchen, media room, another room with a golf simulator, a small gym, and a roomy bathroom. All the furniture was bamboo colored. Ordinarily, she expected fake bamboo-style lunaresin, but Moon was worth billions. So, it seemed likely he imported real bamboo tables and chairs. The side table certainly felt and sounded like wood.

The magical robe Moon wore turned out to be an ordinary slate-blue bathrobe. He was short, barefoot, graying, and barely covered by the robe. He held his hand out as he walked over and smiled through the introductions. Cain appeared from the kitchen as they sat, holding a tray with three bamboo cups, three silver pots, a creamer, and a wood bowl holding sugar and sugar substitutes. Cain's tempo was polished and balanced. Wearing a white tuxedo, he looked like a friendly ghost floating toward them in low gravity—except one who smelled like freshly brewed Earth-grown coffee and carried a tray of goodies.

The coffee was her epiphany, not Moon, and she accepted hers black.

Kate must have furrowed her brow as Cain retreated to the kitchen because Moon answered her question.

"Cain is human. Drone AI is very advanced, but they will never have the warmth of a human butler."

Kate found herself nodding, although she had no experience with butlers, drone or otherwise.

"So, Jin and I have read the report from your private security. Tell us what's not in the report. Was anything stolen?"

Jin was swiping something on his pad. She put her hand over it to signal pencils down.

"This is all off the record."

Moon sipped his tea while he considered her question.

"Look, I don't care if you have a hundred year old Claymore mine in your office safe. To help you, I need to know what's not in the report."

From Moon's expression, she had guessed correctly. Kate knew two truths about the colony's billionaires. They were all paranoid, and they were all collectors. Some collected luxury rockets, some collected art, while others collected sex partners. Moon was on his fourth wife, his youngest yet, but Kate guessed his biggest collection was in his office safe.

She stood up. "Do you mind if I have a look?"

He sipped his tea and then nodded. "It's open. And it's all there."

Moon's office had the same décor as the main room—cream walls and floor, two bright windows on the far wall looking out to a forest, and a wall-size holographic screen on the right. In the left corner, she saw his impressive safe next to his bamboo desk. Its black steel door was half open. To call it a safe was an understatement. Vault or bunker was more apt. As she crossed the threshold, the smell of gun oil crept into her nose. His collection of guns hung on the wall for display. On the back wall, shelves lined with black jewelers felt held more delicate items under glass, including diamonds and gold bars in a bamboo-framed box. He was ready for an apocalypse, except if the apocalypse came to the colony, he'd need to find someone willing to trade gold for oxygen. Unlikely.

After she inspected the contents, she returned to the main room where Cain was refilling her coffee. He glided back to the kitchen before she sat.

"The diamonds, did you—"

"I inventoried them and had my jeweler check. Nothing's missing."

"What about serial numbers—"

"Not all of them have serial numbers. Some are over a century and a half old. But I checked those, too. All there."

"When was the last time they were fired?"

Moon sipped his tea as he pondered the question. "Has to be a few years. Before I moved here. Olicia keeps promising to build a range, but it isn't funded yet."

"Ammo?"

He nodded. "Also accounted for. Every bullet."

She nodded. "Maintenance?"

"I have a smith come in once a year to clean and inspect them."

"When were they here last?"

"Six months ago."

"I will need their name."

"I am sure she has nothing to do with this. I have used her for twenty years. She would not ruin her reputation with her clients. And like I said, nothing was stolen."

"No doubt. I am always on the lookout for a good armorer though. Gotta watch the corrosion, especially with the antiques."

The collection Kate's grandfather left her was paltry compared to Moon's, but she smiled back at him as if they shared a secret.

Jin asked, "What about electronics?"

"I have top security. Impenetrable."

"Nothing is impenetrable. Mind if I look?"

Moon looked at Kate. She nodded, and then he stood up. "I need to unlock the system. Follow me."

Jin stood up and followed Moon into his office. Cain reappeared. As he refilled her cup, now her third, she debated whether she would drink it. If she did, she would need to see the bathroom. The roasted aroma was irresistible, so she found herself surveying the bathroom décor. It was the same as the rest of the suite, with an open bamboo vanity holding two ceramic bowls and bamboo shelves with impersonal curios and towels.

She was not long. They were exiting Moon's office when she came out, with Jin shaking his head.

"They've cloned his server and installed some tracking spyware."

Before Kate could ask a question, a voice summoned her.

"I see one of you here, please?"

Moon shook his head, huffed, and made a big sweeping arc with his hands to wave Kate upstairs. From his scowl, he was well on his way to wife number five.

Upstairs, June Moon met Kate in a pink bathrobe, then waved Kate into her office. The windows played the same forest scene as the rest of the house. But the simulated sunlight reflecting off the pink walls and polished aluminum furniture gave her office an uncomfortable glare.

"I know who did this."

Kate anticipated a confession. Instead, June Moon led her to a bamboo clock on her desk.

"I get them on camera."

Kate chose to wait for the explanation. Interior cameras were not in the security plan, at least according to Moon's security.

"I think he cheat so I bought camera."

"What do you know about the spyware?"

She wagged her finger. "If I do spyware, you think I tell you about cameras?"

Kate picked up the clock and turned it over. As a nannycam, it was unoriginal. It would stand out—at least to Jeong. Lunaresin, not bamboo. There was no obvious way to open it, so she would have to have Jin investigate whatever was inside.

June stared at the clock as Kate tucked it in her armpit. Her facial expression looked torn.

"If it's any consolation, I'd guess he knew about the clock."

June Moon wagged her finger again. "He miss everything in this house."

Kate doubted that. As Kate descended the stairs, Jeong looked up at her, smirked, and shook his head. Precisely the reaction she expected if he knew about the nannycam.

"She thinks she's sneaky."

Kate walked over and handed the clock to Jin. He turned it over and scanned it with his phone. Jeong glared at June at the top of the stairs.

"Maybe she did it."

"I doubt it."

Kate looked over her shoulder to June, who was watching them from the top of the stairs. Her gut was that someone who bought a novelty nannycam didn't install sophisticated spyware. Or fake breaking and entering.

Jin said, "The video is solid. They were in and out in under three minutes. They have masks."

"Sounds professional." Kate paused to watch a short clip of the video. "Any idea who they are?"

"It could be anyone, Chief Devana. Like you, I like to blow things up. Figuratively, in my case. But progress requires scrambling things, you would agree?"

Once again, she found herself nodding. Despite Moon's reputation, in person, he was charismatic. Jin was both nodding and holding back a smirk. The two images he flashed on his phone kept her from kicking him.

"Look at that. A match to two guests in the Apus, room 513."

Moon said, "That was fast."

Jin said, "We have tools private security doesn't."

Tools like luck and Moon's paranoid fourth wife. But Kate would rather be lucky than right any day. She took the clock from Jin, turned it over for inspection, then handed it back.

"Never again will I insult these amateur toys."

Moon said, "I want to talk to them when you arrest them."

"Let us handle this. If we have any questions we will follow up." Kate paused. "Oh, leave everything as it is for now. I don't want them alerted that we know."

"Thank you for handling this. I owe you."

Kate looked back up the stairs to smile and nod to June Moon, who was still watching. "Don't thank me. Thank her. The bamboo clock was her idea."

Simultaneously, both Moons vocalized a sound between agreement and a mating call. The fourth marriage looked hot again, so she said goodbye and led Jin out the door.

Once they were in the elevator, she asked Jin about his smirk. He let his grin get wide and imitated Moon. "*Like you, I blow things up.* You are two peas in a pod."

"His peas are a lot more expensive. Plus, he has more of them. And I am not political."

"Give it time."

She told the elevator to go to concourse level. On the way down, she tried to picture herself in the media. Or running for office. In every image, she saw Rae doing it better.

"I don't see it, Jin. How did you match so quickly?"

The elevator opened, and they took a right on the concourse. It wasn't busy, so it would be a quick walk.

"These two took their masks off in the hall, went down two flights of stairs, then took the elevators. From there, straight to the Apus."

"ID?"

"No hits. But the spyware uses a backdoor typically used by the Feds."

"Feds?"

"Not certain. Everyone in the industry knows about it. Why would the Feds do that?"

"Let's pay them a courtesy call and find out."

"Is this knock or no-knock?"

"Courtesy call. We knock."

As she and Jin walked across the colony, Kate noted how deserted it felt. She was beginning to adjust to the ebb and flow of tourists. Underground, the colony's twenty-four-hour UTC time was an artificial construct. But the lunar calendar still drove rhythms. Visiting topside attractions required lunar day, which at the colony's longitude started two days after the first quarter moon and ended two days after the last quarter moon. Tourists preferred those weeks. Those who weren't going topside could often get an off-peak discount. Any eclipse brought a significant tourist flow.

A lunar eclipse brought peak chaos, with people crammed into the colony like a crowded subway. Immediately after the eclipse, business died because tourists' bank accounts were empty, and their livers were overloaded. The three weeks after the August seventeenth eclipse was the slowest she had seen—first the post-eclipse hangover, then lunar night.

Her calendar said the first quarter moon started Friday the eighth. That meant business—and crime—would pick up Sunday. Looking into the shops, drones and people were using the next four days to restock and recharge.

13

She and Jin made good time to the Apus. When they got to 513, she buzzed the door and identified herself. No one answered, so she tried a second time. Either the room was empty, or the men inside were lying in wait. She would have preferred a battering ram and riot gear, but she decided that the override code and her toe would have to do. She drew her pistol, and after counting down from three, she toed the door open. No one shot at her, so she nudged it open until she saw two men. They wore headphones and sat with their backs to the door, their blue suit jackets slung over uncomfortable-looking resin chairs. They were glued to six monitors sprawled over a yellow portable fold-up table. One screen looked like a video feed of the wall in Moon's office. Another looked like a clone of his computer screen. A third was of the pink ceiling in June Moon's office.

To the right of the monitors, enough half-eaten junk food and takeout cluttered the table to feed a platoon. She shook her head when she stepped into the room and saw their body armor on the bed.

The man on the right startled when he saw her shadow on the wall. He jumped from the chair, flipping it to the floor, then turned and reached for his waist. He shifted his eyes from Kate's gun to Jin's in disbelief, then froze before he drew his sidearm. The agent on the left looked up, then jumped up, performing the same chair flip. But instead of reaching for his pistol, he put his hands in the air, and started talking.

"Let's all relax. We are Federal agents. I'm—"

"Save it. Just keep your hands up." Kate motioned with the barrel of her gun for the left agent to get against the wall. "You know the drill."

The left agent registered a sigh, an eyeroll, and hesitation. He definitely knew the drill. He said, "This is a mistake."

"Absolutely. No sentry at the door. Headphones. Body armor on the bed. Lots of mistakes. Don't make it worse by getting yourself shot in the face." Kate again motioned towards the wall with her gun. "Tell your story there."

In case she had not seen the first melodramatic eyeroll, the left agent repeated it as he put his hands against the wall. The right agent followed suit.

Kate spread their legs and frisked the left agent. She handed Jin the left agent's phone and tossed his two guns on the bed.

"I assume you recognize me from Moon's office."

Right Agent said, "We know who you are, Chief Devana."

Kate didn't like being called Chief Devana. Coming from his mouth, it sounded like a slap.

"Funny, I don't remember a courtesy call. You know, a short message. Like please don't bust two agents during an illegal surveillance op."

She took the headphones off the right agent, tossed them on the bed, then started frisking him. She said, "Unless you're going to tell me you have a warrant."

Left Agent said, "We are undercover."

"Mmmhm." Nothing about the agents' white shirt, pressed blue jacket, and slacks signaled undercover. The Apus' hotel bathrobes were better colony camouflage.

The right agent talked to the wall. "If this is about money, we can pay."

Kate said, "Oh, I definitely think you will be paying."

The right agent had only one gun and a phone. She kept the phone and tossed the gun to the bed.

Right said, "It's not a problem. We will pay the fine."

"Mmmhm. And how much *is* the fine for illegal surveillance?"

The two agents exchanged a glance then the left one answered. "It could be six figures."

Kate whistled. "Damn. Jin, did you hear that?"

Jin was looking over the monitors and shaking his head. Kate unlocked the phone she held and started going through it. She found an image and held it to the right agent's face. She said, "You must be Agent

Bruce Rollins, Homeland Security. Nice to meet you. They are letting anyone into the bureau these days aren't they?"

Kate and Jin swapped phones by tossing them at the same time. She looked at the phone, then said, "And you are Agent John Linton. Nice to meet you too." She turned to Jin. "Jin—what did you think of Agent Linton's offer?"

"I was insulted, honestly."

"Me too. What should we do? Arrest them for attempted bribery?"

"Space is dangerous. I say we take them topside and shoot them in the back."

Kate smiled. "Mmm. Wild West style. Tempting." She stepped back. "Both of you go. I promise if you run now, Jin won't shoot you in the back."

Linton said, "This is a misunderstanding. You're interfering with a national security operation."

Rollins sighed and looked at the ceiling. Kate swiped through Linton's phone, then gave it back to Jin. He shook his head, indicating he hadn't found anything on Rollin's phone.

"What I want to see is the warrant for all this."

Linton said, "Our director will call you. He can straighten this out."

"You can explain when you get back to Virginia."

Rollins banged his head against the painted aluminum wall with a rhythm that reminded her of an intro track for a steel drum band on her and Rae's dance playlist.

"I am telling you Devana, you don't want to do this. It's going to get ugly."

"Banging your head on the wall makes you ugly. What I think is that you two are far outside your mission parameters. How am I doing?"

Rollins and Linton exchanged glances.

"Or maybe you aren't. Either way, I am trespassing both of you and probably doing the bureau a favor."

Rollins said, "Hang on. We can explain."

"You will. To your boss. First, how you got busted. Then you'll have to explain losing six figures worth of Federal Government property—"

Jin was shaking his head and mouthing seven.

"—Or maybe seven figures. *Then* you'll have to explain losing three department issued pistols. Plus attempted bribery. That's a lot of paperwork to swipe, isn't it Jin?"

Jin smirked. "They will need a finger transplant before they're done."

Kate leaned into Rollin's ear. "Without a finger, your prostate will be lonely for a while."

Jin said, "Nah, Kate. *Thumb* up the ass is usually Homeland's protocol."

"Fuck you." Rollin's skull on aluminum reverberated in the hotel room again, this time staccato and louder. Kate didn't stop him. There was no danger that Rollins would put his head through the metal wall. Self-preservation would kick in eventually.

When Rollin's stopped, she motioned them out the door. "So, are you two going to the spaceport voluntarily or do you need an escort?"

They looked at each other.

Rollins offered, "We are investigating threats made by Moon."

"What threats, against whom, and when?"

Linton shrugged. "We have our orders. We told you why we are here. Can we get back to work now?"

"Any more of you?"

Neither of them answered.

"I'll find them too. If Moon is making threats, Jin and I will handle it. This is not how we do things here."

Rollins snarked, "Oh, and how do you do things here?"

Kate smiled her best smile. "You can observe that from Earth. Your Uncle Sam just bought you two tickets home. First class too. Right Jin?"

Jin nodded and grinned ear-to-ear.

"Add to your paperwork how I unlocked your phone and Jin bought your tickets home, courtesy your expense account."

Rollins said, "Fucking hell."

"The longer you're here, the worse it gets. Jin, how is the surveillance between here and the spaceport?"

"We have every square centimeter covered."

He sounded convincing. It was a good bluff, and they bought it.

Agent Linton took his hands off the wall and turned around. He said, "Fine. We are leaving. We need our phones."

Jin said, "No. You don't. Your prints and your face will be enough to board."

Linton hesitated.

Kate said, "Unless you resist and I have to smash your face into the wall. Then you'll be stuck in a jail cell until Jin can upload your new face."

"I'm kinda busy, boss. I have a lot on my plate with Project Orion."

"Won't be a priority. Get to it when you get to it."

"10-4."

Agent Linton huffed, rolled his eyes, and turned towards the door like Axio being sent to his room. Rollins looked at the equipment, banged his head a few more times, then followed Linton out the door.

Kate heard herself yelling after the agents, "Go straight to the spaceport. Swipe right at the boarding kiosk." She sounded like Rae sending Axio to bed.

Kate turned back to Jin, who was grinning. He said, "Fuck I love this job, Kate."

Kate squinted at him. "You wanted to shoot them."

"This is such bullshit. Would you have let me?"

"Some job perks I reserve for myself. Anyway, their fate is worse. They are going to get demoted to swiping left on meaningless paperwork until they're fired." She looked around at the equipment. "What do you suppose this is about?"

Jin found a duffel on the floor by the bed and started shoving equipment into it. "I think they told us. Moon threatened Latham."

"I thought you said he was clean when you profiled him?"

"As clean as twice distilled comet water. Four wives. Three amicable divorces. Not even a domestic."

Kate responded with a smirk, "Maybe he's getting grumpy in his old age."

"According to the file, he's always been grumpy. His second wife described him as a cactus—prickly on the outside, soft on the inside. He fights with his money and his mouth, Kate, not violence. He went on the national server and said he'd take the Latham administration down for incompetence and corruption."

"That's what you think this is? These agents are looking for dirt?"

"One hundred percent opposition research. You never asked me why I wanted to quit Homeland. This is why, Kate. To get ahead, you need to volunteer for side projects like this bullshit."

Kate puffed her cheeks and blew out a breath. "They offered us a lot of money."

"I am not here for the money, Kate. If I ever see that shit here, I am done. And I won't think twice."

Kate patted him on the shoulder. "I'm not here for the money either." She looked over the equipment. "But they will be back. And they won't send plebes."

"How do you want to handle Moon?"

"Does he seem like the type to hide his contempt?"

"Hell no. It's a badge of honor."

Kate shrugged. "Exactly. I say we just go back and ask him what this is about."

On the way out the door, Kate messaged Aria, *spies.* Aria didn't respond, but Kate was sure she'd confirmed Aria's theory.

14

Davis' Drones advertised 'Twenty-Second Century Technology at Twentieth Century Prices.' Kate could not vouch for the prices—everything on the colony was expensive—but she had seen her grandfather's pictures and Davis' shop did radiate the aura of a cheap, twentieth-century bodega.

The owner, Cris Davis, was her partner for a brief chaotic eclipse in February. Then he quit to open this shop, at the center of the adventure wing. Here, tourists lined up to visit early Apollo landing sites, try their hand at mining, or experience the latest craze—surface dune buggy races.

Cris explained to her once that his algorithms determined that tourists were impulse buyers and liked to touch the merchandise. As she approached his deli-style glass counter of electronics and drones, she found herself at the end of a long line of colorful graphic t-shirts and shorts, validating his business strategy. In one corner of the store, a mom was losing an argument with her daughter over a half-open silver backpack with a pink leash dangling out. Inside, Kate glimpsed a curly-haired brown blur and heard a *yip*. The sign behind them read *sale! same-day custom training guaranteed!* The dad and older daughter were holding hands, looking at the top shelf, where a scaled-down hologram of a mining drone proclaimed *delivered to the spaceport hangar same day. Mine your fortune now!*

Kate smiled, thinking, take the drone-dog, leave the miner. Ahead, a boy cut in with a one-sixteenth scale neuroface-controlled miner taken off the shelf and was presenting it to his dad. The dad flipped it over, rolled his eyes, then sighed and put it under his arm.

Cris Davis had been a good partner for a week. But he was better at whatever he did here. There were seven people ahead of her, and it was the off-season. His niche was his own brand of AI that ran on the latest Lunar Foundries chips. Besides tourists, he had a thriving business selling gadgets to businesses—her office had bought some too.

The counter opened up. Customers ahead of her were looking around and waiting. Probably for their kids or partners who had gotten lost among the electronic candy. Kate nodded and pointed, and when no one stepped forward, she pushed her black box through the crowd. At the counter she was admonished by a gruff older woman telling her to wait her turn. Kate didn't think Cris' mom recognized her.

Cris appeared from behind shelves carrying a blue box. When Kate first met him, he had a baby face ten years younger than his biological age, with wiry glasses, short, shaved hair, and buttery smooth brown skin. Since, he had some genetic mods enabling him to ditch the glasses. It subtracted time, but the last eight months had aged his crow's feet about seven years. He looked harried and frenetic. Not unhappily. The kind of frenetic seen in athletes exerting themselves at something they love. He appeared much happier than the week he spent as her partner.

"Mom, this is Kate. You remember Kate."

"The one who made you eat meat."

Kate laughed. Cris smiled at Kate and then shrugged. Cris had been a vegetarian for years until the stress of his assignment here.

"Nice to see you again Mrs. Davis." Kate had already explained that technically, vat grown protein isn't meat. No animals were harmed—except maybe way back when the stem cells were taken. No point re-explaining it.

Cris' mom scowled, then turned to help another customer. Kate lifted her case to the counter and dropped it in front of Cris.

"You could have returned this by drone, Kate."

"This is courtesy of some Federal Agents. You rented them some equipment."

Cris laughed and shook his head. "They messaged me they lost it and begged me not to charge them. They whined about their expense account like I care."

Cris pushed the box back towards Kate. Kate pushed the box forward.

"They threatened to shut me down. Fuck them. Keep it. I'm not refunding their money."

"Pendejo tax. Who said you have to refund their money?"

Cris slid the box towards him and spun it around. "Do I want to know what's in it?"

"Cancer."

"The last cancer shot at me."

Cris Davis came to the colony as her partner eight months ago to investigate theft at Lunar Foundries. They were both contractors, and the case was bigger than they expected. He called what happened a cancer on the colony, and he was right. For two weeks, they had been chased all over the lunar surface, shot at, and nearly killed. After, he made the smarter move. He quit to open this store, saying *this adventure doesn't involve bullets*, while she took this job as Chief of Security, thinking it would be temporary at the time.

She said, "This won't. We caught it early, before it metastasized. Did you know what they were up to?"

"They bought it through the server, and it was delivered to their room. Apus, I think. Popular with the gov types. All I know."

"Someone tasked them with a side project to collect dirt on one of the residents."

"Oh. Well shit."

"And they tried to bribe us."

Cris chuckled. "Because you're here for the money."

"Let us know if you get any more of these fedbois requests."

"Will do. How did the getaway go?"

Kate squished her nose.

"So, not good?"

"High Frontier Grill is fantastic. We had a great time. You should go sometime."

Cris shook his head. "Not a family place. My kids would eat overpriced cheese curds and not appreciate the view. I meant how was the company?"

Kate squished her nose again. "We had a great time."

Cris squinted, then smirked. "How's living together going?"

"Her family is coming. All six in her place."

"Why not use your place?"

Kate pursed her lips. "Yes. Why not? Well, now my place is gone."

"I'd kill someone climbing over people. I love my parents but—" Cris looked down the counter at his mom helping a customer then grimaced.

"It'll be cozy."

"You told her about Kelli."

Kate blinked. "Does everyone know about Kelli for pete's sake?"

"Who else would be running Presidential Security?"

"It's supposed to be classified."

Cris slapped the box on the counter. "And fedbois are not supposed to be spying on colonists."

Kate sighed. "Touche. It went—well she didn't break up with me. She was mad. She insulted me in Latin."

Cris laughed. "I bet. It's your ex. She's gotta be jealous."

"No. Rae is not the jealous type. I am not jealous of her ex, Stuart."

"Everyone is the jealous type, Kate. What did she say?"

"Mad I didn't tell Kelli to fuck off."

"Well yeah. She thinks you want to get back with her."

"Hell no."

Cris investigated Kate's face, then smiled. "Look at it from her perspective. You're Kinetic Kate, who trespasses movie stars and fedbois, but you won't go down in a blaze of glory for her."

Kate opened her mouth. Her lips and brain idled. Finally, "I don't know what that means, go down in a blaze of glory. She's a Brigadier General overseeing colony security, Cris. I can't just ignore her.

"You're still attracted to her."

"I am *trying* to not let my bean run my life—"

Cris looked down the counter to his mother, then put his finger to his mouth. "Don't you have a filter?"

"You weren't conceived in a test tube, Cris. She knows what that is." Kate looked down and winked at Cris' mom. Cris' mom returned a lovable scowl.

Cris shook his head, then smirked. "Back to the question."

"I do *not* want to get back together. Period. It would be jackass stupid. Anyway, the problem may solve itself."

"Because the trip gets canceled? It won't solve your problem."

"Why? I won't—" Rae was right, Kate had a lot of exes.

"It's just a force Kate. Like chemistry. You can channel it to create something." He pointed his oversize index finger at the gadgets on the shelves. "Or, it blows up in your face."

Kate looked around, then stared at the black box on the counter. Definitely almost blew up in her face. But channel it?

"What do you mean, channel it?"

"You've peaked with Rae. Smart, funny, tolerant of all your bullshit. You need something new to conquer."

Sometimes Cris spoke in riddles.

"Rae is not a conquest."

"If anything, she tamed you. Ask yourself Kate, why are you here? Why did you take this job?"

"Every day I wonder, Cris."

Did Rae conquer her? Maybe that was true. Kelli always conflated the oak leaves on her collar with authority. Rae had a small stature but a big brain and a low voice that commanded far more authority. Although Rae could raise her voice when the situation demanded it. Her big voice from that small body made Kate amused and aroused at the same time.

"Why did Aria and Olicia hire you?"

"To protect the colony from going to shit."

"Right. Your brand is safety. This is your house now. If you want Rae to be part of your house, you need to protect it."

"From myself apparently."

"Humans are always our own worst enemy."

Kate looked down the counter at Cris' mom. "How's business?"

"Off the charts. Now, if I could find someone to replace her—"

Kate laughed and yelled down the counter. "It's fine. We love her. Part of the experience here." Then turning back to Cris, "You know you should bottle up your advice—and your mom's—into a therapy bot. Cris Davis Lifecoach 3.0."

Cris smiled and looked at his mom, then turned back, "Some of hers comes with a smack on the head."

"Sometimes I need it."

"First in line to smack you."

Kate smiled. "Rae and Jin are ahead of you. You're back to eating meat again."

Two things Cris never did before the colony, according to his mom: Eat meat, and swear. Kate was positive he did both.

"Obvious?"

"You salivated when I described the food at High Frontier. Does she know?"

"Christ's sake Kate, no. She's the reason. Why does she have to yell at customers?" Cris smiled at his mother, now working her way toward them. "So why are you really here?"

"Special request."

"Turn in fedbois? Done. Free advice. Happy to."

"Not that."

"For everything else we have a form on the server."

"I can't explain this on an eform. It's about my party."

Cris scratched the back of his head.

"Wait, you're not coming? I am sure I invited you and Abby. And the girls."

Cris winced at his Mom with his not-sure-that's-a-good-idea face.

"Dinner. Dancing. There will be a live band—Silicone Jobbers."

If an AI band of silicone robots could be called *live*.

Cris' mom smiled at him. "You go, Cris. I run store."

Cris winced. "So what do you need for the party?"

Kate opened her phone to show Cris a video. He watched it, then squinted at one of the shelves behind him. "I need to get the equipment together. You will need about a thousand drones. I will have to order more,. There won't be sound. Not like in this video. Space is a vacuum, you know that, right?"

Probably something he had to say a dozen times a day to tourists, space is a vacuum.

"Vacuum. You don't say. The Space Force Academy never covered that." She smirked and winked at his mom. "I'll put you and Abby down for the lamb."

Cris watched his mom shake her finger *No*, then walk away.

Cris' eyes rolled and his brain calculated all the customer complaints. Then he said, "We'll be there. Girls too. Put us down for—" Then he made a surreptitious L with his thumb and index finger, and mouthed, *lamb medium rare.*

15

Kate's phone binged. She read Rae's message, running her hands along her white marbled desktop, then rapped her knuckles. Time to go.

Next to her, Jin stood at his desk, absorbed in his work. He wore a light blue oxford with navy blue slacks, the new uniform that the Tourism Board rushed for the Presidential visit. His right hand sipped from a glass water bottle while the other tapped his desktop. Apps on his computer screen flitted left and right in lockstep with Jin's neuroface commands. His screen paused on a blue-on-black code window, and then one of the four monitors on the pewter-gray wall mirrored his computer screen.

"Jin. I am ditching."

Jin's head bobbed as if he was listening to music.

"How are you liking the new uniform?"

Jin stuck his hand out, then turned his thumb down. "They feel like my grandmother's burlap. If the President doesn't come, are we stuck with these?"

She and Jin weren't consulted. She would have voted for something comfortable, like her well-worn blue-and-silver camo fatigues. The Tourism board disagreed and opted for stiff vat-grown cotton in traditional police blues.

When Kate complained to Rae about the rough fabric, Rae waved exaggerated circles, summoned the laundry drone, then uttered something in Latin.

"Rae concocted some fabric softener in our kitchen. She sent our laundry drone off with it and mine came back almost as soft as my fatigues. I'll have her send you some. You done here soon?"

"Nah. Homeland asked me to—"

"There will always be another Homeland request. Take some liberty. The rest of the weekend and Monday too. The advance team should be able to police themselves."

"You've forgotten what it's like."

The advance team consisted of mostly college-aged volunteers. In twenty-four hours, they disembarked to Sodom and Gomorrah, all having signed forms agreeing to no drugs, no prostitutes, no alcohol, and no embarrassing the administration.

"I haven't. Let them weed themselves out. Go home and recharge."

Jin paused to look out the window. Her office's wall-to-wall window overlooked the concourse and hospital one floor below. In the glass, the faint reflection of the Lone Star Flag and US Flag behind her. Outside, hanging upside-down from the hospital's red terrazzo archway, an eight-armed spider drone Rae named Latrodectus colonis, or Lattie. Lattie was doing its job, *brrrrrrrrrrng* letters and numbers into the stone. It attached itself to the archway with four arms, while using two longer arms to etch and polish hospital donor names. With its seventh and eighth arms, it inhaled and swallowed red dust into its swollen abdomen. Windows in its belly exposed its near-full engorgement. Lattie had half a plaque to finish, then would disappear to empty itself.

"Why plaques, Kate?"

"Bodies get aquamated. Plaques are forever. As close to a headstone as you'll find in this place."

"I don't need a plaque. Maybe a dog. You are right though, I need some sleep."

Kate smiled. Jin sighed and shut down his computer. "The threat matrices they sent are all bullshit. Think she's really coming?"

"Above our pay grade. Aria says Olicia's distracted by the ten new missile batteries they agreed to build. More missiles, more buildings."

Jin glanced out the window. Colony foot traffic was scant.

"We should get a dog. I saw one down at Davis' Drones—"

"Dog?"

"To sniff out threats. Cris says the new AI packages are almost as good."

"Military still uses real dogs because fifty years of AI and odor sensors hasn't caught up to billions of years of evolution."

Jin's face fell into his sad puppy pout.

"But ok, let's try it out. Get one of his. It can stay with you."

Jin smiled, staring at the concourse. "It's quiet down there. Going to grab some Uma. Join?"

Directly across from the office, the two most popular eateries, Luna Uma and Lunaburger, served only a handful of customers.

"Love to, but I'm meeting Rae in fifteen. 25 Carina."

"Shit. You take that payoff after all?"

"Scratch and dent. Aria says nobody wants it. Same price as my old place."

Jin smirked, rowing his arms wide to exaggerate his breathing. "Remember, slow square breathing to combat the altitude sickness over there. In, out. Like that. And wave as you fly over."

Kate grinned and waved him out the door. As Jin left, Lattie stopped grinding. It folded its arms and dropped off the archway. Lattie disappeared from the concourse, headed somewhere to empty its belly of red dust.

Kate got up and left her office. She crossed the colony to find Rae at the office of 25 Carina, wearing a smile that was a mashup of happy-to-see-you and I-won-the-lottery.

"Why are we here?" Rae smiled as if she already knew, like handing someone a present when they've already peeked under the wrapping. She couldn't know. Or maybe she did. There were no secrets on the colony. How would she have found out?

After a hug and kiss, Kate escorted them directly to the elevator. "I want you to keep an open mind." Kate pressed sixteen and took Rae's hand, folding their fingers together. "You know sixteen is our lucky number? It's a karmic debt number. Associated with independence and new beginnings."

"That right?" Rae, flashing her mocking-flirting smile.

"I looked it up."

"Didn't cover it in biophysics."

"And this is sixteen cubed."

"Cubed?"

"We met on February sixteenth, and we are going to see 16D on September sixteenth."

Rae had degrees in pathology and organic chemistry. She was not superstitious. But the grin on her face and how she squeezed Kate's hand told a different story.

On the way up, Kate took mental notes. On the third floor, there was a club fitness room, a swimming pool, a sauna, and an esports lounge. On the fourth floor, a golf simulator, basketball court, moonball court, immersive game room, and daycare. Also on the fourth floor, an event room. Fifth floor, gardens and gazebo terrace. The top elevator button was marked R for rooftop terrace. On sixteen, the elevator doors opened to textured latte walls with white trim. The floors and doors looked and felt like natural oak.

"This feels like real wood Kate."

"Heck no. Lunaresin, same as everything else." Kate tapped her foot on the floor. It did feel like wood, but that would be expensive.

At 16D, Kate opened the door. The oak floors continued inside. For a lunar apartment, the size was overwhelming. The main room had floor-to-ceiling holowindows. Upon entering, the windows played a simulated cityscape of downtown San Fransisco on a clear blue day. On the far wall, doors led out to a balcony. The kitchen had polished black lunar quartz countertops with custom Italian-style cherry cabinetry. Fake wood, but a close enough approximation that Kate had to walk in to scratch them to confirm that the cabinets were lunaresin. Kate walked around, counting four bedrooms and a spacious bathroom with a walk-in shower that fit two people.

After they looked around, Kate guided them back to the main room.

"You will like this, Rae."

Kate opened the balcony doors and stepped past the balcony's table and chairs to view the gardens ten floors below. People talked and held hands while they walked among green and pink flowering shrubs inside barrel planters. There was a playground in the corner of the garden. In the center, a white gazebo had been decorated with recently planted green vines. Surrounding and rising from the gardens, twenty-four stories of pristine balconies identical to theirs. At Rae's place, balconies were filled with signs of life—toys, laundry, or dirty dishes on balcony tables. Here, most were empty because 25 Carina was new, and its residents barely moved in.

As they stood side-by-side on the balcony, Rae gaped at the ceiling nine levels above them. "It's a pretty good hologram of the surface."

"Not a hologram. This building is domed, like The Crown Oasis. Lunar nights, they turn the lights off for eight hours a day, so we can see stars."

"This apartment is huge. Why are we here again?"

Kate took Rae's hand. "One hundred sixty-two square meters. You like it?"

"I love it. Maybe? Why?"

"I'd like to live here."

"Someday I can see us living here."

"I mean now. Like tomorrow."

Rae shook her head the same way she told Axio no. "This isn't practical Kate. How much is this place?"

"I can afford it. *We* can afford it."

Rae let go and turned around.

Kate said, "It's a scratch and dent. Aria's explanation didn't make sense to me. But we *can* afford it."

Kate turned around to inspect the floors more closely. If she squinted, she could see some scuff marks.

"It's very practical. Axio has his own room. Your parents have their own room. Meloni has her own room. The bathroom is massive, and the kitchen—"

"You're serious."

Kate squeezed Rae's hand.

"I don't see how we can afford this."

"Aria will give it to us for what we were—I was paying for my old place."

"Why?"

"I don't know. They need to sell it. Squatters. Something. It didn't make sense to me."

"This place had squatters?"

"No. Aria said people were afraid of them. Because it's empty. This place has been used a few times like a bed and breakfast. That's it really."

Rae was silent. Kate turned, resting her forearm on the rail to watch people below walking in the garden. The apartments were quiet except for a couple eating on their balcony.

"I don't need this, Kate."

"I know. I was thinking—what I was doing six years ago." She paused a beat. "I was holed up in a building. Maybe this big. But it was just a bombed out shell in—in a forsaken part of the world. I was calling in drone strikes on some other burnt out shell of a building."

Rae turned around. Another couple came out to sit two floors below. The woman wore a yellow sundress, had her hair in a ponytail, and held a green beer bottle. The man had khaki shorts, a blue t-shirt, and three more beers in his hand.

"My whole squad holed up there."

"Did you lose anyone?"

"Not that time. My point is Rae, I was happy to be alive the next day. I don't need all this either."

"So why move here?"

"Cris said something. He said I should channel my energy into real estate." Kate smiled. "Veni vidi—something."

Rae laughed. "Veni vidi vici villa. Is this about your ex? Showing her you've arrived?"

"What if it was?"

Rae put her arm inside Kate's and pulled herself close.

"You can say no, Rae. Like two-hundred-thirty-nine other people."

"This place is amazing, Kate. But we don't need it."

"It's not really about need, is it? We could live at your parents' place in Silver Cliff and shoot squirrels from their back porch. Right?"

Kate eyed a cat on a balcony.

Rae said, "I spent my whole life trying to get out of the redneck part of Wisconsin."

Kate nodded. "Also beats shooting each other because we are living on top of each other."

"I give you that. Having everyone in their own space is nice. You said this was the same as your old place? How long can we stay here?"

"Forever. Place is ours. If we want."

"Oh."

"Oh—good? Or oh—bad?"

"Both. You know this can't be in my name, right?"

"Because of Stuart?"

"He'll think I have some money I'm hiding. He's a parasite."

"Don't worry about it. We can figure it out."

"He might even sue you. Claim you are hiding money for me."

"Bring it."

Rae's green eyes smiled, curling at the corners, and Rae ran her fingers through Kate's hair.

"And next time I see Kelli, I will tell her to fuck off and punch her in the mouth too. If that's what you want."

"I am not asking you to punch her in the mouth, Kate. Nose maybe. Or pour water over her so she melts."

Kate pictured Kelli in a wet t-shirt, then shuddered. "She's the other witch. I am dropping a house on her. *Bam.*"

Rae laughed.

"You're hot when you're jealous."

Rae poked Kate in the ribs, then turned around to view the inside. "How long have you known about this place?"

"Few days. Maybe a week."

"And you waited until the last minute."

"Sixteen cubed. Our lucky number."

"So, tomorrow. Your loco plan is to move nineteen hours before my parents get here."

"Eighteen, but who's counting. We don't have to. But I booked five drones, more than enough to get it done tonight. Pack like we are going on vacation for a few days."

A family strolled through the gardens below. Two kids screamed and ran ahead of their parents into the playground.

"Well? What do you think? Say yes."

"So, which bedroom is ours?"

"The big one."

Rae looked up at Kate. In the balcony light, her hazel eyes and tawny flecks were warm. Rae scratched Kate's tummy. Then she leaned up, breathy, "We've got eighteen hours. Let's take this place for a test drive."

16

Kate walked into the third-floor apartment above the red-light district, bleary-eyed and feeling deja-vu. The stench of peppermint vape and metabolized alcohol smacked her face as she entered the foyer. Inside, white and red heart-shaped lights weaved around the thresholds, ceiling, and pink walls. Under her feet, the pile carpet needed to be deep cleaned. A bar-height glass and aluminum dinette in the corner was littered with bottles from last night's alcohol and drug consumption.

Seated at the dinette, a man with unkempt black hair, a rumpled purple polo shirt, and a resigned face under a scruffy beard. He was barefoot, in his underwear. The man put on his shirt first before his pants, a poor choice. He could have escaped had he done it the other way around. Jin stood guard at the table, positioned to grab the man's neck and sit him down should he choose fight or flight. Jin's expression was halfway between embarrassment and surprise.

"Sorry to call you on your day off. You—"

Kate found a wall mirror on the left and confirmed her suspicion. Baggy eyes, no makeup, tangled black curls in a half-undone ponytail, and her gray t-shirt and jeans had brown stains from last night's Chinese food. She probably smelled like packing, moving, champagne, and sex because she also forgot deodorant. But the rug had a sufficiently bad cover scent that Jin might not notice.

"Look like shit. I know."

"You look like you haven't slept."

"I didn't. We were up all night packing then getting ready for Rae's family. I was hoping to catch sleep when you messaged me."

"Oh. Sorry."

"It's fine. Rae's parents and her sister are napping because they didn't sleep on the shuttle. You said urgent?"

"Vic is in the bedroom. They had a disagreement about the price. Got heated."

"Who is the vic?"

"Nika Valya. She works for—"

"Shit. I knew I recognized this place. I know who she works for. Where is Greg?"

Greg was Kate's brother, who worked as a bouncer at a club in the colony's red light district, Barely Imprisoned. Mia Breese ran the club, and Nika worked for Mia. As the bouncer, Greg usually handled client disputes.

"Greg pinged me. He didn't want to bother you. But I think you need to see this."

Jin picked up a phone off the table and handed it to Kate.

Kate, read it. "Kody Easton. American University ID."

Jin swiped the air with his finger, indicating for Kate to swipe. Kate read the phone, then said, "Presidential detail. Imagine that, send a bunch of horny interns to tour our fine colony attractions, and they ignore the rules and end up here. What is Nika's story?"

Jin said, "She doesn't want to come out. The family friendly version of her statement is, make him pay, make him leave, make him never come back."

Kody Easton looked defiant. Kate said, "Alright Kody Easton from American University, what is your story?"

"She fucking cheated me."

"If you were fucking, she wasn't cheating you. That's how it works here."

"I can't afford what she charges. It's outrageous."

"Mmmhm. Did she tell you beforehand?"

Easton was silent. A *yes*. Jin nodded and motioned for her to swipe again. Kate swiped through two more screens to find a services confirmation with his thumbprint and a price in big, cherry-red letters.

"Get a copy." She tossed the phone back to Jin. "And *you* get dressed Greg will be up in a bit to help you pack your shit. I want you on the next shuttle."

"I have to tour—"

"You know the rules. Get dressed."

Easton didn't budge.

"I am imagining a conversation with your boss." Kate ran her fingers through her hair and feigned a video call. "Hi this is Kate Devana. Sorry to bother you. Your intern got his name shared all over the server because he shoved his dick in a hooker then didn't pay. Yeah I know, the rules. Unfortunately, he resisted going home. My deputy had to chase him down, taze some sense into him with a billion volts, then drag him to the spaceport. Which unfortunately was videoed and shared by fifty million people on the server. Sorry about the embarrassment he caused to the administration."

She paused to let the mock message sink in.

"How is that conversation going for you so far, Kody?"

Easton remained silent.

"Silence is golden. I am glad they still teach the Fifth Amendment at American University. Now get dressed."

"She cheated me."

"You said that, but you signed the confirm. Contracts are a beautiful thing."

"It's not fair. I thought she was kidding about the price."

"I guess the joke is on you."

"And I don't have to do what you say."

Jin shook his head. "Kate. He's not on the list."

"Not on the list. He signed—"

"He signed the code but he's not on our list."

Jin swiped Kody's phone and then displayed an image of the advance team's code of conduct.

Kate said, "The advance team rules are strict, Kody. Your advance team days are over. If you grovel, he might let you clean the bathroom stalls with your tongue."

Kody looked at his feet.

"Who do you work for?"

Easton didn't respond.

"I can call around if you want. Big group message to all the Directors. Who does Kody Easton report to? He got himself in trouble with a hooker. Pictures attached."

Easton considered the question two beats before he answered. "I work for Bill Caddell, Technology Director for IIRAS."

"I see. I keep hearing that name. Now I am curious. What does Caddell have you doing and why are you not on our list?"

"I am not supposed to say."

Kate said, "Sometimes not talking gets you in more trouble."

"Personnel issues at IIRAS. I am facilitating meetings between staff here."

Jin said, "Meeting planning? Your computer is busted? You can't do that remotely?"

"Off books. They don't want another scandal. Someone got themselves in trouble."

Kate said, "Seems to be contagious."

"I really need to stay. I will pay. I don't want trouble. Is there any way we can keep this private?"

Kate looked to Jin, who shrugged. She said, "Kody, first rule of the colony is everyone knows everyone's business at the speed of light. I don't control privacy." Kate paused. "You go back and tell the rest of the team. Next time I pay a visit like this, I will send you all home."

"I understand. Are you telling my boss?"

"*You* are telling Caddell." She turned to Jin. "Read the message he sends Caddell."

"10-4. I'll hang out here until he gets dressed and is on the way to the spaceport. Should I make him pay?"

Nika's voice screamed from the bedroom. "If he doesn't pay, I want his bony ass charged with theft of services. It's my right."

"I said I would pay, bitch!"

Kate stared at the bedroom wall and puffed her cheeks. She looked back at Jin and shrugged.

Jin said, "I'll make sure he pays and messages his boss. What about Greg?"

"I'll see Greg later and fill him in. If you have this covered, I am going back to our new place to—"

"New place?"

"25 Carina. We moved last night."

Nika came out of the bedroom dressed in a flimsy bathrobe that revealed all her piercings.

"Nika, I think you should stay—"

Nika shrieked *ohmygodyougotengaged* then ran over, her blue hair flapping, and jumped into an embrace. Kate put Nika down and tried to increase the distance between them.

"We are not engaged. We moved in together is all."

Nika stared at Kate's hand, then looked relieved. "That rumor—many girls felt their heart break."

"Just my luck the bitch is friends with—"

Jin squeezed Kody's shoulder, shutting him up with a painful *ow*.

Kate turned back to Nika. "I wish this were a social visit. Maybe it's better if you wait in the bedroom."

"It's my apartment and I have already seen his shriveled up little—"

"For me Nika. Please."

"Well ok. For you Kate. Five minutes though. Time is money. He must pay."

Kate nodded. Nika jumped on Kate again, then floated to the bedroom. On the way she eyed and teased Kody by running her hand down her bathrobe to open it. Then she shook her fingers *No No No*. Jin lifted Kody from his chair by the armpit, then pointed to pants bunched on the table.

Jin said, "I thought you just went to look. Wow, 25 Carina."

"Me too. Sort of. I mean I *hoped*—"

Easton dressed. When he sat to put his shoes on, Jin lifted him back up. He said, "No shoes. You can carry them. Message." Jin paused to hand Easton his phone, then turned back to Kate. "You said it was a scratch and dent?"

"Not very though. Big balcony. The gardens are beautiful. Listen, as much Kody here would love it if we chit-chatted—"

Jin waved her out the door, keeping one eye on the message Easton was formulating. "Go. Get some sleep Miss 25 Carina. I'll deal with this."

As Kate left Nika's apartment, Jin's voice echoed in the hall. "No. Tell him you're going back to Earth."

17

Kate woke without her alarm. A Tuesday, but Earth calendars didn't mean much on the moon, except to dictate tourist ebb and flow. Rays of light peeked under their bedroom door. Scar's shadow purred from the edge of the bed, and somewhere, 25 Carina's muscular fans circulated air through vents. No breakfast smells. No other noises. Rae's family was still sleeping off the time change. Kate rolled, tracing Rae's outline, then closed in to spoon her. Nice and warm. While running her hands through Rae's hair, Rae mumbled between covers and a sleep mask that she wanted to sleep in. So Kate snuggled, waiting for Rae's soft snoring to resume, kissed her, dressed, then snuck to her office.

She grabbed two bags of hot cinnamon sugar donuts and coffee from a kiosk on the way over. Inside her office, she found Jin standing at his desk. As she dropped a bag of donuts on his desk, his look was a mix of *where-have-you-been* and concern. It wasn't the look of *thank you* she expected. He chin-pointed at her pocket, implying that she should read her messages.

She set her coffee and bag on her desk and reached for her messages.

"Shit Jin, sorry. I didn't get any of these."

She slept through two dozen messages. Scrolling through them, some were from Jin, some from the advance team, two from her ex Kelli, and three from 25 Carina administration. Connectivity went down overnight for two and a half hours, preventing the message drama from disturbing her bliss.

"You missed the fun. I had to referee the advance team Director, Director Caddell, and General McMichaels." As Jin talked, he retrieved a donut from a bag, took a bite, then used it for emphasis, dotting each name and arcing the donut from one name to another. "The advance team Director did not know Caddell had sent Kody Easton, so he ripped Caddell a new asshole for not following protocol. Then General McMichaels ripped into both of them for being unprofessional."

He twirled the donut, then landed it in his mouth.

"And?"

"I've never seen adults act like that. Anyway, they recalled the whole advance team." He waved his hand like an airplane taking off, then popped another bite into his grin.

"Recalled just over Easton?"

"Not just. Two more got into it with pros overnight. And a third nearly O.D.'d on amp."

Kate pursed her lips and shook her head as she took a donut from her bag. "They were warned. This ain't Kansas. I ain't Dorothy."

"Most of the drama's over." Jin reached for another donut. "But the advance team Director still wants to talk to you. They will postpone the security team until October 2nd."

"What did you tell him?"

"I played dumb. I said you had urgent colony business." Jin bit off a chunk of donut.

"Thanks. Good job. Maybe we'll get lucky, and this will kill the whole trip."

"I learned from the best." Jin lifted his donut as a toast, cinnamon sugar dusting his uniform. "Oh, General McMichaels stopped by looking for you too."

"Kelli? Here?"

"A few minutes ago. She said she was escorting the advance team off the colony. But she stopped by to congratulate you."

"Congratulations for what?"

"She saw the rumor on the server you got engaged. I didn't correct her."

"I owe you. It was supposed to be your day off."

Jin pointed his half donut out the window, then grinned. "You're welcome. But I didn't say all clear."

Jin was staring out the window. As Kate followed Jin's gaze to the concourse below, her adrenaline went into red alert. The front entrance revolving door spun, with her ex, Kelli, in it and on her way up. Kate looked around. She was unprepared and getting ambushed. But it was fight or flight, and flight was not an option. Kate rushed to concealment, standing behind her desk. Weapons check. Negative. She opened her right drawer, gun. Then her left one, makeup, hair bands, necklace—and her parents' wedding rings. She seized her mother's engagement ring and shoved it on her finger as Kelli walked in.

"Kate, I am glad I caught you."

Kelli was wearing a white blouse under a bell-bottomed pantsuit, the same shade of yellow as the caution light blinking in Kate's brain. Kate couldn't see under the bell bottoms. But Kelli clunked and clodded across the office, then stood nearly eye-to-eye. Kate was tall—one hundred eighty centimeters in flats, or five-eleven as some Americans still measured. Kelli was five-four, which meant under the bell bottoms, Kelli wore boots with eighteen-centimeter heels. Practically stilts.

Kelli crowded her desk. All the extra chairs were in the conference room behind Kate, so she smiled and sat. Her boots, her problem. Even in one-sixth g, they had to be painful.

"Jin said you stopped by earlier. You here to shepherd the advance team back to D.C.?"

Behind Kelli , Jin looked like he wanted to flee. Kate shook her head. She wanted a witness and possibly a backup.

"I stopped by to say congratulations. And talk to you about Easton."

"Thank you."

Kate held her hand out to show her engagement ring. "It was my Mom's."

Kelli turned up her nose. "I remember. Listen, I wanted to talk to you about Easton."

When they were together, Kelli's dismissiveness and chronic interruptions would trigger a fight. Kate studied her Mother's engagement ring, diamonds surrounding rubies, then laughed to herself. Her mom guarding her from the grave. Better than her Uncle Sam's body armor. Kelli had dismissed her ring—her *mother's* ring—and changed the subject. Instead of being mad, she was relieved to move on.

"Kody Easton?"

"Right. Why did you tell him he had to go home?"

"The advance team rules. You know that. No drugs, no—"

"He doesn't work for the advance team Director."

"He works for Caddell, yeah he said."

"And you made him pay."

"Well, I didn't make him do anything, Kelli. I certainly did not make him—"

"He said Jin stood over him, roughed him up, and you threatened him with third degree theft of services."

Kate shrugged. "The vic wanted to press charges." She looked over at Jin. "What was the amount Jin?"

"The amount put it at third degree."

"Christ Kate. For one hour with a whore."

Jin said, "He booked the whole night. We have the confirm."

Kate shrugged again and pushed the donut bag across her desk. "Welcome to the colony. Nothing is cheap here. Have a donut, they're hot."

Kelli turned up her nose as if Kate had poisoned the donuts. "It's outrageous, Kate. This can really blow back on us."

Kate again offered the bag. When Kelli squished her nose, Kate slid it back. She retrieved one to find it cold and dry.

"Well, they *were* hot. Now they're cold. Oh well. You wait too long and that's what happens, right Jin?" Kate looked at Jin, who nodded. He heard the dig and was suppressing a laugh. Kelli appeared clueless as usual. Kate popped half a dry donut in her mouth, enjoying the taste of her apathy. "Anyway, the vic wanted to press charges, Kelli. That has blowback too. It's her right to—"

"Why do you keep calling her the vic?"

"He stole services. She's the victim."

"She's a whore."

Kate finished her donut and slurped some of her coffee. "It's legal here, Kelli. She's considered a professional, like anyone else. I don't like it, but god knows I've done worse for the peanuts Uncle Sam paid. We make them confine it to the red light district, so no fishnets walking—"

"Don't dismiss me. It's disgusting and his mother is a Senator."

"What state?"

"California."

"Then he can definitely afford to pay."

Behind Kelli, Jin chuckled under his breath.

Kelli frowned. "That's not funny."

Kate sipped her coffee. "Consider it a favor. The pros here are ruthless. Like mafia. If he didn't pay, every compromising picture of him since his first erection would be plastered on the server. And then they'd move on to Mommy."

"That's extortion. Chrissake Kate, you are not listening. Why are you taking her side?"

"I am not taking anyone's side. If we don't enforce the contracts, the disputes get resolved with beatings. Or worse. Easton was going to pay one way or the other."

"Why are you being difficult? Senator Easton wants you removed."

"Senator Easton should be thanking me. But if you have a complaint, take it up with Aria Sheppard or Olicia Barron."

"You just don't give a fuck."

"Entitled snots like Easton are a dime a dozen here—"

"There it is. You just don't like him."

"It's not personal, Kelli. He booked a pro, received services, and didn't pay. It's cut and dry. End of story."

Kelli didn't respond.

"Look, Barron's drones work twenty-four-seven to make room for all the ego in this place. Olicia likes the way I run things, and the way I do it, the rules apply to everyone. A contract is a contract."

"Even if it costs you your job."

"Kelli, Olicia Barron is my boss, not Senator Easton."

"Well, I need to take you off the security detail."

"Have you talked to Aria?"

"My next stop."

"Ok."

"What does that mean?"

"It means ok. Go see Aria." Kate hoisted her coffee and blew on it.

Kelli froze. Kate leaned back in her chair and looked over to Jin, who was shaking his head.

When Kelli didn't move for the door, Kate shook her head, leaned forward, and put her phone on the desk. "How about let's call Aria together."

Kelli's boots dragged her whole face into a frown and cemented her to the floor. Aria picked up on video right away. Kate positioned her camera so Kelli could not be seen.

Aria smiled. "Hey you."

"Sorry to bug you, Aria. General McMichaels stopped by. Yesterday we busted Kody Easton, Senator Easton's son—"

"I saw. Messages buzzing all morning."

"The General said Senator Easton was pissed."

"Fuck her and that twerp. Last year he used a fake I.D. and stiffed us in the casino. Next time this happens, I am banning both of them."

"She threatened to have me removed from the security detail."

"She can kiss my ass. Our property, our rules." Aria paused. "But the good news is that this bullshit with the advance team gave me an idea that might get the whole trip canceled. Finally."

Kate stifled her instinct to raise her eyes to watch Kelli's reaction. Instead, she focused on the top corner selfie camera. It couldn't mask her giddiness. "Canceled?"

"Rumor is the campaign is short on cash. We are looking at making them prepay everything. No cash, presto, no trip."

Kate furrowed her brow.

"Deadbeats Kate. Latham administration is full of them, like that kid. They couldn't manage their lunch money. I am not displacing paying customers that booked years in advance with a bunch of deadbeats. They can prepay."

"Right, well I just thought you should know. General McMichaels might be on her way over."

"Thanks for the warning. Oh, congratulations. I heard you closed on that place at 25 Carina. You like it?"

"We love it. It's more than we need now but—"

"You will fill it up soon."

"We already did. Rae's family got here day before yesterday."

Aria laughed. "Speed of Kate. Congratulations. I am happy for you. Glad it worked out."

"Thank you. And thank you—I mean it. We love it. Listen, I'm sure you're busy and I don't want to keep you."

"Yep. Mum is pinging me. Bye."

Kate put down her phone and turned back to Kelli. "You're welcome, Kelli."

Kelli's face got red and her temple veins throbbed. "What's this about trying to get the President's trip canceled?"

Kate restrained her grin. "You heard the same thing I did."

"I don't know if I can work with you, Kate. You are trying to sabotage the President's trip."

"Sabotage is a strong word."

"Barrons don't want her here. That sounds like a security risk."

"Check the server, Kelli. Nobody wants her here. By that standard, the whole country is a security risk. So far, Homeland's bullshit threat matrix is—" Kate looked at Jin, who was rolling his eyes.

He said, "—Political enemies. My opinion, nobody here needs to kill the President. If the election was today, she would lose in a landslide."

Kelli snorted, her boots clunked, and she started for the door. "You know, Kate, when President Latham wins, there will be changes around here." Kelli made a circle with her finger then pointed at the floor. "Starting right here."

After the door closed, Jin affected a high singsong voice, "There will be changes around here. Starting right here."

"Easton is not going home, is he?"

Jin shook his head.

"Let's track him. I want to know why it's so important that an intern stays here."

"Probably just thinks he's entitled."

"That's what worries me. I don't want to be mopping him off the floor because he forgot to pay his pharmacy bill."

"Feeling sentimental boss?"

"No. He'd deserve it. But then I gotta go after the scum that beat him up and make an example of him."

"Above or below deck?"

Jin was asking how many legal lines to cross to track Easton. She said, "Whatever Easton and his boss are into, it can't be legal."

"Done and done." Then after a beat, "The fuck was she wearing? She looked like the wicked witch from the old time movie—"

Kate smirked. "The good witch had a pink dress. My grandfather and I must have watched it a dozen times. The wicked one was green." Kate mock-threatened Jin with her hands. "I'll get you my pretty!"

"And your little dog too!"

They burst out laughing, tears streaming down Kate's face. She couldn't stop. She hadn't laughed that hard in a long time.

18

It took Nate forty-eight hours and three-hundred and seventy-four thousand kilometers to find the right time to sneak into Mylah's phone server to read about his surgery. While she slept under the silver-white bedsheets, he stole a peek.

The lunar hotel Apus was so-so. Not how he saw it in the holograms. Nothing conveyed how cold the aluminum floor felt under the fake rugs as he shuffled around the bed. The shower was tiny, the blue shampoo smelled like dish detergent, and there was no soap. Correction, Mylah said the blue gel was both shampoo and body wash, so he smelled like clean silverware. Although Apus did not offer free eye masks or earplugs to muffle Mylah's snoring, everything could be upgraded for a price. But they paid so much for this suite, they should get everything else free. Life was expensive on the moon, which made no sense to Nate with so many machines providing free labor and running the place. If machines were the future, the future was too expensive. The colony was an experiment that needed to end before it was too late.

Despite the cost and so-so reviews, they let Rily pick Apus because she wasn't happy. Rily moaned about not being included in decisions. If Ben and Rily made decisions, the four of them would be in New York playing video games, cosplaying keyboard warriors. Mylah had no patience for inaction. But to smooth things over, Mylah let Rily pick the hotel. According to Rily, the Apus maximized the review-to-cost ratio for a two-bedroom suite. Mylah said, *Fine. Done. It's just a bed.*

During the few hours Nate was awake for the trip, he rolled his eyes and wondered whether colony wattsuckers had such drama over inconsequential things. But he put that thought aside because he wanted to hold the memory of his dream. Inspirational. His dreams were so vivid after the surgery.

He stood in the dark next to Mylah's bedside table and waited to be sure she was still asleep. The nightlight outlined her curves under the blanket, and her black hair spilled over the pillow. He would leave the Apus a four star review because it was true what people said about lunar sex being so much better. The Apus' bed was amazing for it. It was also true what he'd read about the lunar lift. The low gravity plumped Mylah's tits like an invisible bra. Mylah talked through sex, discussing her plan. Nate wished she'd talk less, but the violence turned her on. Plus, the lunar lift was incredible. He agreed with every word, then ran his thumbs across her brown nipples.

Picking up Mylah's phone and unlocking it made him smile. She didn't trust biometrics, so she still used an old-fashioned passcode, the day they met. She hadn't changed it. It made his skin tingle and he wanted to climb back in bed with her. Instead, he sighed and swiped to his surgery's details. Not hard to find. So easy, it was as if she expected him to look.

He skipped over lab results and swiped to SIDE EFFECTS. Mood swings, anxiety, depression, irritability, feeling overwhelmed, and possible seizures. His neurons were cauterized to prevent PND. What the fuck was PND? He swiped to a search window. Phantom Neuroface Disorder. A condition in which patients experience sensations or communications, sometimes associated with anxiety or paranoia, in a neuroface that does not exist. So, he could hallucinate a connection to his neuroface. He moved on to PRESCRIPTIONS. The white pills had a long chemical name and were something Doctor Bigneedle cooked up for mood swings, anxiety, and PND.

Fuck, he was glad she didn't mention the side effects. If she had told him, he might not have done it. The paranoia, anxiety, and mood swings were all things he felt before surgery. He could add guilt and shame, which were gone now, too. He was glad he did it. Hopefully his mother would be gone soon, like the neuroface. He wasn't even taking the pills and felt ten feet tall and invincible. The hallucinations were going to worry him. But as long as he wasn't having them, he didn't need pills.

Nate closed the medical file and started swiping through Mylah's pictures, finally understanding her plan. Photos were worth a thousand words, especially when the words were uttered in the middle of sex, and he wasn't paying attention. Not the best time to be discussing a plot, unless you're Mylah and the danger excites you. He swiped through images of rocket fuel stored in the maintenance section of the spaceport and the drones fixing the rockets. She took pictures of the omnipresent package delivery drones circling the colony. It was disgusting how these colony socketfuckers lived at the mercy of drones. Some of them would die by drones too. He swiped through images of the places where she planned to plant the bombs. No wonder she was so talkative.

Nate shuffled back around the bed, got under the covers, and sandwiched his head between two of the Apus' skinny pillows to block out Mylah's snoring. Sweet as Mylah was sleeping, after a few days of her snoring, he might have to risk arrest to get earplugs.

Mylah's snoring got louder, and the Apus' thin pillows seemed to capture and amplify her breathing, her snoring, even her heartbeat. Nate tossed, grabbing for blankets and pillows that weren't there. Finally, he heard something in the other room. So he got out of bed and shuffled to the door.

When he half-opened the door, he remembered he was only in his boxers. Rily was pouting from the couch, holding her pad in her hand, wearing an oversized black and blue plaid nightshirt. He turned back to see a white knife of light over the bed that would cut Mylah's sleep short if he opened the door more. Mylah's snoring softened, and she turned away from the light. He stepped out quickly and closed the bedroom door.

"I thought I heard a noise."

"I heard noises earlier." Rily patted the cushion next to her. "Come, you have to see this."

When Rily booked a two-bedroom suite, all four of them together, he knew this moment would come. Rily wanted to be Mylah in all ways, including in the bedroom. His brain hesitated while his double dose of libido jumped to sit beside her.

"What are we watching?"

"I was looking at jewelry and found this." She slid over and leaned on him, holding the pad over his crotch so they could both see a video, and neither could see his arousal.

"What server is this?"

"Remember the woman that demolished Lunar Foundries' chip factory a few years ago?"

"Devana—Major something, Devana?"

"Major Katera Devana. This is her paparazzi server."

The video jerked and shuddered while trying to keep the focus on two women in a crowd, dancing among sparkles of silver and red light from a mirrored ball. In the dark video, he saw shadows of oak barrel planters filled with green shrubs and yellow, purple, and orange mums. It was a garden, except the sky looked black and the lights were off.

"Where is this?"

"Live view from The Crown Oasis' gardens."

"Live?"

"That's her and her future wife tearing it up. Someone is livestreaming her party."

"Didn't she blow up the chip factory?"

Nate remembered reading the headline, hoping his parents had been killed.

"The same."

"I thought she was one of us."

"No. Lunar Foundries got paid by the Feds and used the money to speed up their next generation of chips. She must have been in on it."

Rily zoomed in on a man nearby with smooth brown skin, a clean-shaven head, and a tight shirt clinging to broad shoulders and a muscular chest.

"Him."

"What about him?"

Rily sounded an almost imperceptible moan and hovered her finger over the man's shoulders. Nate touched the flab on his right shoulder. Everyone in this video was a wattsucker or a sympathizer, and Rily was horny for a random toaster on a video screen. This is why he didn't trust her. Rily watched the man dance for a few seconds, then slid the time bar in reverse. The man's hands and arms danced backward. Then, he spun retrograde until he faced away. At that point, she paused and zoomed in.

"There."

"The rose tattoo behind his ear?"

"No dummy. His neck."

Nate squinted and saw the neuroface implant.

"I searched. That's her deputy."

Nate felt his stomach clench. "She's associating with toasters." Why was she surprised?

"Shame he's a toaster. He's—"

Nate watched Rily's face flush. "He's what?"

"I don't know. You think your surgery would work on him?"

Nate shivered and reached for Mylah's throw blanket on the corner of the couch. She was always cold and brought it everywhere, even to space. It took up most of the suitcase and it irritated him. Now he was thankful.

When he finished wriggling the blanket over his legs, Rily covered hers and once again closed the distance and leaned on him, sucking his heat.

Nate unpaused the video, watched the man dance, then paused it. Nate felt his shoulders and biceps. He read it was impossible to build shoulder muscles like that in one-sixth gravity. So, not only was the man a toaster, he had genetic mods. A monster.

"I don't get it. She has a deputy?"

"She lives here at some fancy new place. She's head of security or something. You'll love this."

Rily slid the time bar back about forty-five minutes. He saw faint white specks swirling in a black background. And then, as the blue Earth arced across the image, he realized that the dots were stars and whoever held the camera was panning it across the lunar night sky. A string of tiny multicolor lights appeared in the lower right, moving toward the center of the view. When they got halfway to the center, they began filing into a square the way a marching band files into a flag during halftime. Next, the multicolor lights switched to a blue and silver chevron that pulsed across the view, reflected, whirled like a tornado, then imploded into numbers. 10… 9… 8…

"Are those drones," Nate asked.

"A few thousand. I looked it up. Created by a place here Davis' Drones. Each carries a small sixteen-by-sixteen light board organized into a 2D video display. Wait."

The grid of thousands of drones formed a video display with a heart border. Inside, the drone matrix played a 2D video. A short clip of the couple on a space yacht framed by stars whirlpooled into another image of the couple at an Italian restaurant called Trattoria della Luna.

It agitated his stomach. He had difficulty focusing on someone else's lovesick video memories. Someone protecting wattsuckers.

Nate reached for the time bar and fast-forwarded.

"You don't like it?"

"You do? It's a bunch of socketfuckers and freaks. Who knows if those images are even real. Maybe just AI."

"I can tell they are in love. You can't fake that. That's the colony's Medical Examiner. Rumor is they will get married."

"The alien doctor? The one we protested last year?"

Rily nodded. Nate started to feel lightheaded. Rily paused and hovered her finger over the image of the deputy. "Not everything about technology is bad, right? If we took his neuroface out—"

"He's a magnet dick, Rily. Imagine breeding with a sex robot. Disgusting. You know how horrible I felt with that thing inside me?"

Rily let out a little moan and bit her lip. She was not keeping it secret that she wanted Mr. Magnet Dick inside her, and he wanted to vomit. She started to forward the video slowly, watching Dick dance. He pushed the video and covers aside and got up.

"I'm tired, I am going back to bed."

"Goodnight." She gave him a mocking smirk. The same smirk his mother gave him. His face felt red hot, and the bedroom door slammed behind him louder than he wanted. Mylah stirred.

"What's wrong?"

"I couldn't sleep."

"Just come back to bed."

Mylah lifted the covers. He laid down, his head on her left breast, while she ran her fingers through his hair.

"Your face is hot, Nate. What was the noise?"

He didn't know how to explain his encounter with Rily. "Rily was watching a video of some socketfucker having a party. I started to feel sick."

"Mmm. Let them have their moment of shame. Live by machines, die by machines."

"Phase two, I have an idea for the first bomb."

"Let's talk in the morning, love."

Nate closed his eyes and put his arm around Mylah. He drifted off. He dreamt he was on a white horse named Orion, crashing open the doors of The Crown Oasis to blackness. If Mylah could see his face in the dark, she would see him smiling.

19

"What I don't understand is why the rings were in your desk at work."

Meloni, Rae's sister, was looking across the balcony table at Kate. Her eyes were the same color brown as the tawny flecks in Rae's hazel eyes. Kate was looking at her mother's diamond and ruby engagement ring.

"I didn't trust the drones to pack it."

Meloni smiled. "Jin sent us the video."

"Of?"

"Kelli stomping across the concourse into Luna Uma in her banana suit."

Kate smiled a little. "I didn't watch it."

Kate took another sip of coffee from a blue and silver mug demanding 'GIVE US SPACE,' the 25 Carina marketing slogan. Across the towers, a blue-shirted man and yellow-shirted woman were having an animated conversation over breakfast. Her mouth jabbering, fork waving food. Finally, the fork landed in her mouth. Kate and the man sighed at the same time.

Snapping the box on the engagement ring, Kate said, "Are your parents coming out?"

"Hope not. And don't tell them—"

Rae came out to the balcony with a tray of three steaming bowls. "Don't tell them what?"

Kate's stomach growled, smelling the cheese soup. "Apus has a mass—"

"Oh no, Kate."

"*Hell* no."

"They will drag us." Rae set the tray down. "And I will drag you."

"I plead Judaism." Kate traded her plea for a bowl from the tray. The one piled with jalapenos. "Jalapenos. You know I like it spicy."

Rae twirled and swaggered to the kitchen with the tray, swinging her hips, knowing Kate was watching. Scar, also tracking Rae, jumped on the counter, then licked the tray.

Meloni smiled with her eyes and pointed with her spoon, "It's a Torres family tradition."

"Brat and beer chowder?"

"Fighting Saturday night over what to make for Sunday."

Kate smiled. She won the fight because she was out here during the power struggle. With Rae's Dad, a veteran, complimenting the view and the beer. Then saying, "a fool rushes in there. Don't nobody need to know how the sausage was made. Just mind your manners and compliment the chef later." Then he swallowed his beer and the balcony view and asked, "How much is one of those surface dune buggy rides, Axio sure seemed to love it?"

Kate, now a two-time champ. A spoonful of meat, cheese, beer, and jalapenos, what's not to love about Rae's recipe?

Rae returned, sitting next to Kate. "What are you two whispering about?"

"This is delicious," Kate said, following Rae's father's advice.

Meloni's eyes checked with Kate. Then Rae, stirring her chowder, said, "Thank you. Can we not talk about Stuart today?"

Guaranteeing that they would talk about her ex-husband.

"I will deal with it tomorrow."

Meloni stirred and looked at Kate. Kate was watching blue shirt man bounce a child on his knee while yellow shirt woman took a picture of two sparrows flying between the towers.

"I knew this was going to happen," Rae said, spooning and slurping.

"I think he's bluffing," Kate said, her face flushing from the jalapeno heat.

"Lawyerbots don't bluff, Kate. Not in their training data."

"So, we hire a human."

Rae shook her head. "A human lawyer costs too much. It's impractical. We'll go around about the accusations like always, then settle. He wants me to sell my place. That's what it comes down to. He wants his half."

Meloni said, "What accusations?"

"A laundry list why Kate is unfit." Rae's soup bowl clanged as she attacked the bottom with her spoon.

Kate, to Meloni, said, "A few amusement park rides."

"You let my ten year old son drive a dune buggy on the lunar surface." Rae smiled, half-teasing.

"Safer than what they had at the state fair when I was his age. Roll cages and everything. He had a great time." Then after a spoonful, Kate said, "Your Dad wants to go."

"Of course he does."

Kate, to Meloni again, said, "Also, I helped him with his homework."

"Axio told the teacher the lesson was bullshit," Rae said to her sister. Meloni's head bobbed back and forth watching the volleys like she had a front row seat to a tennis match.

"Axio said *I said* the lesson was bullshit, Rae. Which it was. Teacher doesn't know shit about space flight."

"I'd prefer Axio not swear at the teacher."

"I'd prefer the teacher not teach him bullshit about space flight."

Rae stirred the remnants of her soup and shook her head. "You two. Sometimes I can't tell which of you is the child."

Kate winked at Meloni. "We both are. My toys are bigger, that's all."

Meloni, smiling and spooning her cheese soup, said, "Axio said that to the teacher? Good for him. That school Stuart has him in is awful." Then after a slurp of soup, "Why do you say Stuart's bluffing?"

Rae said, "He's asking for full custody of Axio."

Kate's face was hot, and she was waving her spoon. "This guy who put Axio on a three day tour of the cosmos in February, by himself, because he's too cheap to upgrade, so he can take a vacation with his hook-up du jour."

The custody arrangement was that Axio was with Rae three months at a time. Stuart lived in New Jersey now. Usually, Stuart accompanied Axio and dropped him off at the spaceport. Last February, Stuart sent Axio to the colony early on an economy-class flight. Thirty six hours and a layover on a space station, with the rocketline staff babysitting him the whole time. All the money Rae sent for alimony, yet Stuart was too cheap to upgrade and too horny to wait four more weeks. He didn't bother to tell Rae either, until Axio was halfway to the colony, and it was too late for her to do anything.

Seven months hadn't softened Kate's anger. She tried to put it out of her mind.

"Axio was fine. He travels here all the time by himself." Equally irritating, Rae had a tendency to excuse his behavior.

"For three days, Rae. Point is, Axio is nothing more than a bank account to him."

Rae, shook her head and attacked the bottom of her soup bowl again. "I bet the new one put him up to this. You're right, he doesn't really want Axio full time."

"It's extortion. And a bluff."

"I told you Kate, lawyerbots don't bluff. It's not in the training data, or the settlement matrix. If you ask for something, you have to be prepared to get it."

"That's why we get a human."

"Too expensive, sweetie. I'd spend as much on that as my place is worth. That's what he really wants."

Kate's face was hot. The jalapenos were good, but this conversation was upsetting her stomach. She pushed her empty bowl away, trying to push her thoughts aside too. Now yellow shirt woman had her computer open and was playing something with child number one. Blue shirt man was losing an argument with child number two. He got up and they went inside. Maybe for a second bowl of soup.

Meloni looked at Kate's bowl, empty, then Rae's bowl, also empty, and then hers, still full. "You two are made for each other."

Kate took her bowl and moved to get up.

"Wait for Axio to have some."

Kate looked at Scar sitting on the kitchen counter. Scar meowed, in the same predicament as Kate.

Rae slid the ring box towards her and popped it open. "Wish I had been there to see it."

Meloni said, "Did you see the video Jin sent?"

"No."

Meloni smirked. "She stomped over to Luna Uma. Met with someone. It looked like they were arguing, Kelli poking her chopsticks at him. I don't know what she said but when she left, he swore and tossed his ramen all over the place."

Kate's ears perked. "Argued? Who did she meet with?"

"Jin didn't say. Or maybe he did. Bill Catwell maybe."

"Bill Caddell. Kody Easton's boss."

"That might be it. Whatever you said to Kelli—"

"I said Kody was going home like every other snot that breaks the rules."

Meloni grinned. "Maybe more the way you said it, wearing your mothers engagement ring."

The hairs on Kate's back stood up. Why was it so important that Kody Easton stay here? He was an intern, into something more than hookers and drugs.

Rae popped the box closed, then took Kate's hand. "This place is amazing. Thank you for doing this sweetheart. My parents are having a wonderful time. My mom said, best visit ever."

Meloni said, "Just don't mention church."

"Yeah. Please."

Kate thought again about the fight between Rae and her mom last night. Rae read Kate's mind, saying, "She'll get over it. She knows better than to boss me around in my own kitchen."

Her kitchen. Rae was home. Kate smiled.

20

After lunch, Kate popped to the gym and then down to the esports lounge to play games with Axio until it was time for him to do homework. Her mind wandered back to her office, where she found herself scrolling through surveillance videos of Kody Easton. Jin had done a great job placing trackers and cameras on Kody to fill in the enormous holes in colony surveillance.

She skipped over the filthy parts, fast-forwarding and pausing only to ensure that Kody paid his bill, everything appeared consensual, and there were no assaults. For a Senator's son from California, he was a little conventional. She wasn't judging. She'd seen assets do it all. She smirked. Maybe she was judging a little.

The first video that interested her wasn't from one of Jin's trackers. It was surveillance video from the spaceport.

Kate watched two adults waddle down the skybridge, facing away, in poorly fitting white-on-gray p-suits with helmets off. Inside a red frame, the head of a balding, portly, retirement-aged man ballooned through the p-suit collar on the right. Protruding from the collar on the left, a black sea urchin of unkempt hair in its own red frame. They donned their helmets at the end of the skybridge, never looking at the camera, then climbed inside the charter.

The sea urchin was Kody Easton. Jin had overlayed the red frames with notes on the side. His algorithm had identified the portly man as Bill Caddell, with a ninety-two-point-three probability based on earprints.

Another note had the specs of the rocket they were boarding. A private charter, *Beam Six*, registered with a private military company. *Beam Six* could carry six crew. There was no passenger manifest. This video was a few days old, and *Beam Six* had since gone and come back from the far side lunar station belonging to IIRAS, one of the lunar space agencies.

The second video that interested her was a few hours after Kelli left her office. Kody Easton could be seen holding a folder and knocking on an Apus hotel room. Kate put in her earpods and turned up the sound.

"Doctor Caddell? It's me."

From behind the door, "Who is me?"

"Kody Easton, Dr. Caddell."

After a pause, Easton said, "Maids don't knock, Dr. Caddell. Check the monitor."

After a longer pause, the door opened, and the camera switched to a fish-eye view inside Caddell's Presidential Suite. The spider camera which Jin placed revealed a plush slate-blue carpet, a queen size bed with matching sheets and silver decorative pillows, an oversized oak-colored desk, and a long floor-to-ceiling holowindow set to a view of Dupont Circle in Washington D.C. It looked too comfortable and expensive for a government employee's expense account.

Easton ducked in, dropping the folder on the desk. Easton went into the bathroom as a maid drone exited. Caddell picked up the folder and riffled through it.

Caddell said, "How many copies did you make?"

The toilet flushed and Easton came out of the bathroom. "Are you fucking kidding me?"

"How many copies? And did you number them?"

"You have any idea how hard one print was? I had to ship a fossil from my grandfather's attic and bring it back from the dead."

Caddell didn't appear to be listening. He was paging through the report.

Easton said, "And paper. I had to order that. And I had to code an emulator to—"

"So, just this copy?"

Easton nodded. "Have you been listening to me?"

Caddell swiped pages, as if looking for something specific that wasn't there. "Did you read it?"

"Why did you want this in paper anyway?"

"I don't need electrons floating around in cyberspace. Too easy to copy. Did you read it?"

Easton nodded again. "Fuck yeah. Damn near impossible to copy." He shuffled to the minibar and searched it. "I skimmed it."

"Thoughts?"

Easton pulled a blue and silver bag of water out of the minibar and pushed a straw into it. "Encoding is wrong."

"Ted's been updating the software."

"Good for him. Finally."

"You think it's software?"

"That Sanskrit is your department. Honestly I—"

"It's Python. Not Sanskrit, Kody. Work with me. Software?"

"Just as old. Could be software, but it might not explain the red shift. Or I guess technically its blue shift. The spectral is all wrong. Almost like—"

"How would you test it?"

Easton mumbled through the straw while sucking water. Caddell pursed his lips. Easton mumbled louder, then rolled his eyes and said, "Raw. Data."

"Let's do it."

"Can't."

"Why not?"

Easton walked to the bathroom. He pulled a comb from his pocket and watched his reflection rake his stiff black hair. "I tried. The data is gone."

"What do you mean, gone?"

"Fuck all I know."

"Just gone?"

"Deleted. Erased. Wiped. Fuck if I know how that happened."

"You sure?"

"I checked the archive too."

As Easton groomed himself, Caddell skimmed a few more pages and grinned. Easton exited the bathroom and stood by the door, with no noticeable change in his hair.

"Good work, Kody."

"Good work? Hoff will be pissed."

"She's resigning."

Easton's mouth opened and closed, appearing to debate the next question. "Did you delete the raw data?"

"Shit happens with this old hardware, right Kody? Like fossils, they just erode."

Kate paused the video. Her gut said that the smug grin and evasive answer meant Caddell had erased the data, then sent Kody to confirm it was gone. What data was Caddell deleting, and why?

Kate continued the video. Kody said, "I don't understand why we keep it alive."

"It employs two thousand people in your mother's state, that's why."

"That makes no sense."

"The next Director can pitch whatever they want to Congress. Maybe they will replace all the hardware."

"Next Director?"

"I am retiring. Eventually. Now that IIRAS is returning pictures, no reason for me to stick around. Who knows, maybe your mom will run the agency someday."

Kelli had said that Kody's mom was a California Senator. If she was in line to run the agency, Kate thought that would explain Kody running around with Caddell.

"But the pictures. What about the encoding? And the blue shift?"

"That ship sailed. You said it yourself, a software problem. This report proves it. Ted's been upgrading, that's all."

Easton flashed doubt, then shrugged and reached for the door.

"By the way, did they miss you?"

Easton shrugged. "No nastygram from the advance team Director."

"Well, you are not supposed to be here. So stay out of trouble."

"Fine. Got it."

"You are not here, Kody. I mean it. Invisible. Don't fuck this up."

"What does that mean?"

"You know what it means. One more nasty run-in and you will go home."

"That bitch can't make me go home."

Caddell shook his head and rubbed his forehead. "Your next run in with Devana or her deputy, she will expel you first, call me later."

"My mother told you to have her removed."

Caddell shook his head and rubbed his forehead.

Kate smiled. Now she understood why Caddell was pissed at Luna Uma. Kelli's attempt to keep Easton here and remove her from Project Orion ran into Aria's buzzsaw. Technically, the colony was incorporated in Texas for historical reasons, but it was mainly private property. Olicia Barron developed this place, billionaires financed it, and Aria Sheppard, her daughter-in-law, ran it. They set the rules. Whatever power Senator Easton had in Washington D.C. didn't stretch as far as the moon.

Kate twisted the skin on her ring finger. Her mother had defended her from the grave. Cosmic karma. She should wear that ring more often.

Caddell said, "Have you been following the protestors?"

Kate bolted upright.

"Protestors is one guy and he got here a few days ago. Mostly, he stays in his hotel room upstairs. He stole a package drone. I think I should—"

The hairs on Kate's neck stood straight. Why would protestors need a package drone?

Caddell said, "More are coming. Keep out of sight."

How would Caddell know about protestors coming, let alone how many were coming?

"That dude talks to himself. I think I should report him."

Under her breath, Kate said, "Well, consider him reported, Kody Easton."

Caddell said, "They have a first amendment right to protest like everyone else."

Easton's mouth opened, his brow creased, then he closed it. "Fine."

"Find out what they are planning. Most importantly, when."

"Yeah, whatever. They are going to hold up some placards somewhere."

"Placards that hopefully will embarrass Devana right off this rock."

Caddell probably referred to the protests and counterprotests three years ago after she demolished Lunar Industries' microchip inventory. She got blamed, but the order to do that came from the President. What pissed her off at the time was that the professional second-guessers in Congress ran her name through the mud. The mission was classified, the Pentagon was muzzled, and so she had to sit under the bright lights and be interrogated alone. Demolition was the right call, and her only regret was not doing it faster. At the hearings, no one was there to point to the real culprit, so everyone pointed at her.

Afterward, in her commanding officer's office, he said that if all she ever had to face was tough questions, it was a good day. People under his command had died from bombs and bullets, but never that. He handed her a medal and a heartfelt *thank you for your service* letter from then four-star General Gaby Cruz, both of which had to be locked in a limestone mine for seventy-seven years because the operation was classified. Then, he promoted her and dismissed her with new orders. As she left his office, she resolved to break up with D.C. politics and her girlfriend Kelli, who insisted D.C. was their future. It was the best decision she ever made.

Kate chuckled under her breath. Protestors holding up placards were going to get laughed off the colony. Definitely not get her fired.

Easton shrugged. "Maybe I'll just go ask. Like, pretend I want to join their dumb crusade."

"Dilan is getting fired for messaging them."

Easton opened and closed his mouth, then said, "So, how long will we be here?"

"As long as it takes. Why, Kody, you have somewhere to be?"

"Nah. But in that case." Easton turned on his heels and sped back to the minibar. He stuffed his shorts with bottles of alcohol and amp.

"What are you doing?"

"Lying low makes you my new supplier."

Caddell shook his head as Easton sped out the door. "Stay out of trouble—"

The door slammed. Caddell smiled and turned back to his window. Kate fast-forwarded, then closed the video.

Kate sat back, grabbed a ball from her desk, and then bounced it against the wall. The timestamp on the second video was a few days before the first. Kate ordered the events on a notepad on her phone. Kody Easton gets caught with a pro. He mentioned they were having personnel issues. Kate threatens to send him home, but Kelli tries to intervene. Kelli and Caddell have a fight. Then Caddell and Easton have a strange hotel conversation where Caddell admits to deleting data and asking Easton to follow protestors. A few days later, they departed on *Beam Six*, registered to a private military company. And they mentioned someone named Dilan was getting fired. Maybe that's why they were headed to the far side station, to fire Dilan.

Why would an intern be along for that? Because his mom was a Senator? The hairs on her neck were tingling. The protestors they mentioned, nothing had popped in the threat matrices Homeland was sending. Technically, Caddell was right. They had a right to hold up some placards and get laughed off the colony. Not a true threat Homeland would pick up. But he made it sound more nefarious than placards. Something that would get her fired. She didn't like it.

She scribbled another note for later and underlined it. Jin had placed a spider camera in a private hotel room. She would have to have a conversation with him about that later.

21

Nate stood in his Central Park West apartment in the moonlight. Devana's deputy Jin emerged from his bedroom, his tan skin slick like he had been thinly coated with machine oil. Moonlight glistened his shoulder muscles and pecs. The deputy sneered and lifted barbells, left, right, left, right, left, right, then flung them and stepped closer. No pants. The deputy's brown dick was a plug at the end of a long wire, like a snake hissing at him. Rily came out of the bedroom wrapped in a pink towel, barely covering her thighs, saying, *we are having babies.* Rily opened the towel. Her vagina was a socket, the female end of an electric charging station. Open, ready to charge, but Nate didn't fit. The deputy's snake hissed and crept closer, showing its fangs. It was going to bite him and inject its neurochip. Nate fled through the open balcony door, the deputy a few steps behind, with Rily laughing at him. Nate spread his arms wide and dove towards 72nd Street. He was riding a white Pegasus named Orion. The gold pavement rushed towards him. Starbursts.

Nate jolted awake in a cold sweat. It was dark. The bed was empty. It was difficult to tell how long he had slept. Maybe days. He rolled over and Mylah's side of the bed was cold. His stomach grumbled over the indistinct conversation in the other room. Ben and Rily were both up. He exhaled, letting the seizure pass, then commanded the lights on. His hands trembled while he brushed his teeth and got dressed. "That's what the white pills are for," Mylah reminded him from the mirror. He closed his eyes, blinked her away, then swallowed a pill with water.

Outside the bedroom, he found everyone in their pajamas. Mylah was in the kitchen, holding the suite's fridge half open with her foot while piling breakfast ingredients on the counter. Ben and Rily had swept aside the table and chairs in the dining area. Ben was kneeling with his head inside the rear of a black metallic delivery drone. Rily sat next to him, holding her pad, icicles from her eyes stabbing Mylah. Nate dithered at the threshold. Then his stomach took charge.

"Morning everyone."

No one responded. Rily looked down. Mylah backkicked the fridge closed, then took a knife from the counter. The drone's innards whirred.

Nate shuffled to Mylah, put his hands on her shoulders, and tried to kiss her neck. She shrugged him off and then turned, eyes red and tearing.

"What's wrong?"

She shook her head.

"This is about last night?"

Mylah laughed through tears and tried to wipe her eyes with her forearms. She waved the knife at him, so he stepped back. Her eyes found her sleeve, then she lowered the blade.

"Onions, dummy." Nate peeked behind her, now seeing half an onion on the counter. He laughed. He pointed his eyebrows at Rily and lowered his voice to a whisper. "What's with—"

Rily yelled from across the room. "Mylah thinks I have a crush on a toaster."

Nate pursed his lips, turned to the freezer, and opened it. He hoped to see a new conversation boxed up and ready to be warmed. Although, his stomach would settle for a frozen burrito all the same.

His eyes darted between the boxes in the freezer, settling on a brushed aluminum glint in the rear.

Nate gazed at Mylah's distorted reflection in the aluminum glint and said, "You saw the video? The one with the deputy?"

"I saw enough."

Rily protested. "I do *not* have a crush on him."

Nate thought, methinks thou doth protest too much. Mylah said, "Your—"

Ben interrupted. "—Mylah, can we not talk about this again?" Then he grunted, followed by the scraping sound of metal-on-metal. "There, I think I've got it out."

Nate turned to see Ben holding up a gray metal box and Mylah pointing the knife at Rily. Mylah said, "He's a robot. An android. That's why they're called *magnet dicks,* Rily." Mylah hacked the onion for emphasis.

"I don't think it's a literal magnet. And you should talk. You've had more silicone inside you—"

Mylah picked up an onion to throw at Rily, but Nate grabbed her hand. "Let's all calm down." He took the onion from Mylah and tossed it in the air. He watched its low-gravity arc touch the ceiling, then caught it and set it back on the counter. "You figured out how to reprogram that little robot brain yet, Rily?"

"I think so, why?"

Nate turned and reached in the freezer for the glint, pulling out the aluminum canister of rocket fuel Mylah had stolen. He set it on the glass range top and spun it. "This will be your first delivery. To the deputy."

Rily looked dismayed. "Are you kidding?"

Mylah teased her, saying, "Do you have feelings for a toaster? Been dreaming of doing Kegels on that magnet dick?"

"No. Definitely not."

Nate exchanged a side glance with Mylah, who was smirking approval. He said, "Then what's the problem? One less wattsucker in the world, right?"

"What if we took his—" Rily halted, eyes wide. Nate followed her gaze to Mylah, who was holding the knife at low ready.

Nate gently pushed Mylah's knife arm back to the cutting board. "I told you Rily, it's time to unplug a toaster. Are you in or out?" Nate looked down at the canister and its pinwheel of condensation on the stovetop. He gave it another spin.

"In." Rily's voice sounded meek.

"Ben, you in?"

"He's just a toaster, right?"

"Not just a toaster, Ben. He's the latest model. I was lucky. I had an older model and survived having it out. Barely. I could have had seizures. Or died."

Nate *did* have seizures. And hallucinations. But they didn't need to know that.

"Does this mean we are not doing the protest?"

"The protest is phase one. This is phase two." Nate exchanged another side glance with Mylah. She smiled approval.

“Is there a phase three?”

“I promise.”

Ben was silent.

Mylah whumped the onion, then carved the air with the knife. “Think of it like putting down a rabid raccoon. What’s left of his human brain is sick with a virus. He can’t be cured.”

“In.” Ben’s voice was firm. Committed. “But I want in on phase three.”

“We will all have a role to play in that,” Mylah said, waving the knife like a music director.

“What it is it?”

Mylah talked to the onion. “We are not going to unplug one toaster. We are going to unplug all the toasters around here.”

Rily paled. She asked, “How will we do that?”

Ben’s face was all-in. He was the strong one who could prod her along. On the stovetop, the canister stopped spinning. Nate put it back in the freezer, saying, “When the times comes. Right now, let’s worry about phase two.”

He held his cold hands on Mylah’s shoulders, but she tried to withdraw. He held firm.

“Your hands are cold.”

“You like that.”

“A little lower.” Flirty Mylah showed up, so Nate turned Mylah, put his cold hands on her nipples, and leaned in for a kiss. Mylah put her arms around his neck and kissed him. She tasted like onions. He was thankful to be wearing pants in front of Rily.

He whispered, “You know how to make that fuel go bang, Mylah?”

“Do you doubt my ability to bang?”

“I don’t. I dreamt of phase three last night.”

“Soon.”

“I am so glad to be human again. Thanks to you.”

“It’s Dilan Darcy you should thank. He made this all possible.”

22

Helena smoothed her butterscotch chiffon dress in the bedroom mirror. It made her skin look pale blue. Why did they pick this color for the wedding? Maybe the light at The Crown Oasis would be better.

Nolan came up behind her, smiling at her through the mirror, and put his hands on her shoulders.

"You look as beautiful as the day we met."

"Shut up. I look old and tired."

He kissed her shoulder. "You worried?"

"I haven't heard from Dilan in weeks."

"He said he was getting off the station."

"Bill Caddell is plotting something. I can feel it."

"That Fed woman keeps coming around. Dilan probably thinks the less you know, the better."

Probably. She told Dilan his transmissions off the station were being recorded, so maybe he decided to go dark. That's what she would do. What she'd taught Dilan to do. Still, it felt strange being done to her. By her flesh and blood.

"Try to smile. We haven't been to a wedding in ten years."

"Fourteen."

"Really, that long. Time flies."

"When you're old like us."

"Sixty-four is the new forty-four. I could get one of those injections and turn my gray hair back to its natural brown."

"I like your gray hair. It looks distinguished. Anyway, no genetic mod is going to fix this dress. I look ninety-four. Why would they pick this color for a wedding?"

"You look beautiful sweetie. Try to relax. Bill won't be there. He's not on the guest list."

"Doesn't mean he won't show up. Bill thinks he owns the agency because he's in James Easton's good graces now."

"Right, well, being tight with a California Senator's husband does put you at the top of the D.C. food chain."

"He thinks he's untouchable."

Nolan furrowed his brow and frowned. The look. She was doing something, and he disapproved. "Well, I have news for him. He thinks he's sneaky and deleted the data. He thinks I'm a fool. After thirty-five years of agency corruption, he thinks I don't know how to cover my ass. I know what he's been up to."

"Sweetheart. What do you always tell Dilan? Don't provoke Bill Caddell. He's a snake."

"He is a snake. And someone needs to cut his head off."

Helena took a bag of hand moistener off the vanity, squirted it in her hands, and then rubbed them together.

Nolan rubbed Helena's shoulders. "Well, not you. Not today. Today, let's just enjoy ourselves."

"You think he got to Dilan? We haven't heard from him in weeks."

Nolan shook his head. "Dilan is an adult and can take care of himself. Knowing him, he smuggled himself to a space station and now he and Ted are on a cruise to Mars."

"What if we didn't go to this wedding?"

Nolan sighed and turned to walk out of the room. "You are going to do whatever you want. You always do. Someday it's going to kill you. I am going to the wedding."

23

The videos of Caddell and Easton at their hotel room and then departing on *Beam Six* gnawed at Kate. So many questions. Why was an intern on that ship? Why was the intern following protestors? What was Caddell plotting in her jurisdiction?

She had Jin research him. Caddell owned a multi-million dollar Georgetown mansion in D.C. Six antique gas-powered cars also worth millions. A motorhome. A few ex-wives with generous alimony payments. On the surface, he fit right into the colony demographic. A rich collector. Except, he had never been to the colony. Jin pointed out, billions of people hadn't. True. But Caddell owned all that on the salary of a government agency technology director. And from what Jin said, he wasn't even very good at being a technology director. A technology mis-director, Jin said, because some of the IIRAS technology was as old as the cars Caddell drove.

Jin interrupted her thoughts, walking off the Apus elevator with a silver German Shepherd. Apus was as plain as plain could get, decorated in beige like any other three-star hotel in America. Jin's face, all smiles, the brightest thing in the hallway.

The dog was a drone. She had seen them at Davis' Drones. Jin introduced the drone-dog as Jade.

"Jade?"

"Told you, I got a dog. Silver German Shepherd."

Kate must have looked confused.

Jin said, "Not a real German Shepherd. A drone. Or robot?"

"What's the difference?"

"I don't know anymore. I guess, technically, I can give it commands, so drone. Anyway, flawless. Jade never sleeps. Not really. She's alert while she recharges. And Cris added upgraded visible light sensors, UV sensors, and an olfactory package. Best damn guard dog in the solar system."

Kate looked down at Jade, its mouth all smile, its brown eyes demanding attention, and its pink silicone tongue hanging out. Jade could have been real. Small details gave away that it was a drone. The hair too perfect. Its elbows jerked and servos whirred. Otherwise a good imitation. From a dozen meters away, hard to tell the difference.

Kate asked, "Why Jade?"

"The algorithm recommended it."

"You let an algorithm pick a dog name?"

"You let an algorithm pick me."

Touche. "The algorithm made a recommendation. *I* picked you. What were the other choices?"

"I like Jade. We'll stick with that one."

Kate looked down at the drone, doing an excellent performance of a Silver German Shepherd panting.

"Give her a pet, Kate. Say hi."

Kate looked from Jin to Jade. Both pouted, like she was rejecting them. She relented and bent down to pet Jade. Jade barked and panted.

"She likes you."

Kate shook her head.

"So, why are we here boss?"

"On the video, Kody Easton said protestors are a few floors up. I want to walk around. See what we see."

"Old fashioned surveillance. What are we looking for?"

"I don't know. Kody said one of the protestors talked to himself."

"Half the people in this place talk to themselves."

That was true. Most people were new to the neurochip. Like any new device, even simple ones like the replacement knees and hips she saw people get at the VA, there was a learning curve. It took practice and therapy. Learning the neurochip was like learning a new language or learning to read. Novices often whispered to themselves. Not everyone talking to the air was using the neurochip. Some were just on the phone talking in their earbuds. But the people acting like amateur ventriloquists were the ones with the neurochip.

"We'll know it when we see it."

They decided to start on the top floor and work their way down. Jade sniffed each door while Jin commented on the lack of décor. Except for the numbered plaques on the wall, it was impossible to tell the floors apart. Kate looked up and down the hall, eyeing guests. Jade alerted at several doors. Drugs. She wasn't pursuing illicit drugs, at least not today, although she made notes of the room numbers in case she was called back.

On eight, Jade barked as it exited the stairwell. An ammonia smell. Faint.

"You smell that, Jin?"

"I don't."

"Can Jade identify the smell?"

"Something's wrong with the olfactory package. It says rocket fuel. Can't be right."

No, that was right.

"Can you keep her from barking?"

"Umm—"

"Can't have her barking outside the door."

"Looking up the command in her database."

Kate smirked. "Right. The dog's database."

She and Jin walked around the floor until Jade sniffed under one of the doors and sat, panting and tail wagging.

Kate drew her pistol and stood aside the door. Jade moved to the side while Jin stood at the other side of the door, pistol drawn. Kate counted from three with her fingers. On zero, Jin opened the door with the override code. Kate inhaled. This was beyond stupid. Someone inside could be strapped with a bomb vest and sitting on the sofa waiting for her. Someday she should requisition some riot gear and body armor.

Kate motioned for Jade to go in first and held up a fist for Jin to remain outside. Kate peered over the threshold. Jade wandered around the suite, in and out of rooms, then sat in the middle of the room and barked twice.

"Jade says all clear boss."

Kate holstered her pistol. "Why not just have her speak English, Jin? I mean it's a drone, they can make it however you want."

"People want a dog."

"You wanted a dog."

Jin pouted.

"Not to say I don't like her. It's very realistic."

"They do have an add-on for that. I just think it's weird."

"Petting a drone dog like a real dog isn't weird?"

"You keep insulting her, I am going to have her bite you."

Kate smiled and patted Jin's shoulder. "You ready to search this place?"

"10-4 boss."

As Kate moved through the kitchen, the hairs in her nostrils burned. "I definitely smell the rocket fuel."

"I smell it now, too."

"Find out who booked this place." Kate opened the refrigerator. An ammonia smell smacked her in the face.

"Boss, look at this." Kate turned. Jin was holding up a cracked phone. "Looks like it smashed against pavement."

"Can you get anything off it?"

"Maybe. I don't need the phone as much as the config off internal storage. All the juicy data will be on a server somewhere."

Kate walked out of the kitchen to the dining area. There were random parts in a pile on a table. Under the pile, a paper notebook. She started flipping through the notebook.

"Jin, these look like parts—"

Jin was walking over, nodding. "—to a package drone. Easton said they stole one. I messaged Rae to send one of her techs over asap. See if we can get—"

"—yeah good thinking. Look at this."

Kate flipped to a page in a notebook showing a spaceship hurtling towards the dome of The Crown Oasis. At the top of the page, the title, *The Orionids.*

"Send a broadcast. We need to sniff every package drone at every hotel and casino. Tell them quietly."

"On it, boss. Nathaniel Kirkwood. This room is booked to him."

Kate's phone binged. Rae. She answered it.

"I got Jin's message. I have two patients—"

"—we need a rush job on this, Rae. Prints. DNA. Five-by. Fast, like there is a bomb about to go off somewhere."

Rae sighed. "I'll send Eric over with a handheld. How serious is this?"

Kate flipped another page. A charcoal skull drawing with an empty face and the words, *who is Dilan Darcy?* She said, "We don't want anyone to panic. A stampede for the spaceport could do more damage."

On the next page was a drawing of her, Jin, and Rae titled, *traitors to the human race*. The three of them were in a room with a bomb going off. On the final page, a drawing of Jin. He was naked, in someone's bedroom, with an electric plug coming out of his loins. That one was titled, *magnet dick*.

Kate said, "To be on the safe side, Rae, stay indoors. Tell everyone not to accept packages."

Jin and Kate's phone binged at the same time. A P1 alert. Someone smashing glasses at The Crown Oasis. Shit. Maybe it was too late.

24

Mylah whispered the code in Nate's ear, and he thumbed the panel. Click, unlocked. A smoking grease smell hit him in the face as he opened the door. The kitchen. Drones and machines. Some humans, but it was difficult to distinguish the drones from the people. Arms, cranes, fingers, all dropping things on a conveyor crammed with food and drinks. Or congregating in a corner ahead of him, grabbing items off the belt. Or putting dirties on a different conveyor flowing into the wall.

"In."

In his earbuds, Ben said, "Stay there, wait for us."

If they wanted him to wait, they should have gone first. He took a tray of appetizers off the conveyor and entered the river of servers going upstairs to the wedding. No glances. He'd been afraid the mask looked rubbery coming off the printer, but Rily did a good job with the makeup.

"Going up."

"Wait for us. Don't go yet." Like Mylah letting him be on top, then telling him not to cum. The feeling was there, it was too late. He was up metal grate stairs. They spiraled into a landing. Shoved in the corner, a metal cart with bags of water, coffee, and utensils. He took a steak knife and turned it over in his hand. Thick brown resin handle, serrated, a sharp point. Stenciled 'T5,' for grade 5 titanium. Nice. He could probably cut the neuroface off someone's neck like a skin tag. Or just sever the neck.

He pocketed the knife and made the turn, up more stairs. The bacon on his tray tugged at his nostrils. Smelled good. Grown from a vat, but so was half of New York City food now. Mylah would never know he cheated. He slid a bite of bacon and scallop into the silicone mask's mouth hole and down his throat. Not bad. No glances. He reached for another.

Through another charcoal door and he was on the garden floor. The humidity and the smell slapped him first. Like a greenhouse. The dome covering the hotel and its surrounding gardens was partly mirrored. Lunar night. The inside light reflected off it like a window. He saw a few bright stars, but not the Earth.

"Ben, lights?"

"Ready. Set for ten. Drones are in the air and on their way with the ballistic dummies."

Go time. He took the green slate walkway between barrel planters with orange and red roses. Fake slate. Drone-made. Slippery, he had to be careful. Another pair of barrels, these shrubs with tropical yellow flowers and red, almost orange berries. Earth plants brought here to die. Like the wattsuckers and cyborg sympathizers.

His parents were here? Standing in the walkway, gaping at some purple flowers, a man and woman. The man in a tux, burgundy tie, and the woman in an orange chiffon dress.

He walked up to them. Not his parents, that would have been too good to be true. He took the half-full champagne glass out of her hands. She resisted, he twisted, then he drank it. A gasp. He smashed the glass on the slate. Then he took the man's champagne. Drank that too. The man yelled, waving his hands. He tossed the second glass at a janitor drone trying to clean up. Missed. The broken glass flew everywhere.

He used to do this high. Needed to. Sober, this was so much more fun. Part of his brain wondered if this was a dream or another hallucination. He stepped on broken glass, hearing a reassuring crunch.

The man said, "I'll give you money. Go away, don't ruin this for them. It's selfish and—"

Did they recognize him? He looked down. Blue and green t-shirt. When did he take off his uniform? Didn't matter.

Did they think this was about money? Technology was selfish, not him. Another gasp as he threw the food tray on the woman's dress. Bacon, scallops, oil coating her dress. He offered to lick it off. Yeah, she wanted him to.

A voice in his ear, "Nate?"

A drone got in his way. He knocked it over. Faces screaming at him. He grabbed a plant and threw it at someone coming to restrain him. This was so much more fun sober.

25

Kate returned from the hospital, stormed into her office, then screamed at the top of her lungs. Jin was standing at his desk. He didn't look at her. He took a device from one of the two boxes on his desk, waved it over his pad until it binged, and then moved it to the other box.

He looked up. "Do you want to hit something?"

She did. She looked around. People, metal bolted to the floor, and evidence. Instead, "No."

"Not impressed. Rae said lightning would shoot from your eyes."

Kate smiled a little. Sometimes Jin reminded her of Greg.

"No, laser death rays. But I need my cape." Then, walking to her desk and staring at the Lone Star flag behind it, "But she should talk. Her eyes fillet you. You are on the slab, dissected, organs splayed everywhere, before the anesthesia even kicks in."

"You told me." *Bing.*

She looked at her desk, deciding to stand. Better to think on her feet. "Helena Darcy is dead. She died of her stab wounds."

Jin didn't respond. *Bing.* He moved another device moved from one box to the other. The pewter-gray office paint and two of the far wall's four monitors framed his uniform's light blue shirt, now smeared with salmon-colored food, blood, and remnants of purple mums.

She tossed her phone to him. "I need to know if that's real."

"What's real?"

"Top message."

"Sorry, I couldn't warn you from—shit." He inspected the message from Kelli. "Encrypted. It's real."

"I need to talk to her."

"A good idea?"

"Terrible idea. You're right. She must have known about this. She's a backstabbing bitch and I need to plan out what to say. Why would she send that?"

"Well, *couldn't*, like it was classified, knowing her."

"Is she that petty, withholding information like this?"

She didn't phrase it as a question and Jin didn't answer. Instead, more binging. Maybe the statement answered itself.

"We got a list of attendees and staff?"

"Aria sent it over while you were at the hospital. Geofence warrant for all the devices will take a few days."

"What is that binging, anyhow?"

"Statements went quick, but—"

"Mmmhm. Let me guess. Nobody saw anything."

"Times a hundred and thirty-three."

"Same as it ever was. I told you, meat memory is unreliable. Usually not cooperative either."

"They were cooperative. Well, except for the bride. Mostly everyone was focused on the newlyweds or the protestors." Then, holding up the next device and grinning, he said, "But their devices might have seen something."

He swiped the next device across the pad, waited for the bing, then dumped it into a box.

"They all gave you devices?"

"And quite a few suggestions how to space the protestors."

"How long to process all the video?"

Jin shrugged. "There is a lot here. Even with access to Lunar Foundries' quantum—"

The binging irritated her eardrum. "Know what it sounds like to me? *Bing*, fasten restraints. *Bing*, go for launch. *Bing*, hard count to takeoff. The sound the protestors will hear as they escape. Call up Lunar Foundries. Get them to give you more power."

Jin looked blank.

"Never mind I'll do it. The CEO and I go way back."

"How far back?"

"Long story. I blew up his lab, cost him a trillion dollars, and now he likes me. His algorithm recommended me for this job."

Jin grinned and shook his head.

"When is the next shuttle?"

"Six hours and change."

"What about the private spaceport?" As she said it, she searched. "No flight plans filed."

Bing. "If I were them boss, I'd be on the first ship out of here."

"You hope. They might plan to stay here and create more chaos. We should go down and see who boards. I need to get the passenger manifest."

"10-4. Go together."

"When the warrant comes through, tag faces there without a device."

"Done and done. Two things missing. Helena Darcy's phone. And no murder weapon."

"I'll have one of Rae's techs check the recyclers. Steak knife, my guess. Hopefully the recyclers weren't too efficient."

"There are two drones in the gardens now, sweeping for hair, fibers, DNA, whatever we can suction."

"Are you using the new software?"

"Cris Davis' Genetosweep version 3.2. Done and done. We should have complete workups in a few days."

A few days. The protestors could be gone in a few days. Or worse, they would still be here causing panic.

Then a different bing, this one Aria Sheppard. Jin put it on one of the four wall monitors. A hair band pulled Aria's hair into a tight ponytail and her face into a deep frown.

"Mum is pissed, Kate. Why didn't we know about this?"

Good question. Kate tried on a few lame excuses like, *my ex is petty*, and, *Homeland doesn't share intel*. While she cycled, Jin put a profile of Earth First on one of the monitors. Not much. Worse than a half-assed legend.

"Not much known about this group. Didn't pop on any threat matrices. We do have a lead though."

"Homeland too fucking busy investigating political enemies to check real threats."

Or that.

Olicia Barron's short pixie-styled white hair and purple glasses opened on a separate screen. In the background, Kate could see the black lunar sky and blue Earth through Olicia's floor-to-ceiling window. Maybe a reminder of where Kate could be headed. Too bad, she was starting to like the colony. Although, even Olicia Barron couldn't control the position of the Earth in her window, right?

Olicia Barron wagged her jewelry-laden fingers. Olicia had fourteen rings on ten frail fingers, plus all her metal bracelets. Kate was often surprised they lifted off her desk. "They livestreamed this to the server, Kate. The protest. Everything. And now it's all over the servers that someone got killed. The image is horrible. People will wonder what kind of place we are running."

Yes, image, Olicia Barron's main concern. That Helena Darcy was murdered only a side note. That whoever did this would continue doing it, also only a residual calculation.

Still wagging her jewelry, "We look like fools. Homeland withheld. Someone knew something and they withheld it to make us look like fools."

Kate eyed Jin, food all over his uniform, and the blood and makeup on hers, thinking whoever did this succeeded in making everyone look bad. "Helena Darcy looked worst of all. Being dead."

A nice perk of her relationship with Olicia and Aria, they were from the business school of brutal honesty and had the same non-filter she did.

"Christ, an awful way to go. I won't be surprised if—

Aria cut her off. "What Mum means is—"

"—Excuse me, what I mean is that I won't be surprised if that feckless fat hag cooked this up as an excuse to take over the colony. I am not letting that happen."

Kate inferred the feckless chef was President Latham. The bad blood rotted for decades. The downside of brutal honesty was having to listen to Olicia's conspiracy theories. If President Latham wanted to take over the colony, she would blow up one of the domes or high rises. Let all the air out. Then one person in an EVA suit would come in, waltzing over all the dead bodies.

"I will keep you updated with what Jin and I find."

Olicia Barron's frail pointer finger, heavy with two gem-studded gold rings, lifted off her desk to flick at Kate again. "I want names, Kate. They knew about this, and I want fucking names."

Olicia said names but meant heads. Aria said goodbye and the display changed to black. Kate puffed her cheeks and blew out a breath. Aria had a tough job managing her mother-in-law. Kate collapsed in her chair, its springs jouncing and squeaking, realizing it was a mistake as soon as she did it.

"Kelli can't be the only one that knew." She opened a monitor to Helena Darcy's profile. She flipped through her messages then opened one on the monitor next to Helena's profile.

Rae's tech Eric, who Rae frequently called a miracle worker, had already processed Kirkwood's hotel room. Rae had software that scanned alleles on the DNA and then ran simulations that produced a five-by-five grid of possible faces, or five-by for short. The grid was a metaverse of twenty-five Nathaniel Kirkwoods in different environments. With facial hair. Without. Short hair. Long hair. Kirkwood number thirteen was an image of him with too much sun and heavy drinking. Number nineteen showed him in good health, eating his broccoli and going to the gym. Number twenty, how he'd look if he took supplements.

She studied the five-by, wondering which universe she occupied.

"Jin, how is the analysis going on Kirkwood's phone?"

"I need to borrow the clean room at Lunar Foundries to get the internal storage out."

"I'll ask them to send someone and put a rush on it. When you're done with that, I want everything you can find on Kirkwood."

"How deep?"

"I want to know everything. Who he messages, who he talks to, his playlists, who he fucks, and who he's thinking about while he fucks."

"On it, boss."

"Any luck on the package drone?"

"I've flagged the missing drone. If it moves anywhere on the network, I've got it."

"Good job. Somewhere in there while the algorithms are crunching, go home shower and change."

He looked guilty.

"Downtime is good for your brain. It lets things percolate and filter. Sometimes I come up with my best ideas in the shower."

"I don't want to know what ideas you come up with in the shower."

Kate smiled. She put up Kirkwood's drawing of the skull titled, *Dilan Darcy?*

"I am going to change into something professional, then go see the Darcys. Then to the morgue."

"Rae won't have cause of death yet."

"We *know* cause of death. What I want to know is whether she put up a struggle. I didn't see defensive wounds. Or much food on her dress. Helena Darcy was out of the main melee area."

"What are you thinking?"

"Caddell said more protestors were coming. How many were at the wedding?"

"Hard to say until I process video. Seventeen based on physical descriptions."

She shook her head. "Meat memory is unreliable. I am wondering why Kirkwood has Dilan Darcy's name scribbled down. Why is Dilan Darcy joined up with some random group nobody's heard of before now?"

"On the video, Dilan was getting fired for messaging the protestors."

She sat forward. "So, Dilan Darcy gets a job with the agency where his mother works, then gets involved with a techno-terror group. He's getting fired, while the group he's involved with comes to the colony to protest." Her gut told her Dilan Darcy's DNA would be found at the wedding. She couldn't let the protestors escape. "After the morgue, I want to personally inspect every passenger leaving for the next three hundred years."

"Jade will help with that."

She got up to head out, now wishing she had authorized more than one dog. "Maybe it can sniff out the protestors."

26

Kate opened the door to her apartment and zipped to the balcony to get fresh air. Almost ten stories above her, the black dome barricaded the air from escaping. A thin boundary between space and air, death and life. She exhaled. She was in the middle of something she didn't see coming. Victory disease is what they called it at the academy, a fancy term for hubris and complacency.

Behind her, the place was empty. The floor-to-ceiling holowindows played an illusion. Rae had switched to the vantage of a Toronto high-rise on Humber Bay. A rocky shoreline separated sapphire water from a park filled with crisp fiery fall leaves. Somewhere, a cloudless day. Waves rippled on the water, and autumn leaves blew around white high-rise condos cascading, towards Toronto's cityscape. Not a random selection, Toronto was where Meloni lived.

She didn't believe in an afterlife. But if there was one, her parents and grandfather were looking through the dome, asking what was she doing with her life, and telling her to get her shit together. This was her house. She needed to defend it.

Scar appeared meowing, rubbed her leg, and then licked residual wedding cake from her clothes. He was saying, as one predator to another, whoever killed Helena Darcy thought they got away with it.

Kate left the balcony, Scar following her, then closed the doors and blared metal. None of her neighbors had complained about her loud music. Maybe they shared her taste for hard rock from the fifties. Or the soundproofing was that good. The twenty-fifties were now considered classic, but it was the best era for music—in her opinion. The autotuner fad had passed, key changes roared back into style, and human bands became more creative than the bland AI dominating the decades prior. Real music, real people, with real emotional vocals that even modern AI couldn't match. Meloni and Rae were into contemporary nu AI. Improved but still not gritty enough.

She tossed her dirties at the laundry drone, then guitar-strummed her phone naked to the bathroom. Scar followed like her personal roadie cat.

Before she stepped in the shower, she messaged Rae, *shower then omw Darcys.*

Rae's response was, *having fun*, followed by an image of her face on a screaming, deranged doctor pulling out long spiny hair. Then, *jk. Fine. Darcy scan only. Eric aka miracle worker says half hour. No sign of defensive wounds.*

Kate laughed at the image, then responded with two hearts and a selfie of herself naked in the shower.

Out of the shower and dried, Kate looked at herself in the mirror. She'd let her curly black hair get below her shoulders, trimming just the frayed tips over the last eight months. Flipping through her closet, she found a white blouse, black flats, midnight blue slacks, and a jacket with the right tone. Now makeup. Space Force regulation conservative. As good as war paint. She rechecked the mirror and unclumped her curls.

After dressing, Kate found Premium lunacultured siracha-flavored egg protein with added vitamin D in the kitchen and an organic Earth-style croissant that promised to remind her of a Parisian bakery. She smashed them together and shoved the sandwich in her face while digesting the files Jin sent on the Darcys: Helena, her two husbands Nolan and Paul, her wife Kenna, and the two kids, Dilan and Leyna.

The eggs and the files lacked the spiciness she expected. Helena lived with her two husbands Paul and Nolan and her wife Kenna. There was no acrimonious custody battle over their two now-grown children, nor any legal battles over finances. There were no protection from abuse orders filed by legalbots. Unlike Stuart, Rae's ex, who was a serial abuser of the system. He was worse than a lone star tick dug in for Rae's money.

There was no connection to Nathaniel Kirkwood in the file.

She shook her head reading one of the notes she'd made. She had been to their Cygnus apartment a few weeks ago for a report of an assault. Helena Darcy said everything was fine, but a Fed was sighted leaving the floor. Damn. Another reminder that she had not seen things when they were directly in her face over the last few weeks.

Kate gave Scar the last two bites of the eggs. Scar meowed. Kate agreed, giving Scar a scratch. The croissant was good but didn't remind her of a French bakery. Then Kate cleaned up and headed for Cygnus to see the Darcys.

27

She took the main concourse, stopping only for espresso at a kiosk. While sipping, she planned her interview. Dilan Darcy was a big question mark and also their son. She planned to make them comfortable by making them think *she* was comfortable. Plan A, smile, turn on the charm, flip her hair, and play dumb. "Oh, your son is a protestor, why you don't say," she'd giggle. As if any parent on the planet would concede their kid strapped on a bomb vest and blew up a cafe full of tourists. They'd say, "But my Johnny would never do that". Of course not, unthinkable. She'd flip her curls and flash a big toothy smile.

If that plan didn't work, there were always Plans B, C, and D. Her boots, stun gun, and a real gun. She didn't think it would come to that.

Walking through Cygnus, she noted that it had the same décor as Piscis—sea salt hallways, cold blue and green grays, and faux wood doors with aluminum trim. Plenty of pictures of seascapes and boats lining the halls. It could be Piscis, except for the name. Or, everything on the colony was starting to look the same. If she ever felt homey, she'd move here because the décor reminded her of a chilly Northeastern wind whipping through the hallway that would freeze her hominess in a heartbeat.

Nolan Darcy answered his door with a forced smile and torso-length thin gray hair flowing over a yellow embroidered linen shawl. He wore chocolate-colored linen shorts that exposed his spindly gray-haired legs, bare feet, and toenails as yellow as the shawl. The scents of a thousand candles drifted out of the apartment. Kate caught hydrangea, roses, lavender, cinnamon, apples, pine, cloves, and honey. His apartment was an enticing, aromatic smorgasbord of evidence.

Nolan folded his arms and pursed his lips. Already defensive and confrontational. So much for Plan A. Nolan said, "Paul is on his way to the station. We already gave your deputy a statement. We didn't see anything."

The potpourri of scents carried a meek voice from another room, "Is it Chief Devana?"

Kate still didn't like Chief Devana.

"I am deeply sorry for your loss. I know it's a terrible time, but I was hoping to ask—"

Kenna came to the door with a wad of tissues. Face and nose red, eyes puffy. She had changed clothes and washed the makeup off her face. But she was still sobbing as hard as in the hospital.

Nolan, arms still folded, said "Shouldn't you be off finding who did this?"

Kenna said, "Nolan is obsessed with true crime. He thinks you are here to arrest us."

Nolan said, "The four of us are a family. *Were* a family." Shaking his head, he said, "I still can't believe this. We had nothing to do with this."

"I'm not here to arrest anybody. Helena was missing—"

Kenna said, "Do you know when the Medical Examiner will be finished with Helena?"

"Won't be long."

"I don't want her humiliated by being mutilated and butchered by a—"

Nolan said, "—the Medical Examiner is your wife, right? You can do something about that?"

Kate smiled, but it felt fake. "Dr. Torres has the best scanning equipment money can buy. I am sure she will be respectful. It's important that—"

Nolan pressed. "—but she *is* your wife."

Kate opted not to correct him. "I know this is hard. I was hoping to ask some questions. I am looking for Helena's phone."

Kate peeked into the sweeping studio. She was taken aback at the size. The place was twice as large as the standard Cygnus suite. It looked like they had combined two condos and removed all the walls. For privacy, the space was partitioned with latticed bamboo dividers inset with rice paper painted with sneering pink geishas outlined in black. The geishas were protecting two queen beds set off by dividers, a bathroom, and hiding evidence. In front of the bedrooms' bamboo partitions, a white rattan sofa, a loveseat, and two chairs formed a U around a glass table. All had thin tan cushions that her gut said she wouldn't sit on.

She was probably imagining that the geishas sneered, *the evidence is all here under my kimono*. Hiding devices. Maybe with messages. Or threats. Under the kimonos, proof. When she was stationed in Tokyo, her charm opened a lot of kimonos. Not this time.

"We already told your deputy we don't know where it is."

"Nolan—"

"Kenna, let me speak."

Kate asked, "Was Helena getting threats?"

Kenna and Nolan looked at each other. Neither answered. She took that as a *yes*.

"Have you heard from your son, Dilan?"

Kenna said, "What's Dilan got to do with this?"

Nolan said, "We have no idea what goes on in that brain of his. We haven't heard from him in weeks."

"Any chance he came here?"

Kenna and Nolan looked at each other again. Then Nolan said, "You'd have to ask him."

That sounded a lot like he'd been here recently. Or was here now. "How do I contact him?"

Nolan snorted. He tightened his grip on the door.

"Do you know how he is connected to Earth First?"

Hall light reflected off the door as it shifted and moved. "Leave Dilan out of this. His politics are none of your business."

"You have another child, too—"

"Christ, you people have no empathy. Helena is dead. Probably her life's work at the agency with it. And now you want to take her other son, too." Nolan arm barred Kenna and then stepped back. "Come back with a warrant."

The door slammed with a bang and crack.

Kate shook her head. So much for Plan A. No surprise. Parents don't give up their children easily. They did exactly what she would have done, what her grandfather said to do to protect the family, don't talk to the police. She would have to find another way.

28

Kate huffed so loudly when she flopped into one of the chairs facing Rae's desk that she startled herself. Rae had her auburn hair in a ponytail. Her chocolate-colored shirt had *love is chemistry* stenciled in pink comic sans, above an also-pink stick diagram of a molecule.

Rae greeted Kate with a smile, her hazel eyes smiling too, then returned to something on one of the three monitors on her desk.

"If we get married, Rae, can we skip the protest and murder?"

"Stuart will protest. You will murder him, and I won't stop you," Rae said without taking her eyes off her monitor,

Ha. True. "What's the chemical on your shirt?"

Rae straightened her shirt so that Kate could see *theobromine* stenciled in pink below the molecule. "Key ingredient in chocolate."

"I could use some of that."

Rae looked down at her shirt, then lifted it to flash her boobs. "How about me instead. I am out of chocolate."

"I need both." Kate smiled. A better pick-me-up than Jin's joke.

The shirt went down, and with it, Kate's mood. Rae said, "You know Eric won't have cause of death for—"

"Eric is doing the autopsy?"

"What's wrong with Eric?"

"Nothing. I just thought—"

"I can't. I knew Helena."

"Oh. Damn. I'm sorry." Rae didn't seem distraught.

"Thank you. I didn't know her that well, though. We went to lunch a few times. She talked a lot about her research and the agency. She was passionate about it. It's awful."

Kate sighed. "Apparently I was at Helena's a few weeks ago. I don't remember it. This place—"

Kate paused. Rae didn't respond.

"—this place, Rae. All the simulated windows." Kate pointed to the wall, the window to the morgue. "I can't see the things in front of me."

"Hmm. Metaphysical Kate thinks we live in a simulation."

Rae was mocking her. Why did that turn her on? "Not metaphysical. I'm getting soft. I think the protestors were here for weeks and I missed it."

"I like you a little soft." Rae smiled. "You're not omniscient."

Kate sighed.

"What are you always telling Axio? No one is undefeated. Pick yourself—"

"—up off the floor. Improvise, adapt, and overcome. Oo-rah."

Right, why was she sitting? She stood up.

Silence for a few breaths. Then Rae said, "Eric won't have anything for you for a few days."

"I know cause of death. I am mainly interested in defensive wounds."

"You already know there weren't any."

"I am hoping you—or he—proves me wrong."

"Why?"

"Dilan Darcy, her son, his name was in Nathaniel Kirkwood's notebook with a big question mark. I think this was personal."

Rae didn't respond, still looking skeptical.

"My experience Rae, terrorist groups want the credit. Want to post video of infidels getting beheaded."

"For the likes."

"For the money. Sneaking is bad for fundraising."

"Mmm."

Rae's, *You made a good point, I have to think about it* sound. Not agreement, or disagreement. Her calculations calculating. Simulations simulating.

Kate pictured someone coming up behind Helena Darcy, covering her mouth, then stabbing her four times. "Eric will say one stab to the right kidney. Then one in the back between ribs five and six, puncturing the right lung. Then two stab wounds in the upper abdomen. The attacker missed the heart but lacerated the liver and spleen. The four stab wounds likely happened in that order—kidney, lung, liver, then spleen—two from behind. The attacker is probably right-handed. The stab to the kidney was unnecessary. It would have been excruciating."

Rae reviewed something on the monitor and then smiled. "You know, for a military grunt, you underestimate yourself. Not bad."

"This feels personal. And no defensive wounds. Like she knew her attacker."

Rae said, half-mocking, "So, you knew I wouldn't have the results. And you knew there were no defensive wounds. Yet you're here."

"Maybe I just like staring at your gorgeous hazel eyes."

Rae smiled and batted her eyes. "Flattery will get you everywhere. But that's not it. What did Aria say?"

That wasn't it either. Still, Kate said, "Aria and Olicia think Homeland withheld. Or they've been too busy spying on their enemies to catch real threats."

Rae nodded. "Inclined to agree."

Kate looked around. Rae's office had gone through three phases in the last eight months. First, shiny and new, with unopened boxes around the walls. Next, exponential growth of clutter. Now her office bore all the stains, strains, scratches, and hoarding of the four people whose gloves and protective equipment crowded the shelves. Having outgrown this office in only eight months, it was now in its third and final phase. On the left wall, piled-up empty moving boxes partly covered a window to the morgue, which now was opaque and displayed a picture of Kate and Rae on *Tesseract* five weeks ago.

"When are you moving?"

"The moving drones come later today. The construction drones Thursday, to start tearing out the walls."

Kate let mechanical sounds fill the silence, listening to the rhythm of the hospital. Somewhere water was circulating. The fan in the central air register behind Rae diffused the scent of Rae's lavender conditioner. In front of her, Rae's clicking. Rae liked to type, old style. No neuroface. She said moving her fingers helped her think, that she found the clicking soothing, tingling.

"I'm going to miss that desk."

Rae grinned. "It wasn't comfortable."

"Either time. But we had to try, right?" Kate smiled. They tried the second time to be sure the first time wasn't a fluke. Office sex seems so much better in movies. Even on the moon.

"But my new office is bigger, so—"

Kate thought *yes*, then *maybe,* then *why?* They had a big fancy apartment with a king size bed now. And thousand-thread-count Earth-grown cotton sheets her parents stowed at the last minute. Teal, with matching blankets. Ultimate comfort. Why have sex on a metal desk?

Maybe she was getting old. Shit, homey again.

Rae went back to working on something on her monitor. Then stopped clicking and gave Kate slow side-eyes.

Kate inhaled and held it a few breaths, then let it out. "Kelli knew about the protest. She messaged me, *sorry I couldn't warn you.*"

Rae shook her head.

"I wanted to tell Aria—when she asked why we didn't know—because my ex is a petty officer. A joke but not a joke."

Rae, still shaking her head.

"Jin said maybe it was classified. You know how she is. Pissing me off was just a bonus."

"Helena Darcy was killed."

"What I *want* to do is rip that star off her collar, shove it up her ass, and bust her to private. If this was a personal vendetta."

"Only reason for her to send that is to get a reaction. Don't respond. Petty people do petty things." Then after a pause, "I will fix her. Send me the message."

Kate did, then regretted it. "What are you going to do?"

Rae grinned. "There are no secrets on the colony."

Kate bombed buildings. Rae bombed servers. Kate winced. "Well, hold off a bit."

"Why? The people need to know."

Kate smiled. "Wait till I corral Kirkwood and his thug protestors. And whatever the fuck else is going on here. We don't need a stampede for the airlocks."

"Are you telling me the bomb threat is real?"

"Jin has all the package drones locked down—"

Kate's phone beeped. Shit.

"But what?"

Kate was half out of the room. "But don't accept any packages. And don't wait on me for dinner. I have a hot date with the evening shuttle back to Earth."

Rae, half smiling, "You leaving me?"

Kate blew a kiss. "Never. But I am hoping the protestors are smart and on it. And that I am smarter and catch them."

Kate's phone binged again. *P1. Female, wearing Earth First shirt, brawling. Science Center.*

29

The security broadcast was late, so the clash had shifted by the time she got to the Science Center. Missing a security broadcast was not that unusual. The reception in Rae's office was poor because it was on the lowest floor of the hospital, and the morgue had a lot of metal and shielding. She also ignored a lot of the broadcasts. A fact of life on the colony, drunk and drugged tourists got into a lot of trouble. She only had the resources to respond to the highest-priority calls. Hotel and casino security were equipped to handle the rest. Her office provided backup if needed. But faced with the choice of room confinement to detox and cool off, or a night in her shiny new jail to face charges, guests chose comfortable room confinement.

Helping relieve pressure, transactional disputes and assaults were down substantially since March. The mere threat of her and Jin getting involved deterred a lot of trouble. Clients paid. Knowing clients would pay, pros fees were less inflated, lessening disputes. Although what people got for a one hour romp in the sheets here sometimes made her question her career choices. She'd done worse for less. Her brother Greg did his part keeping rowdy tourists calm too. She couldn't understand why he loved his job, but he did. He said, *All I gotta do is stand around, smile, and look pretty, Katy, like you, and I get paid for this.* She knew standing around was not all he did. Occasionally, a pervert ran into his fist. He called it the family business. He wasn't wrong.

After reading the message in Rae's office, she darted off to I-10, where she grabbed a cart and sped to the fight as fast as she could dodge humans and drones. The drones she avoided easily with a tap of the red *security emergency* button on the cart. An invisible signal swept drones aside like the bow of a boat cutting water. Humans were always the problem. Despite the flashing lights and her yelling *make way*, the humans looked up, muttered, then played chicken with the cart. The cart's programming slowed to prevent hitting people, then accelerated quickly, joggling her like a bumper car at a cheap amusement park.

When she got to the scene, she found tourists milling about outside the Space Museum, eating ice cream and chocolate crepes as if nothing had happened. As she walked around looking for the immense priority one brawl, Jin messaged her. He had brought the woman in the blue-green shirt back to the office.

Whatever brawl happened was over, so she hurried to her office, where Jin sat at his desk holding overwatch on the conference room. He had changed into black jeans and a tight red polo shirt. His one eye was on something on his device, and the other on the open conference room door. He pointed inside with his chin at a disheveled petite brunette wearing a bright green and blue *Earth First* t-shirt and black jeans, sitting at the head of the table and sobbing into her palms.

"Did she say anything?"

Jin shook his head. "Can't get her to stop crying. I think she mumbled, *he wasn't supposed to kill her*, but I won't swear to it."

"Where are the others? We only arrested her?"

"Museum security theater. There was no fight. Just her wandering around. Security saw the shirt and *thought* she was going to start a fight." He paused to roll his eyes and tap his monitor. "I am rerunning footage. She's been wandering around the colony like a zombie, sobbing."

"ID?"

"She's not responsive. I have not run facial yet. No phone or device on her."

Kate watched the woman sob for a few seconds. She'd seen big husky operatives resist knives and electricity, only to cave to powdered sugar.

"Why don't you go down, get three coffees and a box of donuts. Get the ones with the—"

Jin was on his feet. "The yeasty ones with the cinnamon and sugar, done and done."

Kate went behind her desk to retrieve two waters. The Tourism Board gave her a decent budget, so she stocked Icy Comet brand water at the label's recommended sixteen degrees Celsius for maximum flavor.

The mineral balance inside the cool blue and white bag soothed her muscles after the gym. It also calmed nerves like a three-billion-year-old undiscovered narcotic.

As Kate entered the conference room and set the water bags down, the woman did not look up. Her face was familiar, but Kate couldn't place it. Maybe she saw her at the wedding mclcc. Shc was sobbing into her hands, and her long hair was tangled with tears and makeup from running her hands through it. Kate had seen assets shed crocodile tears countless times. Crying could be faked. But makeup in the hair was a detail that pretenders would overlook. The woman was either a famous Bollywood actress, a highly skilled operative, or genuinely heartbroken. Kate dismissed the first two theories. She sat next to her and took a gulp from her own straw. The woman paused her sobbing long enough to look at Kate with baby-blue eyes.

"Call me Kate." Kate smiled and slid the water closer. "Anything I can get you?"

The woman forced a small smile and shook her head.

"I wish I could offer you water from Earth." Kate nodded to the woman's shirt. "But as far as water goes, this is good."

Kate took another swig of water, exaggerating her refreshment with an Oscar-worthy *ahhh.* Jin came in and dropped off two coffees and a warm box of donuts. Kate opened it, filling the room with the scent of cinnamon, sugar, jam, and cream. Warm purple goo dribbled on the tabletop as Kate plucked a donut. Then she pushed the box closer to the woman.

"I don't care what planet they're made. Hot donuts will always be good." Kate took a bite and sounded another melodramatic *mmmm.*

The woman smiled approval and then scarfed one of the donuts. The powdered sugar smeared into her tears and makeup and dusted her blue and green t-shirt like snow. Kate handed her a moist napkin and offered her a second donut. The woman ignored the napkin, opting instead for a cinnamon donut, which she dunked in her coffee. After she scarfed the second donut and half her coffee, she cleaned herself with her forearms and back of her hands like a cat, then looked past Kate as if something else was on the menu.

From behind Kate, Jin said, "I didn't know how you took it."

The woman's eyes smiled, and she bit her lip as she sipped her coffee.

Jin asked, "What is your name?"

"Leyna. With a y."

"I am Jin. Also with a y."

Leyna cracked a flirty smirk through the steam rising from her cup. Kate turned her chair to look up at Jin. There was no *y* in his first name—*Jinho*—until nanoseconds ago. Jin's eyes flirted back, his limbic system in overdrive.

Kate might have mumbled *shit*. She didn't know what Jin's type was. Now she did.

"Thank you, Jin with a y. Close the door on your way out."

Jin opened his mouth. Then he closed the door behind him with a flustered *right*. Kate turned back to Leyna, who had finished her coffee and was now drinking water.

"Who's he?"

"My deputy. Quite a protest your group put on."

The woman looked down at her shirt. She tried to brush the powdered sugar off it. Instead, she smeared dribbled strawberry jam across the planet.

"Oh, I am not with them."

Kate crinkled her brow. "Not a great shirt to be wearing around here, especially if you are not with them. Want to tell me about it?"

"That's just it, I don't know." Leyna's eyes and mouth turned down into an incipient sob.

"Can we start with your full name? And address?"

"Leyna Darcy. Right now I am staying at the *Apus*, room 119."

"Leyna *Darcy?*"

Kate took Leyna's hand as she started to cry again.

"I am sorry about your mom, ok?"

"I didn't know he was going to kill her."

"Who is he?"

"My fucking asshole brother. This is all his fault."

Leyna wiped her tears like a cat. This time, powdered sugar and jam smeared into her hair.

"How do you know it was your brother?"

"Because he has problems and blames her for them, that's why."

"Did you see it?"

"I wasn't there. But I know it was him. It had to be. They had a big fight again. He was messaging that stupid group and he was making threats."

"Messaging Earth First?"

Leyna nodded.

"What was the fight about?"

Leyna computed something in her head before she spoke. "His job. She got him the job. To get him back on his feet while he was at school. We told her it was a bad idea." She paused to sip water. "He was getting fired."

"Where does your brother work?"

"He works on the far side IIRAS station."

"What kind of threats was he making?"

"It's complicated."

"Can you uncomplicate it for me?"

"He was messaging the group. I—" Leyna looked at the door.

"So you think your brother was one of the protestors."

Leyna nodded. "I was hoping to find him. Tell him to stop."

"Dressed like that?"

More nodding.

"Why didn't you report this?"

She shook her head. "I tried. Everyone said there was no way for him to get here. My parents ignored me."

"But you thought there was?"

"It's been done. Hitch a ride on one of the supply ships leaving the station."

"But you didn't see him at the wedding."

"I wasn't at the wedding. I was—" She looked toward the door. "Am I under arrest?"

Kate smiled. "We are just chatting over coffee, Leyna. Jin says you were wandering around."

Leyna, still looking at the door. "I just wanted to talk to him. But—"

Kate waited while Leyna finished her thought.

"—But I couldn't find him."

"How do you know all this?"

Leyna started to answer, then looked at the conference room walls. Then at Kate's clothes. "You think I am a protestor, and I did it, don't you?"

It sounded like a statement.

"Why would you murder your Mom?"

"Because I hate my family. Same as my brother. And here I am in the wrong t-shirt. I didn't do it. And I am not part of Earth First." Then, staring at the door, "I can help you."

"How is that?"

"I know things. But I need to talk to a lawyer first."

Kate puffed her cheeks and exhaled. The carbs and coffee sobered Leyna much quicker than she expected.

She stood. "I am going to step out, Leyna. Someone will be right outside. If you need anything, just ask."

"Where are you going?"

"To get you a lawyer." Kate paused a beat. "Can I call your other mom, Kenna? Or dads? Paul or Nolan?"

"No. Definitely not."

"Ok well—"

"Axyl and Emma Dover."

"How do we contact them?"

"In my—" a pause, then, "I want to talk to a lawyer first. Not a bot either, a human. This is too complicated to explain to a bot."

Kate nodded. "Got it. A lawyer and the Dover's. I'll track them down."

30

Kate closed the door behind her. Outside the office, she found a blue suit wearing short hair and polished black flats standing over Jin and flashing a badge. Jade was in one corner, sitting, ears perked. If Jade could salivate, she'd probably be salivating over biting the Fed.

"Boss, this is Special Agent Milya Bolkov."

"Call me Mia."

"What's so special about you, agent Mia? You dress like all the other Fed clones."

"I can help you."

"The VA paid a lot of money to a therapist who said the same thing, *I can help you*. I dunno, Jin, do I seem sane to you?"

"You turned down a seven figure bribe from those other Feds. On a scale, Harley Quinn."

"Really, not Joker?"

"Not in the remake. The holographic cinematography was great, but AI scripting just doesn't do crazy like you do."

"Fair." Kate turned to Bolkov. "You're still here. So how much are you offering?"

"I am offering evidence. To help you with Helena Darcy."

"What is it?"

Bolkov looked aside at the flags on the wall.

Kate said, "Right. This is a negotiation. You are going to say something like it's classified. Then ask for what we have. Which I naively give you. Then you give us nothing."

"I feel used, boss."

"Very used. How am I doing, Agent Mia?"

"It is classified."

"My report won't be. You can read it when we've closed the case."

Bolkov froze.

"Dismissed, Agent Mia. Come back with some of that illegal surveillance you've been doing—correction, *all* of it."

Bolkov didn't move.

Kate said, "Jade, growl for me."

Jade growled and bared her realistic drone teeth. Bolkov looked at Jade, then muttered *fucking insane is right,* and turned for the door. When Bolkov was gone Kate locked the door then patted Jin on the shoulder.

"Forget what I said about Jade. I like her."

"I told you."

Then Jin looked past Kate as if he were x-raying the conference room. "Anything she needs?"

"A lawyer, a grief counselor, and Axyl and Emma Dover."

"Should I—"

"No, Jin, with a y, you shouldn't. That is Leyna *Darcy.*"

Jin's eyebrows raised.

"And for all we know, she did it. And unless you have a prison fetish—"

"There is no blood on her clothes and no wedding food. If she killed her mother, I'd expect blood on her shirt. And I don't have a prison fetish."

"No judgment from me if you do."

"I don't."

Kate smirked. "Well, we will see." She relayed the interview. "But she's lawyered up."

"If she didn't kill anyone, why lawyer up?"

"Well, one possibility is she did it. Or she was involved with the protestors and doesn't want charged. Or—" Kate stared through the conference room door. "Or she found out while doing something illegal, and she doesn't want charged with that."

"While you were in there, I looked her up. Computer science at Hawaii Pacific."

"So, maybe a hacktivist. We should try to confirm what she said about her brother. Backtrack her movements. I'll have one of Rae's techs get biometrics and evidence off her clothes."

"I can get biomets off Leyna."

Kate pursed her lips.

"10-4. One of Rae's techs will do it."

"We need to light a fire under the DNA. I need to know if Dilan Darcy was there. And we need to search her hotel room."

"If it's ok, I'll wait here. Paul Darcy is on the way. Did you get the video I sent of Kirkwood?"

"Say again?"

Shaking his head, "You don't read your messages do you?"

Did she get a video? "Sometimes I don't get stuff at the hospital."

"*Sometimes*. Well here, look." He fiddled with his computer and brought up a video. "We know where Kirkwood was staying so I backtracked his movements." Jin played a video clip. "Here, he exits his hotel room wearing mask. I tracked him to the kitchen of The Crown Oasis. Here, he is going up the stairs and stopping to grab a steak knife."

Kate stared outside her office window. The concourse was quiet. "Any chance Nathaniel Kirkwood is Dilan Darcy?"

Jin inhaled, then exhaled. "I thought of that, but I don't think so, boss. I did a deep profile on him. His parents died five years ago. They committed suicide off a Central Park West building and left him a lot of money. He's been living in the penthouse he inherited, and been in and out of institutions. I got his medical files. He's known to the NYPD, and I've been able to clip him on surveillance in New York. Hard for him to be in New York and on the far side of the moon at the same time."

"You got his medical records? Legally?"

Jin frowned like a puppy in trouble. "Not exactly, boss."

This was something she'd meant to discuss with him. "You put a spider camera in Bill Caddell's hotel room."

"I did, boss."

"And I am assuming the NYPD surveillance you didn't get through the proper channels."

"So much bureaucracy, boss."

She nodded. "Good work. In case I didn't say it today, really good work."

"I thought I would be in trouble."

"If you didn't own it, you would be. Integrity above all. You can say whatever you want outside these walls. In here, brutal honesty."

"Got it. Thank you."

"You stay here. I am going back to the Apus to see if we missed anything."

"Before you go. Paul Darcy. He'll be here in five minutes."

"He was headed here an hour ago when Nolan slammed the door in my face. Why is he coming here?"

"He wants to update his statement. He says he has a video."

Kate looked at the conference room, wishing she had a second one. Or a third. Paul Darcy might have seen the murderer. Or was the murderer. If it was his son, would he tell them?

"What are you thinking, boss?"

"Something weird about this family. The daughter asks for the Dovers, not her parents. And fingers her brother."

"When I—if I were arrested, I didn't call my parents either."

Kate smiled a little. She knew about that. "Fair. I am thinking divide and conquer. You interview Paul. I will go back to Apus."

"Me?"

"You'll do fine. Focus on whatever video he has. If possible, keep him out here. Don't let Leyna and Paul know about each other. And don't let on we think his son is the prime suspect."

31

The table at *Lunaburger* where Nate sat had a premium view of the traitor Kate Devana's office. Across the concourse, behind the glass office windows, people. Wattsuckers, toasters, all their thoughts mated with machines. Some were typing. Those were the proto cyborgs. His stomach revolted. It didn't matter. They were all aiding and abetting the destruction of the human race.

Nothing would be there in a few minutes. On the second floor, he could see her deputy, Dick, sitting in a chair, resting his meat parts while his cyborg parts did all the work.

He grinned. Maybe Dick was looking for him. But he was right here, looking back, his brain unreachable over the network. They weren't going to find him.

On his right, a drone stopped, turned, dropped his burger on the table, then waited. Was he supposed to do something? It felt like a staring contest, except one of them had sensors and cameras for eyes and cranes for arms.

"Go. Away."

That worked. The drone spun and retreated. Nate peeled open the foil wrapper on his burger and took a bite. He wasn't supposed to be here. Mylah would be mad. Him here, watching, cheating by having a burger. It tasted just like the *Lunaburger* in New York. Same orange sauce, same meat, same cheese that he'd been eating for years. Maybe not the *same* meat. The vats were here instead of upstate New York. Did that matter? Neurochips were the problem. Turning people into machines. Machines didn't need food. And it's not like they planned to buy a farm and grow corn. Or butcher animals. Neither of them knew the first thing about that. So he didn't see Mylah's problem.

The burger tasted good and how could his tongue be wrong about that. The neurochip he knew was a problem, giving him anxiety and depression and hallucinations. Too bad he waited so long. It fried his brain, and he still had issues even though it was out. The white pills were helping. But he wouldn't need them much longer.

He wondered if the colonists even noticed the machines. The metal gnomes hustling about, making it all happen. Drones and robots did everything here. Generate power from massive nuclear power plants. Recycle garbage. Make food and water. Even menial tasks like food service and package delivery.

After the traitor raided their hotel room, Mylah said they shouldn't rely on machines to deliver the bomb. Rily said people didn't pay attention, so they should still use the drone.

Time to find out who was right. A package delivery drone scurried towards the traitor's office. Passing one, two, three people. Nobody noticed.

The traitor came out of her office. Passing a man on the concourse going in. He read her lips. Oh, she was so sad Miss Technology Queen got killed. Poor her. He wanted to scream they would all be dead soon. The traitor said, *let me know if there is anything I can do*. She forgot to say, *for the machines*. Let me know if there is anything I can do for the machines. That's what she meant. Because she sure as hell wasn't helpful to humans.

They parted. The traitor passed the drone. She looked right at it and through it. Rily hovered, saying, "I told you so."

Then the package drone darted for a sliding door in the corner designed for deliveries. He sipped his drink. Wouldn't be long now.

The package drone halted before arriving at the delivery door. Mylah laughed at Rily. "Blocked. See?" Mylah was always right.

The traitor paused and looked over her shoulder. Please, traitor, go back.

The traitor did go back. She did something on her phone and returned to inspect the package drone. She scanned it and then studied her phone. She opened the drone's package door. Empty.

Mylah was right. They checked the test drone. But the fucking cyborg traitor was Major Stupid. Mylah had a backup plan sitting in the corner of Lunaburger. Ha.

He took off his backpack and looked around. A sweet little girl in the corner was playing video games. Her parents were off, not paying attention. He walked over. She looked like a Becky. Becky, the backup plan.

"Hi. That game you are playing. My girlfriend used to play it too. I know an easter egg that unlocks the monster on level thirty-three."

The girl cooed. "Tell me."

"Well, I have to take something over to the police station. It's lost and found. Very important that I deliver it."

The girl pouted. Like Rily did when she didn't get her way.

"Ok. Tell you what. If you help me take this over to the police station, while you're gone, I'll install the add-on."

The girl frowned. Becky the backup plan went to all the best schools and received all the best technology. Maybe even grown in a surrogate uterus like him. Becky didn't like strangers.

"Well, it's up to you. I need to go hand this to that man in sandals on his phone. It's lost and found. While I am working, you can give this to him and tell him to set it on Kate Devana's desk."

"Why don't you do it?"

Smart girl.

"I have money. I live in a big apartment in New York. I don't want the reward. That man looks like he needs the reward money."

He turned to the door. "I'll be back in a little while."

"To help me?"

"If you are still here. Maybe. Sure. If your parents are ok with that."

The girl got up. "I'll do it for you. You sit here and fix my game."

"That's nice of you. Will you be asking for the reward money, too?"

"Oh no. My mommy says we have a lot of it. That man in sandals looks like he needs it."

"Ok good. Well, hurry back."

Nate handed her the backpack. She hurried across the concourse and gave it to the man in sandals, who turned inside to go upstairs. The girl hurried back. Then was grabbed by her mother, who started yelling at the kid. Poor girl. Not that it mattered. They would all be dead soon.

A dog barked on the second floor. Dog? People brought dogs here to die too?

Then a flash and the windows rattled. The building facade still stood. Windows, unbroken. Shit, Mylah said there was enough to take out a three-story building. Or at least blow out the windows. Everyone on the concourse was gawking, like him. The explosion wasn't like in the media. No smoke, no glass shards. What the hell.

Now the alarms were blaring. The fire system drenching the inside of the windows. Liquid, maybe water, was leaking out of the doors and pooling on the concourse.

Now the traitor was running towards her office. He wanted to scream, *too late you cyborg-loving piece of shit. They are all dead.* The traitor hopped to the wall, opened a box labeled *LUNGS,* put a mask on, then skidded across the water a meter. Building occupants were streaming out. Masks on, crowding her, blocking her from going in. She pushed through. He chuckled under his breath. Ha, too late anyway.

EMT drones were forcing themselves through the crowd and into the building. Then firefighters with big red CVFD letters on their yellow sleeves. He should leave. Glancing around, other people were gawking, same as him. So, he waited.

A man came out wearing a mask and carrying a limp woman, also masked. Shit, the fucking deputy. Alive. They fucked up the bomb. Or, Rily liked the deputy too much and maybe she sabotaged it.

EMTs coming out carrying a stretcher. Face covered, he couldn't see who it was. The sandals. The same sandals as the man the traitor stopped to talk to. The EMTs sprinted to the hospital, like the deputy. Shit, everybody was filing into the hospital. Walking. It was Mylah's idea to hit the office, not realizing it was right next to the hospital. That was dumb. By his count, they only killed two people. If that. Mainly though, he blamed Rily. Something went wrong with the bomb.

Now the traitor was coming out. Behind her, a *thunk*. Seals on the door closed. Then a *thump.* In the windows, all the smoke and gas disappeared. Like air getting evacuated.

The traitor went over to a firefighter. Took her mask off. Eyes and nose red, bleeding. Was the stuff poisonous? She grabbed the firefighter's device. The firefighter's jaw moved, lecturing her. She ignored it, instead staring at the pad. The firefighter shook his head as the traitor coughed blood. Maybe the stuff was toxic and would kill her anyway. The concourse's alarm changed, now a silent flashing yellow. The traitor handed back the firefighters' device, coughing blood on it. She took oxygen from an EMT, then walked to the hospital.

He glanced around. The customers in *Lunaburger* still gawking. Time for him to get off this rock and kill everyone. Time for phase three.

32

A blue haze clouded Kate's vision, sirens blared at her, and the world spun. In the smoke, people were running around screaming. An acrid smell like plastic burning filled her nose and mouth and burned her throat. Her face was wet with tears. The glass on her hand scratched her cheek as she tried to wipe them. Her hand was bloody and black with some sort of soot. Nearby, a car was on fire, and a storefront was blown out. The body beside her was her mother, eyes open and glassy, her face bloody and black. Her mouth was open, but she wasn't breathing. Kate's headache was incredible. She reached to touch her mother, but someone was screaming and shaking her. A woman in blue and gray overalls with a Hebrew nametag pulled her away. Kate heard herself scream for her father, who was lying on the curb face down.

Kate gasped and woke to see a nurse in blue scrubs leaving her hospital stall. She blinked. She was in the colony hospital. Her head felt fine. Great, even. The back of her throat tasted like she'd swallowed some bitter tea. She checked herself, finding no soot on her clothes and no blood. Her mother and father were not lying dead next to her.

She exhaled. The dream was a flashback to the bomb that killed her parents at a Tel Aviv café when she was twelve. Now she remembered: She came to the hospital, the nurse put an IV in, and after that, blackness. They must have sedated her. A status window beside her bed said that the Docbot rated her lung damage from the bomb's toxic stew a four out of ten.

Like she told the firefighter who lectured her, she'd had worse on deployment. Shit, she lost time. They sedated her and she wasn't sure how long she'd been out. Another fanatic was trying to bomb humanity back to the stone age and he wasn't going to stop. She needed to move. She rolled off the bed, pulled her IV out, and unplugged herself.

Peering out of her hospital stall's curtain, Kate spied a man and a woman hovering near the threshold of the critical care wing. Through the curtain, she felt like she was eyeing a nefarious reflection of herself from a multiverse. Closely cropped straight brown hair and poses that gave away hefty firearms under their perfectly pressed blue suits. More Feds.

Kate messaged Rae, *help.* She wasn't sure what kind of help she would need, but the hair standing at the back of her neck told her she would need it soon.

She was in stall fifteen. She ducked between the curtains into stall fourteen. This stall had been as unlucky for Paul Darcy as Helena Darcy. After the bomb, the EMT drone brought him here. Now another drone was moving his body to a stretcher for transport to the morgue.

Kate zigzagged through the curtains but paused in stall ten when she saw Leyna Darcy. Leyna's chart revealed that she was stable but in a medically induced coma due to rocket fuel inhalation. She had extensive chemical burns. A note read, *DNA not on file. Marrow biopsy for lung granum.* Leyna would be getting a new lung in a few weeks, grown from her own tissue. If she lived that long.

Kate dipped through the separating curtain to find Jin in nine, arguing through his oxygen mask with two more twin agents. He stood in blue scrubs between the gurney and the curtain, hooked to an IV, with Jade in the corner half burned and in sleep mode. One agent was crowding Jin, while the other held the curtain as if about to leave. Judging from the fog inside Jin's mask, the disagreement was heated.

"What did I miss, Jin?"

Jin turned, surprised under his mask. Kate stepped between Jin and the agent crowding him. Close in, Kate confirmed the firepower holstered under the agents' suits.

"These two are trying to take Leyna."

"Let me see the warrant."

The agent holding the curtain let go to pull out a device and flash Kate. What he displayed could have been a badge or an image of Mars. "I am Agent Stan McCurry. We don't need a warrant. National Security."

Kate didn't care what his name was. After eight months, all the Feds that came here looked alike, as if the government was violating the ban on human cloning and growing their police force in vats, and training them with a political agenda, copy-pasted from a politico's server.

"My jurisdiction. Come back with a warrant."

In her peripheral vision, she could see Jin take pictures and fiddle with his pad.

The agent crowding her said, "We don't need your permission."

"She is in a medically induced coma."

"We will have our own doctor treat her. This is just a courtesy call."

"And I am courteously telling you to show me a warrant or get lost."

The agent at the curtain sighed and reached, signaling that Kate's stalling tactic was failing. So she tried a different approach. "Let's call your super. Last thing you need today is an ass-chewing because you did not follow procedure, right?"

Kate smiled politely. Feds were hostages to procedure. Plus, she wanted to know who their boss was and why they wanted Leyna.

They ignored her and started for the next room.

Jin put up his finger and said, "Wait, now I remember you."

While the agents paused to look at Jin, Rae showed up, trailed by a nursebot. Help had finally arrived, although Kate still did not know how Rae could help. Kate hoped Rae could convince the agents Leyna could not be moved.

"Yeah, you don't remember?" Jin blew the agents a kiss.

The agent at the curtain shook his head. He tapped the second agent on the shoulder, but number two shrugged it off. Rae furrowed her brow and gave Kate *what-is-Jin-doing* side-eye.

"Red Velvet, last year in Vegas." Jin blew another kiss.

Number two took a half step toward Jin. His eyes were big and white and wet, and he glared at something behind Kate on Jin's phone. Kate blocked him. He took another half step. His boozy hot breath provoked her nose. He said, "Fuck you. Where did you get that?"

Her fists clenched, and she smiled a little.

Jin said, "I thought you would remember me. But you were pretty high."

Number two blinked and lunged, jerking like an awkward, off-balance teenager. His department had not trained agents in lunar gravity. She considered letting him trip over himself. She pictured him falling head-first into Jin's gurney, clanging the metal, knocking himself out with a concussion and whiplash.

Instead, she decided to tutor him. She stepped forward, bending her knees to get low, then let his momentum send the bridge of his nose into her forehead. Usually, she'd drive herself into the headbutt with the balls of her feet and thrust, smashing his skull into his eyes and sending him unconscious to the floor. Then she'd follow up with a throat punch or a few kicks. Instead, today's lesson would be a kindergarten playground scrape that would only send him to the nursebot.

As his cartilage crunched, she reached in and unholstered his gun. She stepped back and stifled a grin at the blood pouring from his nose.

"Fuck, that's assault on a federal agent, bitch," number two said, trying to block his nose and cover the blood spatter.

Kate waved them out of the room with his gun. "If I assaulted you, you'd be unconscious. And if you were a Federal agent, you'd have a warrant. Six cameras in this hospital watched you lunge at my deputy. Now let them watch you leave."

Rae interjected, smirking, saying she'd *seen enough,* then instructed a nursebot to revoke both agents' credentials. Kate pointed to the other two agents hovering outside the wing. While a nurse moved to rescind those agents' credentials, number one flailed, trying to help number two stop his nosebleed while also avoiding his elbows. With less gravity to slow blood flow, colony nosebleeds could be especially hard to staunch—which the agents would know if they had better training.

Number two looked through his bloody hand to the nursebot beside Rae. "Can I get help? I'm bleeding."

Kate said, "You said you have medical wherever you planned to take Leyna."

Rae said, "These beds are full of people who inhaled rocket fuel. You'll live. Just keep pressure on it."

Number two looked around at the empty beds. Number one grabbed an elbow and led two away. One said, "You're making a mistake."

"Usually my mistake is not shooting people. Next time, I won't be gentle."

Kate watched the agents walk over to the other two outside, who were now losing an argument to a nursebot scanning their faces. As the four walked away, Kate shoved the gun into her waistband. Then, Kate turned to Rae, who was staring at an image on Jin's phone. Agent Two was almost naked and tied up in leather.

Jin grinned. "I used to do background for Homeland. If you don't want it found, don't post your personal shit on the dank server."

Kate looked away. She'd seen enough. She reached to pat Jin on the shoulder, then retreated as she realized his burns went all the way to his neck.

"Nicely done. How bad?"

"Better than it looks. Doc says I am going to shed like a snake in a few days." He smiled and called Jade to the bed. "On the bright side, I've been looking for an excuse to get new tats, and *boom* here it is."

"We checked that drone."

"It wasn't the drone, boss. Someone handed Paul Darcy a package as he stood outside. It happened so fast. Paul set it down. Jade barked. I rushed everyone to the conference room. Or tried to. The blast threw the door at Paul. Fuck."

Jade woke with a *ruff* and sat up. Her face had escaped damage, but the entire left side of her torso was burned down to bare metal and servos. Jin cupped her face, pet her, and talked to the drone like Jade was a baby. Jade's imitation of enjoying the attention was impressive, realistic, and burned-bare-metal creepy all at the same time.

"If Jade hadn't barked, we'd be dead. Best guard dog in the solar system, isn't that right, Jade?" Jin motioned for her to lie down and roll over, which she did. "I can get her fur fixed, but I am not sure. Has character, don't you think?"

Rae half-smiled. "In a horror movie kinda way, sure."

Kate said, "Did Paul say anything to you?"

"He gave me another device that he found. Said there was a video on it. I hope it survived the blast."

"So, that's three. Can't be a coincidence."

"Three what, boss?"

Rae said, "Kate means three Darcys. Helena, Leyna, and Paul."

Kate said, "We still haven't found the connection between Dilan Darcy and Nathaniel Kirkwood. Except that we think the two of them messaged each other."

Jin said, "And they are not the same person. I confirmed that."

"Well, the good news, I don't think these attacks are random. The bad news, still a lot of Darcys to kill."

"Don't forget the Dovers, boss. Leyna considered them family too. No telling how far out this circle reaches."

Kate nodded. "Listen, I'd like to linger but we need a plan. Next question. Jin, who were these pricks?"

"I got the same flash you did. But they're not on the list Homeland gave us, that's for sure. Facial search for real names will take time. Unless his real name is beedeeessmike153"

"We aren't that lucky. They'll be back too."

"I revoked their creds, love."

Jin said, "I don't think they care, Rae. I doubt those creds were real."

Kate said, "I don't think so either. Contractors. And they won't stop hunting her unless she's dead."

Rae asked, "Why do they want her?"

Kate shook her head. "I doubt they know. Just that they have orders to pick her up."

"Well, she needs medical attention. She can't be transported."

Jin said, "Do you think she's going to die?"

Kate shook her head. "Leyna is stable. I checked her chart. She will need a new lung—"

Rae said, "Maybe not, Kate."

Rae's hazel eyes smiled. Her tawny specks connected into a plan. Kate smiled back, *yes let's do it*. She felt like kissing her. So nice to be on the same wavelength.

Jin looked confused, then horrified. Without hesitation, Rae walked to room ten. Then the alarm blared *code blue, room ten*. Jin's face cycled through a range of expressions as he realized what was happening. Then he muttered into his oxygen mask, *this is a bad plan.*

33

While Rae's tech, Robyn, secured Leyna, Kate received another security message. She kicked herself, realizing that the shuttle had boarded. She had less than forty minutes to launch. The opportunity to pre-screen departing passengers was gone. But the private message offered redemption. It came from one of the two sky marshals on the shuttle. They flagged a pair of furtive passengers wearing green t-shirts under their clothes. The passenger manifest had them seated together in economy class window seats on deck six, 21W, and 22W.

Jin pushed his IVs and electrical leads to the side, then ran the accompanying images, a man and a woman, against images of protestors. The woman had short, black, closely cut hair and looked college aged. The man looked the same age, with long curly brown hair and an unattractive, patchy brown beard. Only the necklines of the green t-shirts were visible under their clothes. No logo was visible, the pair had no warrants outstanding, and Jin indicated no algorithmic matches to the protestors.

It was thin. She felt there was probably a fashion crime here, but based on the photo, she could only issue the man a warning to shave. Still, she'd rather be lucky than right. This message was a stroke of luck, so she replied that she was on her way.

As Kate started for the spaceport, Jin did what she would have done. He told the human nurse he was leaving. After a heated exchange, he said, *if you want to keep me here, you'll have to put me down*. The human nurse said *fine,* and huffed, but made a tactical blunder by calling a nursebot to sedate him instead of doing it on the spot. Before the nursebot arrived, Jin had pulled the IV from his vein and unplugged himself from the hospital machines. He looked like a horror movie villain with his reddened chemical burns, pumped veins, blue scrubs with wires hanging out, and reptilian pupils from the pain meds. Add in the half-burned drone dog, he was a fourteen out of ten on a nightmare scale. No one else challenged him on the way out of the hospital.

Howling pierced Kate's ears on the way to the spaceport. Jade had been trained with all the behaviors of a live dog, including yowling with the sirens on the cart—irritating and amusing but ultimately helpful. Jade's sonic needle perforated the traffic much better than the sirens or Kate's yelling. The humans in the corridor that typically played chicken with the cart instead swept themselves aside with the drones. Jin yelped and cussed too as he struggled to put clothes on over his burns and scrubs. She grimaced each time he swore. She urged him not to worry about it, but he counter-insisted on looking professional at the spaceport. Once dressed, he outfitted Jade in a camo-brown dog backpack, covering her burned fur and bare metal.

At the spaceport, security squinted at the messages she'd received, squinted at Jin, listened to her fast-talking, then shook their heads and talked to the air. Then they said the countdown had been held at thirty minutes due to technical delays—which she surmised was a cover story.

Security waved them through to the gate. There they met a plain-looking middle-aged woman with salt and pepper hair, clothed in a silver and blue *Space Museum* t-shirt, jeans, and holding her badge out. The woman introduced herself as Agent Sarah Li, a Federal sky marshal. She had close-set, roving brown eyes that betrayed her training and experience, and a familiar gait that betrayed a two o'clock bulge at her waist. Kate was so happy about her luck that she wanted to hug Li. Instead, she settled for a firm handshake.

Li shared more images of the passengers, but once again, Jin's search yielded nothing.

Li said, "My partner is watching them. They are in their assigned seats, looking nervous. I recommend we quietly deplane rather than try to take them down on board. We will use a technical issue as cover. You two stay here and grab them on the way out."

Kate asked, "We don't really have enough for arrest, do we? What's suspicious?"

"Well, there is the green t-shirt under their clothes."

Kate and Jin exchanged glances.

Jin asked, "Can you see the *Earth First* logo?"

"No. But it's fucking hot in that cabin and they look like they're going to Alaska." She paused. "Look, I've been doing this for twenty-five years."

Li stood spine straight, shoulders back, stomach in, showing no discomfort from the gun holstered at her appendix. No flinching. Kate did arithmetic in her head while she read Li's body language. Spacelines had not been mass-transporting passengers for twenty-five years. She said *deplane*, which meant Li did airline security before spaceline security. And before that, based on her posture, Li was Army.

Kate said, "Let's do it. What about luggage?"

Jin shook his head. "Hang on—"

Li said, "None. The woman in 21 has a small purse. The man in 22 has two devices in his pocket."

Jin asked, "Devices?"

"My partner thinks one is his phone, the other is one of those fancy new holocameras."

Jin said, "Maybe they checked their luggage. I can—"

"The spaceline searched. No luggage. And when they bought the tickets, they listed a New York address, but this shuttle goes to Vandenberg."

Jin said, "An extra camera and no luggage. For a four-hundred-thousand kilometer trip to the wrong address. Maybe you should have led with that."

Li's close set eyes squeezed together. "I've been doing this since you were precum, kid." She looked at Kate. "New boot?"

"Jin's just inhaled a liter of rocket fuel. He means, we want to be thorough before we toss someone. We've had some false alarms."

Li eyed Jin up and down. "A whole liter. Probably saving a puppy." Then to Kate, "These two are too twitchy to ride my shuttle so we're pulling them from the rocket. Your partner can stand there and be eye candy or question them on the way out."

Kate looked at Jin. He nodded. "Question them."

"Great. Glad we're aligned." Li turned, dripping sarcasm down the skybridge, then disappeared into the rocket. Kate and Jin positioned themselves at opposite ends of the skybridge.

"She was rude, boss."

"They decided to pull these two before they messaged us, Jin. This is her show."

"You trust her?"

"I trust her gut. As much as I trust mine."

"I don't believe in guts. I trust data and algorithms."

Kate thought he did believe in guts, just not Li's gut. "You will. You agree it doesn't add up."

"It doesn't. But they could just be kids going to see friends."

"Better not to speculate. Two people are dead, and we have two hundred sixty-three souls on this ship. Scan every face as passengers come out—"

Their conversation was interrupted by the announcement of a technical delay that required passengers to exit. Boos echoed down the skybridge. A few minutes later, a slow dribble of passengers became a stream.

The first few passengers were caught up in their devices and walked past Kate and Jin. As the line slowed and the skybridge crowded, three dozen eyes rose from devices to look ahead. Kate heard the *vloops* and *dings* of messages passing through the line like electronic whispers. Some passengers stopped to take pictures of the cute silver German Shepherd drone. Then more *dings* and *gloops* as those images were passed through the line. Near the end, two passengers preemptively argued with her, *you can't search my luggage*. Jin messaged that Jade had alerted on drugs that were legal here but illegal in California. The passengers were wrong, she could search them, but she waved them by anyway. Drugs were not on her agenda.

When the skybridge cleared, Jin said they were two short. The protestors had held themselves back.

The marshals messaged *clearing the decks,* then *suspects glued. Move down here.*

Jin furrowed his brow and looked up from the message. Kate shrugged. "Is she set to sniff for explosives?"

"Saved Leyna's life because of it."

Jin sent Jade across the skybridge, then rolled two surveillance drones after her. Five steps down the skybridge, the black drones sprouted blades and flew into the ship. Kate watched the video feed from her phone as Jade and the surveillance drones searched deck by deck.

All the decks were empty except deck six. The protestors were in their assigned seats, holding hands and singing. They had removed their top shirt to expose their *Earth First* shirts. The surveillance drones' fisheye lens flew around the deck, capturing the sky marshals covering the protestors with guns. Jade sniffed the protestors, then sat and barked once.

Kate took a deep breath and exhaled. Then she marched down the skybridge directly to the protestors. When she arrived, they sang and chanted *I am Asher Trift* while glued to the restraints and chair backing. When she read them their rights, they chanted louder. As the maintenance drones closed in to extract the couple from their seats, the man kicked one across the deck. He spat and called Jin a toaster and magnet dick.

"Jin, show him your leads."

Jin wrinkled his forehead, then plucked a blue, still-attached, frayed lead from under his clothes and twirled it in the man's face.

Kate bent over so close to the man's face that she could smell breakfast rotting in his patchy beard and teeth.

"You know it's true what they say. Jin can plug you in and turn you into a toaster. Right Jin?"

Kate winked at Jin. He grinned and licked his lips like he was diving into a Thanksgiving meal. Kate took her knife out and flicked it open under the man's chin. His eyes widened and focused on the point.

"Let's get you out of this seat, shall we?"

She said it breathy, like she was seducing him. His head bobbed up and down and he swallowed. She lowered her eyes to inspect his glue trap. The waist belt needed to be cut. The shoulder restraints were bonded to his t-shirt and arms.

Easy. Kate slashed the waist belt, slipped her knife under his shirt, and ripped it open so he could tumble free. She scored the fabric of his seat around his ass and legs and grabbed the belt of his jeans. The shoulder restraints still adhered to his arm, so she ripped him away, tearing hair from his skin and a wail from his lungs.

Jin handcuffed him. Kate turned to the woman. The woman looked at the now-empty seat with hair dangling from the restraints, then eyed the maintenance drone and closed her eyes.

Kate backed away. The woman remained still, barely breathing, peeking her eyes open near the end as the drone's pinpoint laser painlessly cut her restraints.

When the woman was free, Kate lifted her gently from the seat. "Score one for technology."

The woman put her finger in Kate's chest. "Fuck you. You're a traitor and disgrace to humanity."

Kate seized the woman's hand. Knuckles cracked and the woman cussed as Kate spun her with her finger. Then she tightened the handcuffs until she elicited an *ouch, fuck you* from the woman.

In the woman's ear she whispered, "Drones are coded to be gentle. I'm not. You can think about the irony in my shiny new jail."

The sky marshals assisted with prisoner transport. Once the two protestors were locked up, Kate went upstairs to assess the damage to her office. Kate never thought she would enjoy messaging Rae and Aria, *my jail is full*, followed by a smiley face. She brought up Kelli's message and started a reply—an image of the two protestors in her jail, followed by *fuck you too*. Then deleted it before she sent it.

34

Da-bodt was the sound of the ball Kate bounced off the refurbished blue-gray walls of her office. She was punchy, going on twenty hours without sleep, her thoughts zig-zagging like the ball. Throwing the ball helped keep her awake while reviewing video logs of the interviews with the protestors. She tossed the ball into the corner where the floor met the wall. It bounced off the floor, off the wall, then back over her head, where she reached up and caught it. The two bouncing sounds—the floor, then the wall—formed a trilled sound, *da-bodt.*

Unlike her, the maintenance drones made good use of time. Fresh paint on the walls. New white doors. New titanium blue lunastone desks. The office smelled clean, like detergent. There was no residual acrid odor of the ammonia rocket fuel. The window had been cleaned, and two of the four monitors were replaced. The drones even retired the burned flags and replaced them with a new Lone Star flag and new U.S. flag.

In contrast, her interviews with the protestors were a waste of time.

Da-bodt-bing. The third sound was Jin messaging her as she caught the ball high over her head. He was at Rae's old office and wanted to video. She decided to activate her neuroface. She used her right hand to bounce the ball and her neuroface to swipe green on Jin's video call. *Da-bodt-vloop,* she caught the ball and Jin's video. Her left hand lifted the last mouthful of cold coffee. Three hands, three things at once. Should have been invigorating. Her brain was too tired.

Jin's shaved head filled the right wall monitor. Behind him, she saw Rae's old office wall. She was going to miss that wall.

"Feet up on the desk, Kate. Interviews went that well?"

"That bad. They ranted. Then lawyered up. All I learned was a bunch of new cyborg slurs I didn't need to know. Toaster, magnet dick, goldback, wattsucker, sockfucker—which apparently is short for socket fucker."

Da-bodt. Catch. Perfect throw. "Hypothetically, Jin, where is the line between cyborg and—"

Jin chuckled. "My dad and I always talked about that. Machines have augmented human abilities for three million years. Tools outside our bodies, like spears. Then on our bodies, like eyeglasses and prosthetic limbs. Then inside our bodies. Insulin pumps, artificial hearts, dialysis." He laughed to himself. "Shit, my Dad used to complain, but even he shut up eventually."

"What did he say?"

"He said, cyborgs are enhanced humans, with special abilities. Know what we are without technology, Kate? Naked, in a forest, with no hair, and no claws, and no strength to climb trees to get away from the wolf about to eat us. He'd be dead at forty without his insulin pump and titanium knee. It's evolution. Now we put neurochips in our spine and talk directly to machines. Not really different than typing. We've been talking to machines for a hundred years."

Then her phone binged, *just faster and more direct sometimes.* Jin, showing off. She was out of practice with hers. Using a neuroface was a perishable skill, like throwing a ball, and when she didn't practice, it degraded. She didn't remember her Hebrew after twenty years either. Like language, use it or lose it. Sometimes, she muted it or turned it off for weeks at a time because it overstimulated her brain. Too much binging in her head. Jin was big-brained, able to handle a lot more input.

Da-bodt. "Touche."

He said, "People without a neurochip spend so much time on phones and video games, what's the difference?"

Kate rubbed her forehead. "Maybe we are all cyborgs now. I'm a little punchy. How are you feeling?"

"This swinging magnet dick is starting to slough like a lizard. Docbot's instructions were don't scratch, but man does it itch like a mother."

"You need to get some rest."

"10-4. First, do you want the bad news or the bad news?"

Da-bodt. She caught another lowball to the chest. Kate tried a message over her neuroface, *You could just message me.*

"I could."

Kate was surprised that worked the first time.

Jin rubbed his eyes, stretching the bags under them. His skin looked dry and peeling.

"No good news, huh?" *Da-bodt*. Kate caught the ball up high.

"One set of DNA and prints from Kirkwood's apartment. The phone we retrieved is linked to four servers. Nathaniel Kirkwood, Mylah Wilke, Ben Guerra, and Rily Guerra. Nothing ties to the two we arrested on the shuttle."

"So, the names on the passenger manifest weren't aliases?"

"Nope. Biometrics match their NYU IDs. And nothing ties them to Kirkwood or the Darcys."

"I got nothing from the interviews. The man calls himself Nape, short for Napoleon, the woman calls herself Muriel. They asked for their parents and a lawyer, all of which are on the way."

"What kind of names are Nape and Muriel, anyway?"

"They think they are revolutionaries. It's from a book."

"What book?"

"Not important. My grandfather made me read it."

"I should look it up."

"Don't bother. They missed the point of it anyway. Apparently NYU no longer teaches irony." *Da-bodt*. She threw the ball too hard, and it nearly sailed over her.

Jin said, "I set up an algo to backtrack them through surveillance. Apparently they are very familiar with our blind spots. But maybe I'll get lucky."

There were no secrets on the colony, including the colony's blind spots. For some, a selling point. "I'd like to be getting lucky with Rae right now."

Kate winced, realizing she'd said that out loud. Jin looked down at something, then looked back up at the screen. He wasn't paying attention.

"Right. Well, more bad news boss, no chemical residue on their clothes, nor in their apartment at *Gemini*."

"How can two college kids afford to be staying at *Gemini*?"

"The man's mom is a high-level executive for a battery company. The woman's dad invented some device for cosmetic surgery."

"So, where does that leave us?"

"Civil penalty for being unruly passengers and spaceline property destruction and a basket of maybes. Still working the finances." Jin rubbed his whole face, lingering over his eyes, then yawned. "Maybe these two are copycats."

Kate nodded. "Any hits on Kirkwood?" *Da-bodt.* The ball bounced left, nearly knocking over her coffee.

"What's that sound?"

"What sound?"

"Like a ball bouncing."

"Practicing my moonball. Keeps me awake."

"Moonball?"

"Like handball squash, on the moon." *Any hits on Kirkwood.*

Jin's eyes widened, like he got shocked. Kate rarely communicated with Jin over the neuroface. For some people it felt intimate and intrusive. It was probably a mistake. Jin could program a bot to barrage her brain with jokes. It would be like having her brother in her head, constantly pranking her cortex. A huge mistake.

"You'll love this. He was watching our office from Lunaburger when the bomb went off."

"Please tell me we tracked him."

"I tracked him topside."

Fucking hell. Colony surveillance was spotty. Surface surveillance was zero.

"Don't worry boss. I've got the airlocks monitored. He can't come back without us knowing."

"Good work."

"I am still working on getting the data from his phone. Some of it's strange. He had his neurochip removed."

"Can that be done?"

"Sure. If you like brain aneurysms and strokes. But his problems predate that. He's been institutionalized a few times. We need someone who can interpret these medical records. There are a lot of big words in here."

"Send them to Rae."

"But—"

"You can trust her."

"Rae's office is still processing all the DNA from the wedding. Good news. From the wedding, we did get one unmatched DNA profile that shares fifty percent with Helena Darcy and fifty percent with Nolan Darcy. But it's male, not Leyna."

Kate took her feet off her desk and leaned forward. "Dilan Darcy. Shit."

"His DNA. Not him, at least not on video anywhere. He is not on a single frame of colony surveillance as far back as I can run. And it's four-thousand-four-hundred kilometers to IIRAS far side station where he worked."

"His DNA was at the wedding."

"Not a lot. Could have been a transfer. Maybe Helena had one of his things."

"Or maybe he's one of the protestors. Kirkwood had a drawing of him."

"With a question mark. A theory. No biometrics to—"

Jin's eyes drooped, and he yawned again. Kate fought off her yawn.

"Go home and rest, Jin. Let the algorithms run while you sleep."

"I can't sleep with all this itching."

"Go home, Jin."

"I am sleeping here. Night."

Jin hung up. She imagined him trying to stay awake, then passing out and his head hitting Rae's old aluminum desk. Jin was right. Sleeping was going to be difficult. Protestors were still on the colony somewhere, and one was likely Dilan Darcy. But she had reached the point where caffeine was ineffective. So it was either catch a few hours of sleep or take amp. Amp had side effects, like rage. No one needed to see her rage—except the protestors that bombed her office.

She checked the spaceport departure schedule and then cycled through video feeds of the main airlocks. Entry required biometrics. Now that they had Kirkwood's profile, alarms and locks would trigger when he entered. She wanted to let Kirkwood run out of oxygen and die. She also wanted to find the connection to Dilan Darcy. Her gut told her she was still not seeing the whole elephant. She saw a foot, leg, and an eye, but not yet the entire animal.

The next shuttle departed in fourteen hours. There were no private charters scheduled. She could afford to pick up the hunt after a rem sleep cycle. She messaged Rae *omw home* and a heart. Rae responded with an image of her lying in bed, naked, surrounded by roses floating in the air. The roses were a holographic sticker, but Rae's lust looked genuine. Maybe she wouldn't be getting sleep after all. Kate left in such a hurry she was fortunate the colony's artificial intelligence automatically shut off her office lights and locked the door.

35

Rily's whine was identical to Ben's, except one octave higher. "Isn't it better if we all go together—"

"Definitely not, Rily."

Mylah said, "You saw the violence on the shuttle. That savage Devana assaulted our brothers and sisters standing up against machine violence. She stood by as a drone attacked another of us. The machines are raping our freedom and she's enabling it."

Machine violence. Raping our freedom. Since the protest, Mylah always sounded like she was giving a damn speech. Rily's voice irritated him too, like what he imagined tinnitus to sound like.

Behind Nate, white and silver p-suits and EVA suits hung from the gray walls, ready to use for members of the private spaceport. Outside the door behind Rily, the spaceport's maintenance hangar. To the right, the room where Mylah had snatched the rocket fuel for the bomb. This room smelled like burnt metal. From somewhere outside, a metal grinding noise as a maintenance drone repaired someone's billion-dollar space yacht.

The heart of the machine beast. Which wouldn't beat much longer.

Rily said, "I don't want to be smuggled home. They might force me to—"

Nate saw it in Mylah's face, *so that's where you draw the line, bitch.* A punch would follow. He shook his head, trying to stop her. To tell her *not worth it.* He said, "The smuggler will contact you in a few days. You are posing as—posing as tourists sneaking home."

Nate didn't think it sounded believable. He and Mylah hadn't got this far in planning. But, he only needed them to go along long enough to allow him to skip this rock. He hoped he didn't have to resort to killing Ben and Rily on the spot.

Rily said, "We should go back with you on the ship you're stealing. You'll have plenty of room."

On the one hand, they would be dead either way. On the other hand, they might stop him.

"No. We have to split up. You saw what happened on the shuttle. They are looking for four people."

"But—"

"If we all get arrested together when we land, it's over." Nate glanced behind Rily through the door at a giant gray rocket stretched out under maintenance. "We need to go before our luck runs out."

Ben said, "I told you staying this long was a bad idea."

He never said that. But whatever. Ben's luck had already run out.

Mylah said, "No risk, no reward. Move to the *Aurora* for a few days. It has the most privacy. Check in under new names."

Ben said, "Got it. Anything else?"

As implausible as the story was, Ben was convinced. Nate wanted to crack, *how about go back in time, and convince Rily not to sabotage the bomb.*

Instead, he looked at Mylah, raising his eyebrows and inhaling. "Nope. Be safe everyone. I love you all and see you when I see you—on Earth." Nate added the last words as an afterthought, hoping it sounded less like his final goodbye.

Mylah leaned in for a hug and a kiss. She lingered almost long enough to make him change his mind.

He whispered in her ear. "I want a statue. A big one."

She kissed his cheek and whispered back. "The biggest. Bigger than the Statue of Liberty."

Mylah held his hand, smiling with her eyes, and backed away. "I am so proud of you." She dropped his hand, backed up a few more steps, then turned. He watched her walk past someone's rocket towards the hangar door. Ben and Rily waved goodbye and followed.

Silence. The grinding in the hangar had stopped. The door closed behind Ben and Rily. Then a drone's servos whirred, coming nearer. Hard to tell what direction because it echoed off the metal walls. A black maintenance drone the size of a dog appeared from behind a rack of tools, glided across the floor parallel to the rocket, then disappeared around the corner.

He sighed. Silence again.

He expected to be arrested yesterday. His phantom neuroface had been whispering to him that if they came and arrested him, then it would be proof that humans on this colony could be saved. He wanted to believe it. But it was just another hallucination. In his dream he killed them all. Now he would for real.

He spun and pondered which p-suit to don. Two silver-white suits hung on the wall, *DEVANA*, and *TORRES*. His game of *eenie, meenie, miny, moe* ended with DEVANA so he took Devana's helmet.

A voice behind him giggled. "What are you doing?"

Nate laughed. "Should we close the door in case they come back?"

"They are trotting down the concourse to the *Aurora*. I think Ben is excited to gamble."

Nate shook his head, turning the traitor's helmet over, looking for a way to activate it. "This place. To be honest, I thought we would have to kill them here."

Mylah put her hand on Nate's chest and leaned in to whisper on his lips. "You will. All of them. I only wish I could see it." She kissed him.

"You go get Dilan then don't look back."

"Or I'll be turned into salt?"

"Something like that." Then, pulling away, "How the fuck do I turn this on?"

Mylah grabbed the helmet and hung it back up. "You need her neuroface."

Right, made sense that Devana was secretly a cyborg. Then Mylah grabbed the helmet labeled TORRES and handed it to him.

"Let the traitor's wife watch you kill everyone."

Nate dropped the helmet and ran his hand over Mylah's midsection "We have about twenty minutes while you wait."

Her peppermint breath and tongue tasted good inside his mouth. Her coconut shampoo and hair in his face. She was soft, warm, her arms around him. He slipped his hand under her sweater, at the small of her back, inside her panties. He pictured the violence coming. Mylah kicked the door closed behind her.

36

Kate caught one rem sleep cycle, tossed and turned, then found herself back in her office, watching a video of a man and a woman at the private spaceport lounge. They were the agents that had been hovering outside the critical care wing of the hospital.

Jin spent the night in Rae's office, guarding Leyna. She hoped he was sleeping—if that was possible. His last few messages bordered rambling, which he blamed on itching-caused insomnia. Jin's final message four hours ago was *itching stopped. sleep here,* along with a barrage of surveillance clips and live telemetry of the agents.

Fifteen minutes into the third video, Kate decided the two agents needed names. As the woman agent exited the *Cygnus* fifth-floor elevator and walked down the sea-salt green corridor, Kate recognized the slight limp of an improperly healed ACL injury. Kate had the same injury, although thankfully, hers had recovered fully. She got lucky in orthopedic care. Once with advanced VA surgical bots, and then a few more times with a motivating and busty blond physical therapist that stretched her hamstrings.

So Kate named the woman Gimp. Kate decided the partner was Simp because Gimp dragged him everywhere. Through the casino. Into a hotel lounge. They returned to the hospital, talked to a nurse, and then sped for *Cygnus* as fast as Gimp's knee allowed. Gimp went into the elevators first, and Gimp came out first. No matter how slow Gimp walked, Simp was always one deferential step behind. But Simp wasn't a stingless drone following his queen. At the elevators, when he leaned forward, Kate saw a large firearm hanging out of his pressed blue suit. Kate had no doubt that if Gimp shouted sting, Simp would sting.

Kate wished she had audio as she watched Gimp and Simp walk to the Darcy's apartment. At the door, Simp's back was to the camera, behind Gimp, who faced the door as Nolan opened it. Gimp's hands moved and pointed inside. She read *no* on Nolan's lips, then he shut the door. Kate fast-forwarded to the end of the tape and watched them hobble away triple time.

In the following video, timestamped five minutes later, Gimp and Simp walked into the Apus lounge, to the elevator, then to a room. Jin had overlayed a red circle on the room number, four nineteen.

Later, in a video timestamped a half hour later, the other two agents from Jin's hospital room exited *Apus* room four seventeen. Number one said his name, but she couldn't remember it. Number two had a bloody red gauze on his nose and upper lip that looked packed and taped by an amateur. His boozy breath at the hospital still stunk in her nose. His nose would heal well. They'd said they had a doctor for Leyna, but she knew that was a lie.

The video cut off as they left the *Apus*. She picked them up a few minutes later, hovering underneath her office window, debating. The video was too grainy for the lip-reading AI to make out words, but they pointed at her window repeatedly. Kate checked the timestamp. That conversation happened five hours and twenty minutes ago.

Kate paused the video to check the protestors. On the wall monitor feed, they looked bored but well-fed. Most importantly, they were still in her jail.

When she restarted the video, agent number one won the debate. The bloody, poorly taped pad and broken nose silenced number two's objections, and he looked resigned. They turned, circled into the hospital, and then talked to two nurses. Instead of leaving, they wandered around the hospital. Kate fast-forwarded. At quad speed, they peered behind curtains, in the supply closet, the laundry room, and the break room. They rechecked more curtains, went to the second floor to check rooms, and exited.

Kate smiled. They were looking for Leyna. But she wasn't there.

Five minutes later, they strolled into Cygnus. They meandered through the complex, peeking into the lounge, the gym, the media room, and finally, the pool. Still looking for Leyna. Ha. Rae was a genius.

That's right, Leyna was reported dead, stashed where dead people were supposed to be.

Then they exited the fifth-floor elevator, stopping to debate in front of a picture of a schooner docked at a seaside resort. They faced each other, so, once again, AI could not read lips. Number two kept pointing at the painting, so Kate imagined them headed somewhere. Not soon enough for her. At the end of an animated argument, their arms flopped to their sides. Then they turned and continued towards the Darcys apartment door. Kenna opened the door this time. A few seconds later, Kenna wagged her finger and yelled at them. Kenna's lips and shaking finger were unequivocal, *don't ever come back*. She pointed down the hall, then stepped back and slammed the lunar resin door so hard Kate jerked at the imaginary bang and crack. Good for her.

Kate fast-forwarded. They returned to their Apus room with the tense, dejected frowns of a failed mission.

Kate opened the final video clip and sat back in her chair. The four agents moved through the private spaceport's lounge. On the skybridge, a fifth person joined the boarding party. A man, walking away from the camera, putting his helmet on. The five of them talked. The man turned and looked straight at the camera. The skybridge reflected in his closed visor. Kate felt the dare, the leer, and the grin. Kate chuckled under her breath, *you're the one leaving empty-handed.* All five turned and walked to a ship together, *Beam Six*. Kate rolled back the video. No way to ID the man. She froze the surveillance video, got out her moonball, and tossed it in the air.

Based on the live telemetry, these five were now a third of the way to Earth. Telemetry projected them headed to группа 6 (*Gruppa 6*), a Russian party station in high Earth orbit.

At the spaceport lounge, Kate recognized the worn, detached facial expressions. She wore that look many times. She pegged them as contractors, like her not so long ago. Number five was likely their handler.

Kate tossed the ball and smiled because Jin made a perfect pitch. Kate was a contractor for three years, so she knew the game and played it well. On группа 6, there was no NCO in the next cabin telling them to pipe down or an agency Director worried about a public relations disaster. She imagined that right now, the party of five was fast asleep on *Beam*

Six, dreaming about how to spend their paycheck. A few hours from now, they would wake, and the drinking would start. By the time they got to their cabins on группа 6, they would be too hammered to care about the trackers Jin slipped into their luggage. Later, the prostitutes might find them while going through belongings for something to steal. But on группа 6, the golden rule was *a gun walks behind the snitch.* группа 6 docking protocol disabled eyesight and clipped tongues.

With the agents leaving, she could concentrate on investigating Helena Darcy's murder and the bomb.

Kate realized she'd been humming and had her feet on the desk when she felt eyes peering through her open door. Another pressed blue suit with closely cropped brown hair, wearing polished suede flats, and flashing her badge and credentials. Special Agent Milya Bolkov. Back for round two.

Kate tried not to make eye contact. She could think of seven reasons not to let her in. Like Nolan slammed the door on her, she should slam the door on Bolkov.

Kate bounced the ball around the room, pretending to ignore Bolkov.

Bolkov didn't flinch. She stepped in, her left hand came up and forward and she caught it. Kate closed the desk drawer with her gun, wondering whether she was unnecessarily edgy. If Bolkov wanted to shoot her, she'd be dead.

Bolkov's eyes first ogled Kate's office. Then the four displays with the contractor's faces.

"Play moonball, Mia?"

"I do."

"We should play sometime."

"I came here hoping not to play games with you." Bolkov tossed the ball back and stepped into Kate's office. A decent pitch.

"If you came here to talk to the protestors we arrested—"

"—they lawyered up. I know. Although I saw they talked your ear off anyway."

"Sadly, I wish they had shut up. To them, anyone with a chip implant is a cyborg and a traitor to humanity. We are all apparently letting the machines control us. I learned seven new slurs and got called a goldback. Maybe more, I lost track. Waste of time."

"Copycats?"

"Think so. Of the entitled rich variety. Parents are importing a human lawyer all the way from Earth."

Kate's eyes returned to the frozen contractors' faces on her wall displays.

Bolkov eyed them. "Not ours."

"Would you tell me if they were?"

"I am one of the good girls. You might even say I've been sent as your guardian angel."

Kate shook her head. She would never say that.

"Gaby Cruz sent me. She said to tell you she likes to come home to a clean house."

Gaby. On a first-name basis with Defense Secretary Cruz, using the code *clean house* for a mission they worked together to root out a mole at the Pentagon.

"She said you would understand the message."

The message, *you can trust this one.*

"She told me to share everything we had on Dilan Darcy." Bolkov retrieved her phone, swiped through it, then Kate's phone *binged.*

Kate opened her phone to an encrypted file with an orange and yellow cover and red capitalized words. It was a felony for her to read further. Bolkov looked at Kate's phone and waved her finger, signaling to swipe.

Swiping was going to cost her. Prison time. She would owe a politico for it. Worse than all that, Bolkov would expect to partner up to solve the case.

"What's in it?"

Bolkov looked aside. "Every communication bounced off the IIRAS station feed."

Finally, something useful out of their illegal surveillance.

"Did you read it?"

"Every word."

And she still couldn't solve it. So, there was a piece missing. Kate opened it. She'd written enough intelligence reports to know this one on Dilan Darcy was bona fide. But it was long, and she'd need Jin to parse keywords to distill it.

"My partner will need to see this."

"I sent him a copy."

While Kate skimmed it, Bolkov's eyes monitored her from the edge of her desk.

"Says the agency was trying to get Ted Holden to roll back software. What's that about?"

"Holden was Dilan's boyfriend. They lived together on the station. He did something that threw flags and gave the techs fits. Above my pay grade. We caught an argument between the Darcy kid, his boyfriend Ted, and their boss arguing over a software upgrade. But, prevailing theory is they sabotaged the station."

"Fake images?"

"Techs don't think so."

"Don't *think* so?"

"That's a tech question. But apparently the raw data to prove it went missing."

Kate replayed the video of Bill Caddell and Kody Easton in her head. Caddell said he deleted data. "Went missing? I am not a techie, but I think the term is deleted."

"You never know with this agency. It may turn up on someone's computer two years from now. For sale to the highest bidder."

"Could Dilan Darcy have it?"

"Anyone *could* have it. My grandmother believes in bigfoot. He *could* exist." Bolkov looked at the contractors. "A mystery I can't wrap my brain around. If Dilan Darcy faked the images, he'd want the data out there to prove it. But if the images are real, why hide the data? It's like someone doesn't want the agency to confirm the images are real. Which makes no sense."

"Mmm. What about his threats. They in here?"

"If they came from the station, he encrypted them, and we didn't pick it up."

"Bill Caddell claims Dilan Darcy was messaging Earth First. He was getting fired for it."

Bolkov shrugged. "If so, also encrypted."

"How about Helena? Did she have access to the data? Maybe had a copy?"

"Helena Darcy was a veteran of the agency. Knew all the ins and outs. And this was her baby. If anyone had a basement copy of the data, she did. But again, why hide it?"

"But you don't think the son killed the mother."

"He did something. The agency was unhappy about it, and he was getting fired for it. And it involved his mother. Maybe related to the data. But to travel thousands of kilometers to kill your mother?"

"Don't forget Leyna and Paul."

Bolkov contemplated the wall again.

"But you don't know what *it* is?"

Bolkov shook her head.

"His sister Leyna blames her brother. Says he was troubled."

"Said that?"

"When I went to interview his parents, Nolan said, *the four of us are a family.* Not the six of us. Like the kids are a nuisance. Dilan was enough trouble that they put him in a prison on the far side of the moon. Nolan slammed the door in my face."

"Not a prison. They volunteered. But I get your point. Helena Darcy slammed the door in my face too."

"This family is hiding something and dying over it."

Kate studied Bolkov's face. Agent Bolkov was hiding something, too.

"Could he have smuggled himself here?"

"Those two were good at manipulating the supply logs. They could have smuggled a bear to the station and back."

"I like him for this. His own sister fingered him. His DNA was there. He's had a lot of time to plan this. He's using Nathaniel Kirkwood and these protestors to kill his family."

"To kill his own mother."

"You said it. IIRAS was Helena Darcy's baby. Like—sibling rivalry. But this doesn't say how he got here. Or when. Or most importantly, where he is now."

In the messages to his mother, Dilan Darcy said he would smuggle himself off the station. But how hard could it be to confirm that? Or find him on the colony? Something was staring her in the face. She could feel it just out of reach.

Bolkov turned and stepped to the door.

Kate said, "Thank you. What am I going to owe you for this?"

Bolkov smiled, the marionette lines at the corner of her mouth struggling to lift after years of frowning. Then she pointed to Kate's wall monitor. "I'll get you names of those clowns too."

"Really. I figured you would already know."

"Some other agency." Bolkov retrieved her phone and snapped an image of the contractors. On the way through the threshold, Bolkov's eyes surveyed Kate's office with the same eagerness as on the way in.

"We'll make a good team."

Wonderful. Now Bolkov thought they were a team.

37

Kate bolted upright in bed picturing Kirkwood's drawing of *The Orionids*, the hairs on her arms and neck standing like needles. Her heartbeat pounded in her ears over the sounds of Scar purring and Rae sleeping. In *The Orionids*, he drew a spaceship hurtling towards the dome.

Fuck, she was late. She got up as quietly as she could, dressed, and left. On the way she messaged Jin. He was already in the office and had started the *Tesseract's* fueling cycle. He was thinking the same thing she was.

Kirkwood wasn't coming back.

In the office, Jin was standing at his desk, holding a mug of coffee, and dressed in jeans and a tight green shirt. He looked tanned. If she didn't know better, she might think he had fallen asleep at the beach instead of being burned by caustic rocket fuel. If they had this medical tech when her parents were killed, she would have smooth skin on her left arm instead of a sleeve tattoo over a scar. On the other hand, she would not want modern medicine to peel away her parents' memory. Not even the bad ones.

"How are you feeling?"

"Amazing. The itching stopped. This is what it must feel like to be a snake after it sheds. I'm ready to go bite some shit."

Like-new Jade sat beside his desk and wagged her tail. New Jade, or old Jade with new fur? Impossible to tell the difference.

Kate caught a whiff of maple syrup and sausage. Her stomach grumbled so loudly that Jin paused, furrowed his brow, eyeing her midsection. Better not to eat before flight.

"Kirkwood is not coming back."

"I had the same thought. We had two liftoffs in the last twenty four hours from the private spaceport. One, *Beam Six*, the other a private yacht *Nanosail*. Reported stolen."

"Where is *Beam Six*?"

"Telemetry shows them stopping at IIRAS far side station for two hours eighteen minutes. Now they are almost to the Russian space station."

"Why would they do that?" A rhetorical statement she didn't expect Jin to know.

Jin ran his hands over his head. "It's fucking dark on that side of the moon. They must be insane. You think they went to pick up Dilan Darcy and his boyfriend Ted?"

On the colony's surface, the sun was nearly at noon—The Earth-facing side illuminated at ninety-four percent to be precise—which put the IIRAS far-side station in near total darkness. The kind Earthers hadn't experienced in one-hundred-seventy years because of light pollution.

Even a seasoned pilot could screw up a night lunar landing. Like trying to soft land a submarine on the bottom of the ocean. A lot could go wrong even with the best radar, lidar, UV, and AI. The rocky, uneven surface changed every time a meteor hit. There were unmapped gravity anomalies that could throw the ship off course. The cold night conditions could freeze and glitch the sensors, make them misjudge the distance to the surface.

A nice easy death would be to run out of fuel and free fall, becoming an impact crater. A few seconds to contemplate death. Miss the landing pad, break a landing strut, or scrape an engine, the ship would be stranded thousands of kilometers from people with about nine hours of oxygen. A lifetime to contemplate your stupidity while suffocating.

And for anyone dumb enough to take a night stroll, the Lunar Positioning System, LPS, was unreliable on the moon's far side, unless you had access to proprietary satellites. If you got lost, the ships lights might look like nothing more than starlight or a ship in orbit. While her military EVA suit had a backup celestial navigation system, most civilian EVA suits wouldn't, and, modern Earthers could barely see the stars, let alone navigate by them.

Kate shook her head. "Dilan Darcy comes here, then goes back? I can see him coming here. I can't see him going back. I'd be on the first ride to Earth. Or Mars."

"They are cleaning something up?"

Kate was still not seeing things clearly. The contractors wanted Leyna. Dilan Darcy and Nathaniel Kirkwood wanted her dead. Were the two connected? "Maybe something Leyna knows, that's why they wanted her. Or the agency is hiding its dirt."

"Hiding dirt?"

"The agency hired Dilan Darcy. Maybe knowing he's a big risk. Now he's become a terrorist and they want to hide the connection. Maybe bully Leyna into silence. Then go erase the evidence."

As she said it, she shook her head. It didn't resonate. "We have trackers on the contractors?"

Jin grinned and looked at his phone. Two videos opened on the wall screens. "Four second delay because I had to bounce it through a bunch of servers."

One video view was of a dance club. Red square frames tracked the agents from Jin's hospital room, who were half naked, holding drinks high and squirming. Two naked women, covered in blue and purple glitter, danced beside them, undoubtedly interested in their money, not the black and yellow facial bruise on one and the other's clumsy spasms. She recognized the club. It was on группа 6, which spun fast enough to simulate one-third of Earth's gravity. Enough to dance but not enough to dampen their awkward jerking. She shook her head. She could smell the watered-down drinks, vape, and sleaze oozing through the video feed.

The second video was of Gimp and Simp at a booth in the corner, faces framed with overlapping red squares. Gimp was holding Simp's face, smashing her lips into his, with her bad leg wrapped around him. Gimp's knee was remarkably healed and ready for action.

Kate shuddered and waved the screens closed. "Don't miss that place. How?"

"Do you want to know any more than, I hacked the группа 6 surveillance?"

She didn't.

"Good work. Stays in this office."

On the wall monitor, *Tesseract's* operational screen read nineteen minutes to liftoff. *Nanosail* was in a parking orbit.

"Jin try to get into *Nanosail* controls. Let's talk and walk over to *Tesseract.*"

Jin grinned. "I love a good chase. Can we board him in orbit?"

"Kirkwood doesn't plan to escape."

Jin frowned.

"The drawing he made. Of the rocket slamming into the dome."

"Oh. Shit. He could kill everyone in here."

"Not if we stop it."

"I was going to tell you the other good news. I linked Dilan Darcy to Earth First. He sent them a lot of money around the end of last month. Before Kirkwood arrived."

The evidence against Dilan Darcy was piling up.

"We know when Kirkwood arrived?"

"We do. His prints scanned boarding. And I caught him on surveillance."

"But not Kirkwood's pals, Mylah and the others."

"No. But once we have their prints, we'll get them too. Also in Kirkwood's messages, I found access codes and some plans."

"Now all we need to do is find this fucker."

38

Kate fidgeted with her helmet and ran her hands along *Tesseract's* white leather armrests. With the Presidential visit rumored canceled, her list of demands was also canceled, including the new ride she'd requested. Was she disappointed?

To her right, Jin growled and poked at the dashboard display. A countdown clock and propellant gauge ticked on the dash monitor so slowly she could probably recite all two-hundred-sixty-three pages of the Marine Corp Uniform Regulation in the nine minutes and eleven ... ten ... nine ... seconds remaining. Twice. Or stuff two hot lunashrimp baskets down her gullet. Although it was never a good idea to eat before a rocket ride.

On the way over, Jin's algorithm alerted. Kirkwood had been active on his server and the messages indicated Ben and Rily Guerra were holed up in the *Aurora*, a hotel teeming with security and surveillance. She sent Bolkov to pick them up. She hated to admit it, but it was good to have help and be in two places at once. Not that she trusted Bolkov any farther than she could kick her. If Kate hadn't been able to record every microsecond of Bolkov's imminent raid from eleven different angles, she'd have had a dilemma.

Staring out into the lunar sky waiting for the ship to fuel, she felt the stars staring back at her again. Why hole up in the *Aurora*? A distraction? Maybe both of them were on *Nanosail*. Maybe all of them. Seven minutes and twenty six seconds and damn, she wished this rocket would fuel faster. Her gut said she was missing something more than fried battered protein in her stomach.

Jin cussed and leaned forward, revealing the red racing stripe down the back of his white seat. *Tesseract* was not only thirsty but fickle. He cursed again, then jabbed his dashboard touchscreen.

"This ship doesn't want to recognize my neuroface today."

Jin puffed his cheeks, exhaled, and sat back. *Nanosail's* telemetry appeared on the dashboard screen. Kate's neuroface seemed to be working fine.

She opened the ship's specs on her heads-up display to read through. "Owned by Mauro Wofford?"

"Mining executive. No connection to the protestors." He tapped the screen. "They hacked the registry to rename it *Orionids.*"

"This is a weekend cabin cruiser. One chemical engine, five seats, and barely enough fuel to get them to a retrograde lunar orbit and back."

Kate zoomed out to look for potential supply stations it could use to refuel and hop.

Nothing. It wouldn't have enough fuel to transfer to Earth orbit. Domestic terrorists parked in orbit with nothing to lose made her neck tingle.

The only move was to return to the colony. Likely as a missile.

As the countdown hit six minutes and ten seconds, two things happened. First, *Tesseract's* fuel bar hit eighty-nine percent. And next, *Nanosail's* green waypoint started to move. Deorbiting. Fuck.

"What are the odds we can get a message to *Nanosail*, or better yet, take control?"

"Zero. We are locked out. I tried."

The fuel bar passed ninety percent. Kate reset the countdown to thirty seconds. Then she dismissed the fueling drones. *Clunk-clunk* reverberated in the cabin as the fueling drones unlocked.

"Strap in. I have control."

Kate heard Jin's restraints click. "Confirm you have control."

"*Tesseract* is in final countdown."

"All systems polled green. Except—"

Kate turned her helmet to look at Jin.

"Except I am going to regret breakfast, aren't I?"

He couldn't see her smiling under the helmet visor. *Tesseract's* engines ignited and rumbled. She weighed four times her Earth weight. She could only move her eyes enough to see Jin in her peripheral vision. The skin around her eyes and mouth stretched into an uncomfortably wide grin. Yes, she would miss *Tesseract*. A new ship wouldn't have its oversize racing engines. Plus, if she was going to die today—a fair chance given *Nanosail's* changing trajectory—she'd rather die in these double-padded seats. Four g's felt like a back rub in these.

"Kate—"

Her name sounded guttural. She couldn't lift her arms. She zoomed the telemetry with her neuroface. *Tesseract's* red line was closing the distance on *Nanosail* while *Nanosail's* green arc blinked, recalculating each half second.

Kate. Jin messaging through his neuroface.

Copy. See it.

Kate throttled the engines. *Nanosail* had become a moving target. This was why domestic terrorists in orbit made her nervous.

Her stomach tightened. What goes up must come down, and *Nanosail's* trajectory was now coming down hard, its periapsis dropping two-forty, two-thirty, two-twenty. Yeah, she knew where this was headed.

Why aren't the ship's computers auto-correcting?

Get control of that ship.

Working. Then he messaged, *They don't understand orbital mechanics.*

They understood it. Jin reacted the same way she did the first time she saw it. The mind knew the terrorist plan, yet registered disbelief. Asks, what was killing twenty thousand people going to solve? Three million years of technology, still humans were the problem.

Nanosail's line now intersected with the moon's surface and started scraping across it. Then another dot blinked on the telemetry.

She adjusted *Tesseract's* trajectory to intersect twenty kilometers ahead of where she expected *Nanosail* to hit the surface.

Kate pointed at the red dot. *Rae's p-suit?*

Stole it.

Can you hack her suit video?

Jin spoke, "No. You asked me to upgrade the security."

Well, that was a dumb idea.

"Good thing I left a backdoor." She felt his grin under the visor.

Jin routed Rae's helmet video to a corner of the dash monitor. All they could see was the console dash. *Tesseract's* acceleration tapered off.

"Can you get sound?"

Jin maxed Rae's helmet volume.

Kate said, "I don't hear anything. Blast a message. Tell them to divert."

The camera bobbled. Jin blasted the message again. A blinking light on the telemetry screen indicated *Nanosail's* thrusters had fired. The green dot slowed its scrape across the surface.

Kate already knew where *Nanosail* was going. Enough of the console was visible to see Kirkwood wasn't tracking them.

The red and green arc finally intersected, and a collision alarm sounded.

"Are we really doing this, Kate?"

"Not if you can get control of the ship. If he crashes that rocket into a colony dome, he'll kill twenty thousand people."

Maybe more.

"Maybe he'll miss."

He wouldn't. Unless they collided. She wanted to say to Jin, *on the bright side, we wouldn't feel the impact*. There was no abort or ejection in this ship, nor a way to jump at the last minute. Not traveling ten times the speed of a bullet and with no atmosphere to make a parachute useful. Although it wouldn't be a horrible way to go. Like jumping over water, there were no visual cues for altitude. Just gravel everywhere. With no rushing wind. Like floating, then splat.

No, actually, she didn't want to say that to Jin at all.

He said, "Maybe they'll name an impact crater after me." Then after a pause, "Fuck. I need to get control of that ship."

Kate broadcasted a colony emergency message and then messaged Rae, *I love you.* She heard the message ping in Rae's helmet on the other ship.

She removed her right glove and pressed her thumb to the dash monitor, disabling the collision avoidance alarms and adjusting their speed. This part needed manual confirmation. Her chest and head gained sixty kilos. Then seventy. Then eighty. Her torso compressed against the seat cushion, and her skin stretched. She forced herself to breathe rapidly, sucking air as if from a straw. Between breaths, she squeezed her thighs and listened for Jin's breathing. *Three... four...*

five... Then her weight dropped a hundred kilos, and she listed left as *Tesseract's* thrusters gimballed. Her right shoulder restraint pinched, and her head bounced against the seat. Then weightless again.

"Jin, you with me?"

Life support shut down. He meant *Nanosail's*. Then, *Boom. Airlock blown. Maybe throw it off enough to miss.*

It did. *Tesseract's* computer recalculated *Nanosail's* trajectory. The green circle moved away from the colony. *Nanosail* was tumbling too. In the helmet cam, no one was at the console to adjust trajectory. Jin exhaled and pumped his fist.

"Lunar civilian craft Romeo Hotel Two One Six, this is Ride Base Control. Contact two five nine."

Fucking finally, the military base acknowledging their existence over the coms. Kate smiled. When Aria gave her the *Tesseract* and told her to use it as a cruiser, Kate got to pick the call sign. She met Rae on February sixteenth, so she chose Two One Six. Of course, at the time, she thought this was a temporary gig. She responded, "Romeo Hotel Two One Six switching to two five nine, copy."

"Tango Two One Six, we have you on a collision course. Stand down and maintain separation at twenty-five kilometers."

They weren't on a collision course now, thanks to Jin. Stand down. Ha. She said, "Better late than never, right Ride Base?"

"Tango Two One Six, keep this channel clear. Repeat, stand down and maintain separation at twenty-five kilometers."

Right, no snide comments over the coms. AI has a better sense of humor than military aircraft controllers. Whatever. The elephant on her chest had lifted, so she changed course. *Nanosail* wasn't going to collide with the colony, and they weren't going to collide with it.

"Tango Two One Six, Wilco. Maintaining separation." She adjusted course to fly over *Nanosail* and felt the thrusters obey.

"I've got *Nanosail* cameras onscreen, Kate—Oh. Oh shit." Jin brought up the interior of *Nanosail* to an empty cockpit and cabin.

A new dot appeared on telemetry, moving fast. Out the window, a streak, then a flare and burst. *Nanosail's* feeds became white noise on the dash. The ship vanished with the new dot.

"The fuck just happened, Kate?"

Kate switched camera angles to see a debris field splashing on the moon's gray surface like so many raindrops on beach sand. "Ride Base, this is Tango Two One Six. Splash one. Bullseye. Next beer is on me."

"Roger Two One Six, you're buying. Ahh—General Briggs wants to know if you got a recording?"

Kate looked at Jin. He shook his head.

"Negative, Ride Base. Not a fucking thing." Then she muted the channel.

"They just shot down *Nanosail,* Kate."

They did.

"I blew the airlock, it would have missed."

Also true. Although, Kirkwood could have compensated if he'd been wearing Rae's p-suit. Or on the ship. Ride Base wouldn't know unless they caught the disturbing cabin video. Jin's adrenaline would crash soon, and then he would realize the most unsettling part of the video was that the cabin was empty.

Kirkwood and his crew could have been at the airlock when he blew it and sucked out. Or thrown out as *Nanosail* tumbled. All possible but unlikely. The darkness outside the cockpit ridiculed her. Sneered at her. Her gut had a horrible explanation for *Nanosail's* empty cabin: Kirkwood wasn't on it. Her gut said Kirkwood was still out there plotting, and that he'd bring back fresh recruits and try again.

The far side station needed to be her next stop. *Beam Six* stopped there, Dilan Darcy worked there, and Helena Darcy worked for the agency that ran the station. That station was the connection, and she needed to see it. The face in the blackness outside the cockpit, she could almost see it, hiding in the shadows of IIRAS station.

Kate puffed her cheeks and set course for the far side. *Tesseract* beeped at her because the route she wanted would burn too much fuel. She calculated a more fuel-efficient arc—adding an hour to the round trip—and punched it in.

She exhaled, leaned back, and looked at Jin. "Think they have supplies back there? I could use a drink."

Jin unclicked his restraints. "Feels like a vodka moment to me."

"I'll drink whatever you find back there."

Jin nodded and got up from his seat. After he disappeared into the cabin, she took off her p-suit helmet. Her breath was short, shallow, her adrenaline now dumping into tears. She pictured Rae curled up under covers, her curves silhouetted, her auburn hair spilled onto the pillows, with Kate running fingers down Rae's back and reassuring her it was just someone else's bad dream. But over now.

She let the tears stream, then wiped her eyes and opened the dash camera in selfie mode to check herself. Her skin looked another shade paler than in this morning's bathroom light. Her brown eyes looked darker, eyes sunken. At least she hadn't worn makeup or mascara, so nothing smeared. She took a breath and practiced a smile, making sure to dab the moisture. Her eyes looked puffy. One more fake smile, another deep breath, then she closed the selfie camera and opened a video call to Rae.

39

On *Tesseract's* dashboard drone feed, *Tesseract's* landing lights cut the moon's rocky regolith in black-and-white relief. Ghostly pewter shadow-aliens with pitch-dark grins danced and yawned as the drone's light skated across impact craters. Without light, the sky and the surface were indistinguishable obsidian, and it was cold—the thermal read minus one-hundred-thirteen Celsius. Their position was holding steady at five hundred meters over the surface.

When Kate imagined death, she pictured the moon at night. Humanity's newest graveyard was also its oldest. Meteors, comets, spacecraft, and maybe billion-year-old alien artifacts were dead and buried in those impact craters, never to be found.

Tesseract could be next.

"All I am saying, boss, is they didn't have to shoot."

They did. She didn't respond. She went through the same thing her first deployment. There was no way to know whether Kirkwood had programmed *Nanosail* to compensate for the airlock bursting.

Kate exhaled and concentrated on the video feed, scouring it for the smallest rock—or booby trap—that would damage the ship and strand her and Jin four thousand kilometers from civilization. Maybe for another billion years.

Jin spun the drone to pan the heavy-lift side of the IIRAS landing pad, used for rockets as large as *Tesseract*. Wisps of dry ice sublimed into a fog as the light heated the pad's aluminum pipes and scaffolding.

"All green. Nothing on IR or UV here." Jin paused and looked at the stars outside the cockpit window. "They had no idea what was happening. It could have been an accident. Or amateur mis-programming. From their viewpoint."

"Better safe than sorry." A platitude as unconvincing as when her CO said it. "You hesitate, you die. And with tens of thousands of people at risk—"

On the feed, the pad looked immaculate, swept clean by thrusters. The station's landing lights were out—expected if the station were sabotaged. The wisps of dry ice on the pipes stirred her adrenaline. Cold pipes. The power had been out for some time—certainly more than a few hours. How long was hard to say.

She leaned back in her chair and tapped the monitor. "There. Zoom out."

The drone obeyed, zooming out to reveal a circular ring on the pad where *Beam Six* had blasted debris away.

"They will take all the credit too, boss."

Worse, the military was likely to classify the whole thing. So no one would get credit. A mediabot would say it was just a drill. A test of the anti-meteor defense. Her grade, needs improvement. She wouldn't have waited so long to fire.

Kate studied the drone feed. Jin steered the drone toward the IIRAS buildings. The leady exterior of the two-story equipment shed looked like a metal mausoleum rising from silvery ash. Its red stenciled letters were bleached from thirty years of withering lunar sun.

"You really think protestors stayed behind on this station? There is no emergency beacon."

"First rule of ambushes Jin, they don't look like ambushes."

As the drone camera panned up, the radio telescope on the roof came into view. Jin circled the drone around the shed. He flew over the roof, then returned to the front. The door was open. The drone's light flicked over worn aluminum computer racks inside. Glass cases were shattered, and exposed circuit boards had been melted and fused with the shelves. The destruction looked thorough from the door, but the drone was too large to go inside.

Jin said, "Nothing on infrared or UV. Power is out here too. Inside is ambient, minus one-twenty-two."

"*Beam Six* stopped here for two hours and—what was it?"

"Eighteen minutes. Looks like sabotage."

"No. The racks and the circuit boards are cold. No way that happened in the last few hours. They would be red on thermal. This must be Dilan Darcy's handiwork."

Except her gut told her it wasn't.

Jin spun and maneuvered the drone to the second building with the living quarters. "Maybe they left a manifesto. That would be nice."

Kate's own experience was mixed. Most terrorists thought it obvious why they were killing everyone. None were thinking beyond the bang.

"Look for booby traps first."

The living quarters had the same faded, leady exterior, except it was sunk into the ground and heaped with gravelly gray regolith for shielding. The inner and outer doors of the airlock had been blown open, and its glass windows cracked. Inside, the living quarters looked like another wintry crypt. A half-eaten, now-frozen meal fumed as the light warmed the metal kitchen counter. Behind the counter, the white fridge was open. Most of its contents had burst under vacuum. Dirty laundry peppered the floor. As the light danced over the station's bluish-gray interior walls, a whiff of dry ice gassed from the warmed surfaces.

Jin said, "Drone is too big to go inside."

"Pan the camera."

"Still nada on infrared. Or UV. What is on the walls?"

Jin flicked the drone's light over the walls and waited for the fog to sublime. The letters R-T-H could be seen painted in red block letters. Jin reangled the drone to light EARTH FIRST in block letters on the wall.

Kate sat forward in the chair, then brought up a map of IIRAS station buildings in a small window. "Place is dead. And too small to hide an army. *Tesseract* land here." Kate tapped the center of the heavy landing pad, the same place *Beam Six* had landed. *Tesseract* binged acknowledgment. She felt weightless for a few seconds, then heavier as the thrusters slowed the ship to a gentle landing.

"Doesn't make sense that the power is out, Kate. This facility was designed with a solid state nuke that should be good for a century."

"Cables can always be cut."

Jin made a noise as if he would respond, then turned to watch *Tesseract* descend onto the launch pad.

"You've got that look, Jin."

He didn't, since his visor was down. But she sensed it.

"This place feels creepier than a graveyard on Halloween. You sure this is a good idea?"

Kate shook her head. "Terrible idea. Can you rewind the drone twenty seconds?" She waited for Jin to rewind the feed. "There. To the left of the S. In the shadow. I thought I saw—"

"I don't see anything, boss. Even the best EVA suit would leak some heat in this cold. Both IR and UV are clear."

Cold was bad. Maybe she should move out of 25 Carina. She was not seeing things clearly this month.

Kate studied the IR scan. The kitchen countertop and refrigerator were gray on the infrared monitor. Everything inside was ambient temperature, barely recognizable as separate objects.

"When we land, send out drones to patrol. I don't want anyone popping out of an impact crater to shoot at us."

"10-4."

Kate didn't wait for *Tesseract* to complete the landing sequence. When she heard the baritone whirr of the landing strut motors, she unclicked and headed below to throw on her EVA suit. Behind her, Jin unclicked and followed her.

Kate had donned her EVA suit so many times that her mind wandered while she changed. Coming here to pick up Darcy and Holden made sense. But *Beam Six* only held six based on the specs, so someone would have been left behind. Wait, why was she thinking Kirkwood was on *Beam Six*? That didn't make sense. Kirkwood was on the *Nanosail.* He must have been blown out of the airlock with the others. The IR scan was out of place. Her whole timeline was off. Something lurked at the cold, dark station, but she couldn't see it.

Jin said, "This whole thing is out of place, Kate."

Kate looked at Jin, realizing she'd spoken out loud. Now they were in the airlock. While she daydreamed, she thought of—something, which evaporated like the wisps of dry ice. She watched Jin while he connected the EVA to his neuroface.

As he evacuated the airlock, he said, "You ok, Kate?"

She pressed-checked her rifle as the outer door to *Tesseract* opened. "Let's do this."

Kate looked down over the airlock edge. Based on her Space Force training manual, a forty-meter jump was at the threshold of survivability on the moon. She pictured herself tucking and rolling, surviving the fall, only to have her suit rip on a rock. So she slung her rifle, climbed onto the ladder, and slid down fireman-style, using her gloves' friction on the handrail to slow her. She jumped the last six meters, landing about as hard as if she had jumped off a picnic table on Earth.

At the bottom, her EVA lights rolled a long white carpet across the sunblasted, ashen lunar surface. The moon's regolith wasn't like beach sand, worn and weathered by water and wind. It was more like fine shards of glass or sharp gravel from meteorites pounding the surface over billions of years. The sun's radiation made it electrostatic, so it stuck to everything and tracked everywhere, although her suit's material minimized it. The oddest thing about walking on the moon was the sound and smell—or rather lack of it. Without air to transmit sound, the regolith did not crunch or *shhhft* when she kicked it like beach sand, and the smell of the moon inside her EVA suit was her own lavender hair conditioner, citrus body wash, and adrenalized sweat.

Jin landed beside her with a white drone over his shoulder. It stabilized itself on puffs of compressed air, like an ostrich-sized mechanical parrot.

"Let's shut down and lock up. Don't want anyone to steal her."

"10-4."

After *Tesseract* shut down, Kate turned off her EVA lights and looked up, letting her eyes adjust to the dark. Jin followed, along with the white drone. There were thousands of stars in the sky. Overhead, the Milky Way arced from horizon to horizon like a snowy wedding trellis.

"Never gets old, Jin."

"They don't twinkle."

"Twinkling is because of the atmosphere."

Jin was silent for a moment. "Stellar."

"Breathtaking, yeah."

"I meant that on Earth, *stellar* is used ironically now. Because of light pollution, the sky isn't stellar anymore. Nothing is. You really have to come to space to understand its origin."

Kate laughed.

"What's funny?"

Kate thought about her visit to the colony's planetarium with Rae's parents. There, the light pollution was annoying emergency exit lights and Rae's family tapping on their damn devices.

"Stellar. Yeah you have to come topside to really appreciate it."

Standing still made the hair on her neck stand up. She turned her lights back on and started for the living quarters. "Let's move."

At the end of the landing pad, Jin found several trails of footprints trampled over each other. The drone took pictures, then Jin sent it to follow the tracks. The footprints led to the back of the equipment building, circled around the front, then cut to the living quarters. Kate zoomed in and inspected the prints as the drone circled, but they were too smashed and indistinct to be helpful. After Jin brought the drone back, they walked towards the buildings. The drone kept pace over Jin's shoulder.

"Which building do you want to clear first?"

"Shed. Keep Captain Flint there on watch at the door."

Jin turned his helmet towards her.

"If someone sneaks up, set its alert, Pieces of eight! Pieces of eight!"

Jin's helmet shook back and forth. "I'd check your oxygen."

Kate smirked.

At the back of the shed, heaps of regolith were piled against the outer wall near a hole large enough for Kate to climb into. It was too dark to see its bottom. Jin angled the drone's lights into the pit, revealing two power cables as thick as her arm that had been sectioned with a power saw.

The drone took pictures and video, then they moved to the shed's front. Captain Flint dutifully positioned itself to guard the open outer airlock door. Sandy white regolith had been tracked through the shed and amongst the rows of melted equipment. Kate pointed to a metal bar at the inner door's threshold.

"Jammed open before the power was cut."

Jin turned to her. She could not see his face under his visor but could feel his question.

"Have to jam it open before you cut the power. Otherwise the interior air pressure puts about forty tons of force on this door and jams it closed."

Jin studied the threshold. "You've done this before."

Unfortunately.

Jin then stepped to enter, but Kate barred him with her arm. Instead, she commanded Captain Flint to drop surveillance drones to search the shed. Flint laid three white icosahedral drones that whizzed into the airlock on puffs of compressed air. She brought up the video feed in her heads-up display, ignoring the visible light's impossibly tiny and distorted fish-eye view.

Two things gave away humans—heat and motion. Anything hiding in the corners would show both. She watched the infrared feed, keeping her rifle at low ready in case the shed's occupants ran out. The interior images remained featureless, gray, and still as the drones swooshed around corners, between racks of smashed equipment, up a flight of stairs, then up a second flight of stairs. She switched the IR contrast to *red hot*, hoping to better differentiate between hot and cold.

Nothing.

The drones doubled back down the stairs, seeing two cherry-red human figures framed against a gray and black threshold and holding silvery rifles. Then the drones zipped from the airlock and into Captain Flint's belly. She heard herself exhale over the coms.

Kate waved Jin in. They walked through the racks of melted equipment. Glass encasing the hardware had been smashed. No circuit boards were salvageable. Most were fused to the shelves. Kate's EVA gloves were too thick to finger the equipment, so she unsheathed her knife and poked at the melted computer chips. Nothing pried loose. She scraped residual blue-gray paste off the shelves with her knife. She'd used the paste in a previous life.

Jin walked along rows with a pair of duck-billed pliers and a container. Periodically, he grabbed a circuit board with the pliers, turned it over once or twice, then either put it back or collected it.

"Get samples with the blue-gray paste. Its unburnt thermite."

Jin turned another circuit board over with the pliers. "Personal experience again?"

"Specialized and printed for vacuum welding or demolition. High temperature, self-sustaining if properly ignited, with its own source of oxygen. Easy to steal from one of the colony's myriad construction sites."

Jin put the circuit board back on the rack. "So, yes."

"You think we can get anything off this equipment?"

"Doubtful. This tech is older than I am. But I know a guy at Lunar Foundries who's a history buff."

Kate nodded on her way to the back of the shed, where she found open metal stairs. She climbed them with her rifle high in case the drones had missed something. Her rifle's light invaded the dark corners of the second floor, finding only two more equally demolished equipment racks and more blue-gray paste. She climbed the second flight of stairs, rifle high, to the roof. The dull metal and glass radio telescope wafted the same puffs of dry ice when the light warmed its surfaces. The telescope appeared in order, except that its cables had been cut too.

She tracked downstairs, double-checking the corners with her rifle light. Jin was outside the shed, lifting the evidence container into the belly of the drone.

"You know Kate, I almost wish he hadn't got shot down. I'd like him alive so I can fucking kill him. Who does that, tries to kill so many people?"

She patted him on the shoulder, awkward in an EVA suit. Then she started towards the main building. Captain Flint advanced ahead of her, its floodlights lighting the chalky gravel heap blanketing the main building. She sent more white surveillance drones inside. But, like the shed, all she saw on IR was her and Jin in cherry red, framed against the outer airlock as the drones exited the building.

Kate descended the ramp to the airlock, sweeping her rifle light around the threshold, then across the interior. The hair on her neck stood. Blue-gray stains marked where the outer and inner airlocks had been breached.

Inside the living quarters, behind the half-eaten meal on the counter, an aluminum mug sat on its side with a tea bag hanging out, its contents now sublimed. The frozen pants and underwear on the floor were faded from vacuum and direct sunlight exposure. Shit. That was a big problem. Her rifle light scanned the wall, lifting ghosts of dry ice into space. Green block letters—ASHER TRIFT—had been spraypainted on the steely walls. Under that, EARTH FIRST.

With two feet inside, an alert binged. A priority one security alert from the colony. She ignored it because her rifle light's arc froze at the station manager's desk. A body. Two bodies. What her gut expected to find.

"Kate—"

"I need to message Rae."

"Kate—it's Bolkov. *Aurora* was a dead end. No Ben and Rily Guerra—"

"Someone needs to tell her that's not what a priority one alert is for. We have a bigger problem."

Jin took a step in and doubled the illumination on the desk. "Jesus fuck."

She lowered her rifle to the floor and pushed his rifle down too. "Gotta preserve them."

40

"TURN IT OFF! TURN THE FUCKING POWER OFF!"

The station's lights flicked on, and Kate was blinded. Rae could yell when necessary, and that big voice from her tiny body made Kate smile. Rae was an auburn-headed David, and the world was Goliath, not expecting the slingshot. Her best slings were polished and delivered in a foreign language, often Latin, leaving her enemies bewildered and concussed for days.

This time though, the yelling was pointless. Rae's EVA suit electronics automatically modulated the volume.

As Kate's eyes adjusted, she saw no one reacting, not even to Rae's ghostly white waving arms framed against the blown-out airlock. Rae's wild gestures reflected in Jin's EVA visor as he casually looked up from his pad. Rae wagged her glove at something behind Kate, so Kate turned to see Rae's intern, Eric, swiveling.

Behind Eric, ASHER TRIFT and EARTH FIRST in green and blue block letters covered IIRAS' station living quarter's dull, metallic gray walls. The ceiling's LEDs emphasized every ding and dent on the once-polished aluminum kitchen cabinets. Frozen jeans and underwear peppered the floor and metal bunk beds. An icy half-meal in a metal bowl on the kitchen counter wisped and smoldered cold gasses.

Kate's eyes finally adapted to the brightness enough to see the streaks of fog streaming from the body beside Eric.

Kate turned back to Jin. "Jin cut the power."

"They just—"

"ERIC, get those bodies in a GODDAM BAG!"

"They won't fit Doctor Torres. This one's stuck to the—"

"COVER THEM THE FUCK UP."

Kate lifted her rifle and prepared to shoot the lights out. "Just cut the fucking power, Jin."

Jin muttered into the coms. The lights flickered, then surrendered. The living quarters were pitch black except for the dull red light on Rae's helmet. Lights beyond the blown-open airlock scattered off the gravelly lunar surface and framed Rae as a mystical red shadow.

Kate smirked. Hot, spicy, jalapeno Rae was the best Rae, as long as Rae wasn't pointing the flamethrower at her.

"ERIC use the BIG bags—"

Kate slung her rifle and walked past Rae to the cargo cart near the door. She suppressed the urge to say something that would turn up the heat.

"—and everybody out except for YOU and YOU and YOU."

With the back of her head, Kate felt the point of Rae's ethereal shadow glove, so she knew she was the third *you*. Still, she half-swiveled to confirm it. Then she took big bags from the gray metallic cargo bin on the cart. Her EVA gloves were clumsy, and she grabbed too many extra-large body bags. She tried to pull them apart, but the static electricity turned them into a tangled mess.

"Kate. What was the first thing I told you? Don't. Disturb. The evidence."

"I—" Kate finally separated two crumpled bags from the mess in her hands. "—Roger. No power until you say so." Rae wanted the lights off because they would heat the surfaces, causing volatile compounds to sublimate in the vacuum of space. And evidence.

"And keep everyone out of here, Kate. They are trampling shit everywhere, kicking up dust and touching things. I will never get a time of death if they keep contaminating my crime scene."

Kicking up dust was impossible to avoid on the moon. Regolith was electrostatically charged and adhered to everything. But Kate inhaled and bit her tongue. What she wanted to do was take Rae's helmet off, run her fingers through that auburn hair on fire, taste her salty tongue—yeah, there was no way for that to work here. Not the most appropriate time. But Kate thought it better to concentrate on the compartment of her brain with Rae in it than the other one, closer to her lizard brain, which was visualizing all the medieval ways to hurt the person responsible for this crime scene. That gratification she'd delay until after Rae confirmed the time of death.

"Roger. Keep people out. Why don't I stand outside and guard the door?"

Special Agent Bolkov's shadow hovered near the inner airlock threshold. "I will stay. I need—"

Kate balled up the bags and tossed them to Eric, then crowded Bolkov out of the room.

Bolkov protested. "I need—"

Kate arm-barred and stepped forward. "—to let her do her job. She's very good at it. You heard her, everybody out."

"Don't disappear, Kate."

Kate felt Rae's eyes and her suit's red lights on her back as she walked out. Without turning, Kate nodded and gave a clumsy, gloved thumbs-up.

"And wipe that smirk off your face."

With her back to Rae, wearing an EVA suit with a mirrored helmet, there was no way Rae could see her face. They had only been together eight months, but it was like they'd been mind-melded, and Rae could hear her thoughts. Kate's smirk changed to a grin. With that auburn hair on fire, Rae was definitely the woman for her.

Outside the door, she stood guard while watching Agent Bolkov walk up the ramp, past a mobile light tower, then follow a well-worn trail across the regolith toward the equipment shed. Maintenance drones had put up three light towers, arranging them so the equipment shed and living quarters were lighted, as well as the gravelly path between them. Under the lights, the slate-gray equipment shed looked less spooky than hours ago. Now, it was just another worn and weathered gray building rising from the moon's surface.

Two more of Rae's white-EVA-clad interns stood near the shed facing each other. If they were chatting, they were on a different frequency so the rest of the group wouldn't eavesdrop. Agent Bolkov walked up to them and pointed inside the shed. The interns nodded, and Bolkov disappeared through the blown-open airlock.

Beside her, silver-gray boxes were open, with their equipment sprawled everywhere.

Silence in the coms reminded her that her stomach roiled.

It took Rae and her crew just under four and a half hours to arrive at the far side station. Aria provided a cargo rocket. Rae showed up with four interns, Agent Bolkov, and Aria. They descended from the cargo rocket all cheery, like a victory party. The interns first, Aria next, then Rae, and finally Agent Bolkov, who gave her a pat on the shoulder after jumping the last meter. After the people, a caravan of maintenance drones exited from the cargo hold and darted in all directions. Three zipped behind the shed to get the power back on. The rest set up the mobile tower lights and moved Rae's equipment to the main building.

While Kate waited for Rae's crew to arrive, she could only feed her face and take a nap. She went through every compartment in *Tesseract* but only found stale snacks and coffee. So, she and Jin ate what they could find, and she had a double espresso followed by shuteye. Usually, she would wake refreshed just as the caffeine kicked in.

Instead, she tossed and turned with her stomach torn inside out. Her timeline on this case was all wrong.

At the equipment shed, the two interns split up. One walked around back while the other went inside the shed. Kate took a head count and checked the sensors. Video feed from a drone overhead showed Aria supervising the maintenance drones behind the shed. Jin was on the roof, bent over and pulling equipment apart with tongs. Bolkov's red dot was inside the equipment shed near one of the intern's yellow dots. Another intern was walking towards Aria. The last two were inside the quarters with Rae.

Surrounding the station, desolation and cold on UV and IR, maybe for hundreds of kilometers. No pop-up attacks were imminent.

"Kate. You want to come back in?"

Kate went inside to find the bodies bagged. Cool red lights and holocameras on tripods stood around the room. Interns had put the frozen clothes and half-eaten meals into bins and now scraped paint off the wall into containers.

Rae waved her to a desk while shining a purple light over a monitor. "Positive ID on Dilan Darcy and Theodore Holden. I will need to thaw them to be sure, but it looks like vacuum decompression. Explosive, judging from the blood spatter on the computer monitor."

Blood spatter fluoresced under Rae's purple light. Rae let Kate get a good look, then picked up the monitor and put it in an empty bin.

"How long did you say the contractors were here, Kate?"

"Two hours and change."

Rae looked at the body bag in the shape of a chair and closed the lid on the bin. She uttered something breathy.

"I didn't catch that."

"I need to get a scan to read internal temp, but they might be frozen to the core. They've been here much longer than eighteen hours."

Kate turned and studied the inner airlock. Kate tried to do the math in her head, but her stomach acid ate at its lining.

Agent Bolkov appeared at the threshold. "They must have stolen the thermite from a colony construction site."

She already knew that. Kate burped. "Protestors didn't do this."

"Don't overthink it, Devana. They studied hard for this assignment. One turned himself into a human missile. You found rocket fuel and circuit boards that tie to the missing drone and the bomb set off in your office. DNA proves Darcy was at the wedding. And a bullet-proof money trail ties them all together. You've taken four most wanted off the board and two more we didn't even know about."

Bolkov's count was off. Kate's brain and stomach differed by how much. Bolkov figured Kirkwood and his crew went out of the *Nanosail's* hatch, but that's not what happened.

She said, "Why kill Darcy and Holden?"

"Loose ends."

The acid in her stomach said no, that wasn't it.

Kate turned to Rae. "My stomach doesn't feel right about this."

"Occam's Razor, sweetie. Maybe your stomach doesn't feel right about the junk you ate on *Tesseract*."

Kate looked at the black hump, formerly Dilan Darcy. "If he was at the wedding, how'd he get back here?"

Jin was not in the room, but he had been listening. "I am searching for all the trips to this station. Maybe they hacked the registry like they did *Nanosail*."

But how many could there be? Kate looked around. "Why come back?"

"Maybe the manifesto." Jin's face wasn't visible, but Kate could hear the smirk in his voice.

Bolkov said, "Again, loose ends. To kill Dilan Darcy. Probably Darcy was keeping a list of other cells."

No, that wasn't it, either. Kirkwood was alive, and Dilan Darcy didn't kill his mother. Something else happened here, but she'd need time of death to confirm it.

"Love, Eric and Robyn need help carrying the bodies out of here because we can't get a drone in. We are done with evidence collection. When the bodies are out, you and Agent Bolkov are free to search the place."

Jin, over the coms, said, "Does that mean I can turn the lights back on?"

"Yes, Jin. Once we get the bodies out of here."

41

Sunday morning, after sleeping fitfully, Kate sat on her balcony with a mug of coffee and a slice of peanut butter fudge pie. Yeah, Rae made it for dessert. Yeah, simulated daytime was ten a.m. Other people had their rituals, this was hers, dessert for breakfast one week a month. The sugar didn't soothe her cramps. But for each brief mouthful, she could forget her dark dream of IIRAS station. In her dream, she was inside IIRAS station living quarters alone and the lights were out. A fat white termite walked over Dilan Darcy's frozen body and laid thousands of eggs. When she reached out to smash it with her glove, she woke up. She was sure her dream was telling her to find the termite before it laid eggs.

This morning, 25 Carina residents were out on all twenty-five floors, eating brunch and coffee on their balconies, walking their drone pets or in rare cases real pets, or letting their kids buzz toy drones over the heads of pedestrians in the garden gazebo below.

Meloni sat across the table, in a cycle of swiping and watching videos on her pad. She had her ears in and was watching—something. Kate sipped her coffee, ignoring the messages on her phone. She'd tried and failed to short-circuit its interruptions to get sleep.

Kate scooped from the fudge layer. Meloni looked up and took one of her earpods out, saying, "I want to surprise Mom and Dad and take them to the show at the Galaxy. You and Rae saw it?"

Rae's parents weren't here either. Usually, they locked themselves in the bedroom Sunday morning and attended virtual church. This morning they left early, for in-person service. It was inevitable that they'd hear about it. Fortunately, by the time they did, Kate had come up with a good story to get Rae and Meloni out of going. She said it was for those fifty-five and over. A half-true generational jab that went over their heads.

"Yeah, The Solar Fountain. Our first date."

"How was it?"

"Amazing."

"And the show?" Meloni smiled.

Kate let the joke slip by and Meloni pouted.

"Sorry. Yes the show was amazing too."

"Still have cramps?"

Kate nodded. For the last twenty-four hours, her intestines twisted between bouts of diarrhea and cramps—which could have been something she ate on *Tesseract*. Or her period. But it wasn't either. She needed to know when Darcy and Holden died.

Kate heard her phone bing again. A third bing made her jam her coffee mug on the table to grab her phone. She thumbed it with her left hand while scooping more pie. "Jin. He's at Lunar Foundries and want me to hear from their historian who examined the chips we recovered." Kate was aware she was mumbling through a mouthful of peanut butter.

"It's Sunday." Meloni eyed Kate, shook her head, and then returned to watching a video. "You and sis work too much."

"Normally we don't. This is—"

"Is what? You should be resting, Kate. You jailed the protestors. The mediabots are saying you broke the back of a terror network. Give yourself a break."

She didn't do any of that. Kirkwood was missing and Helena's killer was unidentified. Kate tried a break. She also tried working. Her paperwork was still in draft, incomplete, and she lost three esports games to Axio, which she should have won, except she kept checking her phone to see whether Kirkwood was arrested instead of watching Axio's oncoming attack. Her gut told her Kirkwood wasn't going to be arrested where he was. But she couldn't be sure until she got time of death.

Kate said, "My Mom used to say when criminals and terrorists honor Shabbat, I will too. Besides, we are fifty meters underground, four hundred thousand kilometers from Earth. Days and seasons don't mean much."

"Rest does. It's unhealthy to work seven days a week." Meloni stared at Kate shoveling the pie into her mouth. "You know that's my recipe Rae stole from me."

"She said it was passed along generations."

"Yeah. The younger one passed it to Mom, then Rae stole it. Generations."

Kate chuckled through a spoonful of fudge. "Well, it's amazing and I might steal another piece. Then I am hoping the historian finds something that might help us track the rest of the protestors."

Meloni huffed. "Axio is fine here if you need to go, Kate."

Kate scraped the last glob of peanut butter fudge off the plate. She licked the spoon, then rose. "Are you sure?"

"I don't book clients on weekends. Well, unless the markets are melting down. But that's rare. Go."

"I really appreciate it."

Meloni sighed and lowered her eyes to her pad. "No problem. Make plans and then everyone cancels at the last minute. A Torres family tradition."

Kate picked up her mug off the table and slugged her last mouthful of coffee. "Axio has homework due tomorrow. I told him no esports til it's done."

Meloni's freckles smiled with her brown eyes. Kate saw Rae reflected in Meloni's dimples. "What is that look for?"

"Axio is lucky to have you."

"He's a good kid. He deserves better than that—" Kate looked over her shoulder to see if Axio was nearby. "—than you-know-who. I'll probably stop by the morgue too."

"Maybe a wasted trip. Sis complained this morning it would take two weeks to thaw those corpsicles you brought her."

"Not the coldest she's recovered. She's magic with her scanner."

Meloni picked up her coffee and grinned. "I will make sure Axio does his homework so you two can christen her new office."

"She told you about that?"

Meloni smirked over her coffee mug. "You did. Just now."

Wow. Touche. She walked into that one.

Kate toasted Meloni with her mug, then scooped up her dishes to put them in the washer and sped out the door.

42

On the concourse, Kate squeezed between bleary-eyed visitors and their rolling suitcases. On weekends, fresh tourist squads replaced the beaten casino refugees. Families marched in geared formation: two bleary adults, two to four kids dressed in *I love you to the moon and back* graphic shirts, shoes with light-up planets, pillows for the long ride, backpacks, frontpacks, and stuffed green aliens velcroed to torsos. Some kids jumped, exploring their superpowers in low lunar gravity. Others held an older hand while gun-pointing at shops' holodisplays of Halloween costumes.

Scraping past a display of a gold-and-black Martian superhero reminded her that Axio wanted to be the red-white-and-blue alien from that holomovie for Halloween. She couldn't remember the character's name. In front of the display, she became a tourist. She scanned, checked inventory, and rejected all the upcharges. She used her lunar resident discount. She bought one for Axio and one for herself. Nothing for Rae, who could be the scary doctor from the movie. Ha, that joke wouldn't go over well, especially if Rae couldn't find something at the last minute. So she backed out and bought something for Rae, too. Then, she resumed working.

Near the spaceport, shoulder-to-shoulder squads of smiling arrivals churned with dazed and confused departures. In, out, and around. She rushed through the whirlpool. On the other side, she made a right turn, swam to an elevator, and her destination.

The front entrance of Lunar Foundries bustled because of its unique artwork. When the rock was excavated to rebuild the factory after Kate blew it up, geologists discovered a rare seam of green-purple-and-blue-streaked labradorite. Designers incorporated it into the architecture, using Lunar Foundries' drones to carve busts and sculptures into the colorful rock. Lunar Foundries' entrance had become an art museum, where visitors pondered each piece and took selfies.

Kate buzzed past the tourists and security, pausing only long enough to kiss her ring finger and touch her favorite exhibit, the sculpture *Selene*, a towering relief resembling a grapevine. *Selene*'s roots appeared cultivated in blue regolith. Its knotted blue-green vine blossomed at eye level into iridescent purple and blue grapes representing various space outposts and colonies. Overhead, starships and space stations flew among its leaves. For luck, kissing and touching the grape symbolizing the lunar colony had become a colony ritual. She felt lucky, smiling when her ring finger touched the stone.

Past security, she turned left down the main hall to find Jin in the hall with two other people. One was a short man with a wrinkled grin, thin gray hair, and spectacles covering yellowish-brown eyes. Doctor Apul Mulawarman, CEO of Lunar Foundries. The other had a shiny red bald streak, cotton-ball-white tufts of hair, and a smile that looked like Christmas. She recognized him but couldn't recall his name. His badge read Doctor Mac Oviedo.

Doctor Mulawarman stuck his hand out first. "Good to see you, Kate. When you are not blowing up my lab."

He winked, grabbed her, and pulled her in for an awkward hug. She was much taller, he felt frail, and technically, he was one of her bosses. But he hugged warmly.

Dr. Oviedo jutted out his hand. "Major. You don't remember, but we've met."

Kate smiled and shook Dr. Oviedo's hand. "Call me Kate. I am not Major anymore."

Jin said, "We were wrapping up." He pointed into an office with a stack of nine monitors inside. "Dr. Oviedo gave us the whole history of IIRAS."

Oviedo said, "Frankly, it was a miracle it launched. And as you could probably guess, by that time, the technology was fifteen years outdated. The agency pushed for the launch anyway, despite internal concerns. The director then was afraid of delays, because more delays would likely kill the project on the hill."

Kate sighed. She remembered that Oviedo could be long winded and confusing. How to politely stop a historian from reciting history? She held up her hand. "Ok. Pretend I am just a military grunt from Texas and dumb it down."

Dr. Mulawarman smiled and talked over his glasses. "Someone at the station swapped chips. You've recovered three generations of chips. One is really old, the originals. We didn't make those. The other two we manufactured, but they were never designed for the station."

"Why would someone do that?"

Oviedo said, "Sir—how can you—"

Dr. Mulawarman said, "Now that Kate's here, I'll explain it. It's a piece of history—a piece of *classified* history—but we are all friends here, right?" Seeing nods, he continued. "We contracted with the agency almost two decades ago to replace the original chips. We promised big cost advantages because we were here, so there was no requirement to heavy-lift the product to lunar orbit. But, we went through several design changes. They had a lot of demands." Dr. Mulawarman waved his finger back and forth and shook his head. "Unrealistic. Engineering is about tradeoffs, and an agency flush with money doesn't think it needs to make them."

As he talked, his face flushed, and his temples throbbed. He paused to take a breath. "After five design changes, the agency IT director finally signed off, and we manufactured our first run. Except he denied signing off and stiffed us."

Jin said, "Who is he? What do you mean stiffed—"

"Bill Caddell. Rejected the changes and didn't pay. So we never shipped. Legal wanted to pursue them. I wanted to sue the fu—" Dr. Mulawarman looked at Kate. "—pardon me. Ollie talked me out of it. She had much more experience than I did. She said all the agencies are like this. Be a team player. So we did."

Ollie was Olicia Barron. Kate crumpled her forehead. Kate had never seen an agency not spend money. "What happened to the chips? And funding?"

"Chips, we recycled. Funding, I don't know. Ollie was right. We got another contract with the Defense Department and recouped our losses." He pointed to the monitors inside the office. "I checked. We made those—eight, nine years ago. A cheaper commercial product not designed for space, so there's no radiation shielding. They would not survive long in the harsh conditions on the far side very long."

Jin said, "I don't understand why someone would do that. Someone replaced the old chips with these new ones, but not the ones you designed specifically for the station. "

"Those old first-generation chips were never designed to last this long. They are forty years old. Nor the second generation you found. That station must have been close to a blackout. Someone was trying to hold it together with duct tape and glue, with the newer chips."

Kate snapped her fingers. "On the video. The argument between Dilan and Caddell, Dilan said, what's a Georgetown mansion go for these days. And this should have been done years ago. The chips were never replaced properly, because the money went to his pocket."

Jin said, "I saw all his properties. His antique cars. His lifestyle. I wondered how he could afford that."

Kate said, "In the videos, Ted was accused of upgrading the software. And Caddell deleted some raw data."

Oviedo glanced at the monitors inside his office, frowning. Six eyes waited for him to speak. "I ran filters on the images they released." He paused in thought again. "Images are just bits of zeros and ones. Data. The signal comes into the station, the chips decrypt and translate the signal, then the scientific team examines them. Thing is, the station managers are responsible for the hardware. They are there to manage it, and are the ones physically replacing it when it goes bad."

"Dilan Darcy and Ted Holden were the station managers. You are saying they'd take the blame for installing the wrong chips," Kate said, studying the pink and blue diagrams on the monitors inside Oviedo's office.

"With the station destroyed the way it was, they'd get blamed, yes. But—I ran the images through a filter. Someone manipulated them with AI. "

Jin said, "The images were faked?"

Oviedo shook his head. "Not faked. More like blurred. Although I'd need the raw image data to be sure."

Dr. Mulawarman said, "Ted would have to upgrade the software to be compatible with the chips. The chips would decode the signal at a higher resolution. If those were released, it would prove the station had the wrong hardware."

Kate said, "So someone would have to manipulate the images. But then why delete the raw image data?"

Oviedo kept shaking his head. "There is not enough computing power on the station, so the image manipulation happened after they were relayed to Earth."

"Which would trace to Caddell. So Caddell had to delete it to cover his tracks." Kate nodded as if she understood the diagrams on Oviedo's tower of screens.

Oviedo continued, "Someone would have figured it out. The AI he used doesn't understand astrophysics. The doppler shift was wrong." Oviedo sighed. "But without the raw image data, there is no proof."

Mulawarman shook his head. "Such a tragedy. Aria sent me the site survey. This used to be humanity's greatest achievement. We are going to fix this and get it operational."

Kate's phone binged. "Maybe there is another way to prove it without the image data. Rae has time of death." Kate looked at Jin. "We should explain this to Bolkov."

"Boss?"

"It's been right in front of me the whole time, and I didn't see it. She came to investigate Caddell, not the protestors. Dr. Oviedo, can you send us a summary? "

Oviedo looked at Mulawarman, who said, "Mac will send you whatever you need."

Kate reached for Oviedo's hand and shook it. When she reached for Mulawarman's hand, he pulled her in for another awkward hug.

"Always good to see you, Kate."

43

Stepping into Rae's new office, Kate felt static electricity. Maybe more than her old office because of its immense size. Her new office was a level up from her old office, literally and figuratively. Construction drones had cut a hole in the floor, welded stairs, rearranged the walls one floor below, then sandblasted the scars and painted the walls a milky latte color—all while humans slept.

An open metal rail on the right-front corner just inside the threshold guarded steps down to her old office, now part of an expanded morgue. The right wall was almost entirely a window. In it, Rae hovered over a scanning machine shoved into a corner, her auburn hair in a messy bun and wearing green scrubs. The window was an illusion, a live view of the morgue downstairs. Three steps into the office, the window changed to pictures. A wood-framed summer shoreline view of Lake Winnebago was pinned between pictures of Rae's staff—dressed in pink, purple, or blue scrubs. At the far end, near Rae's desk, was a still image of her and Rae clinking wine glasses at High Frontier Grille. To Kate's left, the construction drones installed five fog-blue cubicles, leaving space for five more. Charcoal moving bins stacked four high occupied four cubes, while the fifth held half-installed shelves. A fountain of multicolor personal effects and safety equipment sprayed from the containers and decorated chairs and desks.

"Should we go down to the morgue, boss?"

While she surveyed, Jin arrived, standing close enough for her to catch the clean smell of gym soap. Jade trotted through the door and sat between them, its pink silicone tongue hanging to the side.

"Her message said wait here." Kate glanced at Jade, not remembering the dog at Lunar Foundries.

"They remodeled her office quick." Jin followed Kate's eyes to Jade. "I stopped. She needed a walk."

"Barron's construction drones don't get union breaks." Jade panted at Kate and feigned a bark. "And Jade is a robot. She doesn't need a walk."

Jin reached down to pet Jade, who wagged her tail. "Did you hear that? She called you a robot. Get her, Jade."

Jade grinned at Kate, then barked. Kate gave Jade a scratch behind the ear.

"Do that many people die here that she needs a big office?"

Kate shrugged. "Space is dangerous."

Between the suicides, mining accidents, and overdoses, Rae complained she did not have enough time lately for research.

"Something bothers me, boss. You cost Dr. Mulawarman a trillion dollars. Yet he hugged you twice."

"Long story. I'll tell you sometime."

Jin looked at her and shook his head, smirking.

"We need to scour all the surveillance of Caddell. Everyone he met with."

"Done and done. I started that before I headed here."

Agent Bolkov walked into Rae's office. "Did I miss the show?"

Kate crinkled her face. "No. She said to wait here."

Bolkov pointed to an image in the window. "That your engagement party?"

Kate looked at the wall and realized the images had cycled to a group picture of their party at The Crown Oasis' gardens. Her, Rae, Rae's parents and sister, Axio, Kate's brother Greg, Jin, and Cris and Abby Davis, all smiling and holding their wine glasses in cheers.

"We aren't engaged."

"But I heard—"

A closing door echoed from downstairs. The wall display changed to a holovideo of a translucent heart and lungs, illustrating red and blue blood perfusing the organs with each heartbeat.

Rae stomped up the stairs, then opened the gate to step out. "Agent Bolkov. Jin. And my lovely life partner. Just the three I wanted to see."

Kate twisted her ringless finger. She glanced at Jin, who was staring at his feet. He heard the sarcasm too. Rae didn't like working on Sundays.

"You can call me Mia—"

Rae ignored Agent Bolkov. She trudged over to her desk, walked around, and then flopped down. She touched one of the six displays at her desk, changing the wall display into a graph with a bunch of red and blue points and a curved black line through them.

"Agent Bolkov, how much do you know about space radiation and its effects on organic matter?"

Professor Torres was picking on the plebe. Jin was probably relieved he wasn't it this time.

"Well, it's bad."

Rae sighed. "Let me put it this way. There are lots of ways to date a body. But when my sweetheart brings me a lunar corpsicle at minus one hundred ten degrees Celsius, radiation degradation is the only way."

Bolkov said, "There were two bodies."

Pro tip, don't correct the Professor on the first day, especially when the day was Sunday, and it was the Professor's day off.

Rae ignored Bolkov, saying, "Jin when did Darcy send the money to Earth First? It's in my notes but—"

Kate felt the temperature drop in Rae's already icy voice.

While Jin read his notes off his pad, Kate rocked forward, hands in her pockets. "You're going to tell us Darcy was dead before that."

Rae shook her head. "Gold star. But detention for spoiling it. I'll see you after class."

"You probably need to explain it to them."

Bolkov said, "Explain what?"

Rae changed the display to a three-dimensional rendering of the inside of IIRAS station living quarters, with cabinets, clothes, and the bodies of Dilan Darcy and Ted Holden slumped in their chairs exactly as they discovered it.

"Eric stayed up all night to get this simulation finished. Normally I'd ask him to present, but he crashed. He told me to tell you he likes single malt, chewy."

Kate nodded. "Noted."

Rae played the simulation, explaining cosmic radiation ionization intensity and how it sloshed around the IIRAS station living quarters.

Blue fluid entered the open airlock and turned green, yellow, and red as it bounced and diffused around the room. Soon the interior was purple, with the bodies of Dilan Darcy and Ted Holden drowning as if the station had sunk into an alien ocean.

Rae said, "It's mainly high energy protons, which as you know Agent Bolkov, cause damage. To paint. To metal. Especially to organic matter like exposed skin."

Above the simulation, a bar showed the time.

Jin asked, "The scale is days?"

"Eric used this simulation to backsolve how long the bodies were exposed. The ionization damage of the bodies matches the simulation at about twenty-one days. We can also triangulate with other—"

Bolkov said, "Due respect Dr. Torres, your model could be off."

"Usually the biggest problem is exposure to unfiltered sun. But warming and sublimation were limited here since they were sheltered, so we can be precise. We accounted for uncertainty."

"You're saying Darcy was dead before he sent money. That's not—"

Rae paused the simulation to a purple smear. "Not me. The science is saying Dilan Darcy died September twenty-second, give or take forty-eight hours."

"If he was dead, how could he send money to Earth First?"

Rae shot Kate a look, *please get her out of my office.* Kate relayed to Bolkov what Dr. Mulawarman had told them. Then she said, "The sabotage on the station wasn't done in two hours. It would have all been hot on infrared. The clothes were faded from unfiltered sunlight. I knew that was a problem. And the bar, jamming the shed open before they cut the power. This was a professional job."

Bolkov folded her arms. "What about his DNA?"

"Transfer. Jin's been saying that from the beginning."

Kate would have to make that up to Jin. He was right all along.

"But the money came from Dilan Darcy's account."

Jin said, "I am looking into it. Probably spoofed."

Bolkov was shaking her head. Kate turned to Jin. "Where are Nolan and Kenna Darcy?"

"Packed up and took a shuttle to Vandenburg."

"Good. Did we recover Helena's phone from them?"

"They claim they never had it. We never recovered it."

"Pretty sure they don't. What about Paul's phone?"

"A grainy video of a protestor three feet from Helena Darcy. And another figure. No high probability match."

"Where is Leyna?"

Jin pointed to Rae. Rae said, "Oh, I forgot to tell you. We moved her out of hiding back to a hospital bed to prep her for her new lung."

"Are we lucky enough that she's awake?"

"You are always lucky. She's awake."

"That's our next stop. Jin, you take Bolkov."

Bolkov clenched her teeth. "What about you?"

"Professor gave me detention. I'll be right behind you. Five minutes."

Jin turned and darted down the hall. Jade ruffed and bounced out of the room. Bolkov shook her head, then sped after Jin.

Kate watched Jin open the stairwell door. When they were out of sight, Kate closed the office door. Rae's face had softened, and the room temperature went up. "Thanks for cracking this on a Sunday."

Rae smiled. "Thank Eric and Robyn. They did all the work. Robyn likes red by the way."

"You ok?"

"Bolkov annoys me. Like I don't know how many bodies are in my goddamn morgue right now. And I am grouchy. I had to be in early because a double suicide and an overdose came in. The overdose *couldn't wait*, because politics." Rae rolled her eyes.

"Politics?"

"Not a big deal. They wanted the prelim and toxicology before it hit the media. How are your cramps?"

Kate looked at the purple blot on the wall. "Gone now. Thanks to two slices of peanut butter pie."

"I hope you saved me some."

"I stashed some in the back of the fridge for you."

Kate heard a door closing downstairs. She walked over to kiss Rae before someone came up the stairs.

"Oh, I forgot one thing, Kate. The paint. Eric said everything matched except the paint."

"Matched, you mean the age?"

"Everything had the same exposure, except the paint. It was fresh."

"Fresh? Like how fresh?"

"It hadn't even cured. I'll get him to narrow—"

"—No need. We know when that happened." Kate studied the simulation, its alien purple fluid rippling inside the station, then went through construction equipment inventory in her mind.

"Kate, that's only possible if—"

"—what I was thinking too. You're the best. I love you." Kate pressed Rae's lips against hers, then flew after Jin and Bolkov.

44

Jin and Agent Bolkov were delayed, so Kate was the first to arrive at the hospital. She exited the elevator on the second floor to see Annelle Gray clicking down the hall wearing Milan's latest pewter-colored pantsuit, a white blouse, and shimmering silver bling platform pumps.

Kate frowned. On every second floor of an Earth hospital, there would be a window, maybe made of thick glass, but one that Kate could shoot open to defenestrate Gray. Kate pictured Gray's mouth open in shock, her platform pumps scintillating in the sun, and the pantsuit flapping on the way down. The colony hospital was two hundred meters underground, so she'd never have that pleasure here.

Gray paused and tilted her head towards Kate, her blond ponytail and fifty thousand dollar Italian clothes posed against the off-white wall. With one hand, she held a single-serving juice bag. The other held up one index finger. "Right back."

Gray clopped to a door, opening and closing it. Kate did quick arithmetic in her head. Gray's fees were astronomical, and she billed in ten-minute increments. Kate couldn't afford even one of Gray's clicks across the floor. She could not fathom how Leyna Darcy could afford sixteen clicks for a juice box plus a return trip, when a nurse would do it for free.

Jin stopped beside Kate. "Boss, she's the asshole celebrity lawyer. A lower level of hell than she's used to visiting?"

"Asshole celebrity lawyer is a triple oxymoron, and I think this is my punishment, not hers."

"You mean it's redundant."

Kate looked at Jin, her mouth half open.

He said, "Oxymoron is contradictory words. Asshole celebrity lawyer all mean the same thing." He grinned and half-unsheathed his tazer. "They mean I get to use this."

Kate pictured a crackle and then one of Gray's out-of-control clients yelping and jumping back. She smiled.

Bolkov was now beside Jin, "Who are we tazing?"

Gray rematerialized from the room. "So you want to talk to my client."

Kate said, "Shouldn't you be somewhere taking out celebrity trash?"

"You are defaming my clients."

"No. Just defaming you. Why are you here?"

"You are here to interrogate my client, Leyna Darcy. I am here to accept your offer of total immunity on her behalf."

Kate's brain blanked, unable to find the best cuss. Maybe all of them.

Gray reacted to Kate's blank stare by shifting her weight from one foot to the other, causing her hips to sway opposite. In her peripheral vision, Kate saw Jin's eyes swing with the action.

Bolkov said, "We haven't made one."

Gray looked at Jin, smiled, and bit her lip. "So make me an offer." Jin's shoulders squared.

Kate looked at Jin. "Sure. You can have my deputy Jin for a night in return for a full statement."

Jin flushed and glared at Kate. Kate grinned and shrugged.

"Sadly, no deal. Not even for two nights."

Jin pouted. Really? Kate shuddered. Not that she'd made better choices at his age. She turned back to Gray. "So what does Leyna need immunity for? We haven't charged her with anything."

"You might link her to the Darcy murder and bomb."

Kate exchanged glances with Bolkov, then said, "The investigation hasn't gone in that direction. Best case, we charge her with bad fashion choices for wearing an Earth First t-shirt."

"But you think she can help you. That's why you're here. So, immunity."

"For what?"

"Life. The Universe. Everything."

Bolkov said, "Can we stop the games and be more specific?"

"She wasn't involved in the Darcy murder. She wasn't even in the gardens. And she didn't bomb herself."

Kate looked over at Jin, who shrugged. She looked to Bolkov, who mouthed *no*. Turning to Gray, she said, "First, tell us something we don't know."

"Against my advice, she is willing to consent to a search of her phone and provide access to her private server. She says she was masquerading as an Earth Firster—I will let her explain it."

"Where did this phone come from?"

"It was stashed in her bedroom safe at Hotel Immunity. Password, immunity."

Bolkov asked, "Why do we give a shit?"

"Off the record. My client claims she was investigating her brother. She may have come across files of interesting agency transactions."

Jin said, "So computer crimes. She hacked into government files."

"Some of which may be classified. Maybe a little breaking and entering too."

Kate looked at her toes, which were hidden inside black flats. Unlike Gray, she hadn't polished her nails in two weeks. Annelle Gray's perfect salon pedicure and glittery white polish came with a manicure, spa treatment, and an enormous bill probably larger than Kate's mortgage. Gray knew what was on the phone and only took cases for one of two reasons.

Leyna Darcy did not have money—or at least not enough to afford Gray—which meant it was the second reason. Gray took quite a risk, clicking through the hospital in fifty-thousand dollar clothes, where all sorts of colorful biologicals lurked ready to ambush her outfit. For nothing, hopefully. If Kate agreed to the deal, they would get Leyna, but Gray would walk out without her prey. Although Kate's intestines registered disagreement.

"We have a deal—"

Bolkov protested. "*We* do not."

"We do."

"Or else what, Devana? You don't have jurisdiction—"

"Or I trespass you off this rock and the rest of us listen to Leyna."

"That's obstruction."

"And I am very good at it. Do you want to close your case?"

"What case? I am here—"

Jin said, "Don't bullshit us. If you were investigating the protestors, you'd be gone."

"I was. And you can't—" Bolkov inhaled, puffed her cheeks, and mouthed *fuck* at the ceiling.

Kate said, "You knew."

"I didn't. Only a hunch. There was no proof." She folded her arms. "Still isn't. I think we are getting played."

Jin said, "You don't give a shit about a low-level computer crime. That's not why you're here. You'll sentence her to a cubicle farm on some space station where she can be a pet, tortured by your agency's data requests for a few years."

"Sounds personal."

Jin puffed his chest. "Also none of your fucking business."

Kate put up her hand to stop Jin. "Ok, so trespass it is. I can close your case myself."

Bolkov exhaled slowly and unfolded her arms. "Fine. For the record, I object, and I didn't think he'd go this far."

Gray started swiping her phone with one very long silver-polished nail and then walked over to show it to Bolkov. "Paw."

Bolkov sighed and pressed her thumb to Gray's phone.

Gray manipulated her phone, flipped it around, and then brought it to Kate. "Paw."

Kate scrolled the immunity agreement. "Axyl and Emma Dover?"

"Good for you for reading the fine print. Half my clients don't."

"I told you Devana, we are getting played."

Kate ignored Bolkov, instead raising her eyebrows at Gray.

"It's a package deal. In case someone gets ornery and flings a conspiracy or facilitation charge." Gray shoved her phone closer. "Paw."

Kate reread the agreement, scrolling up and down and double-checking it. "Before I sign—I should warn you that you are wasting your time."

"Rarely."

"The movie you think you own from what Leyna knows, won't get made."

"It will. I will be your agent, and you will play you."

Kate laughed. "Nooooo thank you."

"Why not? Nobody will tell it better. You are photogenic and have presence. Tell me what happened up there."

"Classified. You know that."

"So it wasn't a drill."

Kate didn't respond. Her face felt hot.

Gray smirked. "You'll say yes. I can't tell you why. Maybe to make that fat mortgage of yours. Maybe to control the narrative about yourself." Gray waved her hands over her head to highlight an invisible marquee. "Imagine a hologram of a washed-up actress, lying about your life in front of a billion people."

Kate shook her head.

"Or maybe AI. A total hallucination with a made-up avatar."

Kate's cramps returned.

"Everybody says yes, Kate. As your agent, I will get you the best deal. Make sure you are in control. Now c'mon, paw."

Kate scrolled again to make sure she was signing the immunity agreement. Then shook her head as she pressed her thumb to the screen. "When I'm dead."

"The only way to guarantee that is to sign with me. Otherwise—" Kate felt a sharp stab in her stomach.

Gray grinned, swiped her phone, and then swooped to Jin, biting her lip. "You can paw me later."

Gray retrieved a phone from one of her pockets and set it in Jin's hand. Kate imagined she heard static electricity jumping from Gray to Jin, frying the electronics.

"It's unlocked. I'll message you the password to her server." Gray lingered, then pivoted in a runway turn to the hospital room. "My clients are ready to see you."

45

"I am thinking about a sleeve to cover my scars." Leyna fidgeted with the octopus of IV drips and wires protruding from her pink flowery hospital gown. Her gurney, IV, and monitoring equipment were sandwiched between taupe bench seats along the left and right walls. Leyna was half-upright on the gurney and blanketed with hospital-standard death-gray sheets.

Jin smiled from the corner beside Leyna's gurney. "There's a good artist in my building. Graduated CalArts."

"You have one, don't you Major?"

"Please call me Kate, Leyna. Yes, I do." Kate rolled up her blouse sleeves to show Leyna her shoulder and arm tattoos. "Built up over time. Mom and Dad inside the Star of David was my grandfather's idea. I got this one in the Marines. This one I got when I graduated the Space Force Academy—"

"What does Semper Fi Semper Supra mean?"

Jin smirked. "It means she's always faithful to being cavalier."

Kate smirked and shook her head.

"Are the skulls how many people you've killed?"

Kate thumbed the tattoo of her Mom and Dad. "No. Those are to remember friends, who've died."

"Oh. I'm sorry."

Kate smiled. "Don't be. Not your fault."

"Your parents were killed too?"

"Yes." Kate exhaled, then rolled her sleeves down. "And don't worry about scars, either." Kate smiled and expected a smile from Leyna.

"How is Jin? I wish he were here."

Kate looked around the room for help.

Annelle Gray wasn't here. She bailed after springing her trap, saying it was too crowded and that she wasn't needed. A blessing. Bolkov hovered at Leyna's right foot, flashing I-told-you-so lips.

Kate's frown settled on Axyl and Emma Dover, sitting along the right-side bench holding hands. Emma's other hand rested on the bed, comforting Leyna.

This was the fourth time Leyna had asked where Jin was.

Jin shifted a half-step forward, into her view. "I am right here."

Leyna turned and looked up. Her face lit up.

Emma patted Leyna's hand. "The doctor says her short-term memory will take a while to come back from the concussion. He says the low gravity makes bruising worse."

Kate nodded and tapped her skull. "The blood doesn't drain right. I've had a few of those too. You'll get better."

Leyna looked up at Jin. "Em says you saved my life, Jin."

Instead of telling the story for the third time, Jin said, "I will make something you can watch, so you won't forget."

"That would be nice. Can you put your hand here, on the rail, where I can see it? That way I won't forget you're here."

Jin put his hand on the rail. His eyes widened as Leyna's hand snared his.

Bolkov asked Emma, "What about her long-term memory?"

Emma looked at Leyna, who said, "Before the bomb I remember everything perfectly. I remember Paul. I remember Jade barking at the delivery drone. I remember the doctor said I will need a new lung."

Axyl said, "They took your stem cells a few days ago. The doctor said it's almost ready for transplant."

Kate blew out a breath and looked at the Dovers. "Did you tell her about the station?"

"We told her about her brother. If she remembers—"

"I remember. Rest in peace little brother, god knows you need it."

Kate said, "Little brother?"

"The way we grew up, it was always like I was the big sister, even though he was older. I had to take care of him."

"I know this is hard. We are sure your brother did not kill your mother. The timing is wrong."

"I know. I was in shock when I came to your office. You think Bill Caddell killed my mom and my brother and Ted."

"What do you think?"

"That makes a lot of sense. I started investigating my brother over the images."

Axyl said, "When I tested them, I found problems, like the redshift."

Jin nodded. "According to the historian, the images were manipulated. The hardware on the station was never upgraded. Caddell embezzled the money."

Mia added, "But without the original data we have no proof he was involved. Caddell deleted the raw image data."

Leyna fiddled with her sheets, covering herself. "He didn't. The raw data is on my server in an encrypted folder."

Kate said, "You got the raw data—how?"

Leyna looked at Axyl, who nodded. "It's ok to tell them, sweetie."

"It is. You have immunity." After Kate said it, she looked at Bolkov, who had her arms folded, flashing *this-better-be-worth-it* back.

"My mother had it. I copied it from her server."

Emma gasped, "How did you—"

"From her apartment. She keeps everything unlocked there."

"Child, you broke in?"

"Technically Em, my prints were still in the system. But then Paul caught me and deleted them. But he forgot to change the override code. I thought he and Ted faked the pictures. That's why I thought he killed my mom."

Bolkov asked, "Why don't you tell us what else you found."

"I found Dilan's donations to Earth First. I also found access codes and expense reports. That's when I really got scared. I thought my brother was a psycho terrorist."

Jin asked, "How?"

Leyna looked to Axyl for approval, then continued. "I hacked into his server and his diary."

Bolkov frowned. "Why didn't you report it?"

Axyl replied, "We tried to. Paul and Helena blocked us. The agency gave us the runaround."

Leyna moved her wires around. "So I decided to pretend to join Earth First to see if I could get close. I found messages that they were planning something big—a protest. A big group of them. I never found them, though."

Kate said, "I think there was no *they*. That's why you never found *them*. It was only ever Nathaniel Kirkwood."

Jin and Bolkov both looked at her. Kate said, "Please continue."

Bolkov said, "You mentioned expense reports. Tell me about those."

Leyna puffed her cheeks and exhaled. "The expense reports, whew. Well, Ted was faking them too."

Bolkov asked, "Did you only find Ted's fake reports?"

Leyna scrunched up her face. "No. How did you know that?"

"Tell me."

"His boss Caddell and his little minion—"

Kate asked, "Who is the minion?"

"Kody Easton."

Kate looked at Jin. "Have security pick him up and give him a metal detox."

Jin looked at his pad and grimaced. Kate turned back to Leyna. "I apologize. Please continue. Your brother's boss and his little minion's expense reports."

"What is a metal detox?"

Kate pictured Easton's arrest. He would be high, with a prostitute, need to detox, and likely antibiotics for the STD he didn't know he had. Kate shook her head to erase the image.

"It means jail while he sobers up."

"Oooh. Can I come spit on that condescending little fuck? I hate him."

Kate chuckled, glad Leyna was feeling better. "Probably inappropriate."

Jin said, "Also too late." He paused to look around. Ten eyes waited in silence. In a private message, he said, *OD'd yesterday.*

Kate nodded. "Right. Rae said politics."

Everyone looked at Kate, confused. Kate gestured to Leyna. "Please continue." Then she sent Rae a message over her neuroface, *Easton not an overdose.*

"Caddell's boss and his minion were also faking invoices and reports. They were pretending to buy things, but they never did."

Bolkov asked, "Like what?"

"A lot. Circuit boards. Equipment. Enough to replace everything at the station. Honestly, half of it I didn't recognize. Rocket parts, I think."

"So, Caddell faked buying from Lunar Foundries after he—"

Leyna said, "No. The reports had invoices from a company called ES Aerospace."

Bolkov said, "ES Aerospace? Are you sure?"

"They are all on my server."

Kate flashed Bolkov a questioning look. Bolkov said, "Shit. ES Aerospace is Jim Easton's company. The minion is his kid. Senator Barb Easton is his wife. They are laundering all the money through his company."

Jin said, "All that money went to Caddell and Easton."

Bolkov said, "Why would Dilan and Ted fake the expense reports?"

"For my brother, it was a fuck you to Caddell. He thought it took away from what Caddell could steal. Only, my mother found out."

Leyna glowered at Bolkov. After a long pause, Bolkov said, "I went to Helena with a video of Dilan and Ted arguing with Bill Caddell. She slammed the door in my face."

Leyna fiddled with her IV and punched a button on the gurney. "Dilan and Ted planned to spend the money they stole on a trip to Mars. Not like Caddell could turn them in."

Kate said, "What about Paul? Did he know?"

"There are no secrets between them. Plus, Paul caught me, so he probably figured out what I was doing. Nolan probably knew too."

Kate looked at Jin. "The unidentified figure on Paul's video."

"On it."

Leyna looked at Jin. "You think he killed my Mom."

Kate looked at Emma Dover, who returned a glare. She didn't need a neuroface or AI to translate Emma's face. Emma Dover was asserting her unhappiness that Caddell tried to kill Leyna too.

"I am sorry about your family, Leyna. Yes. He's a suspect for all the murders."

"Did Dilan suffer?"

"No. It was instant. Space decompression."

"I'm glad. He suffered so much. He deserves peace." Leyna's eyes got moist, and she reached for Emma's hand. Then she said, "I found a report dated the 20th. Caddell expensed ES Aerospace for a rocket and security to fire Dilan and Ted and escort them off the station. That didn't make sense because they *wanted* to leave. They should be on their way to Mars. After mom was killed I just—" Leyna's eyes watered, and she squeezed Emma's hand.

"Boss, the rocket they hired is *Beam Six*."

Bolkov ran her hand over her face. "Is he that arrogant, expensing a murder?"

"He's been getting away with this for years. Not just embezzling—laundering it through Easton. And his plan worked, except he didn't count on Rae cracking the timeline." Kate looked at Bolkov as she said it, imagining a *thank you* for nailing her case on Caddell. When it didn't happen, she wondered why Bolkov was here. Not Caddell. Or not entirely Caddell. Then the answer smacked her in the face.

Bolkov asked, "You really believe that gibberish?"

Kate tugged her ring finger. "I bet my life on her. It's not gibberish, Mia."

Someone knocked on the door. A human nurse in baby-blue scrubs peeked in. "Time for her meds." Kate nodded, and the nurse came in, squeezing around Bolkov. "I need to give her a sedative. The doctor wants to make sure she sleeps. Leyna, how is your pain?"

Leyna looked at her hand. "The pain button doesn't work. Can Jin stay?"

The nurse fiddled with Leyna's IV line, then injected something into the bag. "The doctor wants you to sleep for a solid nine hours." The nurse looked around the room. "No disturbances. Your friends are welcome to stand around in the dark."

Jin sandwiched Leyna's hand on the gurney. "You'll be safe here."

"I should help you go through the reports. There are so many."

Kate waved Jin to the door. "You have been extremely helpful, Leyna. Let us do the investigating from here on out. You need to get rest."

Kate thanked the Dovers, then waved Bolkov and Jin out of the room. Kate exited last and closed the door behind her.

46

Once the door closed, Jin said, "Caddell hired those four fuckers at the hospital that tried to take Leyna."

That wasn't all he did. Kate nodded, looking up and down the hall. It was empty except for her, Jin, and Bolkov. "Who did Caddell meet with while he was here?"

"Nothing unusual. Kelli you know about." Jin smiled. "Helena Darcy. Kody Easton. One unsub at Lunaburger. Otherwise he mostly kept to himself."

"Do we have video of the unsub?"

"Yes."

Jin turned his pad to show a video of Caddell seated in the Lunaburger across from her office eating. The man across from him wore a mask. He was stealing fries from Caddell's plate, waving them, then eating them. There was no audio but the lip reading AI translated.

[Man] "How many does it hold?"

[Caddell] "Six."

[Man] "That'll do. I'll take it."

[Caddell] "Take my friends with you."

[Man] "How many friends do you have?"

[Caddell] "Four. I'll take the shuttle."

[Man] "More than I thought." Then, after the man chewed more of Caddell's fries, "Sure, why not? It's a party. Two hours."

[Caddell] "Fine"

The man stared at Caddell until Caddell picked up his phone and typed something.

[Man] "Also tell them I'm the captain. They take me wherever."

Caddell thumbed something on his phone.

[Caddell] "Can I give them a name?"

[Man] "Are you dumber than a doormat? I mean you are a doormat. My cute sweaty little doormat. But don't be as dumb as one."

Caddell thumbed his phone again.

[Man] "This is a new experiencc for you?"

[Caddell] "No. Not really."

[Man] "I didn't think so. I feel like in different circumstances we would have been friends."

[Caddell] "I have a son your age."

[Man] "Yeah but I can see it in your eyes. You're staring out over the cliff, thinking people shouldn't step off. Wattsuckers are disgusting. Our meeting was karma. The universe defending itself."

[Caddell] "I'm just sick of this place. These people. This food. I just want to go home."

[Man] "I'll send details where to send the money. Remember, every month. I feel like I should remind you what I have. But I also feel like I won't need to. You'll get home, relieved to feel gravity again. You'll start thinking of the payments as a donation. We call ourselves the Orionids."

The man stole Caddell's last french fry and waved it like a conductor.

[Man] "Who knows. You bump into an old friend. Except they aren't your friend anymore because now they talk to machines through a wireless interface in their fucking neck. Or they've been infected with a virus to get rid of gray hair and glasses. You'll feel different. Happy to know the money is making a difference. You'll think of yourself as one of us. Maybe up your donation."

[Caddell] "I don't give a shit what you call yourself. Just go. They don't know who you are so they might not wait."

Kate reached and stopped the video. "That's Nathaniel Kirkwood."

"Hard to tell with the mask, boss."

"He said wattsucker. Kirkwood is blackmailing Caddell. Paul's video has the three of them together. Kirkwood caught Caddell murdering Helena during the protest, then used it to take *Beam Six*. Are the trackers on the contractors still active?"

"Yes. Still on группа 6."

"Verify they are there, then let's fire up *Tesseract*."

Bolkov said, "Aren't we getting ahead of ourselves?"

"Kirkwood is on группа 6 with the others. Caddell's four friends are the contractors. They went back to the far side station to paint the graffiti, then to группа 6."

"Went back? How do you know?"

"More of Rae's flowery math. They brought special paint, and it was fresh."

Bolkov folded her arms. "So what if it's fresh?"

Jin said, "Can't just paint in a vacuum, Mia. What they use for that is more like epoxy. Hard to find, even here. They went back knowing they would arrive to a blown out station. That's the only reason to take that kind of paint."

Kate said, "Something that's been bothering me. Why four contractors? The answer is, they needed four to destroy the station."

Bolkov asked, "Why go back just to paint graffiti?"

"I think Caddell used the protestors as a cover story, then somehow it became a real story. He planned to blame them, but Kirkwood comes along at the last minute and says, no, it doesn't look like we did it because we would have graffitied the station."

Kate looked around, there was nothing in the hall to punch. "I want these four fuckers and Kirkwood. And Caddell. Where is Caddell?" She wanted the Eastons too, but that would be more complicated.

Jin said, "Caddell left on a shuttle five hours ago. Economy. One layover. He'll be on Earth in thirty-one hours."

Enough time to do what she needed to do before he landed.

Bolkov said, "What about the other three protestors?"

Kate said, "I don't think they exist. Jin, did we ever see other protestors on video?"

"No. Witnesses reported multiple protestors but fuck if I can find them."

"Meat memory is unreliable. And we never found any other DNA or prints at Kirkwood's apartment. Did Rae get back to you about the medical records?"

Bolkov glared at Jin. "You hacked his medical records?"

Kate shook her head. A strange red line for Bolkov given how much illegal surveillance she handed over. Kate asked, "What was the diagnosis?"

"She said layman's terms, multiple personality disorder, possibly a rare side effect of Phantom Neuroface Disorder. She thinks all the messages on the server were only ever Kirkwood talking to himself. She said, possibly related to having his neurochip removed. He was delusional too. He thought his parents were alive, but they died years ago, committing suicide off the Central Park West building he inherited."

Bolkov said, "Jesus, Kirkwood was hallucinating? All those messages were him talking to himself? Because he had a neurochip put in?"

Jin shrugged. "I've never had any problems with mine."

Kate said, "I turn mine off sometimes for weeks at a time. Too much stimulus. When I do it's like a part of my brain is asleep, like when you wake up and your arm has pins and needles, except in your skull. Am I going to start chewing my fingers off?"

Jin said, "I don't think the neurochip installation is the problem. Having nanowires ripped out of your brain is hella bad idea. Rae said she'd need a scan. "

Kate grimaced. "Like a self-inflicted lobotomy. He's dangerous and we are going to get him before he tries another attempt on the colony."

The hospital door swooshed open, and Axyl and Emma Dover exited. Axyl reached out for Kate's hand. "We are really grateful you are handling this."

Kate must have been squeezing hard, but Axyl didn't retreat. "We are glad she is recovering. She'll be safe here." She let off the pressure, but he held firm.

Emma said, "Will she? What about the four that came for her?" She pointed to Jin's pad. Jin turned it around and hid it. "They were at the hospital. That's what the nurse said. They were coming to finish the job, weren't they? That's why she woke up hiding in the morgue, isn't it?"

Those weren't questions. The Dovers weren't naive.

Bolkov said, "They step foot on the colony, we'll get them."

Emma Dover glowered at Bolkov and pointed at Jin's midsection. "Bill Caddell has money. God knows how much stashed. He could send any *four fuckers*, isn't that right?"

Emma's face shook and squeezed, as if getting the word *fucker* out was a once-in-a-lifetime event. It was a not-too-subtle hint the Dovers had been listening at the door.

Axyl squeezed Kate's hand again while sizing up Jin. "Will you be guarding her?"

Another non-question. Kate looked at Jin and Bolkov. "I will find someone, yes."

"She feels safe around your deputy."

"I need Jin to help the investigation. But my brother Greg is thirty centimeters taller and a hundred kilos meaner."

Emma looked relieved. "Thank you. It means a lot to us. She is like our own daughter."

Axyl let go, then they walked down the hall. When they were out of earshot, Kate caught Jin smirking.

"What?"

He put up two fingers. "Two. Two centimeters taller."

"I meant compared to me. And he *is* meaner than you."

"Why don't you just put him on the payroll already?"

"He's happy keeping pervert ass out of that strip club."

"Plus, you are mean enough for all of us, right?"

Kate smiled and imitated Rae's Dad's Wisconsin accent. "You betcha."

Bolkov said, "Back to Caddell. I need to see those reports. If we can prove he sent money and codes to Earth First, that's a free upgrade to domestic terrorism."

"Done and done. I can trace the messages. Is this above or below deck?"

Bolkov said, "I assume you mean legal. It needs to be legal."

Kate said, "Do all the investigating you want. I am going to get all five of them."

Bolkov threw up her hands. "*Going* to get them? Why? We should lure them back."

Jin said, "How would you lure them back?"

"Let them know Leyna is alive. Encourage them to come back and finish the job."

Kate put up her hand. "No."

"It's not—"

Kate stared at Bolkov until she blinked. "No. They will come here expecting an ambush. They outnumber us, and we can't even guarantee the same four will come. Sometimes the bait gets taken, Mia. We are not risking Leyna's life."

"Amen, boss."

"So you're going to группа 6."

"We hunt them there. They are drunk, high, and think they are safe."

"That's a Russian space station—the state department—"

"The state department can suck my bean. I don't work for them anymore. Anyway, the cartels run it. So it's hard to call it Russian."

"You can't just—"

"You can't, maybe. I can do whatever I want. I'll ask for forgiveness later. You can stay here and guard Leyna."

Bolkov folded her arms. "Hell no."

Kate looked at Jin.

"Hell yes, I am in boss."

Kate watched Bolkov's face rotate through disbelief, frustration, and fear. "Fine. I am coming too. If these assholes killed Darcy and Holden and can finger Caddell, I want to talk to them."

Kate sized up Bolkov. "Have you been trained on space ballistics?"

"In a simulator."

"Not the same. There are only two seats in the cockpit. You have to ride in the cabin."

"What the hell kind of—" Bolkov exhaled. "Fine. Cabin."

"Ever done 8gs?" Kate looked over at Jin, who was holding back a smirk.

"No. Do I look like a fighter pilot?"

"When did you eat last?"

"About an hour."

"Go puke your lunch up then meet us at the private spaceport in about a half hour."

"Seriously?"

"Or, puke in your suit on liftoff and swim in it for sixteen hours. Your call."

"Sixteen hours?"

"Six there, eight back."

"Just two hours to interrogate them?"

"I don't plan to stay long enough to interrogate them, Mia. We are dragging their asses back here."

"You are fucking nuts. They are not coming voluntarily."

Kate shrugged. "Up to them. This is an all-volunteer mission. High risk. Are you in or out?"

"Do I have a choice?"

"Always. You can stay here and guard Leyna."

Bolkov inhaled, then puffed her cheeks and nodded. "This is insane. But I'll see you in thirty."

Jin watched Bolkov scurry down the hall. "She's never flown with you. Mia has no idea what she's getting into."

Kate smiled and patted Jin on the shoulder. "Since you're not the boot around here anymore—"

Jin pumped his fist. Then read Kate's face and frowned.

"—I need to tell you something." She explained her real problem with boarding группа 6. Then said, "You can back out."

"I go where you go." He looked down the hall where Bolkov had been. "You going to tell her?"

"They won't do anything to her. She's not worth anything to them."

"I feel honored."

"So, it's important they don't know we are coming. And Plan E, I need you to rig *Tesseract* to blow."

Jin grinned. He was as loco as she was.

47

"I have control."

"Confirm you have control." Kate sat back, letting Jin pilot.

Jin fired the attitude thrusters, centering Earth's blue and white horizon in the cockpit window. Then *Tesseract* rotated, spinning the Earth until its blue horizon was above them.

"Do you miss it, Kate?"

Kate had not been to Earth in eight months. She caught her faint reflection in the black stripe across the cockpit window, between Earth's blue grin and the dash. Past Kate would see her current self as a helmeted alien in a pressure suit. Unrecognizable, with a serious job, a fancy apartment, and trying on her mother's engagement ring—even if only for ten minutes.

"I miss—I miss real ice cream. But—" Kate studied the layers of white clouds above her, dotted with fat cotton balls. It was an overcast and rainy day somewhere on Earth. Up here, it was always sunny. "—but I wouldn't trade."

"Yeah, me neither. I definitely don't miss living in one of these floating roach cans like группа 6."

Although группа 6 was a silver-gray dot on the horizon, it filled up the dash display in front of her. Kate was here a few years ago. Since, two new rings had been added. Six massive rotating rings in total. Each spun on a rim of stationary scaffolding connected to a long axle. Docking modules protruded from the axle between rings like colossal insect spines, the kind that injected addictive toxins, and then sucked money and energy. Ships stuck to the docking needles, paralyzed, many of them empty husks.

An engineering marvel thirty years ago, группа 6 had been abandoned, then purchased by an oligarch, and now the cartel that ran it was remodeling. At each end, drones constructed the seventh and eighth rings in a meticulously choreographed dance traveling twenty-thousand-kilometers-per-hour through space. Four supply ships hovered, two on each side. A line of white drones like space termites crawled through space to the bare metal bones carrying materials. They transferred them to construction drones clinging to the scaffolds, then returned.

The drones not only vacuum welded the panels over bones, they also confirmed each part's weight and position and sent the data back to a central computer to orchestrate load balancing. As drones fabricated the far ring, drones on the near end assembled a mirror image. Every nut and bolt was positioned to prevent группа 6 from destabilizing like a lopsided high-speed tire dismounting in a death wobble.

The slightest off-balance force would turn группа 6 into a meteor in the upper atmosphere and send its shards crashing to Earth. Not that she would lose sleep if this place burned up, but detonating *Tesseract* to turn группа 6 into a bolide was plan E, and she had four other escape plans before that.

Kate zoomed in to supervise Jin's docking protocol. A dotted green line ended at a green dot at the center docking module of группа 6, farthest from the construction. It would have been her choice.

"You promised me 8gs."

Mia's voice echoed in Kate's helmet. In the window, Kate glimpsed Mia's reflection. Her body was stretched through the cockpit threshold, floating in zero-g, with her arms stabilizing her body against the walls.

Kate switched the display to survey the docking ports. "Maybe on the way out. We'll need every molecule of fuel to get out of here. Did you get what you needed off Leyna's server?"

"Defense Department has reviewed the raw images. They are going to take over the station. I have orders to confiscate all the raw image data and delete the copies. You two need to sign a non-disclosure."

Kate nodded. That made sense.

Jin shook his head. "Everyone wants those images. What's in them?"

Mia didn't respond.

Jin paused a beat, looking at Kate, then said, "I want to know what's in the image data."

Kate said, "Ninety-nine percent of the declassified satellite data from forty years ago is fucking ancient riverbeds or images of Russia and China giving us the middle finger."

"I don't see your point." She didn't answer. After a long pause, he said, "You are saying someone is out there four light years away giving us the middle finger."

"If we are lucky, that's all they are giving us. If we are even luckier, it's just ancient riverbeds on a distant planet."

"But it's proof—"

Kate shrugged.

Jin shook his head while swiping through docking screens. "The Pentagon gets to hide this forever?"

Kate said, "Not forever. A building full of analysts will spend a year working up a threat assessment. Then it goes in a limestone mine for seventy-seven years. After that, they'll declassify it."

In a limestone mine, in a box, probably two rows over from her classified medals.

Mia said, "One hundred and thirteen now."

Damn, Kate was never going to see those medals again.

Jin said, "No way the Pentagon keeps this a secret for a hundred years."

Kate shrugged again. "It's already the worst kept secret in history."

"You knew."

"This isn't my first rodeo in space." She smiled under her visor.

"People should know."

Kate shook her head. "Why? What would happen?"

"We'd go there. Shake hands, share technology." He paused to look at Kate, then shook his head. "Then wipe them out and colonize the planet."

Kate gun-pointed her finger toward him and mouthed, *bingo.* To Mia's reflection, she asked, "What do you think, Mia?"

Mia nodded. "The Pentagon eggheads say the history of civilization is that the more technologically advanced one wipes out the lesser one. If they are more advanced, we don't want them to know our location. If they are less advanced, we don't want them to know we are coming. And the Pentagon *certainly* doesn't want to telegraph our capabilities."

"The fact that we haven't heard anything is proof they don't know we're here." Looking towards Jin, Kate said, "Or that there's no intelligent life. Intelligent life would have recognized us as the neighborhood assholes and wiped us out first."

Jin looked out the window. "We don't know they aren't trying. It would take a thousand years to send a fleet, right?"

"I wouldn't bother with a fleet. I would launch a big fucking meteor and smash the locusts. And I would start with группа 6." Kate pointed out the window.

The cylindrical, gray reflection of the группа 6 docking column was a warped white stripe in Jin's visor. He swiped across the controls and put a port within the crosshairs. Then he sent Kate a private message over his neuroface, *We should keep a copy and do our own 'threat assessment'. We are out here on our own.*

He said *threat assessment* sarcastically as if he forecasted the Pentagon would screw it up. Kate was impressed he'd been able to project sarcasm over his neuroface. He was right, too. She responded, *roger that.* Swiping through control screens, she said, "For now let's worry about the more immediate threat, humans killing each other."

Jin looked up at Mia's reflection in the cockpit window. "So, what will happen to Caddell?"

Mia said, "Unfortunately, we can't prosecute him because the image data is classified. I'm pissed about that. So this could be a wasted trip."

Kate said, "He killed people. And he will keep doing it. Prosecution is not what I have in mind."

Kate pointed to a ship docked on the module two places over from the center. "Get close."

Mia's reflection asked, "Close to what?"

Kate zoomed the display to show the ship's markings, *Beam Six*. "So, not a wasted trip."

Mia said, "You think they are still here?"

"We used to call this place Upyr 6, the Russian word for vampire, because it sucks everything you have. It's hard to leave—until you run out of money. Then you can't leave fast enough. If you owe, they confiscate your ship and you burn in."

"Burn in?"

Kate scrolled the display to show round coin-like objects dimpled on the docking module. She kept scrolling until she found a slot with the empty imprint of an upside-down cone, the shape of early-century lunar capsules. "Burn in, they send you back to Earth in one of those."

"Oh. Escape pods? Do they work?"

Kate shrugged as if Mia could see through the p-suit. She hoped they worked, since that was Plan B and C. "Probably. But at that point, your choice is to be killed on the station or take your chances in that."

Jin said, "I doubt people self-report they are alive to the cartel either. Like, Hi honey, I'm home, I still owe you money."

Kate nodded.

Mia said, "How are we getting in?"

Jin smirked. "I think we just knock."

"You don't just knock on группа 6."

"We do. I called ahead and made a reservation."

Kate said, "Jin means he hacked in and gave us a cover. We're just—" Kate smiled at Jin as if he could see under the visor. "Three more contractors on vacation, right?"

He nodded. Kate switched back to *Tesseract's* docking display and gave Jin a gloved thumbs-up.

Mia said, "Do I need to go back to the cabin and buckle up?"

Jin looked up, the space station reflecting in his visor between a sliver of Earth and a fisheye view of the dashboard display.

"Don't move. This won't hurt a bit."

48

Before the docking clamps' clunk and clatter reverberated inside the ship, Kate had swum to the cabin and removed her p-suit. Jin and Mia followed. Kate opened *Tesseract's* hatch and peered into the space station from the threshold. The docking module extended to a narrow, cylindrical back dot to her right. To the left, the module passage ended. The walls were dirty, as if peppered with smoke. Down the corridor, left and right alternating doors led to other ships. Counting from her memory of the exterior, the seventh door led to *Beam Six*.

Bolkov said, "We need to crawl all the way in zero-g? That must be—"

Kate pointed to a nylon handle above her sliding along the corridor. "—three hundred meters. But no, grab one of these handles as they go by." Then, she shoved herself towards it. She caught it and held on, letting the loop pull her forward. Kate looked between her feet. She watched Mia push off, miss the loop, float in zero-g, then right herself against the wall. Mia crawled around to grab the next handle as it passed. She jerked, her body stretched out, then the pulley dragged her a few meters behind Kate. Jin, taller than both of them, simply reached on his tiptoes. One hand grabbed a loop while the other held onto the hatch. The pulley yanked, and the hatch door slammed shut. He let go of the hatch and allowed the lift system to propel him.

Kate counted the doors as they passed. When she saw number seven approaching, she let go of the loop and grabbed the handrail, her feet swinging to a stop. She put her hand out for Mia, who caught it and twisted wide. Kate reined her in. Jin stopped on the far side of seven.

"You get control of the ship, Jin?"

The display on Jin's pad cycled through screens as he gave it commands from his neuroface. Then he nodded. "Have it."

"Vent the cabin. Count to twenty. Then repressurize and open the hatch."

Mia's mouth opened, then closed.

"They'll live, Mia. Unfortunately."

Kate heard metal squeals, groans, and punching from the other side of the hatch as *Beam Six* depressurized. She counted in her head. At twenty, she heard a hiss, a clunk, and then the hatch to *Beam Six* drifted open.

"Mia, you wait here. Cover the door."

Mia's mouth opened and closed again, then her forearm tensed as she gripped the handrail. Kate clasped the threshold and pulled herself inside with a breaststroke, floating near the ceiling. The interior of *Beam Six* was small and bland. Six seats, all facing a tall one-hundred-eighty-degree cockpit window overlooking rings three and five of группа 6. One of the front seats was fully reclined, with a blanket and pillow velcroed to the next seat over. Blue liquid droplets floated around the cabin.

"Not here."

Jin peered through the threshold, eyeing the blankets. "Someone's been sleeping here. What's the blue goo?"

Kate pointed to a silver bag velcroed to the armrest beside the pillow. "Looks like a sports drink exploded when we depressurized. Let's close the hatch before it floats out."

Kate swam along the ceiling into the corridor and closed the hatch behind her. "Is *Beam Six* fueled?"

"Nope. Empty."

"Probably burned it all getting here. Disable it anyway, just in case."

Mia said, "They're stuck here."

"No. There are a hundred other ships they can steal. They are here by—"

Kate almost said *choice*, but that wasn't the right word. She pursed her lips, shook her head, and hopped on one of the loops. She watched Mia climb the wall and reach for one. Jin waited for Mia. With two eyes on his pad, he reached up and one-handed a hoop.

At the end of the corridor, the dot was now a door to the center axle where all the docking spokes ended. There were rings to the left and right.

Jin called out, "Right. Second ring. Trackers are pinging from five-ninety-four and five-ninety-five but—"

Kate grinned and winked *I-told-you-so* at Mia.

"—It looks like they are in a club nearby boss, Space Moscow."

Mia said, "Isn't that a chain?"

Kate said, "Run by the same cartel. Here the drugs and faces are harder."

The opening loomed in front of Kate. She let go of the lift, letting her inertia propel her. She swung her arms wide, sliding her hands along the walls and calibrating the friction to slow herself through the door. Then she found a loop going right and hung on. Her body stretched out as the lift moved. She looked between her feet. Mia reached through the door and grabbed a loop. Jin came through feet first, landed against the wall, then pushed off to propel himself toward them. He was showing off.

Loud laughing and talking echoed off the walls, and then Kate saw people ahead. They were drunk, high, mean, and on a collision course. She opted to duck into one of the docking spokes as she passed. Then, with one hand on the edge, she leaned out and snagged Mia, pulling her in.

Jin smirked, shrugged, and kept going. He put one arm forward like a blocker. Kate smiled and shoved off behind him. She looked between her feet to see Mia snatch a pulley.

Ahead, she heard *fucking hell mate*, and *bloody moron*, then passed two drunk men clinging to handrails and giving her a middle finger. Kate ignored them. Through her feet, she saw Mia pass them, exchange words, then flip them off.

Forward, Jin was disappearing into a side passageway. She let go of the loop, slowed her momentum on a handrail, then gripped hard and swung feet first into the corridor. Mia floated by the door, eyebrows raised and mouth agape. A second later, she reappeared, using the threshold for leverage and swimming through the hatch.

A thruple entered the corridor behind Mia. Two men and a woman pushed through the door and took up the entire passage so no one could pass them. In front of Jin, Kate spotted more people, and an elevator. They were in a long line, entering a sick amusement park.

She pulled herself towards Jin and motioned for Mia to close ranks. At the end of this corridor, the elevator would accelerate and align them with the ring. They would hop, step, and trip forward to one-third Earth's gravity, then descend stairs into a migraine. Kate felt a tug in her intestines. Getting into группа 6 had been easy. Getting out wouldn't be.

49

Walking around ring three to Space Moscow had been like a dizzying tour of a cramped Russian boat in the center of a storm. группа 6's rings were like massive hamster wheels, rotating to simulate gravity, with an upside-down horizon forty-five paces ahead. People were the hamsters. The floor continually fell to meet her feet, while at the horizon, maid and maintenance drones appeared to drop from the ceiling and then zig-zag underfoot.

She passed an endless series of nondescript gray portals and black windows leading to something seedy or dangerous. The cleaning drones toiled and whined, gray paint peeling from overheating motors, swelling their bins with the dirt they vacuumed from the floors and vents. группа 6's drugged and zombified inhabitants appeared at the horizon shoes-first, then legs, then torso, and finally their yellowed and bloodshot eyes. Sometimes they bumped and kicked the maid drones, other times their eyes stabbed Kate's gut. A few offered sex for money. Or money for sex. But none yelled *Devana!* She felt relief each time they passed. группа 6 was surreal, treacherous, and nauseating.

Mia wasn't shaky, which Kate attributed to inexperience. Jin wasn't shaky either, but he was taking Kate's lead.

They were a third of the way around when Jin paused mid-stride. Shouting and screaming echoed ahead.

Jin said, "Surveillance cut."

Kate waved them forward. "Perfect. Let's move."

Jin followed. Mia furrowed her brow and stalled but then followed two steps behind.

When they got to Space Moscow, the bouncer was cleaning up a brawl. A man and a woman smeared the floor, bloodied, punctured, and not breathing. Another man stood nearby, nursing a deep red gash.

The bouncer's clothes were bloodied. The weapon he held was hidden by his forearm. He wiped it on his pants in one long gleaming streak, then sheathed it in a thigh pocket.

As Kate walked by, the bouncer made eye contact. She looked aside, beyond his face tattoo and scars, peeking in the door to a back corner, where she thought the contractors would be seated.

She kept walking, but her heart raced because Mia slowed to rubberneck the carnage. Slow was dangerous and Mia was three steps behind. Kate slowed until she could wrap her arms around Mia, then bit her lip and kissed Mia full on the mouth. She let her tongue probe around, listening for the catcalls, then released and drove her forward.

"Christ Devana."

"Keep. Moving."

"To where?" Mia ran her hand through her hair and fluffed it.

Jin chuckled. Kate looked at him, and he shook his head. "I'm moving boss."

Kate said, "Gimp and Simp are still in the club."

"Next time you could buy me a drink first. Or warn me."

Jin choked words through his smirk. "The other two are in five-ninety-four."

"Five-ninety-four it is." Kate side-hugged Mia and smiled.

The three of them continued arm-in-arm. Periodically Kate checked группа 6's windows, eyeing the faint reflection for followers or unusual interest. The bouncer was watching the crowd at the threshold of Space Moscow. The crowd's eyes fell on the bodies pooling in blood.

Forty-five strides later, they were out of the bouncer's view, so Kate dropped her arms. Mia sighed and touched her hair again.

Jin chuckled again. "You going to be ok, Mia?"

"My husband will be fine."

"Not what I asked."

Kate lifted a backhand fist to shush them, then pointed to a worn silver-on-black placard on the door thirty paces ahead. She motioned for them to walk past the door. Twenty paces beyond, she checked the hall, empty, then they crept back to five-ninety-four.

There was no way to know what was on the other side of the door. The pair could be asleep. Or having sex with prostitutes. Or something else nefarious while one held a shotgun to the door. *Blam, blam, blam.* First, she would be dead, then Jin, then Mia.

Kate motioned for Jin to take the side of the door with the lock, while she and Mia took the opposite side. Jin put one finger up. Then as his hand morphed to thumbs-up, she heard the door's solenoid click. She put her fingertips on the door and slid it into its wall pocket. It was dark inside. The light from the hall was a problem, but there was no shotgun blast.

Kate peered around the threshold and prayed thank you to whoever invented night eye masks. The pair had splurged for the extra-large soft black ones with stereo speakers, the kind that were perfect for drowning out lights and snoring. Or for masking Kate while she danced and sang her way into their stateroom.

Kate motioned for Jin and Mia to wait. She tiptoed in, using the hallway light to inspect for weapons. The cabin was tiny and messy. Two twin beds occupied the middle of the room, leaving barely enough space to walk around. A gun could have been stashed under heaps of pants, in a backpack, or in one of the open drawers spitting shirts and underwear. But, she guessed under the bed or pillow.

She motioned for Jin to come in and stand over the far side bed. Mia stepped in. Kate signaled for her to close the door, pointed to the lights, and put three fingers up. Then, she stood over the other bed. She recognized the broken nose on number two from the hospital. It had not healed well, so he snored like a chainsaw.

Kate counted down with her fingers. On zero, Mia flipped the lights. The combined reaction was more loud snoring. Kate put her knee on Two's chest, her gun to his neck, and ripped off his face mask.

"Jesus Fuck. I told you I'd pay you."

It took a few seconds for Two's eyes to adjust. When his pupils constricted, he focused on Kate, struggled for a half second, then opened his palms when he saw the gun. "Who the fuck are you?"

His hands reached for the pillow. Kate pressed her gun to his carotid and whispered, *don't move*. He froze. His breath had a sickly sweet metabolized alcohol smell. She felt under the pillow, retrieved a pistol, and handed it to Mia.

"You know who I am. Palms on the headboard."

He complied, saying, "You are going to be in a lot of trouble for this. You'll never get off this station alive."

"Says the guy with the gun to his chin. What's the bounty on me up to?"

His face looked blank.

"Well, right now, you're the only one who's seen me here. And if I shoot you in the face, it stays that way." He looked at the barrel of her gun and swallowed. "Or, maybe you tell me all about how you killed two sweet innocent people on a science outpost."

"We were never at any science outpost."

"We have you on video leaving for the far side observatory. You, sleepy here, the woman with the gimpy leg, and her shadow."

"You're insane."

"What's your name?"

"My name is fuck you bitch."

"Boozy. You smell like a Boozy. You know how this game works, right, Boozy? Jin there wakes up your partner, Snoozy. Then we have a debate about whose idea it was to kill Dilan Darcy and Ted Holden. He'll say it was your idea, you'll say it's his. The winner gets a ride home, the loser gets to stay here and bleed like a snitch."

"Eat my ass. You aren't going to shoot. I am not telling you shit."

Kate shrugged and looked at Jin. "Wake Snoozy."

He shook Snoozy and then ripped his mask off. Snoozy opened one eye and squinted around the room. "Did we buy a—"

Boozy shouted, *Devana!* and then pushed Kate off the bed. Mia screamed, *gun*. Three blasts reverberated off the tiny stateroom's walls. The muzzle flash blinded Kate and her ears rang. When she stood, she checked herself. She wasn't bleeding. Neither were Jin or Mia. Mia had her gun on Snoozy, whose brains were on the headboard and mattress. Boozy had two holes in his chest, two center-mass shots, one to the heart. He was coughing and pumping too much blood from his chest to be saved.

As the ringing subsided, it was replaced with Mia pleading, *NO NO NO NO*. Mia didn't lower her weapon. Kate stood beside Mia with her arm around her waist and then pushed the muzzle down.

Jin said, "I didn't see the gun."

Choice reprimands replaced the tinging in Kate's ears. But now wasn't the time. They needed to move.

Mia caught her breath. "I am so sorry. I saw—"

"—he had a gun, I know. Good shoot." Kate squeezed between the beds and took Snoozy's gun from his hand. She unloaded it and checked it twice.

Jin said, "I have no fucking idea where that gun came from."

"Where do you think it came from?"

"Between the mattress and the headboard?"

Kate tossed the pistol on the bed. "Piece of shit jammed on him. You are lucky to be alive." She looked at Mia. "We all are."

Mia remained fixated on Boozy. Her eyes were wet. Kate put her hand on Mia's shoulder. "Jin, can you search the beds?"

Kate backed Mia towards the door while Jin stumbled over shoes, clothes, and luggage. He slid his hand under Boozy's pillow, lifted his head, and then pulled another gun from between the headboard and the mattress.

"Good save, Mia." Kate rubbed Mia's shoulders.

The water was flowing down Mia's cheeks. "I don't know how to write this up. I am going to be fired."

Kate looked at Jin. He unloaded the gun, then shrugged. Kate wiped Mia's tears. "What happens on группа 6 stays on группа 6. Right Jin?"

"10-4."

"But the sound—"

"They'll think someone didn't pay their tab. Happens all the time."

Jin climbed over Boozy's body to grab a phone he'd spotted. "Like the club. Right?"

Kate nodded. Jin pressed the phone to an ash-gray finger and then waved it and smiled.

Kate pointed to a computer splattered with gore. "Unlock everything. Grab and go. We need to move."

"It's—I don't have—"

Kate pointed Mia to a shirt and backpack on the floor. "Wipe it off and stuff it in. We need to move."

Jin asked, "What about the guns?"

Kate didn't answer. Instead, she grabbed a backpack off the floor and stuffed a laptop in it.

"10-4 boss. Take the electronics."

50

When they returned to Space Moscow, drones were smearing coagulated red muck across the floor with their mops. Patrons walked across the slop, leaving tracks of red footprints up and down the grayish corridor. Before Kate exited five-ninety-four, she'd scanned her bloodstained clothes and checked the closets. But she decided against stealing clothes and changing. Bloodstains were like an invisibility cloak here. Even the bouncer of Space Moscow looked past the three of them and waved them in.

Space Moscow's black walls hid the filth at the tables and booths while green and purple tube lights framed it as a reminder. Although Space Moscow was decorated like a retro dance club, there was no music, only a high hum in her ears from the ventilation fans interacting with her gunshot-induced tinnitus. She detected a bleach smell, ozone.

She spotted Gimp and Simp, still at a back right-corner booth occupied by a tabletop arcade game. She ducked to the left and motioned for Jin and Mia to grab an empty booth nearby while she pushed her way to a counter lined with blue string lights.

The back of the bar was mirrored and lined with shelves of unlabeled liquids refracting the club's neon colors. The bartender dressed in skin-tight, midnight-purple spandex with vertical orange stripes and a wig of green string lights. His head dipped in acknowledgment as she shoved the last centimeter to the counter.

Stripe floated down the counter, checking with each customer until he got to Kate. His ice-blue eyes mirrored the blue counter lights.

"Three Iced Bounties."

Stripe's blue eyes blinked, and he took a half step. She tapped her finger on the bar.

"Real coconut."

Stripe's eyes blinked again, and Kate felt like prey.

"Real coconut. Big upcharge."

Kate smiled at Stripe's unexpectedly perfect English and tapped her finger on the bar again. "I'll pay."

"Do you want to run a tab?"

"We won't be here long."

Kate watched Stripe retrieve cups of espresso and then glass jars with cocoa powder, ice, milk, and shredded coconut. The last time she'd tasted natural coconut was in Cabo San Lucas, eight months ago. February felt like a lifetime ago. After quitting the military three years ago, she took a job in the private sector, spending her nights dancing, and her days investigating corporate types who felt entitled to pad their early retirement fund with company money. For three years, no one shot at her. She had a platoon of girlfriends and no responsibility. In February she boarded a flight to the colony with a healthy olive skin tone, thinking she had the best job in the world, that it was a mistake that they'd assigned her to investigate an engineer at Lunar Foundries for a second time, and that she'd be on the first flight home once they realized the mistake. Now, her skin flashed caution orange under Space Moscow's LEDs. She wanted to call Rae and Axio and tell them she was safe.

Stripe mixed ingredients with the skill of a professional street magician performing the three-shell game. He dusted the cocoa powder into the espresso, added milk, swished, then swirled the mix over the ice and garnished with the coconut. She monitored his hands because the secret to the three-shell game was that the pea slid in and out of the shells while the magician covered it. She did not want anything extra slipping in.

After he slid the drinks towards her, she swirled a coconut strand in the latte and tasted it.

"Best Iced Bounties in the solar system right here." She winked at him, thanked and then paid him triple. Once for the drinks, twice as a tip, and the third to remain invisible. He said happy hunting and moved to the right.

In retrospect, she miscalculated and should have tipped more. Later she learned Kirkwood also paid Stripe as a lookout.

Kate scooped the drinks and forced her way to their booth. Jin was engrossed in his pad, which covered a smutty arcade game begging for money from under the glass. She set the drinks down, then slid in.

Mia pulled her drink closer. "What's this?"

"Local special."

Jin dragged his drink across the table, eyes fixed on a video. "They recorded everything at the station. The two you call Boozy and Snoozy are laughing while they blow the airlocks."

"I won't lose sleep." Kate raised her cup. "To Mia saving our asses."

The three of them clinked and sipped.

"I can't tell who's who in EVA suits on the video. There are three suits at the station. The third is pudgy."

Kate said, "Caddell."

"Likely, boss. But hard to prove."

"What I'd like to do is—"

Jin paused and looked at Mia. When she didn't finish her sentence, he asked, "What you'd like to do is what?"

Across the club, Simp and Gimp were engrossed in a game.

Mia agitated her drink, staring into the whirlpool for a few seconds, then said, "I want to see Caddell burn for what he did."

Kate saw a path through the crowd that kept Simp and Gimp boxed in. She raised her glass. "I'll drink to that. To Caddell burning."

The three of them clinked. Kate downed a mouthful of coconut and iced coffee, then got up. "First things first. Time to move. Mia, you take Gimp. Jin, you box them in. I'll take Simp."

Mia said, "Which is which? I can't tell them apart."

Kate said, "Gimp is the woman with the bad knee. Simp is her shadow love toy."

Mia nodded. Kate took her drink and folded her way to Gimp and Simp's booth. The pair was too absorbed to notice Kate and Mia slide into the booth. Kate poked her gun into Simp's abdomen. Simp looked up and elbowed Gimp. Then he put his palms on the table.

Kate looked at Gimp. "How's the knee, Gimp? Hands on the table like your boy toy here."

"Fuck you. Why are you here?"

Kate chin-pointed to Jin, who had squeezed into the booth next to Mia. "We have video of you at the station, killing two people."

"Bullshit."

Jin lifted his backpack. "Wanna see?"

Simp wiped his forehead. "Fuck Deb, I told you this was a bad idea."

"Shut up, Cookie. It's bullshit because we weren't at the station, were we?"

Kate shook her head. They didn't look like a Deb and Cookie.

Simp nodded. "She's right. We stayed on the ship. We had no idea until the four of them got back."

Mia asked, "Four of them?"

Gimp said, "McCurry, Lee, Caddell, and that dumbass kid."

Kate looked at Jin. "Which one was McCurry?"

"McCurry was *brains*. Lee was the broken nose."

Kate looked back to Gimp. "Who was the dumbass kid, Easton?"

"I think so."

Mia looked at Kate but directed the words to Simp. "Your partners have told us their side of the story, why don't you tell us yours?"

Kate nodded. "Not that it matters, right? The getaway driver still gets charged with murder."

Simp jerked from an elbow to the side, then Gimp talked. "They are not our partners. And bullshit. They didn't talk."

Jin had retrieved his pad from his backpack and had turned it to show Gimp a thumbnail. "Want to hear them laughing as they kill Darcy and Holden?"

Simp sighed. "We should just tell them, Deb." He jerked again from another elbow.

Gimp said, "We didn't know. We signed up for property crimes, not this."

Kate said, "Funny. So did I. Yet here we are."

Simp looked at Gimp, who shrugged. He said, "Please understand, we only started in August."

Kate motioned for him to continue.

"Easton–senior–hired us to extract two people. Dilan Darcy and Theodore Holden. It was a rush job. He said they had been fired."

"What about Helena?"

"Never mentioned her. When we got to the colony all we were told was that it was a hostile termination. We would need to breach the station and take them to Earth. When we got there, McCurry told us to stay on the ship. We had no idea what they were doing. When they got back, they yelled *go* so we lifted off."

"You left without Holden and Darcy," Kate said.

"In hindsight—" Simp paused and looked at Gimp. "—In hindsight, maybe we should have known what the plan was because there were no empty seats."

Simp jerked. This time there was a kick, not an elbow.

"When did you find out?"

Gimp sighed, "A few days later. McCurry caught me going through his phone." She nodded towards Jin. "I saw that video. He said if we wanted to stay out of jail, I should shut up and follow orders."

Simp said, "At the end of the week we got a bonus. Bigger than the contract called for."

"And then?"

Gimp said, "And then nothing. Caddell had us lay low and treated us like his personal butler. Get food. Do his laundry. "

Jin smiled. "His laundry? On the colony the drones do it."

"What I tried to tell him. McCurry said, if he wants us to be his maid, shut up and spend his money. Until that terrorist thing at the wedding."

Kate asked, "You weren't at the wedding?"

"We were playing cards in the hotel. All four of us."

"Caddell?"

Simp said, "He had an invite to the wedding. When he came back, he had McCurry dispose of some things."

"What things?"

"I didn't see. It looked like a duffel. With some clothes in it."

"Do you know what he did with it?"

Gimp said, "He was supposed to destroy it."

There was silence. Gimp and Simp looked at each other.

Mia said, "But he didn't."

Gimp said, "Not exactly."

Kate said, "He hid it."

Gimp cleared her throat. "We want a deal."

Kate shook her head. "No."

"No. Just No? Then no we won't tell you where the duffel is."

"You two dragged us all the way to this hellscape. Door number one is you talk. Door number two is we leave you here."

Gimp said, "Sounds good to us."

Kate winced. "McCurry, the brains of your operation, right now his thoughts are splattered across the back of a headboard. His partner, Mia here broke his heart. This place is brutal on witnesses. You'll burn-in in a cardboard box."

"No one knows."

"I know. And the bartender knows. When we get up, everyone will know."

Simp's eyes darted across the crowd. "I put a tracker in the duffel. He hid it on the surface." Simp slid his phone to Jin.

"Cookie—"

"Screw you, Deb. I want out of this place."

"I am not going to prison."

"It's better than being mopped off the floor."

Kate looked at Jin, who was swiping through Simp's device.

"On it, boss."

Kate put her palm up. "Let's not bicker. The future for you two is very uncertain. What happened after the duffel? What about Leyna?"

Simp said, "McCurry told us to scoop her up."

Mia said, "Convenient now that McCurry's dead. Can you prove any of this?"

Gimp and Simp looked at each other, then Simp sighed. "Holden hacked into our ship. While the four of them are at the station, we were—"

Simp glanced at Gimp, then held out his hand to ask for his phone back. Jin slid it over. Simp swiped it, then turned it to show Kate a video of Gimp and Simp bouncing inside *Beam Six*.

"Looks uncomfortable."

Gimp said, "It was."

Simp looked at her, hurt.

Kate tapped the phone to stop the video, then slid the phone across the booth to Jin. "But your knee looks fine. So Nathaniel Kirkwood tracked you here?"

Gimp said, "Not exactly."

Simp said, "Caddell messaged us that Kirkwood was the captain. To take him wherever he wanted to go."

Gimp said, "First he tried to recruit us. Then he tried to buy weapons from us. Now—"

Simp said, "Now he's blackmailing us. He has proof Caddell killed that Darcy woman. And he has that video of us killing Darcy and Holden."

Kate said, "Probably more than that."

Gimp and Simp froze, mouths open, staring at a point towards the door. Kate turned as the crowd parted. A pistol connected to an arm wearing a new nose, new ears, red hair, and green eyes.

Kirkwood. Holding a gun. Shit.

Kate and Jin rose at the same time. She dived towards Kirkwood but wasn't fast enough. Two steps from Kirkwood, she was blinded by the muzzle flash.

She tackled Kirkwood between shots three and four. She was wrestling the gun from his hand when she heard Jin yell *Kate*. Kate wrestled Kirkwood into a chokehold and squeezed until he stopped struggling. When she turned to the booth, latte-colored milk had spilled and mixed with blood spatter on the table. Simp was under the table, which was shoved forward. Gimp slumped forward, face in gore, dead. Jin hovered over Mia, yanking her out of the booth.

"Mia is shot."

"Take Kirkwood."

Jin lay Mia on the floor and switched places. Kate checked Mia. Two shots, one to the carotid and one to the temple. Kate turned to the crowd, then uttered something in Russian. The crowd's eyes turned away, but she saw the bouncer walking over.

"We have to go, Jin. Now."

"What about Mia?"

"She's dead."

"Shit. Well we can't leave her."

Kirkwood announced his consciousness. "Fucking wattsucker. Get off me."

"Get him up."

Jin lifted Kirkwood by the armpit, his whole hand wrapped around his bicep, so hard Kate thought he'd tear his arm off. "You are coming."

"The fuck I am."

Kate said, "The alternative is I shoot you in the kneecaps and leave you for the animals."

Kate pointed her gun at Kirkwood's knees. Kirkwood stared at the weapon. Jin leaned down and hoisted Mia's body over his shoulders with a groan. Blood dripped down his back. Then he pointed his pistol at Kirkwood.

Kate crouched down to see Simp under the table. She waved him out with the barrel of her gun.

When Simp stood up, the bouncer was already looking him over. Kate stepped between them. "These are mine."

The bouncer eyed Kate. Shit. Did he recognize her?

"You registered?"

She exhaled under her breath. "Stsyapan will get his forty percent."

"Is sixty. You make mess in room ninety-four."

They already found the bodies. New management was more efficient than the old. She didn't have a lot of time before they identified her. Jin's surveillance hack was good, but not permanent.

"Forty five and he can keep *Beam Six*."

It was fun to negotiate with money she didn't have and didn't plan to deliver. The bouncer stood silent, squinting at her.

"C'mon Jin, we are late." Kate pressed the muzzle into Simp's back and shoved him forward. The crowd parted, and they walked out of Space Moscow.

51

They inched a hundred paces beyond the club before the corridor echoed with loud voices. Kate had bought time. Not a lot. The clamor could be a posse gathering, and they were leaving a blood trail in the corridor that the maid drones were not cleaning fast enough.

"Jin, we aren't going to make it. Not like this, with these three."

"You are going to die, bitch."

"I die Kirkwood, we all die."

"I'm ready to die. You're not getting off this station."

"I am open to ideas, boss."

Kate eyed a door with Russian above it. лифт, *lift*. Behind that door, stairs and an elevator to the center axle. Two doors beyond the lift, round portals on each side. Escape pods.

"How's surveillance?"

"Still down."

Kate pointed to the portals, then shoved Kirkwood toward an escape pod. Jin walked over and opened the door. "Kate, there is only room for two."

"Perfect. Kirkwood, you get in." Kate booted him in. Kate wanted to bang his head against the threshold, but they didn't have a lot of time. Kirkwood stood there, looking around. The inside looked like an early-century space capsule she'd seen at the Smithsonian.

Kate took Mia's feet, then nodded to Jin. Jin lowered Mia off his shoulders. Kate thrust Mia feet-first into the escape hatch. "Kirkwood, take her feet. Move her to the pod."

"Fuck you."

Kate shrugged. "Okay. We will do this the hard way." Kate laid Mia's feet across the hatch threshold, then climbed over and into the escape pod. Kirkwood shrank back. The escape pod was cramped. Kate reached out, lifted Kirkwood by his carotids, and squeezed. Kirkwood punched and kicked for ten seconds, then went limp. Kate counted five more seconds, then lowered him onto one of the chairs and strapped him in. Then, she hoisted Mia's body into the other chair and strapped her in.

Simp tried to step into the pod, but Kate pushed him out and shut the hatch.

Simp stared at the closed hatch. "Did you?"

Kate had an assignment for Simp. Did she want him to believe she was merciful, or cruel? Maybe both. "No. I want Kirkwood alive."

"Boss, is this a good idea?"

"Can we make this touchdown somewhere on the East Coast?"

Jin pointed to a panel beside the hatch. Kirkwood was conscious again, beating and cursing from inside the hatch. Kate had a lot of questions that she wanted to ask him. Mainly, whose idea it was to bomb her office, Caddell's or his. She could scream questions through the door, make Kirkwood believe he'd get a reprieve for telling the truth, then send him to burn in anyway. Or knock him unconscious and try to drag seventy kilos through the station in zero-g. There was no time for either. And it didn't matter. Kate opened the panel and punched the GPS coordinates for the east coast of Florida. She touched ok to confirm. The pounding reduced to a hiss and then silence.

"One away." Kate exhaled a little.

Simp said, "What about me?"

Yes, what about him. Kate shoved him forward and pointed to another escape hatch on the opposite side. "You have an assignment." Kate explained what she wanted Simp to do.

"What happens if—"

"Do you doubt I can find you anywhere in the solar system?"

Simp shook his head and swallowed.

"I've become lazy. And homey. If I have to leave the comfort of my balcony, I will be very pissed. Understand?"

He nodded. Instinctively, she said, "I can't hear you." A mistake. He shouted, "Yes *sir*," so loud she checked the hall to see whether anyone heard.

She pushed him to the escape capsule. "Make it your life's mission."

"And after?"

Kate shrugged. "Maybe you got caught up in a hurricane you didn't see coming. Maybe your case goes to the bottom of my pile. I have a big pile, right Jin?"

Jin nodded.

"Hopefully, I *never* have a reason to go digging for it. Understand?"

He nodded again. Kate opened the hatch and pointed the muzzle of her pistol inside. Simp studied the interior like he was climbing into his own coffin, then stepped in. As Simp strapped himself in, Kate opened the control panel and punched in coordinates. The hatch swung closed. She pressed *ok* and the airlocks hissed.

"Think he'll do it?"

"Fifty-fifty. How are we on surveillance?"

"Someone is in trying to reboot."

"When we get to the top of the stairs, can you shut down the ring?"

A gunshot cracked, and Kate felt the ricochet at her feet. Jin went first into the stairwell. Kate backed through the door, taking potshots at the feet appearing at the horizon, then closed the door and shot at the lock, hoping to jam it. Once at the top of the stairs, they ran to the elevator as metal screeched and clunked. Kate lurched backward as the ring stopped. She felt lighter, then weightless. She swam along the walls to the elevator. The elevator door closed to cracks of gunfire as someone tried to shoot the stair door open.

Her weight returned. The elevator moved.

"Jin, can you see where they are?"

"Surveillance is still off. But I've activated the fire system. They are locked out and getting pissed on."

Kate exhaled a little more. Incredibly, they were still on Plan B. "Well, that should send them scurrying. It's going to be a long crawl to *Tesseract*."

The elevator opened. Kate peeked out and the corridor was clear. Thank god, she hated hand-to-hand combat in zero-g. Kate waved Jin out and grabbed a handle.

They passed three clueless drugged guests, each time Kate's stomach and fists clenching and then relaxing. Two lefts, a right, no one in sight, then they were passing *Beam Six*, with no time to search it. Once in

Tesseract, Jin had it undocked, and they were pulling away before they were clicked in.

Once they were away, Earth rotating in the cockpit window, Kate exhaled. "I thought we'd have to shoot our way out."

"Actually, you thought we'd have to threaten to detonate *Tesseract* and hold the whole station hostage while we escaped."

"I had two plans left before E. Maybe next time. I want to see this place burn."

"We can go back. Steal a ship and detonate *Tesseract*."

Kate laughed. She brought up a search window. Two escape modules deorbiting. On track. Heat shield stable. She sent an alert to the Coast Guard.

Jin smiled. "I've almost been killed twice in the last week. Would now be a good time to discuss the pay scale?"

"Three times. One was your own fucking fault," Kate said.

"I—"

Kate's harshness echoed off the cockpit walls.

"We will work on that. Like I always say, I'd rather be lucky than right. Today we got lucky." She rapped her armrests. "Plus a little Jinho Knight magic. A lot of magic."

Jin smiled. The ship's engines increased, rumbling. She felt an adrenaline crash coming. "Is that really what you want, more money, Jin?"

"I wouldn't say no. But right now, what I want is to cuddle with Jade then take a shower. How about you? What are you going to do when we get back?"

Kate looked at the blood on his clothes, then hers. They hadn't even donned their p-suits. She had an extra phone too. She looked at it and realized it was Kirkwood's phone and she didn't recall taking it. She handed it to Jin.

He inspected it. "Locked. Simple password, no biometrics."

He'd have it cloned and unlocked before they left Earth orbit. On it, he'd find video proof Caddell stabbed Helena Darcy. Caddell would never be prosecuted, and she wasn't going to waste rocket fuel chasing him to Earth. She'd send her message a different way.

Kate pressed Rae's avatar on the console.

"Kate—where are you?"

"*Tesseract*. I just wanted to say I love you and tell you we are on the way home."

"Why are you covered in blood?"

"Oh. I kissed Mia and she got killed."

"You what? You are not making sense. Agent Bolkov is dead?"

"I need to call her husband." Kate started to feel heavy as the thrusters accelerated. "I will call you after we're cruising."

"Kate wait. Are you ok? Are you coming straight here?"

"Straight there." She looked at Jin, who was holding up four fingers. "Jin says four hours. Love you. Give Axio a kiss."

"Love you. Come home safe."

The call closed. Kate said, "Four hours?"

"You promised 8gs."

Right. Mia was dead.

52

Kate wanted to watch the video of Caddell from her balcony. Jin was watching from their office. Simp had placed seven spider cameras on Caddell's thirty-ton motorhome. A 360 view outside and inside. He stripped all the metadata, encrypted the video, and bounced them across a few satellites. Seven videos on her handheld were crowded, but she didn't want to miss any action.

Inside the motorhome, Caddell was in the driver's seat. Plush leather, almost as nice as *Tesseract's* seat. Caddell checked his mirrors and pulled out. Crunching gravel gave way to the purr of asphalt. The leather-bound wheel spun under his palms as he made a wide right. He looked relaxed driving such a big rig.

On the side views, mossy gray post-and-rail fences accelerated until they were a blur. On the left side, cows grazed between patches of melting snow. On the right, deer wandered among the cut-down corn stalks searching for leftover kernels in the mud.

Caddell's dashboard display interrupted the country scenery.

Jin messaged her, *James Easton calling.*

This ought to be good. Thankfully, the audio was high quality.

Caddell thumbed the steering wheel, declining, but Easton called back. Caddell thumbed his wheel again, this time answering.

"Jim. Hey."

"Why did you decline my call?" Easton was calling audio-only. Wherever he was, he didn't want to be seen. The green frame surrounding Easton's empty gray avatar on the dash lit and blinked with the volume of Easton's voice.

"I'm on the road."

"You driving? Where are you?"

"Virginia. Driving is a lost art, Jim. I'm about to pull over for breakfast, can I—"

"You're going to kill someone. Let the computer drive that behemoth."

Kate laughed under her breath. He already did kill people. Helena Darcy. Dilan Darcy. Ted Holden. Paul Darcy. Kody Easton. Some by proxy because he used Nathaniel Kirkwood and military contractors. Some like Mia Bolkov were caught in the crossfire.

"It's peaceful, Jim. You should try it. Rockets kill people too you know."

"What the fuck did you do?"

"I let nature take its course. You should too."

Caddell was so blasé. *Let nature take its course.*

The left and right side views had changed to yards and driveways. Here there was no sign of frost. Mowerbots wended along the driveway edges and circled the omnipresent Virgin Mary birdbaths and political signs to attend to the grass.

Easton said, "It's all over the servers."

"Just rumors. It's classified, Jim. President Latham won't allow a panic."

"Cruz resigned, Bill. The trip is off. The whole team disbanded. Now Latham has asked for an investigation." Easton's green frame blinked yellow and red as Easton raised his voice.

"Well, the way she runs things I wouldn't worry."

"Your professional opinion or that of a retired bystander?"

Caddell checked his mirrors, paying more attention to the road than the conversation. "The agency is tied up in a neat little bow for Barb, Jim. But my professional opinion is that she should hedge her bets."

"Is it Bill? Tied up? You promised me Devana would be gone." More red blinking from Easton's avatar.

"From the pictures, the protestors did a number on the station. Set the agency back a year. That's on Devana. Give it time and trust the process."

"Barron Industries got the rebuild using Lunar Foundries new line of hardware. Says they can do it in a quarter of the time at a third of the cost. The station will be fixed by January." Easton sounded resigned.

Kate pictured him in a car, sunk low in the seat, with his eyes peering over the door.

"Hype."

"Drones Bill. Fucking drones. Half the savings is they don't need to lift it with our rockets because they are already on the fucking moon. Jesus. We needed this contract."

Kate said to the video feed, "And Caddell won't be skimming. A nice savings there, too."

The audio was one-way, so Caddell didn't hear her sarcasm.

Caddell said, "How did they put in a bid so quick?"

"They were allowed on site and did a survey. Devana brought them. Like goddamn locusts. This is your fault, Bill."

That's why Aria wanted to come to the station. Aria never overlooked a business opportunity.

In the motorhome's rear view, the sun hovered just above Simp's silver car, reflecting off the sunroof. He followed Caddell a little too closely for her comfort, but Caddell had not noticed for a dozen miles.

"Drones can't do what people do, Jim."

Easton's avatar blinked red. "And the goddam leaks. Have you seen them?"

"I shut down my accounts. Half of what's online is the hallucination of some conspiracy AI."

"It's the other half I'm worried about. How did they get the fucking expense reports to leak? They are going to lead right to you, and then to me."

Kate considered giving Leyna a job, but Cris Davis scooped her up first.

Caddell was silent. On the side views, yards changed to clean brick storefronts. His dash console beeped. Two traffic lights ahead at the corner, it looked like Caddell planned to get breakfast at a travel stop.

A siren wailed in the background on Easton's side of the call. That would be the multistate manhunt closing in. The Eastons panicked, resigned, and were now fugitives.

Caddell said, "Where are you, anyway?"

"Barb and I are taking a vacation. After Kody, we felt—"

Yes, probably a very long vacation in a tiny cell. Or an urn. She didn't imagine the manhunt ending well. They usually ended with gun battles.

"Good for you. You need one."

Caddell had zero remorse over Kody Easton. For some reason, that's the murder that pissed her off the most. Helena, Paul, Leyna, she could wrap her mind around the evil plan to protect himself. The over-the-top plan to use the protestors to cover it up, whatever. It might have worked, except he didn't count on the solar system's foremost expert in extraterrestrial forensics, Rae, cracking the timeline. Or Jin's hacking prowess.

But there was no reason for Kody. Kody needed help, not an overdose. Caddell tossed him aside like a piece of garbage. Now here he was, casually telling Kody's father he needed a vacation.

The Marine in Kate wanted to be in the coach, in Caddell's bedroom, waiting for him. Knife him the way he did Helena. Look into his eyes so he'd know it was her. But she was also a Guardian, and this plan was Mia's wish fulfilled. He was a roach, not worth the rocket fuel anyway, and this message wasn't for him. It was for all the other outlaw roaches that wanted to infest her jurisdiction.

Kate messaged Simp, *execute*.

Caddell spun the leather wheel, turning wide and slowly into the travel stop. The parking lot was empty except for three cars at the front with silver umbilical cords connected to chargers.

After a long silence, Caddell said, "The agency is clean Jim. Delete, redact, reupload, that was the plan."

"None of that happened, Bill."

"It will. Give it time."

"Not something we have. Leyna Darcy is alive. Did you know that? She got a download from her mother."

"Alive? Fuck." Caddell braked.

"We needed that contract." Easton's side of the call whistled. There was a gust of wind, then more sirens. Easton said, "We gotta go. Now."

Easton hung up. Caddell slowed the motorhome, pulled around the building, and parallel parked against the far curb, occupying five spaces.

The side video caught Caddell stepping off his coach and stretching his arms.

In Virginia, it was a beautiful morning. Behind the travel stop, farmland with a dark green cover crop rolled into the Appalachians and a crisp blue sky.

On the colony, it was a beautiful afternoon. Below her, a family was strolling in the gardens. In the gazebo, she saw Rae, Axio, and Rae's family having a picnic. It looked like they had everything spread out over the bench. Above her, the obsidian domed barrier between life and death remained intact.

Caddell meandered to the rear of the coach, where he opened up a storage compartment and retrieved a charging cable as thick as his wrist. It looked heavy. He dragged the cable to the charging station, then swiped his phone to pay.

On the rear video feed, Simp parked as far away as possible, near the exit, while maintaining a line of sight. The motorhome's inside camera caught Caddell walking inside, up the stairs, yawning, and stretching. Then closing the bedroom door.

Dirt nap time.

Simp waited fifteen minutes, got out, then snuck behind the motorhome's fast charging station. Kate heard whirring as Simp popped off the back panel.

Five minutes later, Simp had two cameras set up, livestreaming from inside the travel stop. He sat at a table overlooking the motorhome from safety. A woman strolled over to refill his coffee. She looked mid-sixties, with long gray hair in a ponytail, with a too-tight faded green graphic t-shirt that squeezed her skin and was trying and failing to hold her ample aging breasts. She spoke over curls of steam rising from the pot of coffee in her hand. "Dat yours?"

Simp said, "In my dreams."

Kate studied the feed. The waitress had her eyes on the multi-million dollar motorhome, probably hoping its occupants would come in, sit at her table, and leave a big tip. She never glanced at Simp.

"I feel like french toast today. And bacon, crisp."

The waitress nodded and walked off.

Halfway through Simp's breakfast, smoke wafted from the underside of the motorhome. A cup of coffee later, the spider cameras cut to white noise, and the fire department struggled with a lithium battery fire over a thousand degrees Celsius, hot enough to cremate William M. Caddell.

Simp's livestream cut. Then he messaged, *splash one.*

Kate closed the feed and looked up at the obsidian dome holding back space, then inhaled. A great day for a picnic with her family.

53

Kate smelled fresh bread. The crowd was light at Trattoria Del Luna but all smiles. Behind Rae, she caught a woman in a black and white uniform, her blond ponytail bouncing towards them with a breadbasket in one hand and a flask of red wine in the other. Kate squeezed Rae's hand across the black-and-white checkered table.

Kate's phone binged.

Rae smiled, her hazel eyes the same cheery shape as the wine in her glass. "How did they meet, anyway?"

"Jin says Kirkwood was protesting at Foggy Bottom when Caddell stopped at a light. He was driving his antique gas guzzler. They talked and Kirkwood handed him a flyer."

"I really wish they'd send me his brain to scan."

"Maybe in thirty years. You think his neuroface caused this?"

"I don't think the neuroface caused this, Kate. Yanking it out—" Rae shook her head. "—don't do that. Scar tissue maybe triggered something. I'd need a scan." Then after sipping her wine, "You would say, Kirkwood was a grenade and Caddell pulled the pin and tossed it here."

Kate tasted her wine. Trattoria Del Luna wasn't crowded today. Smells of cheese and marinara sauce tickled her nose.

Kate said, "I went back to talk to Kenna Darcy. She finally let me in."

"How was she?"

"I told her they would name the repaired station after Helena. The Helena P. Darcy Interstellar Observatory. That seemed to cheer her up. She said it's what Helena would have wanted."

Rae looked away.

"You didn't like her."

"She was devoted to her research."

"But?"

"She was cold. I was afraid telling you would—I don't know."

"Everyone deserves justice, right?"

Rae smiled. "That your campaign slogan? You going to start walking around here with your cowboy hat and call yourself Sheriff?"

"Giddy up pardner." Kate smiled.

Rae bit her lip and tilted her wine. "I like it."

Kate squeezed Rae's hand.

"Speaking of justice, the new lawyer says Stuart's lawsuit is DOA. She got an expedited hearing. So Axio will be here for the holidays."

Kate gulped her wine. Rae squinted. "I thought that's what you wanted?"

"It is. Axio being here for the holidays is fantastic."

Rae continued squinting.

"It's the cost, Rae."

"Gray isn't charging for this."

How a dealer gets you hooked on the latest rage-inducing drug: The first hit free. Lawyers were infuriating. The need for one, more so.

"It cost my soul." Kate swigged her wine, smiled a little, and looked away. "If I had one."

Rae squeezed Kate's hand. "Thank you for doing this."

Kate studied the tawny specks in Rae's eyes, then sighed. Warm brown today, the same color as her hair.

"She wants to go on offense with Stuart."

"Offense means what?"

"Sue him back. Get Axio full time."

Of course she did. Kate's phone binged again.

You'll say yes. I can't tell you why, Gray had said. Not seeing lies onscreen, check. Avoiding the priority one trashed-room distress call for the actress playing her, check. Of course, Kate wouldn't play herself. But Jin could vet who did, a bonus.

All of that. But mostly, she said yes to see Rae smile, because now she would get Axio full time.

"Are you going to get that?"

Kate relented and looked at her messages. "Mia's husband. About the funeral."

The server arrived to exchange the empty carafe with another full carafe. They exchanged smiles, Kate mouthed *four* to the server, and then the ponytail bounced away.

"What did he say?"

"I don't get it—" Kate sniffed her wine, watching two servers behind Rae. A man and a woman, one of them the server with the ponytail. They were chatting and laughing like they were having fun. "—he said how much Mia loved working with me. How she looked up to me, and how great Jin was. And you. Called you Doctor Einstein. He said he'd never seen her so excited about a case."

"Doctor Einstein?"

"Because all your fancy science finally nailed Caddell." Kate slurped her wine and shook her head.

"And that bothers you?"

"I was nothing but mean to her, Rae. She risked her life and saved ours. In return, I was mean to her and treated her like *them*. She didn't know what she was getting into."

"Mmm." Rae sipped her wine. "I think she knew what she was getting into. What did you say to him?"

"Same thing I always say. Which is never enough. But always sounds better than the alternative—beloved wife and mother gunned down by a senseless sociopath because I wasn't fast enough. You know she had three kids?"

"I didn't. What are you going to do?"

Kate rubbed her forearm. The skin under the new tattoo for Mia Bolkov would be irritated for a while.

"Take her ashes in *Tesseract* for an 8g spin. Then let her husband cry on my shoulder. Tell him what a hero she was and that I made her death count."

Kate slugged her wine and poured another. Before Kate could continue, the server's blond ponytail bounced over and dropped a plate of four shrimp crostini, each drenched in something creamy. Rae picked one and bit into it.

Kate smiled at the server and mouthed *two*.

It was a good thing that she was interrupted. She didn't want to talk anymore shop. She wanted to put October behind her. November was going to be a much better month.

After swallowing her crostini, Kate said, "Aria said the Presidential visit is officially canceled."

"Was it ever really on?"

"They paid for The Crown Oasis garden to be cleared, now it will sit empty. Aria refuses to rent it because then they have to refund the campaign. She'd rather screw the Latham administration. But, Olicia is concerned about the image of an empty garden."

"Wow, a real travesty."

Kate finished her wine, then nodded to the server. "A parody of a problem I know. But we should help them with that."

"Oh?"

The server with the smiling bobbing ponytail brought over a bottle of Prosecco. Rae's face lit up as it dropped. Her hazel eyes smiling *yes* into the green bottle. Kate retrieved two ring boxes from her lap.

Yes, November was going to be a much better month. So good, she would even wear a dress.

Thank you for reading! Please leave a review on Amazon or Goodreads.

Receive newsletters and advance notice of future books in the series: click https://wyattwerne.com/signup, or scan the QR code below and sign up.

Acknowledgements

Thanks and love to my wife Alison, who read versions and provided insights.

Thanks to my beta readers, especially Susan Collins who helped make this version readable and provided valuable tips on self-publishing.

Thanks to my wonderfully talented, amazing, humble editor Hayleigh Burnett (www.editingfox.com) for tearing her hair out over my missing verbs, spliced commas, and last nanosecond changes.

But mostly – thanks to all my readers! Stay tuned for the next book in the series.

www.ingramcontent.com/pod-product-compliance
Lightning Source LLC
Chambersburg PA
CBHW020554310726
48979CB00008B/1209/J

* 9 7 9 8 9 8 8 7 2 5 7 2 5 *